BRING DOWN THE SKY

CONTENTS

ISBN: 979-8-9885735-3-1 (paperback)

ISBN: 979-8-9885735-2-4 (ebook)

Bring Down the Sky

Cover by Maria Spada.

Map of the Continent by Shivnath Productions.

Bloodrune art by Alex Spreier.

To every man whose work feels thankless and unending

"And for Grimsdalr, the Task of the Sentinel: So long as your watch remains unending, you shall be the bastion between the Waking World and the one beyond."

Teachings of the Church of the Triad

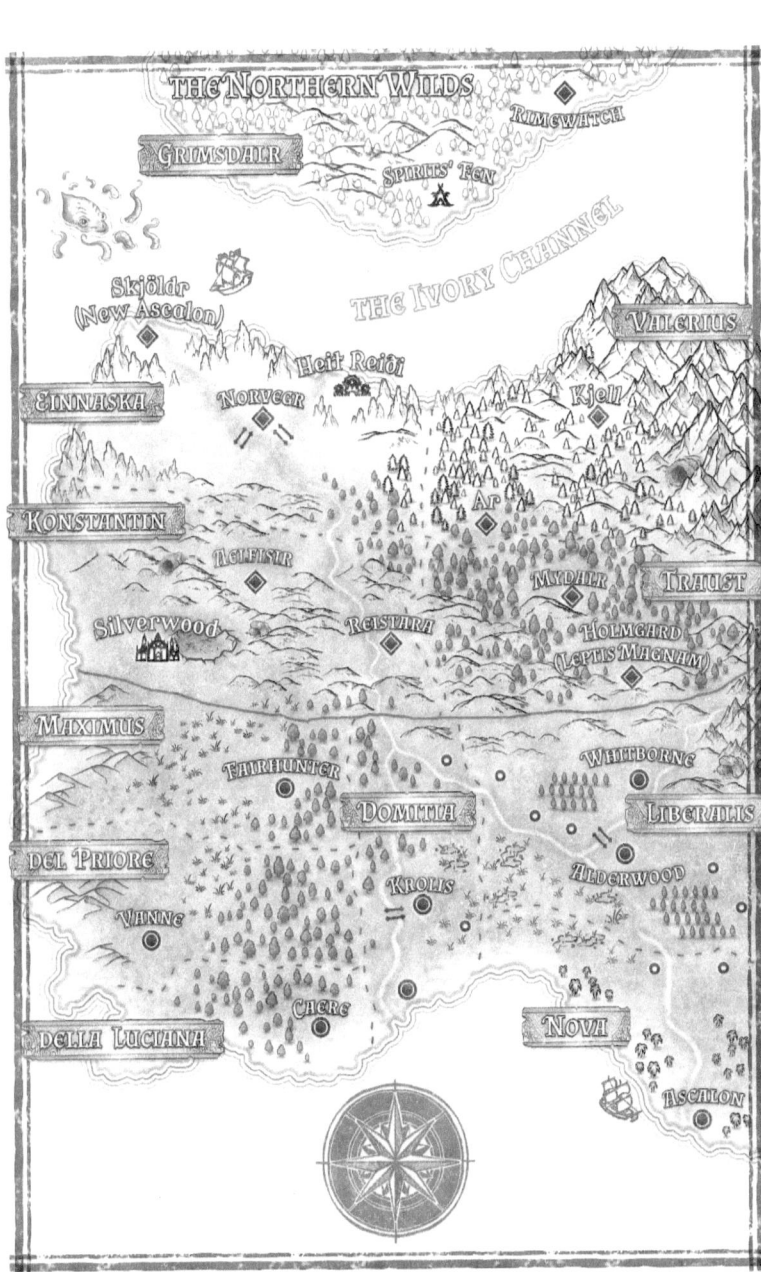

DRAMATIS PERSONAE

The Valerius Family

Living

Frelia Helm's Grace Valerius—former Grand Duchess of Valerius Territory, former Krakenguard, current Swordmaster at the Silverwood Military Institute.

Deceased

Einar Winter's Heart Valerius— Grand Duke of Valerius Territory, died in the Tyrant's War at the Battle for Heit Reiði. Father to Frelia and Diarmuid.

Hana Holt Defender Valerius—Grand Duchess of Valerius Territory, died of plague. Mother to Frelia and Diarmuid.

Diarmuid Iron Valor Valerius—Frelia's older brother, died in the Winter War.

Brenn Seladalr—Frelia's maternal aunt, former spymaster for the Kingdom of Kaldr. Died in a blizzard.

The Caecillion Family

Living

Vendrick Caecillion—theCount of Caecillion, former Queenmaker, former Spymaster of the VolsiniiImperium, current Headmaster of the Silverwood Military Institute.

ClarissaCaecillion—the Countess of Caecillion, Lieutenant of the Caecillion blacknetwork, sister to Vendrick.

Sulpicia "Deadcut" Verona—former Imperial General, current Governor of Northern Volsinii. Mother to Vendrick and Clarissa, ex-wife of Vittoro.

Deceased

Vittoro Caecillion—Former Spymaster of the Volsinii Imperium, father to Vendrick and Clarissa, political lieutenant to Ironfang.

Lucia della Trova—Prima Donna of the Opera Imperalis, Unseen agent assigned to pose as Clarissa Caecillion. Also Clarissa's ex-girlfriend.

The della Luciana Family and Retainers

Living

Elias "Ironfang"Della Luciana—Imperator of the Volsinii Imperium and General of the Imperial Army.

Markus della Luciana—former Queenmaker, Captain of the Imperial Watchers stationed at the Silverwood Military Institute, and prince of the Volsinii Imperium. Ironfang's son and brother to Galeria and Faustine, half-brother to Orsina. A Silverwood contemporary of Frelia and Vendrick.

Orsina della Luciana—Grand Mistress of the Bloodrune Hunters and the Duchess of della Luciana. Ironfang's oldest daughter and half-sister to Markus, Galeria and Faustine.

Galeria della Luciana—Baroness of Lysander. Ironfang's daughter, half-sister to Orsina, and sister to Markus and Faustine.

Faustine della Luciana—student at the Silverwood Military Institute in the Violet Owls House, Ironfang's daughter andsister to Markus and Galeria, half-sister to Orsina.

Drogari—Orsina's bodyguard.

Deceased

Titus della Luciana—Ironfang's oldest son by his first wife, killed in the Tyrant's War.

Gaius della Luciana—Ironfang's younger son by his first wife, killed in the Tyrant's War.

The Grimsdalr Family

Living

Thera Bones' Defiance Grimsdalr—former Margravine of Grimsdalr Territory, former Krakenguard and fiancée to Hägen Einnaska, currently trapped in the form of a garmr. Frelia's childhood friend and a Silverwood contemporary of Frelia and Vendrick.

Deceased

Herja Ancestor's Truth Grimsdalr—Margravine of Grimsdalr Territory, died in theT yrant's War at the Battle for Mydalr. Mother to Cillian, Thera, and Kjeld.

Jari Shield Wall Grimsdalr—Margrave of Grimsdalr Territory, died in the Winter War. Father to Cillian, Thera, and Kjeld.

Kjeld Grimsdalr—Cillian and Thera's older brother, died in the Winter War.

Cillian Wilds Guardian Grimsdalr—former Margrave of Grimsdalr Territory and Krakenguard, died after being captured during the Battle of Spirits' Fen. Frelia's childhood friend and a Silverwood contemporary of Frelia and Vendrick.

Liesel Shades' Defiance Grimsdalr—Thera's daughter, born during her incarceration with the Unseen. Presumed dead.

The Einnaska Family

Deceased

Hägen Falling Stars Einnaska—King of Kaldr during the Tyrant's War, Frelia's childhood friend and a Silverwood contemporary of Frelia and Vendrick. Brother to Reina.

Reina Einnaska—Crown Princess of Kaldr during the Winter and Tyrant's Wars, possessed of the Einnaska Bloodrune, known as the Butcher of Eastborne. Sister to Hägen.

Njal Einnaska—King of Kaldr during the Winter and early Tyrant's War, father to Hägen and Reina.

Silverwood Staff and Students

Living

Edmund Blightsen—White Magicmaster at the Silverwood Military Institute, former Krakenguard. Frelia's childhood friend. A Silverwood contemporary of Frelia and Vendrick.

Claudia Campagna—Loremaster at the Silverwood Military Institute.

Lucian Corvinus—Cavalrymaster at the Silverwood Military Institute.

Hrolff Gellir—Wyvernmaster at the Silverwood Military Institute.

Tiber Marcellius—Black Magicmaster and Deputy Headmaster at the Silverwood Military Institute, an old man who has been there since Frelia and Vendrick were students.

Torhild Olsen—Roguemaster at the Silverwood Military Institute, revealed as Unseen during the summoning of Lord Muninn.

Perseo Ossani—Axemaster at the Silverwood Military Institute, cousin to Siegmund.

Favonia Sabine—former Imperial Watcher, current Lancemaster at the Silverwood Military Institute.

Livia Serrana—Archerymaster at the Silverwood Military Institute.

Applus Vitellus—Tacticsmaster at the Silverwood Military Institute.

Leon of the Titanheart—Captain of the Cost Effectives, Frelia's former mercenary band. A Silverwood contemporary of Frelia and Vendrick.

Owen Gundalf—student at the Silverwood Military Institute in the Violet Owls House, Kaldiri.

Karina Hunter—student at the Silverwood Military Institute in the Violet Owls House.

Ellie Mattingly—student at the Silverwood Military Institute in the Violet Owls House.

Siegmund Ossani—student at the Silverwood Military Institute in the Violet Owls House, cousin to Axemaster Ossani.

Valente Secundus—student at the Silverwood Military Institute in the Violet Owls House, possessed of the Domitia Bloodrune.

Christel Vilulf—student at the Silverwood Military Institute in the Violet Owls House, possessed of the Traust Bloodrune.

Deceased

Brigitte Konstantin—Krakenguard during the Tyrant's War, possessed of the Konstantin Bloodrune. Killed in the Massacre at Kollavik. A Silverwood contemporary of Frelia and Vendrick.

Julia Liberalis—A Queenmaker during the Tyrant's War, killed at the battle of Fort Frostmaiden. A Silverwood contemporary of Frelia and Vendrick.

Roland Sferrazza—A Queenmaker during the Tyrant's War, killed by Vendrick in the post-war. A Silverwood contemporary of Frelia and Vendrick.

Caecillion Black Network

Living

Talis Mitri—physician and former Queenmaker, currently studying Bloodrunes for the Caecillion Black Network.

Athos del Priore— former Queenmaker, Captain of the Watchers stationed at Heit Reiði/Serpentbrook Hold. A Silverwood contemporary of Frelia and Vendrick.

Irirangi of the Kingfisher—former Queenmaker, current Queen of the Rippling Isles. A Silverwood contemporary of Frelia and Vendrick.

Deceased

Hazel Stonebreath Mitri—Talis Mitri's wife, possessed of the Háski Bloodrune. A Silverwood contemporary of Frelia and Vendrick and Free Cities native.

Octavia Nova—Crown Princess of Volsinii during the Tyrant's War, possessed of the Nova Bloodrune. A childhood friend of Vendrick's, and Silverwood contemporary of Frelia and Vendrick.

Legendary and Mythological Figures

Lady Daybreak—First of the three sister Goddesses of the Triad, said to have taught humanity to work the land and gave them fire, and it is from her that all things begin. She is the ruler of Solivallr, the final resting place for the souls of the brave.

Lady Twilight—Second of the three sister Goddesses of the Triad, said to have taught humanity to rest and the secrets of the sea, and it is from her that they learned balance, and measure. She is the ruler of the Sapphire Fields, the final resting place for the souls of the diligent.

Lady Midnight—Last of the three sister Goddesses of the Triad, said to be the bringer of endings—death, decay, and winter,—mother of garmur, and ruler of Hell, the final resting place for the souls of the wicked. It is also said she will begin the end of the world, known to the Kaldiri as Heit Reiði, if she is ever unsealed from Hell.

Lord Huginn—Lady Twilight's raven, governing thought, and the legendary Guardian of Konstantin Territory.

Lord Muninn—Lady Twilight's raven, governing memory, and the legendary Guardian of Traust Territory.

Lord Geri—known as "Geri the Greedy One," one of Lady Midnight's wolves in Kaldiri legend and the legendary Guardian of Einnaska Territory.

Lord Freki—known as "Freki the Ravenous One," one of Lady Midnight's wolves in Kaldiri legend and the legendary Guardian of Valerius Territory.

The Kraken—legendary Kaldiri giant squid that lives in the Ivory Channel.

The Sightless One—a shadowy figure which lives in Ironfang's mind.

The Watcher— legendary Kaldiri hero who is said to have become a mighty bear rather than join his ancestors in Helheim, so that he could become the Guardian of the Northern Wilds.

Saint Victrix Domitia—progenitor of the Domitia Bloodrune.

Saint Randolf Einnaska—progenitor of the Einnaska Bloodrune, once-sea raider and eventual first King of Kaldr.

Saint Eydis Grimsdalr—progenitor of the Grimsdalr Bloodrune, legendary guardian of Solivallr.

Saint Einar Háski—progenitor of the Háski Bloodrune, known as the first proper Grey Mage.

Saint Klaus Konstantin—progenitor of the Konstantin Bloodrune, a village doctor.

Saint Edmund Maximus—progenitor of the Maximus Bloodrune.

Saint Cornelius Nova—progenitor of the Nova Bloodrune, eventually the first Imperator.

Saint Sigvaldi Traust—progenitor of the Traust Bloodrune, once-Thane and eventual first Count of Kaldr.

Saint Hana Valerius—progenitor of the Valerius Bloodrune, once-Thane and eventual first Grand Duchess of Kaldr.

CHAPTER ONE

ONCE, WHEN VENDRICK CAECILLION had been a gawky preteen, his tutor had made him memorize a poem. He had chosen Imperator Aurelius IX's *Musings on the Dreaming of the World*. He had forgotten most of it in the intervening years, although he could still feel the cadence in his bones if he read it, like slipping into an old sweater he'd forgotten he owned. The last line, though, had burrowed into the back of his mind and lived there ever since:

And I press on, lightless, until the work is done.

"Lightless," Vendrick muttered as he sent a Singularity pellet careening into a man's chest, "until the work is done."

The hard knot of arcane energy cratered the Imperial Watcher's banded armor and splattered the wall behind him with gore. Vendrick twisted his fingers, and the Singularity pellet zipped back towards him, freezing in place just before his raised, open hand.

Some of the Imperial Watchers clustered in the foyer stared at him in wide-eyed shock. They knew him as the Headmaster of Silverwood, a composed man who was made of hard angles and sharp decisions. But other Watchers knew him as the Viper of Ascalon, and while they stared at their newly-dead comrade with disgust and horror, they weren't surprised.

"Muratori," Vendrick called out to the next name on his list, calm as you please, "you stand accused of abetting the Unseen. How do you plead?"

An Imperial Watcher across the room tried to hedge. "Abetting the *what*?"

"The Unseen," Vendrick repeated flatly. "The apocalyptic blood magic cult whose atrocities I frankly don't have time to list at present."

"Apocalyptic?" Muratori squeaked. "You know nothing of—"

She shoved her hands over her mouth, but it was too late.

"Ah," said Vendrick, "guilty then."

Like a cornered prey animal, Muratori lashed out: "Do you think killing me matters? That when the Sightless One comes, he won't leave you to fight the darkbeasts with all the other unbelievers? And when the Grand Huntress finds Valerius and Vilulf, that she won't—"

Vendrick flicked his fingers, and the Singularity pellet whizzed across the room. It caught Muratori between the eyes before she'd even had the time to draw her sword, and she slumped across the table, blood pooling beneath her.

Across the room, one of the greener recruits began to retch into a flowerpot.

"What is the meaning of this?" thundered the lieutenant as he came rounding out of his office.

Vendrick held up the hand keeping his spellbook open, and there, glittering on his middle finger in the torchlight, was the fox-head Imperial Seal. It was a heavy ring he hadn't openly worn in many years, and, like Aurelius' poem, felt like coming home to a place he no longer recognized.

The lieutenant froze. "You aren't authorized to carry the Imperial Seal, Caecillion."

"Am I not?" Vendrick asked coolly, annoyed but not surprised. The Imperator had revoked Vendrick's right to use it when Vendrick had resigned as his Spymaster, but the average citizen didn't know that. "Someone should probably tell the Imperator."

Purple, arcane energy dripped from Vendrick's fingers as he yanked his Singularity pellet back from Muratori's corpse. It arced and doubled back on itself, sliding through the air as though reality itself couldn't abide its presence.

The lieutenant ducked out of the way of the first pass, but Vendrick reversed course and smashed the knot of arcane energy into the back of the man's armor. The lieutenant began to convulse, a black, ichor-like substance foaming from his mouth. He fell to his knees, coughing and retching black froth.

Vendrick's gaze flicked up to their third in command, a thin woman who was nearly old enough to be his mother. "Clean house, if you would," Vendrick told her over the dying lieutenant. "You've lost three of your number this morning, and likely more of the treasonous bastards will show themselves in an hour, or so."

She stared in horror at her lieutenant, now lying on the floor, unmoving. "Headmaster Caecillion," said the once-third, now-first in command, "what is going on?"

Vendrick paused, debating how much to say. "Have you heard of the Unseen, Ricci?"

The Watcher shook her head no.

"Then as I said, they're a blood magic cult with designs upon Silverwood," Vendrick said. "They are enemies of the Imperium, of Silverwood, of myself, and of anyone who wishes the world to remain intact."

He gestured to Muratori and the dead lieutenant. "These two belonged to it. And that darkbeast Valerius killed last night that I'm sure you've heard the rumors regarding?"

The Watchers at least had the decency to look embarrassed.

"Summoned by one of their number," Vendrick added. "Now if you'll excuse me, I have other business to attend to, and you have corpses to bury."

He left the spluttering guardsmen to deal with their own rot, and Vendrick hurried down the hall to the Captain's office.

This was the strangest, trying-on-last-summer's-clothes feeling yet. Vendrick had grown up alongside Markus della Luciana, served alongside him as a Queenmaker during the Tyrant's War, and worked with him as the Captain of the Imperial Watch stationed at Silverwood for years now. None of that was to say that Vendrick had ever *liked* the man—Markus was a useless twat—but he had always been. It was like a light fixture or commemorative statue had suddenly been decommissioned.

That Markus had summoned the massive darkbeast Frelia was currently butchering out in the field was neither unexpected, nor news, but Vendrick had to be sure. He did nothing in half-measures, and it was why he was so effective a Spymaster.

Lightless, he thought, *until the work is done.*

He approached a lectern that sat, unassuming, between a bookshelf and a weapons rack. Faustine had told him the secret that lay behind it, and warned him that the contents were "horrifyingly nasty," to use the teenager's own words.

Vendrick had told her he expected no less, and that she should get some sleep.

The textbook sitting on the lectern appeared to be a swordsmanship manual fifty years out of date. Not quite old enough to be considered antique, not quite modern enough that the average professor would want to use it to teach. And Markus wasn't even a professor.

Vendrick flipped through the book for a moment until he landed on the diagram of the *posta di domina* sword stance. The illustration showed a man with his sword raised overhead, as if to cut directly downwards at an enemy before him. Vendrick carefully reached out with one gloved finger, and pressed the tiny swordsman's face.

A mechanism clicked softly in the lectern, and then the bookshelf beside it swung open easily into a dark, yawning stairwell. Just as Faustine had said it would.

How long has this dugout been here? Vendrick wondered acidly as he began the descent. Had it been built under his nose, or was it repurposed from something that had come before? The idea that Markus had managed renovations of this nature while Vendrick had been just sitting over in Salonia Hall rankled him like a festering boil.

Markus was a known entity; a fool who thought his name would protect him. If he'd managed to build this himself, then not only had Vendrick and his black network missed that, but he also hadn't noticed that an Unseen plant was impersonating his own little sister.

And if he hadn't caught that either, how many other things had he missed?

Volsinii military units were built on trust. They had to be, by design. If you didn't trust that the soldier beside you was going to do his duty, or that the general giving orders would support her troops in the heat of battle, you did not have a unit. At most, you had a handful of warriors who would probably die at the first enemy encounter.

He knew that, but still, trust didn't come easy to Vendrick. His baby sister was among the select few he would, if pressed, admit that he trusted. No wonder, when he could count his friends on one hand and have fingers left over. No wonder he hadn't asked her their code question from the very moment he'd become suspicious. No wonder the Unseen had used her. He had gotten complacent.

Vendrick would rectify that mistake. He would clean house here, and then he would liberate Clarissa from Serpentbrook Hold and ruin every Unseen he found on the way out.

The smell began to hit him then. Acrid and pungent, like sewage in high summer. His boots touched solid ground, and in the soft semidarkness, nothing moved. Vendrick waited a moment, eyes raking the room, then pulled the kerchief tied around his neck over his nose and mouth. He drew a quick rune in the air before him with his other hand, the purple, arcane light vivid in the gloom. He completed the rune, and then a magelight bloomed at his fingertips.

Green, brackish light slid over a granite laboratory table stained with both black darkbeast ichor and the much more familiar ruby red of garden-variety human blood. A sewer grate had been set into the corner for experimental runoff, but normally that meant alchemical reagents that had been mixed with coffee grounds or silver to ensure they were inert.

In Markus' laboratory, it apparently meant severed flesh.

All-too-human lungs poked out of the bin beside the grate, and although decay had begun to set in, Vendrick could still make out bits of intestines here and bone fragments there.

"Lightless," he muttered beneath his kerchief.

Who had these bones been? One person, two, a family? How many people had Markus murdered to build the monster Frelia was currently dissecting aboveground?

Because that's exactly what had to have happened. Faustine had corroborated it, and even if she hadn't, Markus had turned tail and run the instant he had an out in the fight on the hillside. And nothing screamed guilt quite like running away.

Vendrick sighed, and then immediately wished he hadn't. The stench was eye-wateringly strong, and he had work to do.

He began to case the place with a professional's practiced eye. Ignoring the laboratory table and organic detritus for a moment, Vendrick surveyed supply cabinets and desk drawers and the like. He found piles of surgical implements—well-kept and clean, which was a terrible sign—and medical accoutrements, as well as stacks of journals and folios that Vendrick would have killed to have the time to sift through.

He was just making a mental note to have his black network divest the place more thoroughly when he opened the last supply cabinet.

The rusty smell of dried blood hit him at once, and there was a row of vials neatly slotted into a rack on the top shelf. The vials were empty but for a reddish residue that it didn't take a genius or a Spymaster to identify.

But what was the point of holding onto dirty blood vials? They couldn't be reused like that, and the neat stack of clean syringes beside it implied...

Oh. Vendrick's mouth fell open as he realized.

These were bloodrune vials. It was the only logical explanation for why Markus hadn't cleaned them. How much blood did he need to do... whatever it was beastminders and the Unseen did with bloodruned folks' pilfered blood? Vendrick didn't know, but if the levels of residue were any indication, it wasn't a lot.

His mind first went to Frelia. *His* Frelia, as of maybe six hours ago. He hadn't even slept, too focused on clearing out the winter ball and making plans and preparations during his last night as Silverwood's Headmaster. He'd checked in with her several times, and continued to find her hacking away at the enormous corpse of the bird-like darkbeast they'd taken down together.

It wasn't exactly the most auspicious or romantic start to a relationship, but he could fix that backstage later. Besides, she kept shooing him away so she could do her own lightless work.

His mind went next to Christel Vilulf. Their bloodrune had erupted earlier in the school year, and although they were a competent swordsman, they didn't have nearly the experience Frelia did. In many ways, if Vendrick left Silverwood, Christel would be a sitting duck.

Valente Secundus came to mind next, the other bloodrune-bearing student at Silverwood. He was a scion of the Secundus family though, so even if he had the Domitia Bloodrune, he had protections that Christel simply didn't. Valente was a nobleman's son that would be quickly noticed as missing.

Vendrick shut his eyes and breathed in sharply. He had never been more certain of his decision than at this exact moment. The professors would be flabbergasted, the students gutted, and the students' families, outraged, but better all that than leaving this place a wide-open target.

The Silverwood Military Institute was no longer safe. And it was that simple.

Vendrick's gaze traveled down the supply cabinet shelves, passing over scalpels and scales and rolls of gauze, until it arrested on a crystalline lump nestled in a heavy cloth. Vendrick was reminded of crystal balls in diviners' shops, except that the lump was uneven, and ruddy red like a blood clot. And if he squinted, he could just make out a small, glowing rune set deep into the center of the thing.

"That's a bloodrune," Vendrick muttered, "or I'll eat my boots."

He had seen bloodstones before, of course. They powered everything from enchanted weapons to ever burning wall sconces, and his sister was an enchantress, for the Saints' sake. But he had never seen one with a rune inside it, let alone a Bloodrune.

With the kind of care typically dedicated to baby animals, Vendrick slid his gloved fingers beneath the cloth nest and lifted the bloodstone to the level of his eyes. It pulsed with faint, arcane energy, and the rune inside swirled as though caught on a breeze. He wrapped it in the cloth, and then sealed the bundle shut with a roll of gauze for good measure. Vendrick had sat through too many lectures on the dangers of touching unknown arcane artifacts not to.

Frelia was going to want to see this, and he had no idea how she'd react when she did.

A clock on the wall began to chime softly, and Vendrick glanced over to the sudden sound.

Six o'clock. It was nearly dawn, then. Time to put everything in motion.

With one last glance about Markus' laboratory, Vendrick slipped the bloodstone bundle into an inner jacket pocket and headed back up the stairwell.

His black network would have to take care of the rest.

CHAPTER TWO

THE HILLSIDE BETWEEN THE boarded-up Silverwood chapel and the Imperial Watchers' barracks reeked with the smell of burning hair and rancid meat.

Frelia Valerius had been awake all night, hacking off portions of dead garmr to throw onto the pyre she'd stayed up to stoke. Her shoulders burned with exertion, and she'd had to clean the axe and re-sharpen it about four times. She lost track after she'd barely reached the monster's ribs and had to go for the whetstone yet again; there was still too much corpse to burn to worry about the weapon she'd need to destroy at the end of the night, anyway.

Not for the first time, she cursed that she couldn't just burn the whole thing on a pyre in one go. The smell was awful, like every thrice-damned battlefield she'd ever walked and then some. The black-feathered corpse was a monstrous raven, big as a house and twice as sturdy.

Lord Muninn. The Guardian of Traust Territory. Lady Twilight's Raven. The Lord of the Slain.

Dead by her hand—or, well, as dead as legends ever really got. And good riddance to the poor bastard. It hadn't been roused by normal means; it had been summoned by a Volsinii beastminder, twisted beyond recognition to a purpose it hadn't been built for.

Like me, Frelia thought grimly as the axe bit into the raven-garmr's breast again.

Dawn was starting to lighten the horizon just over the roaring pyre, and Frelia wondered if Vendrick was faring any better than she was. She may have been stuck on "butcher the monster corpse" detail, but at least she hadn't had to explain to the entire Silverwood winter ball why everyone needed to go to ground immediately. The students, the faculty, the Goddesses-damned Imperator...

Ja, Frelia would take butchering the garmr corpse over that.

Vendrick had come out to check on her sometime between the dismantled talons and lower belly. Offered up fresh coffee, a jug of water, and leftovers from the winter ball dinner.

Also? Merciful Goddesses, he was awful now that he had free rein to flirt. It was kind of fantastic.

Ichor suddenly sprayed out of an artery, despite the corpse having been dead for hours. Frelia ducked her head and jerked out of the way, managing to avoid being completely doused. Ichor caught the hem of her dress, and she stooped to cut it off. She'd throw the scraps of her winter ball gown on the fire alongside the chunk she was working on.

When it came to garmur, Frelia Helm's Grace Valerius was certain of two things: they hunted in packs, and dead ones only ever brought more. So until the beast was back in Helheim where it belonged, she wouldn't waste time changing clothes or getting sleep or showering.

By the looks of it, she had about half a corpse to go.

She freed a chunk of the raven's breast about the size of a wyvern-saddle and dug the axe into the corpse further up the breastbone. Frelia put both arms around the loose piece and, eye watering from the stench, hauled it over to the pyre.

White-hot embers sprayed and spiraled toward the sky when she threw her burden atop the smoldering pile of wood and meat. The sewage-and-rancid-meat smell kicked up again, and she grimaced. Frelia didn't bother to cover her nose and mouth, though; her hands were filthy and her clothes weren't any better. She simply turned away from the pyre, coughing, and trudged back towards the corpse.

She was exhausted. When she'd had to butcher-and-pyre these things in the war, there had been more than one person doing the damn work. Other Krakenguard, usually, or someone's house knights, or, hell, even local villagers. Frelia was alone out here, as she had ever been.

Her father's voice came to her, as if to scold: *a loose sled dog is a lost sled dog.*

"I am not a loose sled dog," Frelia muttered to Muninn's corpse as she hefted the axe again.

And she wasn't—least, not anymore. She had *volchya* again now, even if it consisted of her students and a defrocked cleric and a former spymaster and his little sister. That was at least a sled team, wasn't it?

"I am a professor, dammit," she muttered. "At least for another twenty minutes."

Her bones began to rattle against each other, each rib and tooth a cacophony. It was a feeling as familiar to her as her own breath.

Rumbling. It meant a live garmr was near.

Frelia released her grip on the axe and left it embedded in Muninn's side. She reached for the legendary sword sheathed at her side—somehow, impossibly, hers—and drew as her eye scanned the horizon.

Lake Silverwood was still, off in the distance, and the barracks were quiet and unassuming. Vendrick was down there causing trouble, last he'd said, but you wouldn't know from looking at it. Frelia's gaze traveled over the dirty snow of the hillside, the burning pyre, and over to the broken wall outside the chapel.

Four green eyes burned like unholy fire in the predawn light as they stared Frelia down from just inside the curtain wall.

Like all garmur, this one was massive. Easily the size of a horse-drawn carriage, she was built like a wolf, and so heavily scarred that patches of her hide had never grown back right. Violent, red scars slashed up her flanks that hadn't yet healed.

But the green of her eyes was hollow. A ring around a much more human, muted brown.

Every instinct Frelia had screamed at her to run, to fight, to gut this monster and throw it atop the pyre, too. Before it could eat someone, or destroy something, or call on its friends.

The effort it took Frelia to release her grip on her sword was inhuman.

"Thera Bones' Defiance Grimsdalr," she called over to the beast, "don't fucking sneak up on me like that!"

The beast made a hoarse noise almost like laughter. But it hurt too much to hope, and Frelia tore it out at the root. Thera might be somewhere in there, but this *thing* wasn't her unblood sister.

"Well if you're going to just stand there," Frelia called over to her, "make yourself Saints-damned useful! Eat some of Muninn, or something."

Beast-Thera made that hoarse noise again, and started to lumber towards where Frelia stood beside Muninn's corpse with her hands on her hips. But then the beast froze, halfway across the hillside, all four eyes narrowing at something towards campus.

It reminded Frelia of the times Thera had stood up in her saddle, staring out across the horizon at something none of the rest of them had seen. Usually Cillian would have readied the Blink rune as soon as he saw the change in his twin.

The Blink rune...

Frelia had held onto the Grimsdalr Blink for a long time, now. She'd refused to teach it at Garmur-Killing 101, but if Muninn wasn't an end, but a beginning... there were several people she could think who needed to know it. Last night's fight had shown her just how vulnerable she was—how vulnerable they *all* were—without Cillian around.

Frelia had held onto the Grimsdalr Legacy, sure, but it wasn't hers to give.

"Thera..." Frelia began quietly.

Beast-Thera's ears pricked up to signal she was listening, but she didn't take her eyes off the direction of campus.

It was easier, somehow, not to look into the beast's inhuman eyes. "...I think I need to teach Vendrick the Blink Rune. Probably Edmund, too."

Frelia expected an explosion of protests, a curtain wall of negation and 'how dare you's.

What she got was a soft, firm, *"Agreed."*, and Frelia was struck by the reminder that Cillian had been the choleric one.

A second later, Thera bolted towards the chapel's curtain wall again, and Frelia was alone on the snowy hillside.

Shapes began to appear out of the early morning gloom, and it took Frelia a truly stupid amount of time to realize she recognized them, given that she knew they were supposed to be coming.

There was Axemaster Ossani, whose enormous shoulders were impossible to mistake, and Archerymaster Serrana, who somehow looked even more severe in the early morning light than she normally did. They were assisting old man Magicmaster Marcellius as he shuffled along like his leg was paining him this morning. And behind them was an even more familiar figure in cleric robes that had been dyed green years ago.

"Good morning, Frelia!" Edmund Blightsen called out.

"Nice corpse you've got there!" Axemaster Ossani interjected.

"You haven't been working all night," Edmund added, "have you?"

"You see anyone else helping?" Frelia shouted back.

"Why didn't you say something?" Magicmaster Marcellius gently chastised. "Once the students were seen to, we could have assisted."

Frelia didn't know how to say *because I don't trust enough of you* in a sentence that was remotely polite, so she said, "Wasn't thinking about it."

Edmund came over to stand beside Muninn's corpse with her, studying the broken ribcage through his round glasses lenses. "Is this... who I think it is?"

Frelia nodded, hefting the axe into striking position again. "Muninn, Lord of the Slain."

She punctuated the raven's title with an axe to the neck.

Edmund blanched in the early morning light. "How did it get here? And... why attack?"

"Excellent questions." Frelia buried the axe in a second cut beside the first, working more of the creature's flesh free of its bones. "That's why Vendrick called a faculty meeting at the ass-crack of dawn."

"You look dead on your feet, Valerius," Axemaster Ossani said, coming over to join them at the beast. "Gellir and Campagna should be arriving shortly with coffee, but in the meantime, let me do what I do best."

He held out his hand with a winsome smile.

"*Ja,* pretty sure if I stop moving, I'll just fall over." Frelia crouched and began to tug the newly-hewn section of monster free. "Thanks, though."

Ossani made a face, and then moved to draw the axe holstered on his belt.

"You don't want to do that," Edmund said, making a negating motion with his hands. "Whatever you use to cut this thing apart will need to be burned afterwards."

"Why?" asked Archerymaster Serrana from across the way.

"Garmr blood always draws out more of them," Frelia said dully. "And it's almost impossible to get the smell out of the metal."

Saints, she'd thrown out so many swords over the years. Frelia heaved, and the newly-freed chunk of garmr-flesh came loose.

"I'll handle that," said Edmund softly, and his signature orange magic began to bloom at his fingertips. "Marcellius, would you kindly check on the pyre?"

Edmund drew a languid rune in the air before him as Magicmaster Marcellius made his way over to the pyre with Serrana's help. The old man's own green magic ignited as he drew a rune across the foot of the pyre. Marcellius' hands were never so steady as when he was casting magic.

Edmund finished his rune a moment later, and then orange magic dived for the chunk of garmr-flesh in Frelia's arms. She let it go, and smiled tiredly as the meat began to float towards the pyre.

Ossani whistled. "That's handy."

"Keeps your clothes clean," Edmund said, squinting at the meat as he concentrated.

A moment later, Marcellius completed his own rune, and the pyre roared to life so fiercely, Frelia felt the sudden heat blast across her face.

"Sorry!" Marcellius' gravelly voice called over. "That wasn't supposed to be quite that fierce..."

Frelia laughed, and a moment later, Edmund did too. "Burn the whole thing to ash, Marcellius," she called over. "It's the only way through."

"You had a good start, then," he said, and it echoed of all the black magic classes Frelia had taken as a student.

The floating chunk of neck meat thumped down atop the pyre, sending cinders spiraling skyward, and then the cycle began again.

True to Ossani's prediction, Wyvernmaster Gellir and Loremaster Campagna arrived three chunks later with a huge thermos full of coffee and a stack of tin cups, respectively. By the time they'd sorted out drinks and explanations for everyone, the rest of the faculty had arrived, and the most familiar figure of all was hiking up the side of the hill from the Barracks.

"Ah, good," said Vendrick. "You're all here."

He looked about as tired as Frelia felt, but there was a manic energy behind his eyes that was probably keeping him upright. She wanted to ask what the hell he'd gotten himself into down in the Watchers' Barracks, but knew better than to ask that with an audience.

"Come about, all of you," Vendrick said, gesturing for everyone to circle up. "And tell me what you know of the Unseen."

CHAPTER THREE

FRELIA WAS STARING AT Vendrick in unmasked surprise, and he tried not to let it burn a hole in his resolve. This had to be done, and he had to give enough information to make it plausible.

Don't you trust me? A little voice in the back of his mind wanted to ask her, but Vendrick viciously squashed it.

Trust was a loaded word, and he wasn't about to lend it any more ammunition.

"Aren't the Unseen the..." Ossani seemed to look around for a charitable word. "...folks who worship Lady Midnight, in Ascalon?"

"Just call them a cult," Frelia muttered. "It's what they are."

"There's no need to be rude," began Lancemaster Sabine, who had always been a thorn in Vendrick's side. She'd been an Imperial Watcher, once, and was far too familiar with Markus della Luciana.

"Correct on both accounts," Vendrick interrupted over her. "Now, I've no idea what they want with Silverwood, but they're the reason we keep being overrun with monsters."

He gestured to the half-decimated garmr corpse, and the assembled faculty grimaced.

He was also lying. Vendrick knew exactly what the Unseen wanted with Silverwood—the folks with bloodrunes who attended and taught here. But he didn't have the time, inclination, or backup for *that* rabbit hole.

"How do you know it's the Unseen?" asked Tacticsmaster Vitellus, whose background was so blank, Vendrick could paint a portrait on it. (Which led Vendrick to believe that Vitellus wasn't the man's actual name.)

"Right, and I have family who attend the Church of Midnight," Cavalrymaster Corvinus said. "I can't recall my mother saying anything sinister about it."

"Patience, all. I'm getting there." Vendrick held up his hands in a placating gesture. "Additionally, to those of you who had the dubious pleasure of speaking with my sister last night at the winter ball—"

A small chuckle ran across the assembled faculty, but Vendrick kept his facial expression neutral.

"—you should know, that wasn't my sister at all. It was an Unseen agent, wearing her face with magic."

He watched for the professors' reactions. Frelia was, as well. Most of the faculty looked genuinely surprised, and Marcellius even looked horrified. Sabine looked like she wanted to argue, and Vitellus' horrified look was paper thin. But Corvinus' surprise was genuine, and grim understanding was dawning across Ossani's blunt face.

"Something you want to tell us, Ossani?" Frelia barked.

He startled. "Just that she seemed odd last night," Ossani said. "She and my sister hit it off so well at Stonebreath and Mitri's wedding that they're in the same opera-watching group, now."

"Exactly," Vendrick said. "That's part of what tipped me off."

Marcellius moved his hand away from his mouth to ask, "What does a religious group want with poor Clarissa?"

"Excellent question," Vendrick said. "I intend to find out."

It rang with the finality of cannon fire.

"That said," Vendrick continued, "I called you all here to discuss next steps."

"Next steps regarding what, your jumping at ghosts?" Lancemaster Sabine asked.

For a moment, Vendrick debated how honest to be. Too blunt, and he'd spook the skittish ones. Too delicate, and he wouldn't bring the gavel down with appropriate force.

He turned to look directly at Sabine, and the woman took an inadvertent step back.

"Sabine," he said in his best oh-come-now voice. "We have been assaulted twice in our home by the very monsters we supposedly have a contingent of Imperial Watchers to keep out. If I didn't know any better, I'd suspect they're involved."

It dawned on the Silverwood faculty, one by one, that Vendrick Caecillion had never ceased to be a spymaster. It was in his blood, and bones, just like a bloodrune. He watched as the realization dawned on each of their faces—except for Frelia, who had never thought of him as anything different.

"Preposterous," sniffed Sabine, although sweat had beaded in her hairline.

"Their Captain is a beastminder," Vendrick said, "who attempted to prevent Valerius from slaying Muninn last night and then promptly ran when he couldn't."

A hush fell across the meeting. Most everyone had always agreed that Markus della Luciana was a shithead, but there were whiny, spoiled brats, sure—and then there were criminally dangerous men hiding behind that façade.

Frelia was staring at him so hard, Vendrick could feel it boring into his chest. He was sure she wanted to ask what the hell he'd found down in Markus' laboratory, but that was certainly too blunt for this crowd. At least she realized that.

"That garmr corpse is a lit fuse," Frelia said, pointing to it. "Until it's burned to cinders, we're all at risk of more of them showing up."

"What about your wards, headmaster?" Loremaster Campagna said, and she sounded almost pleading. Poor thing. She was a historian, not a soldier.

"No ward is perfect," Vendrick said. "They will all break eventually, and it's not wise to be on the inside when they do."

"That's why white magic wards need to be re-laid every so often." Blightsen spoke up for the first time in the entire meeting. "Which isn't an issue if the caster is on hand."

Frelia was the only one who didn't immediately turn to stare at Vendrick in horrified surprise.

He smiled, wryly. "You're getting ahead of me, Blightsen."

"You're not leaving," Campagna said, "are you?"

"My talents are required elsewhere," Vendrick said, "and Silverwood is no longer safe. Last night made both of those facts abundantly clear. So as of four forty-five this morning, I have resigned."

"Now who's running away?" Gellir said, and Vendrick could practically smell the sour fear wafting off of him. "You were just insulting della Luciana for that!"

Vendrick didn't rise to the bait.

"Oh, I'm not running," Vendrick said. "And rest assured, I have set plans in place for your continued safety. Now, Marcellius." Vendrick turned to look at his deputy headmaster. "You are now in charge, so I suppose the following is a proposal."

"Consultation," Marcellius managed.

Vendrick smiled, but it was tired and thin. "Indeed."

"Of course you have a plan," said Archerymaster Serrana, and she sounded sadly fond. Like someone readying to put down a beloved warhorse with a broken leg.

"I do nothing without one," said Vendrick. "Now, Silverwood has a multitude of emergency protocols, one of which is for plague. It details the quick evacuation of the student body, as well as faculty and staff, while minimizing the risk of exposure to infected persons. The latter is, obviously, not important in this scenario, but the evacuation is. We will send the students home with a letter of credit for the second semester, which may be redeemed at a time in which Silverwood is deemed safe once again."

"So it is running," Gellir said, with sadness and distaste.

"It's target minimization."

It wasn't Vendrick who said it, but Frelia.

"And dunno about you," she added, staring down Gellir, "but I know *ech er seiða*. It doesn't matter how we feel about it."

It was one of the handful of Kaldiri phrases Vendrick knew. *This is war.*

"How does the evacuation work, Caecillion?" Ossani asked.

"By end point," said Vendrick, grateful to bring the conversation back around to the point. "We will group students based on where they need to return home to, and send them off in batches. All the Ascaloni students, for example, will go with whichever professors are returning there. Prefects are to be informed of the protocol first and assist faculty in the exodus."

Ossani nodded. "Sensible, but what about the students without a home to return to?"

"And the faculty," muttered Gellir.

"There is a boardinghouse in Silverwood Town that will take those persons in," said Vendrick. "It's named in the paperwork."

"And who determines when it's safe to return?" Campagna asked, her fingers twisting and twitching at her coat sleeves.

"The headmaster and Captain of the Imperial Watchers," said Vendrick. "So, Marcellius and whoever replaces Markus della Luciana."

"Oh, it's one darkbeast!" Sabine bristled. "Do you burn down a home when you find a single cockroach in the cellar?"

"It's three, actually," Vendrick said. "And we've even got an exterminator living among us."

He glanced to Frelia, and belatedly, so did everyone else. She didn't like being the center of attention any more than Vendrick did, but you'd never know by looking at her.

"There's never one cockroach," Frelia said, "or one garmr."

Slowly, the other faculty began to nod. Vendrick was relieved he didn't have to further argue for the necessity of the evacuation protocol—

But then, that was why he'd requested the meeting take place on the hillside, beside the butchered corpse of a darkbeast.

"Also, I've been wondering," Vitellus said, "Valerius, why are you burning a garmr corpse when there's a beastminder on staff?"

"Can't find him," Frelia said cheerlessly. "And I'm not going to stand here and let us paint a target on the walls again."

"There is no target from a dead monster," Sabine huffed.

"Yes, there is," Blightsen suddenly said. "And it's painted in their blood."

The former cleric was shaking, but his voice was steady and his hands were clenched tightly around his tin coffee mug. He wasn't looking at anyone, keeping his eyes trained on the sloshing liquid in his cup.

"I was at Kollavik, in the medical tents," Blightsen added in a quiet whisper. "I won't live that again."

For a moment, the entire hilltop was silenced by Blightsen's naked pain. The Massacre at Kollavik was why the Kaldiri knew dead garmur attracted more, and it was called a massacre for a reason.

Then Marcellius said gently, "And we aren't asking you to. That is why we will evacuate."

"We'll *what?*" came a new voice from over by the main path.

All eyes fell to Markus della Luciana as he strode up the hillside, looking like he'd been thrown off the Silverwood battlements and scraped back upright into his boots. His curly brown hair was scraggly, his olive skin sallow.

"Well, there you are," Vendrick said like he'd finally discovered the rock in his boot. "I've been looking all over for you."

"I was in my office," Markus snapped.

"Really?" Vendrick tilted his head like a curious dog. "I searched there. Quite thoroughly."

Markus froze mid-stride. "At what time?"

"Immediately after the fight with this thing," Vendrick said, gesturing to Muninn, "And again just now."

Markus opened his mouth to lie, but Vendrick wasn't finished.

"Care to explain the human remains I found in there?"

Shock fell hard and fast across the hillside. Jaws dropped and gasps rang out, and Marcellius stared at Markus in horrified disappointment. Vendrick grimaced in secondhand shame; Marcellius was the father figure to every mage who had ever come through Silverwood, after all.

"I beg your pardon!" Markus screeched. "I will not stand here and be accused of murder by the Viper of Ascalon."

"He didn't say you killed them," Ossani pointed out. "Just that he found remains in your office."

"If you are seriously accusing Captain della Luciana of what I think you are," Sabine hissed, "then the Imperial Watchers would have to search his entire office!"

"As well they should." Vendrick smiled. "And I will inform them to make certain to check behind his bookshelf when they do."

A vein pulsed in Markus' temple, and for a brief moment, Vendrick savored the feeling of getting under the bastard's skin.

Then the stench of carrion rot drifted lazily across the hillside, and Vendrick wrinkled his nose.

"Headmaster Caecillion," Markus said, "I have been more than patient with your—"

"Oh, that's another thing," Vendrick said. "I am no longer the headmaster. You will need to direct any Silverwood inquiries to the deputy headmaster, Magicmaster Marcellius."

For just about the only time in his entire life, Vendrick saw Markus shut his mouth. It lasted a few, beautiful moments while the gears in Markus' head turned and he tried to process what he was hearing.

"I can't believe this." Markus blinked a few times. "You are a liar and a murderer and who in Hypogia would hire you?"

"Shut up and let the man talk, della Luciana," Frelia snapped.

"You will speak to a scion of the royal family with the respect he is due," Markus barked, "or face consequences, Valerius."

A muscle in Frelia's jawline twitched, but Cavalrymaster Corvinus interrupted to say, "Della Luciana, *please*. Let us be civil."

"Oh, civil, is it?" Markus sniffed. "Well, I wish to hear why Caecillion has abandoned his post."

Vendrick resisted the urge to dig his thumbs into his temples. How much to let on that he knew, how much to keep close to the vest...

Well. There was one thing that would shut him up.

"Do you recall," Vendrick said after a moment "speaking with my sister last night?"

"Of course," said Markus. "Why?"

"That was not my sister." Vendrick kept his facial expression hard as ice. "It was someone wearing her face."

He waited, but Markus' facial expression gave nothing away. "What proof have you?"

"I watched her face fall off," Vendrick said flatly. "But my point is—"

"Well, then where's your imposter?" Markus interrupted.

"Actually," piped up Marcellius, somewhat apologetically, "I've also been wondering that."

Frelia sounded disgusted as she said, "Got eaten by a garmr last night."
It wasn't even a lie.

Most of the faculty looked horrified, but Markus sniffed and said, "Well that's convenient."

"Oh Saints," said Serrana quietly.

Frelia nudged the woman's shoulder in a way that was probably meant to be comforting. "It's what they do."

Vendrick refused to glance towards the ruined wall near the chapel. There would be no explaining Thera without tipping all their cards, and Vendrick wasn't prepared to play that hand just yet.

"So now there's no body," said Markus flatly. "Really, Caecillion, do you expect us to just believe a story like that with no proof?"

"Yes." Vendrick spoke so abruptly that Markus startled. "And frankly, it's not my concern whether you believe the truth or not."

Somewhere in his periphery, Frelia and a few others snorted.

"I will launch an inquiry into this!" Markus hissed.

Ossani shot Markus a withering look. "Why, so you can prove Valerius slaughtered a darkbeast that your Watchers couldn't?"

Markus seethed. "My Watchers are perfectly capable of defending Silverwood."

"Then why didn't they?" Frelia asked.

"I warned you—" Markus rounded on Frelia. "—to speak to the royal family with respect."

"It's a fair question."

Everyone turned to stare at Magicmaster Marcellius, who had never looked so frail and so old as he did just then.

But the mage didn't falter. "If they are truly capable of defending Silverwood," Marcellius continued. "then why was a professor required both times we were attacked?"

"I am incapable of being everywhere at once," Markus said acidly.

"You were in the academic quad at the beginning of the year!" Ossani said. "Not to mention the ballroom last night. There's no way you couldn't have known, if Valerius did."

Marcellius' eyes narrowed uncharacteristically. "Particularly since I would presume the head—err, Caecillion, I suppose—informed the Imperial Watchers after he himself was made aware?"

"I did," Vendrick lied.

Markus' grey gaze swiveled to Vendrick. "Who'd you tell? It certainly wasn't me."

"Ricci," Vendrick said, figuring the woman would be too frazzled to contradict him if Markus actually got around to asking. "I was then told there were guardsmen patrolling the grounds and I needn't worry about Valerius' paranoia."

"Enough, della Luciana," Ossani said. "The longer we waste time here, the more chances there are for even more darkbeasts to show up."

"I'm working on it," Frelia huffed, gesturing with the axe towards Muninn's corpse.

"Keep going," said Blightsen, still too quietly even for him. "I'll help you get it onto the pyre."

"I did not authorize this," Markus snarled. "You will cease this Kaldiri nonsense at once while we get to the bottom of Caecillion's insanity."

"*Ja*, well, me and my nonsense can multitask." Frelia shouldered her axe again and glanced to Vendrick. "So Marcellius, Caecillion, what's the battle strategy?"

"As I had said," Vendrick began smoothly before Markus could insert himself into the conversation again, "we will be evacuating based on the Silverwood plans for plague."

"We're going to what?" shouted a new, much younger voice.

All the adults turned to see a gaggle of Silverwood students stopped dead in the middle of the towpath. Some were carrying axes, and others, thermoses or travel baskets from the mess hall. Vendrick recognized them at once, even without their uniforms.

It was Frelia's homeroom.

CHAPTER FOUR

Professor Valerius recovered from the shock first.

"What in Helheim are you lot doing here?" she called over to the Violet Owls, and Faustine smiled.

Leave it to the Professor to make cursing feel like home.

"We came to help you with the monster corpse!" shouted Siegmund Ossani. He was enormous, with hands and feet too big for his frame.

"How do you know about that?" Professor Ossani shouted back. Faustine still didn't know how they were related, exactly, but she was pretty sure they were cousins.

"Faustine and Christel told us!" Siegmund called back. "What are all the professors doing here?"

The adults all looked around at each other uncomfortably—even Markus, whom Faustine hadn't noticed was there, at first. Her stomach fell at the realization. The last thing she needed right now was any of her bloody family.

Then Headmaster Caecillion sighed. "I suppose the news was bound to get out eventually."

Markus' eye about bugged out of his head. "You cannot seriously just drop this information on—!"

"As of this morning," the headmaster interrupted, "I have resigned. Magicmaster Marcellius will be overseeing the evacuation of the Silverwood Military Institute."

Faustine stopped dead in her tracks. "You... what?"

Silverwood was only safe because Headmaster Caecillion was running it, and Faustine knew that for fact. It was the major reason Markus hated the man so much. The Unseen couldn't very well waltz in and steal kids with bloodrunes while the Viper of Ascalon was overseeing their welfare.

If he wasn't going to be there anymore... then neither would kids like Valente and Christel. Faustine had to work not to look at either of them in horror.

"Whoa," said Siegmund. "Why?"

"Siegmund!" Professor Ossani said, but he was laughing.

"Because we are evacuating," the headmaster—or, well, Not-Headmaster—said. "Silverwood is no longer safe, and last night's episode made that abundantly clear."

All eyes went to the half-butchered monster corpse on the hillside, and Saints, this was too much like that day in the academic quad.

"Well, make yourselves useful, Little Owls." Professor Valerius cut into the conversation as if with a sword. "Siegmund, Owen, Faustine, Karina—you lot have the axes, *ja?*"

All four of them nodded.

"Come with me," the professor added. "I'll show you where to cut. Everyone else, I hope you brought clothes you don't mind ruining. Caecillion, keep going."

Explanations of prefect duties and lanes of egress and overall organization washed over Faustine, even as her arms burned with exertion and Markus repeatedly tried to derail the conversation. Her borrowed axe sunk into the darkbeast's flesh with a gross squishing sound, over and over, until whatever part she was supposed to be hacking off fell away. Then Valente or Christel would appear in her periphery and haul the chunk of now-unidentifiable meat over to the pyre. Ellie was helping Professor Blightsen keep it burning high and bright, and whenever a new portion was added, the air would clog with burning hair and rancid meat.

Then the cycle would begin again.

Why can't you burn the whole thing at once? She remembered someone asking at one of the Garmur Killing 101 classes.

Professor Valerius had said the Kaldiri had tried that at first, but found that the monster would take days to burn and attract more darkbeasts the whole time it did. So they took to hacking them into pieces to speed up the process.

Faustine noticed that Markus was arguing against evacuating—and of course he was. His entire purpose for the family was to find bloodruned folks at Silverwood and inform the Unseen.

Cushy job for a rank failure, Orsina had muttered the day Father had told them Markus was going to Silverwood.

She'd gotten smacked, then, and Faustine was pretty sure her oldest sister still had the scar on her cheek to prove it.

And then the Not-Headmaster was saying, "Any questions?" and the professors were beginning to disperse.

Faustine had a lot of questions. Where was she supposed to go, back home with Markus and Ironfang? Where was Christel supposed to go, they didn't even have family to go back to. What about Professor Valerius, and Professor Blightsen, and all the others who didn't, either?

And then a shadow fell across her face, and Faustine's hands froze on the axe.

She glanced up to find Markus, lanky and looming in his banded, Imperial Watchers' Armor, glaring right at her like all this was somehow her fault.

It was his typical facial expression.

"You will return with me to my office," he ordered. "I shall deal with you there."

Faustine shifted her grip on the weapon, wishing she could use it, but knowing better. And though her hands shook and her voice was little more than a whisper, she said:

"I won't."

Markus recoiled like she'd struck him, after all. "I didn't ask your opinion, and this is not optional."

"Markus..." said Not-Headmaster Caecillion warningly.

"I'm not going." Faustine's voice was louder this time, solid.

"I haven't the time for this," Markus snapped. "You are going to stick that axe in the ground, bathe, and then gather your things and meet me at the inn in Silverwood Town before dinner. And then we are leaving, apparently."

Faustine felt the eyes of her classmates on her, but still, she couldn't stop. Not now that she'd started. "I didn't say you couldn't go."

Markus' hand curled around the haft of the axe, and he leaned in to hiss, "This temper tantrum is an embarrassment to the family. You will return to Caere, and you will learn your place in this world if I have to tan it into your hide myself."

"You will not." Faustine couldn't believe what was coming out of her own mouth, but once she'd started, she couldn't stop. "I'm not going to your office, I'm not going back to that empty villa, and I'm not going anywhere with people who threaten me!"

Fury flashed across Markus' face a half-second before his hand moved. Faustine shut her eyes and braced for pain, but it never came.

Cautiously, Faustine opened one eye to see that Professor Valerius had caught Markus' arm in a grappler's hold.

"You will not," Professor Valerius growled, "threaten my students."

"You have no right." Markus yanked his arm out of the professor's gloved hand. "This is a family matter."

"I know," the professor said, bringing up her fists in a grappling stance. "That's why I'm walking up to the Senate and demanding it."

Not-Headmaster Caecillion loosed a barking laugh.

"Stand down, both of you," Magicmaster Marcellius said. "Clearly tensions are high, but surely we can—"

He cut himself off with an alarmed shout when Markus began to draw a rune. Faustine had probably seen her brother cast a thousand times at this point, and rose-gold magic alit his narrow face as Markus began drawing the crisscrossing lines and jagged swirls that made up the runic language.

Then he cried out in pain as the world began to smell of ozone. Professor Valerius' eye widened as she bolted forward, slamming into Markus just as his stolen Bloodrune went off.

He didn't fall right, as though he were somehow heavier or sturdier than he should have been. It didn't stop the Professor from scrabbling at his breastplate, digging her fingers into the lip of his collar—whatever it took to bring him down.

Faustine yelped and backstepped out of the way of the tangle of flailing limbs and grunted curses. Other professors were shouting too, now, and Axemaster Ossani rounded on them, bellowing, "Oi, oi!"

And then Professor Valerius howled. Genuinely, outright howled. It was rage, and it was grief, and it was a single note more gut-wrenching than anything Faustine had ever heard.

Axemaster Ossani froze, his jaw hanging open. "What the hell, that's not..." He paused, blinked, and then shook his head. "That can't be a bloodrune?"

"You fucking zychnik," Professor Valerius spat, *"I will bleed him from you myself!"*

She lunged for Markus again, but this time Axemaster Ossani caught her by a fistful of her cloak. "Oi, Valerius," he said, "easy!"

"Under the authority vested in me," Markus began raggedly, dusting off his kilt and staggering to his feet, "by the Senate and Imperator, long may he reign, you are hereby—"

"I thought your family was runeless, Faustine." The voice was quiet, and cut through Markus' bluster like a knife.

Christel's golden hair shone in the early morning sun, and their blue eyes were locked on the bloody, wounded eye in Markus' face. If anyone had a right to know about the bloodrune-stealing, it was Christel Vilulf, but after Faustine had done exactly that last month, the truth made her throat gum up.

"We are," she managed, and she looked helplessly over to Not-Headmaster Caecillion.

His face was, as always, a cool, neutral mask, and his voice was even when he spoke. "Valerius? While you're just standing there—kindly confirm what's in Markus' eye."

"Bloodrune of the Sentinel," Professor Valerius ground out immediately. "Grimsdalr, granted to defend the innocent against Lady Midnight's children."

She lashed out with a swift kick, slamming her boot into Markus' shin. The Watcher Captain shrieked and flinched away, only for Axemaster Ossani to grab a fistful of his cloak, too.

"For all the fucking times this thief has done that," the professor snarled.

"If Faustine's family is runeless," began Owen Gundalf, one of Faustine's Kaldiri-born classmates, "then that can't be her brother... right?"

He looked from professor to professor, but all of them stared at Markus' ruined eye in visible shock.

All of them, except the Not-Headmaster, that is. (And Faustine was really going to have to ask what to call him now. Count? That felt stilted.)

"That's... not how Bloodrunes work," Owen added. "Right?"

He put more weight behind the question the second time.

"Right," Professor Valerius growled.

"So..." Loremaster Campagna looked so pale, Faustine wondered if she might faint right there. "...then who is wearing Markus' face?"

"Oh, I don't have to answer to the likes of you," Markus snarled, and he wrestled out of Axemaster Ossani's grip.

Red-gold arcane light shone from his fingers a second before a rune caught Professor Ossani square in the chest. The big man was blasted backwards across the hillside, and the concussive force threw him into Archerymaster Serrana and knocked them both over.

A shock of Dark Fire whizzed past Markus' shoulder, missing by a hair's breadth, and Professor Valerius yanked Faustine out of the line of fire. Markus was suddenly drawing again, and the Not-Headmaster followed suit. Arcane light dripped from their fingers as they raced to complete their runes—a mage's duel in every way.

Markus winked out of sight an instant before the Not-Headmaster's dispel rune blasted at nothing, and silence fell across the chilly hillside.

"Fucking hell," the Not-Headmaster muttered. "Blightsen, check on Serrana and Ossani."

But Professor Blightsen was already there, rolling up his sleeves and pressing his hands to foreheads and wounds.

CHAPTER FIVE

IRONFANG WAS DECIDEDLY NOT having a good morning.

So, the summoning of Lord Muninn had been a raging failure. Ironfang wished he were surprised. He had warned Markus not to underestimate Valerius and Caecillion. That for all their myriad flaws, they remained competent combatants, for the bloody Saints' sake. Valerius had survived with the Bloodrune Hunters on her heels for most of her adult life, and Caecillion had retired as an Imperial spymaster. That had only happened once before in the entire history of the Volsinii Imperium, and it had been five hundred years ago.

So now Markus had completely wasted a vial of Traust blood and didn't even have the garmr to show for it. The Unseen would continue to work without Valerius' bloodrune, and with Caecillion's intelligence network breathing down their collective neck. Without even the courtesy of keeping him at Silverwood!

Fantastic. This was exactly why Ironfang trusted his last living son with a grand total of nothing.

Last night had been Markus' last chance. If Ironfang wanted something done right, he'd apparently just have to do it himself. He didn't have long before the Sightless One would throw a fit about this latest blunder, and Ironfang could only hope he was far from Silverwood when the Old One decided to start complaining.

With any luck, he'd be halfway back to Ascalon by the time the migraines started, and Orsina would be Ascended at Serpentbrook Hold. Clarissa Caecillion would be out of his hair for good, and Vendrick would be unbalanced enough to make messy mistakes that allowed the Unseen a crack at him and Valerius.

All would be well. Ironfang could still salvage this. He just needed--

Elias.

It was only years of practice that made him keep moving. Ironfang was becoming aware of an unnatural chill slipping into his bones, and the hairs on the back of his neck were standing on end. He shivered, knowing he had only moments to get out of sight before his mental interloper became obvious.

Failures, failures, tsked the voice.

It felt like the fetid air of an open grave in the back of Ironfang's mind. Like every awful thing the world had ever taken from him. Like Ironfang's formative years and Vittoro Caecillion's failed Ascension.

The Sightless One's voice always felt like death itself.

My Lord, Ironfang mentally replied, even as he hustled across the academic quad, *to what do I owe the honor?*

Sudden pain cut across Ironfang's mind, blooming like a migraine but sharp like physical agony. He tried not to cry out as he slipped beneath the eaves of Salonia Hall, clutching his head in his hands.

I give you Drogari, whispered the Sightless One in Ironfang's mind, seething. *I give you the knowledge of my children and their births. I give you time plentiful, and the power of the gods. And yet, you fail me!*

My Lord, Ironfang thought, trying not to sound desperate, *we are working—*

Silence!

The whispered word sparked stars across Ironfang's vision, and he immediately squeezed his eyes shut. He pressed his forehead to the cold stone pillar beside him, willing the pain to go away, or at least subside.

I have given you every tool to succeed, the Sightless One whispered, hammering nails into Ironfang's psyche with every word. *Why do you fail me?*

My Lord! Pained tears ran down Ironfang's face, catching in his beard. *My Lord, I beg your patience just a little longer.*

I have been *patient,* the Sightless One snarled, *for millennia.*

We're only mortals, Ironfang tried.

You are not.

Ironfang knew, from past experience, that blaming his subordinates' obvious incompetence would get him nowhere. The Sightless One wanted results, and seemed to labor under the delusion that Ironfang could hop across the continent and be everywhere at once. (Ironfang's theory was that the Sightless One could do that, once he were freed.)

We have seven of the nine bloodrunes, my Lord, Ironfang told it, instead of any of that. *With plans to gather the remaining two before spring.*

The Sightless One went silent for a long, terrible moment. And then the pain between Ironfang's eyes eased, just a little. *Which two remain?*

Háski and Valerius, Ironfang said at once.

Soft laughter began to filter across the quad, and Ironfang wasn't even certain it was in his head.

The fighters, the Sightless One whispered, amused. *Of course.*

Ironfang was not a tentative man by nature, and it rankled him that the Sightless One could reduce him to such a state. Orsina had *better* return with successful news from Serpentbrook Hold, or Ironfang was going to have to look into his other, less desirable options.

But for now, Ironfang just said, *We know Valerius' whereabouts as well as Stonebreath's. It won't be long now, my Lord.*

Ironfang waited for the cold to recede, for the pain to stop. The Sightless One could hop into his mind at any moment, but he didn't typically stay long.

Then the Sightless One said, *I have another task for you. Two, in fact.*

Ironfang eased himself away from the pillar, glancing furtively around the quad to make sure he was still alone. *My Lord?*

I require a sacrifice, the Sightless One said. *Make it so.*

Ironfang sighed. The Sightless One was demanding those more and more often. Could a divine being be greedy? Did they even operate with such vices and virtues as greed and charity? Or was there another reason it was demanding living flesh so often, now?

And you shall have one, Ironfang said smoothly. *Even now, the Unseen prepare an Ascension in the north.*

Not that one, the Sightless One said. *One from you* personally, *Elias. Or have you forgotten the cost of failure?*

This time, Ironfang really did freeze. He considered his options, his possible answers.

No, my Lord, he finally said. *I have not.*

Good. Make reparations, and then I shall grant you purpose.

Ironfang rubbed at his temples as he hurried away from Salonia Hall, trying to sort through what raw materials he had access to. He didn't have a day to waste in the woods going after a deer or elk, didn't have the time or patience to snare a rabbit or squirrel, and didn't have a horse or wyvern to spare. He supposed he *might* have a spare child, but that would be more trouble than it was worth, at the moment. If he offered Markus to the Sightless One, there would be no one left for the Old One to inhabit if he decided to vacate Ironfang's mind.

Unlikely, but worth holding onto. For the moment, anyway.

Did Silverwood Town have stray cats or dogs? One of those would work, if Ironfang could catch one. He detoured to the Silverwood mess hall and came away with a pouch full of cut-up sausage leftover from breakfast.

He hadn't even had to lie; it *was* for the strays of Silverwood Town.

By mid-morning, he was sitting on a log near the edge of the town, wedged between the butcher's quarter and woods, coaxing a skinny-looking setter out of hiding with bits of sausage.

Dogs had never much liked Ironfang. They usually growled at him as though he, personally, were going to steal their food and murder their puppies. But that had quieted in recent years, no doubt thanks to the Sightless One, and this dog let Ironfang scratch absently behind its ears as he surveyed the forest. It wasn't exactly the old growth forest of the Northern Wilds, but it would do.

With slow, deliberate movements, Ironfang rose to his feet. The hound didn't run off, which he took to be a good sign. He set off into the forest, whistling for the dog and holding out another piece of sausage.

It trotted along beside him, munching on its last meal, as Ironfang slipped into the Konstantin forest. He didn't know where he was going—not exactly—but he hadn't needed to worry about such mundane things in years. The Sightless One would let him know when he stumbled across a place where the seal between worlds was thin.

In no time, he was good and lost, deep in the woods and off the beaten path. Getting out was going to be a complete pain. Still, Ironfang pulled up short when he felt the mist tug on his bones. The dog stopped too, sitting back on its haunches and sniffing the air as though it had scented prey. Ironfang studied the unnatural silence, and he could just barely make out the midday sun over the tops of the dark trees.

Then he felt it. A whisper of power unlike anything in the Waking World.

Ah, he thought. *Hello, my Lord.*

The hound continued to pant beside him, and for a long moment, Ironfang wondered if he'd been forsaken after all. The thought left a hollow pang in his chest, empty and numb. Again? Was he going to have to suffer this vast loneliness, cut off from the world, *again?*

Then the Sightless One whispered, *Proceed.*

At once, Ironfang dropped to a knee. The dog turned to him, already nosing his hand for more treats. It was a handsome setter with a shaggy, spotted coat and an eager disposition. A good dog for a huntsman in the coming days, once it was properly fed again.

The dog began to whine as Ironfang drew his dagger, but he coaxed it forward with small scratches behind the ears and another bit of sausage. The dagger slipped soundlessly into its chest and its throat, and though the blood that fell onto Ironfang's hands had to be warm, he felt nothing through his gloves.

The setter collapsed onto the forest floor, and silence reigned.

Then the dog began to retch, convulsing where it lay. It vomited its heart, its lungs, and a number of other organs Ironfang didn't care to identify, before the dog drew shakily back up to its feet.

Its eyes were burning, hollow and green.

He left you a gift, said the Sightless One.

Although Ironfang was long since used to the grimmer aspects of the divine, it took him aback. *In this... muck?* He forced himself to look down at the pile of newly-made-garmr vomit. *I don't see anything.*

Try again, little one.

Ironfang steeled himself and began to sift through the garmr-vomit with the tip of his knife. The smell nearly did him in as he pushed around the detritus of a once-living creature until there, in the center of it all, lay an unidentifiable fleshy lump. It was red and lurid, almost obscene-looking amongst the rest of the mundane gore.

At once, Ironfang knew.

With wordless reverence, he lifted the lump out of the muck and cradled it like a newborn. He turned it this way and that, studying its peaks and crevices in the dappled sunlight.

Now, said the Sightless One on the breeze, *you know how garmur work, I trust?*

Ironfang swallowed audibly. *I... don't suppose I could cook it?*

The Sightless One laughed, though it was more like a breathless wheeze on the wind.

"Thought not," Ironfang said, not really to the Sightless One. It wasn't the first disgusting task the Old One had given him, and it wouldn't be the last, either.

You know the cost of failure, said a voice in the back of his mind. Ironfang didn't know whether it was his.

Ironfang rinsed off the fleshy lump in a nearby creek, the Sightless One laughing in the back of his mind the whole time. But Ironfang had standards, thank you very much, and also vomiting the thing right back up seemed like it would sort of defeat the purpose. And Ironfang had not connived his way onto the Volsinii throne just to be deterred by a measly lump of garmr meat.

Steeling himself, Ironfang swallowed the slimy, fleshy lump whole.

For a moment, nothing happened. Ironfang felt a bit like an idiot as he knelt there on the forest floor. He was the Volsinii Imperator, for the Saints' sake, and he had far more important things to do than scrabble in the dirt. Surely the Sightless One knew that? He'd been the entire reason Ironfang had orchestrated war against Kaldr in the first place.

Then something white-hot burned through his insides, and Ironfang began to convulse. He pressed his bloody gloves to his mouth, willing himself not to throw up.

Easy now, said the Sightless One. *You're already Hypogean; it won't kill you.*

But still, the lump burned all the way down Ironfang's throat. *Water,* he needed water. He splashed creek water onto his feverishly burning face, tried to drink but the liquid boiled in his mouth.

I'm sure it hurts, though, the Sightless One added, almost as an afterthought.

The sheer agony almost made Ironfang regret this entire endeavor. Almost.

It felt like hours before the burning died down, before Ironfang could breathe without fearing he'd vomit. The burning knot that had slid down his throat and boiled his stomach had settled into a warm ache, and Ironfang found he could drink this time without vaporizing the water in his throat.

Now, said the Sightless One, *open your senses.*

Ironfang sat back on his haunches and closed his eyes. He tried to let the world wash over him, tried not to focus on any one sound or smell or let his thoughts cloud over with to do lists and notifications that this body part hurt, that one did.

And then he felt them.

He felt a garmr curled up near Silverwood, snoozing although the creature did not actually need to sleep. He felt the remains of two dead ones over near Leptis Magnam, and wondered what in the gods' name had killed them.

Here in Konstantin Territory, the vestiges of their bloodrune buried deep in the earth sang to him like an operatic aria. Ironfang drew on that power, drank it in. He felt more garmur pacing through the remains of Valerius Territory, felt a huge knot of hell's children deep in what could only be the Northern Wilds.

Ironfang opened his eyes, and was surprised to find tears streaking down his face. *Thank you, my Lord.*

Use it well, said the Sightless One. *I have another task for you.*

CHAPTER SIX

BY THE TIME EDMUND had seen to the injured, Frelia had calmed down the Violet Owls, and the other faculty had left to begin the evacuation protocol, it was well and truly daylight.

Frelia stared at the sliver of sunlight like it had personally offended her. She had been awake far too long and was in desperate need of a shower, nap, and food, in that order. Unfortunately, she had yet to reach Muninn's head and shoulders, even with the Violet Owls' help.

She became vaguely aware of a shadow on her right, and glanced over just in time to see Vendrick come to rest beside her.

"How are you doing, love?" he murmured, and his hands fluttered like he wanted to reach out to squeeze hers but didn't want to get garmr ichor all over himself.

Frelia paused to actually take stock of herself. Every muscle in her body ached, and her exposed skin was going numb from the way garmr ichor burned.

"Been better," she said. "Also been worse. You?"

"I'll live." Vendrick grinned, but it was thin and worn. "And so it's agreed, we should probably do a better job of looking after one another?"

"Probably." Frelia lowered her voice to add, "What are we going to do about Faustine, Christel, and Valente?"

"Same thing as before Ironfang stuck his nose where it doesn't belong." Vendrick leaned into her personal space to the point that Frelia could feel the warmth emanating off his skin. "We'll evacuate Christel and Faustine somewhere safe, and Valente too, if we can swing it."

Frelia's eye cut to the chapel. "What about Thera?"

"I've been thinking about what to do with her, too. And I think I've got it." She felt his eyes on her, bright and calculating. "We'll send Christel and Faustine with Thera and a certain professor to Talis Mitri's laboratory. They can be gone before Ironfang's morning coffee even gets cold."

Frelia's brow furrowed as she watched Owen and Karina hack away at Muninn's corpse. Siegmund was throwing water over his head like this were a rugby tournament, and Ellie was nearby with another jug of it. Valente and Owen were still hauling chunks of meat over to the pyre, and Faustine supervised, her fingers still loosely curled around an axe to keep them from shaking.

Her Violet Owls. Her responsibility. Her kids.

"Did you say laboratory?" Frelia asked. "As in, beakers and vials and alchemical ingredients?"

"I did."

Frelia waited for him to add something else to that, but he remained silent. She was going to have to poke him. "Why would we send them to an indefensible office?"

"First," said Vendrick, "because it's not indefensible. I have plenty of the black network stationed there, plus it's an alchemical lab; there's a basement. Second, because it's run by Talis Mitri and his wife, Hazel Stonebreath."

He said it with finality, but Frelia had no idea who that was. Not Hazel—she knew her from Silverwood—but the other name. "Who's Talis Mitri?"

"An old friend of mine," Vendrick said. "A talented physician and white mage who served in the medical tents during the Tyrant's War."

Frelia's eyebrow rose. "Is he a cleric?"

"Decidedly not." Vendrick sounded amused. "But he wasn't a Queenmaker, either, and at the moment, I think his laboratory may be the safest place for a handful of teenagers we can't keep a direct eye on. Also..."

He trailed off, to the point that Frelia glanced over to him.

"Also, what?" she pressed.

Their eyes met, and the acid-green was a gut punch to her soft, squishy underbelly. "Also," Vendrick murmured, "I have him researching bloodrunes, and he would absolutely love a docile darkbeast."

Frelia's hackles rose. "She's not a science experiment!"

"Nor would Talis treat her as such," Vendrick agreed. "But she is intelligent. And, I would bet, enough so to want to return to her actual body."

Four green garmr eyes burned in the back of Frelia's mind, and she closed her own eye against it.

"Can he do that?" she asked.

"Dunno," Vendrick admitted. "But if anyone can, it'll be Talis and Hazel. They're brilliant. Also, I figure we—"

Vendrick cut himself off abruptly, and Frelia glanced up to find Edmund hustling towards them, his pale face blotchy and his breath coming out in puffs.

And despite his very obvious exhaustion, he was a cleric by nature and trade, and still asked, "Do either of you need patched up again?"

He had already seen to the knife wounds in Vendrick's arm and shoulder, plus the battery of bruises and lacerations Frelia'd gotten. Frelia had never heard Vendrick curse so loudly, colorfully, or vehemently than she had while holding his arm steady so Edmund could yank the knife out and stop the bleeding.

"Not unless you have a spell to wake me up," Frelia said tiredly.

Edmund made a sympathetic noise. "I think there might still be some coffee left? But, um, as your healer I would really recommend actual sleep, instead."

"*Ja,* it's on the list." Frelia waved him off.

Vendrick snorted. "Thank you for your assistance this morning, Blightsen."

"I'm a healer." Edmund looked taken aback. "That's what I'm for."

"There's a reason we always had a cleric on hand in the war." Frelia clapped Edmund's shoulder a few times, and though she tried to be gentle, he winced anyway.

"Two clerics," Edmund reminded her. "Hägen just never formally took up the cloth."

"Which makes him a healer," Frelia said, "not a cleric."

Edmund laughed, and it sounded about as tired as Frelia felt. "So, um, what's the plan for...?"

He trailed off, flicking his eyes towards the broken chapel wall. And Frelia was reminded of all the times Edmund had sewn her or Thera back together, and her heart twinged painfully in her chest.

"We were just discussing that, actually," said Vendrick. "What were your evacuation plans?"

"Hadn't gotten that far," Edmund said, his eyes narrowing just a little. "Maybe visit my mum in Olicana. Why?"

Edmund was kind, sure, but he wasn't dumb. The ones who thought so usually assumed kindness was a weakness, and not a life's calling.

"Would you consider an escort mission?" Vendrick asked quietly.

"Me?" Edmund was visibly taken aback. "Wouldn't Perseo Ossani or Hrolf Gellir be more suitable for something like that?"

Vendrick cocked an eyebrow. "Why would you say so?"

Edmund sighed. "Why do you think, Caecillion?"

"I think," Vendrick said, deceptively lightly, "you are aware of the Chapel situation, Faustine's situation, Christel's situation, and possess the very soul of discretion."

Frelia immediately knew what Vendrick was getting at. "Besides, you're also the least controversial Kaldiri on staff, Edmund."

She left unspoken *so we can trust you to hate the Imperator and his men.* Edmund laughed, just a little. "I'm only half."

Frelia opened her mouth to argue that his da had been the last Einnaska King's seneschal, but Vendrick said, "Can we count on you?"

Edmund made a face. "Can I have some time to think it over?"

"Err..." It was probably just an eternity of Volsinii politics that kept Vendrick's face neutral.

Still, Edmund fixed him in a pointed, owl-eyed stare. "I knew it. What's the issue?"

"Things are already in motion," Vendrick said. "Frelia and I need to leave before Ironfang collects himself, and so do Faustine and Christel. Valente, as well, if I can make it work, but I doubt I can sneak a scion of the Secundus family out from under their nose."

Frelia looked at Vendrick in growing horror. "What about *sleep,* Vendrick? Breakfast? Showers? We've been going since yesterday morning."

"I brewed a stimulant for that last night." Vendrick pulled open the edge of his jacket to reveal a vial of tangerine orange liquid nestled in an inside pocket. "Three sips of this, and you won't need to sleep for a week."

"Is that Bitterbane extract?" Edmund's eyes narrowed in suspicion. "That's been illegal for a decade for good reason, you know."

"Conveniently, you'll note, made so after the Tyrant's War. And Frelia, you realize there's a good chance we'll walk into another fight, right? Little point in bathing until after that."

"Sure," she said, "but my clothes are ruined and garmr ichor burns."

Vendrick recoiled. "It does?"

"Yes," Edmund piped up, "like stinging nettles."

Vendrick blinked, and very pointedly looked Frelia over from head to toe and back again. "You're drenched in it."

"*Ja*, why do you think I want a shower?"

Vendrick made a face like he both wanted to protest and smack her for being so reckless.

"And we also haven't talked about what the plan is for after we get into the stupid fort," Frelia said. "And you haven't told me what kind of fort it even is."

Vendrick's stare became guarded. "It's... Serpentbrook Hold, Frelia."

"*Ja*, and that means nothing to me." She rolled her eye, exasperated. "Is it a motte-and-bailey? A stone tower keep? What kind of garrison does it have, what defenses? Running headlong into hell is my thing; *your* thing is planning everything meticulously. What the fuck has gotten into you?"

Vendrick's jaw fell open, and he looked to Edmund. The cleric suddenly found a smudge on his glasses worthy of his full attention, and was furiously rubbing the hem of his sleeve over the lenses.

Vendrick heaved a breath, and did her the courtesy of meeting her eye. "Frelia," he said quietly, "Serpentbrook Hold was renamed after we captured it in the Tyrant's War."

Ice began to creep down Frelia's spine. "So, what, is it Fort Frostmaiden?" She could handle that one, at least.

Vendrick shook his head. "No."

"Fort Knaerwood?" Worse, but not impossible.

Again, Vendrick shook his head.

Frelia's stomach fell into her boots as she hissed, "Heit Reiði?"

"I'm... so sorry, I thought you knew."

For a moment, Frelia could only stare at him in numb, dumb shock. Then she bundled her cloak in her arms, pressed her face into it, and screamed.

"I'm so sorry," Vendrick said again when she emerged.

"Shut up," Frelia snapped. "I am..."

She cut herself off, abruptly, and tried to swallow around the growing lump in her throat.

"...I'm not letting you go alone. So it's moot."

Vendrick looked like he wanted to reach out to comfort her, and so Frelia took a step back to both spare him the garmr blood and her the feeling of breaking into a million little pieces. Goddesses, she felt like she was going to be sick.

Heit Reiði.

She was going back to Heit fucking Reiði.

Vendrick kept speaking, but he may as well have been underwater, for all Frelia understood. This couldn't be happening, couldn't be fucking happening. She had sworn never to set foot in that wretched place again, and yet here it was, laughing in her face and looming on her horizon. Frelia had no desire to see where everything had fallen apart, let alone walk its halls and break its defenses.

She startled when a hand landed on her shoulder, her own reaching for her sword hilt.

"Frelia, talk to me," Vendrick said, squeezing her shoulder gently. "You're hard enough to read on a good day."

"Is it the eyepatch?" she tried to joke.

"No, it's the fact that you always look like you're debating a murder." He paused. "And the eyepatch."

"Even if you leave now," Edmund put in as delicately as he spoke to dying men, "you won't make it all the way to the northern coast in three days, Vendrick. I'm sorry, but... your sister will be dead by the time you get there."

"No, she won't," Vendrick said swiftly. "I've got a homing rune attuned to Athos del Priore."

Edmund's jaw fell open in a little, round 'o' of surprise.

"So if he's still himself," Vendrick added, "then I can get us there, *now*, with whatever is on our backs."

"Which I need to pack, too," Frelia reminded him.

Saints, she was tired. Bitterbane extract was sounding like a better idea the longer she stood here with no end in sight. Even if the one time she'd ever used it in the war, she'd had a panic attack and a week of nightmares.

"Tell me what you need," Vendrick said. "I'll get your things in order while you're cleaning up."

The idea of someone else going through Frelia's shit normally made her skin crawl. With Vendrick, though, it mostly gave her a vague sense of unease, like when she used to ask Thera to braid her hair or Cillian to hold her up so they could stumble home from the pub.

Frelia didn't like needing other people. It was a good way to end up disappointed, if not dead. And besides, the Valerius were bred to be the war dogs of Kaldr. She was supposed to *be* needed, not the other way around.

Vendrick's voice brought her sharply back to herself. He was arguing with Edmund, now. "I'm not letting them murder my younger sister, Blightsen."

"No, she's your *volchya*," Edmund agreed. "You have to go, if there's a chance."

Vendrick paused, ire cooling somewhat. "My what?"

"*Volchya*, sorry," Edmund said. "It's a catch-all term for close friends and family."

"People you give a damn about," Frelia croaked, and it echoed with her da's voice in her ears. "Literally, it means wolfpack."

Or owlets, she thought, a little sourly, and glanced over to her students again.

Ellie had moved onto throwing water on Owen's face, and he was blushing like mad under her attention. Faustine was laughing at something Karina had said, and Christel had stacked three slabs of meat atop each other to carry them over to the pyre. Siegmund had four, and Valente was jokingly heckling the both of them as they struggled towards the pyre, ready to step in if someone fell.

They were good kids, even the Volsinii ones. And Frelia didn't like that she wouldn't be here to guard their backs from Ironfang and his scheming.

But what else could she do? Vendrick was her *volchya*, too. And if he was, then so was his sister. And Clarissa faced the certainty of death without their help; the Violet Owls only faced the possibility.

One life, or two, or three, or three-thousand, she had told Vendrick once. *How are we supposed to calculate the worth of that?*

And he had answered, without hesitation, *By triage.*

Well, if Edmund could triage in war, Frelia could triage in peacetime. Even if it was only technically peace.

"Goddesses preserve me, but alright." Edmund drew in a deep, tired breath. "I'll take this escort mission."

Vendrick breathed in audible relief. "You're a bloody Saint, you know that?"

"Not quite," Edmund said with a small smile. "I want to ask you questions about this shadow war and what in Lady Midnight's hell you've gotten my dear boneheaded friend—and now me—into."

It took Frelia a second to realize he meant her. "Hey!"

"I suppose that's fair enough," Vendrick said with a laugh. "Come walk with us while we finish laying plans, and tell me—what would you like to know?"

Something unreadable flashed in Edmund's ordinarily kind eyes. He glanced over his shoulder to the Violet Owls, and to where Axemaster

Ossani was supervising them, and said, "Tell me everything, would you kindly?"

"You two do that," Frelia muttered, already on the move towards her students. "I'm going to go say goodbye for once."

CHAPTER SEVEN

FAUSTINE WAS TIRED, BUT it was the good kind of tired, where you could see the work you'd done and feel like you'd properly accomplished something. Most of the raven-like corpse was either on the pyre or in pieces ready to be thrown on it, and even if they had to burn their clothes afterwards, it meant everyone would be kept safe.

Faustine could live with that trade.

"I'll take it from here, Ossani," said a familiar, Kaldiri voice from somewhere to Faustine's right, and she glanced over just in time to see the professor coming towards them.

"Hi, Professor!" Karina called as their Swordmaster approached. "We're almost done."

"I see that," Professor Valerius said. "Good work, all of you."

Faustine was unable to keep from smiling. It was so rare that she ever was praised for her work, and it was only ever at school. It was why she liked it here.

Silverwood isn't safe, a little voice reminded her.

Faustine's stomach flipped as she realized, if she couldn't stay at Silverwood and had told Markus off, then where was she supposed to go?

Maybe she could stay with Karina's family? Or Ellie's? That would probably put them out, though, and Faustine couldn't do that to them.

Valente and Siegmund were from noble houses that would turn her over if Ironfang demanded it, and Owen was from Northern Volsinii and Faustine didn't want to put him in danger like that. And Christel didn't even *have* a home to go back to—what were they going to do?

Maybe she could just go with the Not-Headmaster and the professor, wherever they were inevitably going together? Christel, too.

"Are you okay, Professor?" Christel's voice yanked Faustine out of her spiraling panic. "You seem kind of... stiff."

Professor Valerius' face tugged into a sad half-smile. "I came to say goodbye, little Owls."

At once, Faustine dropped her axe and scuttled over to the professor. She was only a few steps ahead of the others.

"What do you mean, goodbye?" she asked around the lump in her throat.

The professor gestured for them all to gather 'round, like this was the middle of a sparring drill and she'd noticed everyone making the same mistake. Faustine took her place beside Owen and Karina in the huddle, resisting the urge to throw her arms around their shoulders like usual because everyone was covered in burning darkbeast blood.

"I wish I could tell you the headmaster was the only one resigning," Professor Valerius said. "And I wish I could tell you that when you return for the second semester, whenever that will be, I will be there to make you run laps and hold your swords correctly."

A bubble of laughter burst in Faustine's chest, and it left tears in its wake.

"But I won't," Professor Valerius said, her voice unusually quiet. "So this is goodbye, little Owls. I am proud of each and every one of you—even you, Siegmund—"

The big guy laughed so hard he hiccupped.

"—and I know you will do yourselves proud, when the time comes to fight."

Although she didn't say it, Faustine had a bad feeling that time was now, actually.

"What about the grappling unit?" Karina asked, scrubbing tears out of her eyes. "I was looking forward to learning more of that that..."

"You never taught me how to do the lance-twirly thing," Owen protested, his chin wobbling.

Professor Valerius' voice was rough, too. "You never got a hundred on an exam."

"I was working on it..." Owen glanced to his boots, and kicked at an invisible clump of dirt.

"Where are you going, Professor?" Valente asked, shifting from foot to foot probably as much from the conversation as the darkbeast blood that had gotten on his leg. "Mercenary work again?"

"Probably." She nodded, and then sighed. "Don't forget what I've taught you all about garmur—"

"They're big, hungry, and angry," interrupted Ellie, a statistical first.

"And there are a couple different sizes!" Christel interjected. "The small ones, the big ones, and the stupid-big ones."

"Where there's one," Valente added, "there's always more, 'cause they hunt in packs."

"And you gotta kill them with fire!" Siegmund pointed to the pyre across the way.

Professor Valerius blinked at them for a moment, and then, inexplicably, started to laugh.

"You'll all be just fine," she eventually managed to say. "Goddesses protect you, until you can do it yourselves."

She spread her hands as if offering a benediction, but found herself hugged instead. Karina squeezed hard enough to make the tendons in her arms stand out, and then let go of a bewildered Professor Valerius, looking a bit sheepish.

"Sorry," Karina said. "It just seemed like the right thing to do?"

"Go hit the showers," Professor Valerius said with a smile, gesturing over her shoulder at the dorm. "I'll take care of the rest of this."

The Violet Owls took their time disappearing, each one wanting to say goodbye to the professor in their own way. The rest kept fanning the flames and butchering Muninn, breaking its bones now to make sure they'd burn.

"It's kind of like a chicken, don't you think?" Faustine asked when it was finally her turn to speak to the Professor alone. "Maybe that's strange to say, but it's what I keep thinking."

"That's not that weird; it *is* a bird," said the Professor. "It gets weird when you realize a bird carcass isn't all that different from a human carcass."

Faustine blanched, and the Professor winced.

"Sorry," she said. "I'm clearly not running on enough sleep."

"Err, Professor?" Faustine ventured after a moment. "Is everything okay?"

Professor Valerius sighed. "I've been trying to figure out how to ask you that, *yishka*."

Faustine figured that was Kaldiri, but she didn't speak it. "I beg pardon?"

"You just saw a lot last night," the Professor said. "And I don't care if you've seen it before, you're still a kid. And I wish I'd had someone ask me how I was doing, after the first garmr I saw eat someone."

Faustine stared at her for a moment, mouth open in shock. For all that Professor Valerius looked intimidating—and did she ever, what with the eyepatch and black hair and Kaldiri furs when it was even remotely cold outside—she was still the only adult who regularly seemed to care about what happened to Faustine.

It was why Faustine had no idea what to say to her.

But Professor Valerius seemed to take her silence for something else entirely: "I guess I probably should have sent Edmund to check on you.

He's..." She seemed to search for a word. "...much better than me with this kind of thing."

"No, no, it's okay!" Faustine hastened to add. "I'm just surprised."

The Professor raised her eyebrow, and Faustine had the absurd panic that she somehow hadn't studied for some exam. "I didn't realize this was so out of character for me."

"No, no, not for you!" Ugh, Faustine was making a mess of things, damn. "It's just... well... people don't really ask me if I'm okay."

Silence fell.

"I'm going to throttle your entire family," the Professor said, "starting with your shithead brother."

Faustine felt like crying again. Part of her wanted to ask if the professor would really do that, just to hear her say it. But she knew even without asking that Frelia Valerius would.

Professor Valerius could do anything.

"I'm sorry he stole your friend's bloodrune," Faustine said, even though she knew it was an absurd thing to say.

"Going to go out on a limb here," said Professor Valerius, "it's not your fault. What happened, though?"

Faustine told her about how della Trova had injected the Grimsdalr Bloodrune into Markus' arm a few days before the winter ball, and how he'd been using Grimsdalr blood to make darkbeasts for years.

By the time she finished, Professor Valerius' jaw was gritted so hard, Faustine could see the tendons in her neck standing out. "I'm... going to kill him," the Professor said. "I swear it on the graves of my parents, my aunt, and my older brother."

"You'll probably have to get in line," Faustine said, trying to joke. "I think a lot of people want to do that, including my father."

"That reminds me," the Professor said, "you're ignoring the question and this wasn't supposed to be an interrogation."

"It's okay," Faustine said, genuinely. "I like being helpful."

But the professor just shook her head. "What's going on in that head of yours, little owl?"

"I..." Faustine froze. "What do you mean?"

The professor kicked at a loose bone near her foot. "The first time I watched someone get eaten by a garmr was at the battle of Fort Frostmaiden. I threw up in the middle of a damn battlefield; Cillian had to cover me."

She shook her head, annoyed at her younger self.

"And for days, I felt the crunch of that thing's jaws snap shut over my comrade's bones whenever I shut my eyes. I think that specifically might be a bloodrune thing..." She patted at her side, just above her right hipbone. "...But even my runeless friends didn't sleep well for weeks."

Oh. That's what the professor meant.

Faustine tried to smile, but it cracked her face like an eggshell and suddenly there were tears instead. "What do I do, Professor? I can't go home but it's not like I can go with any of my classmates."

"About that," Professor Valerius said, dropping her voice low. "After you clean yourself up, pack quickly and get to the Headmaster's suite. It's still Vendrick's for the moment, and he has a plan for that. I told Christel the same."

Part of Faustine wanted to tell Professor Valerius the truth about what Faustine had done for Markus. But another part of her couldn't bear to see disappointment in Professor Valerius' eye, and what if she stopped answering Faustine's questions? What if she had to stare down an eternity of living like a hermit without even Professor Valerius to write letters to?

Also, there was the terrifying monster corpse she was cutting up, sure, and there was also Headmaster Caecillion dueling someone with as much ease as Faustine braided her hair in the morning. But there was also the fact that Professor Valerius kept calling him his given name, and he kept using hers.

And if there was one thing any self-respecting fifteen-year-old Volsinii girl caught onto, it was that.

"So are you and the Not-Headmaster..." It was ridiculous, absolutely absurd, and also, Faustine wanted to *know*. "...together now?"

Somehow, unthinkably, Professor Valerius turned violently red. "Shit."

Faustine screeched with triumphant laughter, only just stopping herself from clapping her hands over her mouth because they smelled awful. "Is that a yes?"

"Ugh," said the professor. "That obvious, eh?"

"You keep calling him 'Vendrick'," Faustine pointed out, feeling weird even as she said it.

"And that's enough for you Volsinii? Helheim."

"I'm happy for you," Faustine said, and she meant it. "Even though he's kind of terrifying."

The professor snorted. "He's really not, once you've seen him passed out on a stack of library books at three in the morning during exams week."

"Wait, wait, wait," Faustine said. "You met at Silverwood?"

"*Ja,* alchemy class," Professor Valerius said. "Used to have black magic study group over there." She gestured towards the lakeside, where students still spread out blankets and homework when the weather was nice. "I was your age, or thereabouts."

It was so delightfully, absurdly normal. Faustine felt a little bit like she'd just seen behind the scenes at an opera. "Wait, if you met at Silverwood when you were my age, why..."

She cut herself off abruptly. She could ask Ellie why she hadn't gotten around to dating Owen yet, but she couldn't ask the professor!

Professor Valerius cocked an eyebrow. "Why did it take us until now to get our shit together?"

"I wasn't going to say *that...* "

The professor only laughed. "Because he's Volsinii, and I'm Kaldiri, and there was a war, Faustine."

Faustine sobered immediately. "That's... fair."

She glanced over to the pyre, where darkbeast meat roasted and then turned to ash.

"It's not a ridiculous question." Professor Valerius sighed. "But I can't say I recommend two decades of unresolved sexual tension any more than I do fighting garmur, so is there anything else you want to ask before I tell you to go shower again?"

"Professor!" Faustine spluttered.

"What?" Professor Valerius appeared genuinely confused for a moment before she rolled her eye and reached out to rough up Faustine's hair. "'Sex' is not a dirty word, Faustine. It's a completely normal part of a healthy, adult relationship. And many unhealthy ones."

Faustine couldn't help it; her jaw dropped. "You're... not embarrassed?"

"Of what?" Professor Valerius asked. "That I find a man attractive? Shocking, truly. Never happened before in the history of the world. Definitely doesn't factor into how annoying I find him."

Faustine laughed, and she couldn't help but think that she would have much preferred having Professor Valerius for an older sister, rather than Orsina or Galeria. Orsina was too cold, and Galeria was too wishy-washy. They'd certainly never joked with her about boys.

"Can... I ask you something, professor?" Faustine said.

"I am literally telling you to do that, so go for it."

Faustine winced. "I meant not about darkbeasts, or anything?"

"Oh." Professor Valerius seemed to shrink a little. "I guess. But I'm not great with emotional shit, Faustine. You know that."

Faustine didn't bother to mention she didn't have anyone else to ask. "What do I do about my father? He's not just going to let me leave, you know."

Professor Valerius' face was grim. "Leave that to Vendrick and me. He's got a plan to keep you safe, and I have a sword."

Faustine stared at her for a moment, not daring to hope. "But I belong to the della Luciana family."

"No," the professor said sharply, "you *are* a della Luciana. You *belong* to yourself. Understand?"

"Not really," Faustine admitted quietly.

"It's just like what I told you about the concentration exams. It doesn't matter what Ironfang wants from you. *You* have to live with your choices, not him."

"But I..." Faustine faltered. "It's one thing to study things he's not fond of. That's not really going to matter after graduation. This is..."

Treason, she left unspoken.

But she didn't need to say it; the professor knew. "It's not without consequences," Professor Valerius agreed. "Your da will be mad, and probably the rest of the family, too. But your alternative is screaming on the inside for the rest of your life."

Suddenly Orsina and Galeria made a hell of a lot more sense. Galeria had several small children and a household to run as its baroness, and even though Orsina's husband had died mysteriously and very young, she had never remarried and thrown herself into the Bloodrune Hunters instead. Rumors swirled that she'd even killed him to do it, though nothing had ever been proven.

Faustine had never shed a tear for either of her sisters in her entire life, but suddenly she felt like crying for both of them.

"Put it to you this way, Faustine," Professor Valerius said. "You know that feeling you get just before we begin sword drills? The warning bells in your stomach, or maybe the back of your head?"

Faustine nodded. They'd been going off all morning.

"That feeling doesn't only show up during combat," Professor Valerius added. "Listen to it everywhere. It's your body trying to save itself."

CHAPTER EIGHT

THE SILVERWOOD HEADMASTER'S SUITE was equipped with its own kitchen, bathroom, and balcony, and so Frelia, Vendrick, and Edmund had fallen back there to finish strategizing and clean up. It had been a while since Frelia had showered privately, and it was a shame she didn't have the time to savor it.

Or take a nap afterwards.

"Vendrick," said Frelia, sticking her head out of his bedroom once she was clothed again, "come here a second."

He turned away from where he and Edmund had clearly been talking over coffee, pinking slightly. "I beg your pardon?"

Frelia resisted the urge to roll her eye. "I want to talk to you about something before Heit Reiði."

She'd mentally chewed it over all through her shower. They were leaving Silverwood to deal with the Unseen, and that meant fighting was on the horizon. And Frelia didn't trust the Unseen not to throw a wad of garmur at them after the past semester. It was practical, logical, and frankly stupid not to.

Frelia also knew Vendrick had a few fire spells in that book of his, but he didn't have the most garmr-killing spell of all: the Grimsdalr Blink. She'd shut down all attempts to bully her into teaching it during Garmur Killing 101, but at this point, she had no choice. Thera had even agreed with her. There was no logical reason to keep mentally chewing it over, except that it felt so wrong.

"What is it?" Vendrick asked, shaking her out of her thoughts.

Frelia fell back out of the doorframe and gestured for him to follow her inside.

Vendrick did, a little uncertainly. He was already dressed in a mages' coat and had his spellbook holstered at his hip, the silhouette she knew all too well from the Tyrants' War.

It startled her, to stand at his back and only see the enemy.

"Frelia?"

She let out a breath and then turned to face him. "I think you should learn the Grimsdalr Blink."

Vendrick stared at her for a long moment, and anxiety began to churn in her stomach.

"Are you certain?" he finally asked, so softly it burned.

Was she certain she wanted to teach him Cillian and Thera's family secret? To trust a Volsinii man with Kaldr's singular advantage over the Garmur? To release her white-knuckle grip on the past and knee-jerk desire to protect anything Kaldiri?

"As I'll ever be," she got out.

Vendrick nodded, slowly. And then he reached one gloved hand out to squeeze her arm.

"Then I'm honored," he said.

"Don't be so Volsinii." Frelia felt herself redden. "And get me some paper."

Vendrick rolled his eyes, but while Frelia had been expecting a scrap of an envelope or something, what he pulled out was his spellbook.

"What's the first stroke?" he asked. "That's how I have this thing organized."

Frelia tried to remember where the rune started, gave up, and brought her hand up as if to cast. She went through the motions—one looping line, another, *another*—and then said, "Here."

Vendrick nodded, and began flipping through the pages of his spell book. "Fits right in after the one for 'Ethereality.'"

Frelia blinked. "For what?"

"Become invisible."

Frelia's jaw dropped. "You can do that?"

Vendrick laughed, self consciously—"Not well."-and set his spellbook down on his bedside table, smoothing the blank page flat with his gloved hand.

"Wait, wait," Frelia said, "so could you turn us invisible and *then* warp us to Heit Reiði?"

The idea of running invisibly through the keep under the Volsinii's nose was a lot less daunting than the alternative.

"Technically, yes I could." Vendrick made a face like he'd just stepped in something wet while wearing socks. "But I'd need about a week of free time to figure out how to stack the runes appropriately and make sure all of us ends up where it's supposed to be."

Frelia harrumphed. "Dammit."

"Agreed, we'll stick with plan A." Vendrick pulled a pencil from his inside jacket pocket and held it out.

Frelia stared at it uncomprehending. "What do you want me to do with that?"

"Draw the... Grimsdalr Blink rune?" Vendrick's eyebrow rose.

Frelia's eye widened. Mages were about as protective of their spellbooks as mother bears with their cubs, or Frelia with her family shield, once upon a time. She had never so much as touched a spellbook, other than to hand it to its owner in combat.

Something deep in her soul softened. "You don't want to do it yourself?"

"You're the expert, here." Vendrick's smile was too soft to be teasing. Stunned, she took the pencil from him and moved to stare at the blank page of his spellbook. Shit, that was a lot of white space. And how did rune diagrams work, again?

She flipped one page back to remind herself, and caught Vendrick flinching out of the corner of her eye. "Sorry," Frelia said, and she meant it. "I'm trying to remember how rune diagrams work."

"Typically," said Vendrick, a little stiffly, reaching over her to point out the various parts of his Ethereality diagram, "you draw the rune in its entirety in the upper left-hand corner, and then beneath that, each of the various steps to draw it, with little arrows."

Right. Like kids learning their letters.

Frelia lifted her right hand again, walked herself through the Grimsdalr Blink, and then began to draw on the blank spellbook page. There was silence, but for the scratching of the pencil. And it was strange, not having to immediately drop into another fight after drawing the Grimsdalr Blink. Frelia was pretty sure she'd never so much as thought about it in the setting this tranquil.

And then it was done.

Eye on the page, Frelia drew the rune once more with her hand in the air, just to make sure, and then held the spellbook and pencil out to Vendrick. "Okay. That's it."

She felt something try to catch in the corner of her eye, so she kept talking.

"When you draw it, it'll feel like someone is trying to squeeze all your insides out through your pores, and probably give you a migraine. You'll need to visualize piercing your way back through the tear it'll shove you into."

"You, in a general sense," Vendrick asked, "or you, as in me personally?"

"Uh," said Frelia. "Both? That's why I use a sword. Or an axe. Or whatever else is to hand—I'm literally piercing back through to the Waking World."

Vendrick nodded, like this was all very normal. "Anything else?"

Frelia opened her mouth to tell him that according to Grimsdalr legend, the blink rune tore a hole in the veil between worlds, but what came out was a pained sort of noise that made her clap a hand over her mouth.

"Right." Vendrick's voice was soft again, like a warm blanket and dammit, she needed a nap. "That's probably not a fair question."

"You're a mage." Frelia tried to force herself to move her hand off her mouth, but failed. "Of course you want to know what you're casting."

"I," said Vendrick, "am an interloper, and I know it."

She risked a glance up, and found herself snared in acid green eyes. Something uncomfortable and squishy tightened in her chest and dammit, she didn't have time to unravel it right now.

"I know what this rune carries." He held up his spellbook and shook it a little, for good measure. "And I know this wasn't an easy thing for you. But I *will...* "Vendrick leaned into the word, just a bit. Just enough. "...build a world where you can openly share it again. I promise."

The only thing worse than Vendrick's flirting, flung like precise knives wherever Frelia was still unarmored, was when he dropped it and said what he was honestly thinking. *Because I love you, you fucking dorchya!* had rung in Frelia's ears for hours, mocking her with its sincerity, and it had only gotten worse since last night.

He hadn't said it again. Vendrick Caecillion wasn't stupid, even if he did like to tease the Wolf of Kaldr. But he didn't have to, now that she finally had all his pieces laid out before her.

"So shall we test it?" Vendrick asked.

"Good idea." Frelia nodded, and finally shook her hand loose. "There probably isn't room in here, though. Unless you want to punt yourself through the door and into your living room."

"That'll work," Vendrick said. "What kind of magic is the Grimsdalr Blink?"

Frelia blinked. "The kind you can cast?"

Vendrick snorted. "Like, is it grey magic? White magic? Black magic?"

It occurred to her, then, like a sharp kick in the kidneys. "I have no idea, although I probably did at some point. Why?"

Vendrick's neutral mask didn't move. "It makes casting easier, when you know what to power it with. But I've muddled through before, and certainly can do so again."

He squared his shoulders and then went to stand at the foot of his bed, facing his door like an enemy combatant. He raised his hand to casting position like a maestro just before a symphony begins.

"I should be on the other side." Frelia's feet were moving. "Just in case."

"Good thing Blightsen's here." Vendrick was trying to joke, but all it did was shove a knife further into those bruised kidneys.

What would Edmund say to this? Did he even care about the old ways anymore? He affected a Volsinii accent, for the Saints' sake, he had no right to judge her.

Frelia opened Vendrick's bedroom door and got herself out of the Blink rune's approximate way.

"Everything alright?" Edmund asked, standing awkwardly near the hallway to the kitchen with his coffee.

"Not really," Frelia said, "but get ready to possibly heal Vendrick if this doesn't work."

She refused to believe it wouldn't. *Refused.*

Edmund's face darkened, just a little, and he set his mug down on the nearest flat surface. "What are you two doing?"

Frelia held up a finger, and then she felt it. The sharp, astral tang in the air that heralded magic. She could easily imagine the jerk Vendrick must be feeling behind his navel, now, the kaleidoscopic tunnel the Blink Rune was blasting him through like a cannon shot.

And then, there he was, sliding sideways out of literal nowhere and skidding across his carpet. Vendrick managed to catch himself just before the front door, one arm braced against the doorframe.

"That's..."he said, apparently and for once at a loss for words. "...*oof.*"

He was amazing, is what he was. The most gifted mage of their time, easy. Frelia had never known anyone to look at a rune once and cast it without some horrible side effect blowing up in their face. And doing it on no sleep and jittery from caffeine and Bitterbane?

Absolute insanity.

But there he was. Hale and whole. (Or something like it, anyway.) That squishy thing in her chest was starting to migrate towards her guts and dammit, she did not have time for this!

"And you use that to fight monsters?" Vendrick pointed to where he'd come from, as if to indicate the tunnel he'd just come out of. "In the middle of combat?"

"Crazy, isn't she?" Edmund asked, although he was smiling.

Vendrick looked to Frelia with a new gleam in his eye. "Bloody incredible."

There it was again. What he was really thinking.

Frelia felt heat rush to her face. "Are we getting your sister, or what?"

CHAPTER NINE

ATHOS DEL PRIORE WAS just sitting down to lunch when Frelia materialized over his shoulder.

The knights across the table from him blinked at her a few times, and then one of the older ones blanched. "...General Valerius?" she said.

Athos whipped around, his hand going to the hilt of his axe, and shit, did he look like a garmr had chewed him up and spat him out again. If Vendrick were to be believed, the Queenmakers' brawler had gone grey long before he'd even hit thirty, and though he was still a brick shithouse of a man, he seemed off, somehow.

Athos' blue eyes widened in horror at the sight of a one-eyed, fully-armored Frelia Helm's Grace Valerius.

"...Frelia?" His voice seemed somehow less booming than she remembered, the lines in his face much deeper.

Tired, Frelia realized with a jolt. The automaton engine that had once been Athos del Priore was tired.

"The ghost of," Frelia said.

Astral energy snapped behind her, just like Vendrick had said, and then the man himself was looming over her shoulder.

"Just kidding," Frelia added. "We're real."

"Good morning, Athos," Vendrick said, and it wasn't pleasant.

Athos choked on his coffee. "Shit, Vendrick!" he spluttered. "I didn't know you were coming."

"Neither did I, funnily enough."

Silence fell across the Heit Reiði mess, and Frelia refused to look around. At least, not longer than it took to mark the exits. The place hadn't changed at all, except the banners were the wrong color, now. She had to keep her focus, and even if the Bitterbane staved off the exhaustion, it still lingered on the edges of her senses, waiting.

"Can I..." Athos looked to be at a complete loss. "...help you, somehow?"

"I hear you've a prisoner I would very much like to meet."

All the color drained from Athos' round face. "I don't have any prisoners right now."

"Don't lie to me, del Priore. You don't do it nearly well enough."

It rang across the flagstones, though Vendrick had not raised his voice.

"You'll only make it worse for yourself if you fight me," Vendrick added. "I'm certain you know who held this fort before you."

All eyes in the room flicked to Frelia, and she ground her teeth. *Hold steady, Valerius.* Athos was the only one of their graduating class who loved the old tales as much as Thera and Roland. Knighthood to him was borderline idolatry. He wouldn't tell his men to open fire—yet.

"So whether or not you're honest," Vendrick said, "I'll get what I came for. It simply needn't get messy."

Athos stared at them for a moment, terror mounting in his eyes. "Vendrick," he finally said, "they'll kill me."

"Most likely," Vendrick agreed. "But I'm still merely considering it."

Athos recoiled. "You were a Queenmaker!"

"So were you."

They stared each other down for a long, icy moment.

"What'll it be, del Priore?" Frelia's hand tightened around the hilt of her sword. "Death or dishonor?"

Athos turned to look at her, his eyes sadder than he had any right to be. He had only ever known Frelia as a sparring partner in the Silverwood training grounds or an enemy general, after all.

"I thought you were dead, Frelia," he said.

"It's not for lack of trying on your friends' part," she snapped.

Athos' blue eyes flicked between Frelia and Vendrick for a long moment. She couldn't read his expression, so neutral and Volsinii as it was, and she wondered if Vendrick could. And then Athos raised his hand and made the Silverwood sign for "strike" overhead.

At once, Frelia tackled him into the table.

"I always thought better of you, Athos," Vendrick muttered, and Frelia felt the snap of Astral energy against her back.

The blink rune shot her forward across the mess, and Vendrick fell back from the arrows that struck the ground where Frelia had just been. They would have perfectly pierced her heart, if he hadn't warped her.

Frelia still didn't know how she felt about teaching him the Blink Rune, but there was no arguing that it was already proving useful.

Vendrick was moving, drawing runes as quickly as he dared. Frelia sprinted for the heavy double doors to the mess hall, vaulting over tables and shoving confused Volsinii out of her way. Her back felt naked without a shield, and truly, this place was a nightmare arisen from the grave.

An arrow whizzed past her face, and Frelia didn't pause to mark the sniper. It wasn't ultimately going to matter; not now that Athos had declared war. She and Vendrick didn't have to fake pleasantries and good faith. She could bury the Volsinii who had taken Heit Reiði from her, and Vendrick's spy network would mean she could walk free after.

Hesitation, after all, had never been the issue.

Still, she didn't feel better when she slammed the mess doors shut behind her. Arrows peppered the heavy wood with muted thunks, and Frelia took off down the hall again. Everything was so familiar, here.

From the chips in the tile to the alcoves off the main drag to the smell of hunter's stew and hard-baked rolls in the mess hall.

She met back up with Vendrick in a conjoining hallway, viscerally shaking. Already, there was sweat pooling across Vendrick's brow. There was some sort of viscous gunk spread across the door to the mess beside him, and it pulsed with faint, arcane energy.

"That ought to hold a moment," Vendrick said. "Lead the way."

Frelia tried to breathe normally as they stormed the halls of what had once been her fort. She tried not to recall that her father had liked to hold court in that alcove, and she had usually lurked in that one to get away from him.

The worst part was, Frelia wasn't even sure that, if she'd known he would die defending the gates, she would have done anything differently.

Voices began to echo in the hall in front of her, and Frelia immediately flattened herself into the nearest alcove, dragging Vendrick with her.

"...And I do hope everything is in place for the ceremony," came a clipped, Volsinii voice.

"Nearly there," came a Kaldiri voice that made her blood boil. How dare her own people support this heresy! "Just a few more runes and then it'll be time to drag the prisoners into place."

"Finally," said the first voice again, and this time Vendrick tapped her shoulder.

Frelia had to crane her neck backwards to look at him, pressed together in the shallow niche as they were. She nearly missed it when he mouthed, "Orsina."

Anger exploded in her chest, and Frelia had to physically hold onto Vendrick to keep herself from launching at the Bloodrune Hunters' general. Fury was good, though; it was familiar and comfortable and, hell, at least Frelia had something to blot out the nauseous anxiety and broken memories.

The voices continued down the cross-hall, and neither Frelia nor Vendrick so much as breathed until they had completely faded.

"I will behead that bitch," Frelia growled.

"If it gets to that," Vendrick murmured, "I'll hold her down for you."

They slipped soundlessly down increasingly twisted hallways, until the air grew cold and daylight died to fiery wall sconces.

"Nearly there," Frelia muttered.

The crypt at Heit Reiði was meant to be a temporary holding facility for casualties and final resting place only for unknown soldiers. It had never been locked during Frelia and her father's tenure, but there was a large padlock staring at her from the door now. Frelia supposed it had been wartime when she'd held the fort. There would have been little point in locking the crypt, just to turn around and unlock it twenty minutes later.

"That didn't used to be there," she muttered.

Vendrick was already reaching for the thieves' tools in his inside coat pocket. "Watch my back."

She made a face. "You don't need to ask."

Vendrick made short work of the door's lock. He caught the heavy padlock as it fell away, laying it silently beside the door. He fell back behind Frelia to let the melee fighter go in first, and she pulled open the heavy iron door with uncomfortable ease.

The musty smell of old wood and rotting bones hit her full force, and Frelia immediately moved to cover her nose and mouth with her shirt. "Well," she said grimly, "these haven't been moved out like they're supposed to."

The crypt hadn't been built to house this many remains. They were stacked several high in the alcoves running along both walls. Had the Volsinii returned the bodies of her fallen brethren, after Heit Reiði fell? And what had they been doing with the dead since then?

"Saints, that's awful," Vendrick said, and Frelia wasn't sure if he meant the smell or the desecration.

As they sunk deeper into the maze of half-assed graves, Frelia realized, no, Athos had definitely not been burying people properly. It struck her as incredibly odd. Athos del Priore was the only person Frelia knew that tied with her da for the crown labeled 'entirely too concerned with honor and duty.'

He'd been assigned to Heit Reiði after the Volsinii had stolen it, so why hadn't he returned the Kaldiri remains back to Skjöldr, all those years ago? It was one of the oldest provisions in the rules of engagement. What did he gain by keeping them here, besides disrespect? Frelia shook herself of the thought like the dog they called her, and then she smelled it.

Fresh blood.

It had a distinctly metallic smell wholly unlike the decay of the rest of the crypt, and although Frelia's instincts screamed at her to fall back, she pressed forward. Vendrick grimaced behind her a moment later, but he didn't falter, either. His hand was poised over the spine of his spellbook, tucked into its sheath on his belt.

It was a good thing Frelia was already breathing through the fabric of her undershirt, or she might have gagged when she pushed open the door to the prison. It reeked even more strongly of blood, piss, and the unwashed. The guard on duty only had a moment to yelp before Vendrick's Nettle spell sank into his neck like poisoned needles.

"I expected," Vendrick said quietly, stooping to relieve the convulsing guard of his keyring, "so much more of Athos del Priore."

"Why?" Frelia glanced down the hall towards the cells, but no one else came running from around the corner. "I know he made honor a personal battle, but..."

Vendrick straightened back up to his full height, keyring in hand. "He asked to be stationed here after the war because he couldn't stand the Unseen."

Frelia blinked at the news, her mind whirring as it tried to process the new information. "Then why is he helping them now?"

"Excellent question."

Frelia drew her sword as they approached the cellblock "So did you tell Athos about the Unseen, or did he learn himself?"

"I told all the Queenmakers towards the end of the war, one by one," Vendrick said as they set off down the first row of empty cells. "Most were appropriately horrified."

Frelia's sword hand gripped the hilt more tightly. "And the ones who weren't?"

Vendrick's face tightened. "There's a reason you don't hear much of them, anymore."

She knew better than to ask where they were buried.

As they rounded the corner to the second cellblock, an arrow whizzed between them. It grazed Vendrick's cheek, and he immediately began drawing a rune across Frelia's back. The cellblock was a straight shot; there would be nothing to stop her from slamming into the guard if he drew the Grimsdalr blink.

She felt the familiar snap of astral energy behind her navel a half-second before it pelted her forward with the force that had once wrecked garmur. All around her, the prison crystallized into a many-layered diamond before she crashed back into the Waking World. She rammed her shoulder into the guard, his un-armored head cracking against the stone wall behind him.

"You have something of ours," Frelia snarled as she gripped the man's throat. "We want her back."

"Third cell, on the right." The guard immediately pointed down yet another side hallway.

"Thanks," Frelia said, just as Nettles stabbed into the man's eyes.

She cut his agony short with a sword to the gut.

"Much obliged." Vendrick's voice drifted by from down the hall. "I was trying not to hit you."

"Appreciated," Frelia grunted.

The guard's directions led them down yet another dimly lit hall, and there, in the third cell on the right, was a woman.

Her chestnut brown hair had been shorn above her ears, likely to prevent lice, and she was dressed in rags so dirty it was impossible to tell what color they were meant to be. She dragged herself into a sitting position at the sound of approaching footsteps, groaning. And though one of them was swollen partially shut, she had eyes of the brightest green.

If a touch lighter than Vendrick's.

She blinked hard at their approach, and then managed in a heavy, hoarse voice, "Vendy?"

Frelia fought the urge to laugh. That nickname was ridiculous.

"Good morning, Clary." There was guarded relief in his voice as Vendrick began testing keys on the cell lock. "Remind me, what was it I used to tell you before every society party you insisted on attending?"

The woman's surprised laugh was wheezing, guttural. "Don't get belligerently drunk or sleep with strange folk, and if I needed a fast exit, the Viper of Ascalon was always available."

The lock clicked open, and genuine relief broke across Vendrick's stern face. "*Merciful Saints, Clarissa, don't worry me like that again!*"

She gasped another laugh as Vendrick scooped her into a fierce hug—dirt, lice, blood, and all. "Just keeping you on your toes," she said, and her arms shook as she squeezed Vendrick's back.

"There are better ways to do it." He patted her cheek a few times. "How are you feeling? Can you stand?"

Clarissa grimaced. "Not well, on either account."

"How about run?" Frelia asked from her position in the hallway.

"Even worse?"

Clarissa squinted at her a moment, confusion in every line of her dirt-streaked face, and Vendrick prompted, "That's Frelia, Clarissa."

At the blank look that earned him, he added, "Frelia *Valerius*."

It took another moment, but then recognition sparked in Clarissa's eyes.

"Oh, Saints," Clarissa said as she allowed Vendrick to loop her arm around his shoulders. "How's the Traust kid doing?"

"Better than you," Frelia said over a choked noise that may or may not have been Vendrick laughing.

Clarissa grimaced as her older brother dragged her to her feet. "Please tell me that we don't have to fight our way out of here, Vendy."

"Well," he said, "if it makes you feel better, I suppose I don't *have* to say it."

"Can you fight?" Frelia asked.

"Generally speaking, yes." Clarissa sighed in pain as she balanced on shaking legs. "Currently, I don't think I could summon so much as a beetle."

Frelia studied Vendrick's younger sister as she emerged from her cell, took note of her bare feet, thin face, and general trembling. *No*, Frelia decided, *definitely in no state to fight*.

Which left them a single option. Not a good option, mind, but the only one Frelia had.

"Hold her steady, Vendrick," Frelia ordered, tugging her sleeve up to her elbow. "I have a grand total of one idea."

"That's more than I have," he muttered. "Short of warping her out to Irirangi."

"Don't you dare send me to the Rippling Isles!" Clarissa screeched.

Frelia drew her dagger. "Then hold still."

"What is that for?" Clarissa and Vendrick both asked at once.

"Calm down." Frelia poised the blade over the newly-exposed skin of her forearm. "It's for me."

She grimaced as she made the first cut, and then a second, larger one so that blood began welling up from the wound.

Her very much runed blood.

"Frelia," Vendrick hissed, "what the hell?"

Frelia ignored him and tried to focus. Her father had handed this spell down in case of emergencies only, and Frelia hadn't so much as thought about the spell rune in a very long time.

War does funny things to you.

"Clarissa." Frelia tugged off her right-hand glove with her teeth, and spoke around it. "What do you know of bloodrunes?"

"Very powerful," Clarissa said warily, "very terrifying, and I'm glad our family doesn't have one."

"*Ja*, about that." Frelia dug her pointer finger into the wound she'd just made, like dipping a quill in ink. "You're going to be borrowing mine."

"I'm going to be what?"

Frelia gestured with her free hand. "Vendrick, turn her face towards me."

"*Frelia?*" Clarissa's voice jumped an octave.

"It won't hurt." Frelia raised her bloodied finger up to Clarissa's face. "Or, well, won't hurt much. You'll be able to draw on my power and its, for a bit. Don't scrape it off."

Clarissa stared at her with eyes as wide as tea saucers—at least the one, anyway. "How is that possible?"

"Blood magic," Vendrick hissed, and it wasn't a question. "I thought the Church of the Triad had wiped it all out, minus the Unseen."

"Not quite," Frelia said, and began to draw.

Clarissa flinched as Frelia drew the claw-like Valerius bloodrune on her cheek in quick, firm strokes. The swordswoman muttered in Kaldiri as she drew a fast rune in the air before her, icy blue arcane energy trailing from her bloody fingers.

Clarissa gasped, and suddenly clutched at her arm.

"Your pain is my pain," Frelia said. "And mine is yours."

"Hang on." Vendrick shooed Frelia away from her new arm wound. "Wouldn't that just make it so that you both can't fight?"

"I guess not," Clarissa said, patting at Vendrick's arm around her shoulders. "I feel... almost fine."

"I've felt better," Frelia said, and oof, was Clarissa's pain blinding for a moment. "But also worse."

It wasn't like Clarissa had taken a war axe to the chest, after all. She was just hungry and coming off torture, felt like.

Vendrick studied his sister warily as he let go. Though she swayed for a moment, she stayed on her feet. "Is there anyone else down here, Clarissa?" he asked.

"No, I've been alone for weeks."

It was little relief to know that the Unseen weren't keeping a ton of living people down here. Frelia and her da hadn't kept many prisoners either—just the occasional spy or attempted deserter. But Frelia was pretty sure the only reason there weren't more people down here was because they were in worse places.

"Better alone than dead," Frelia said.

Clarissa and Vendrick both winced.

Vendrick glanced to the bloodrune on his sister's cheek. "Do we need to give Clarissa a minute with that?"

"I'm feeling pretty okay, honestly." Clarissa stretched her arms over her head as if to prove it. "But I can barely think straight and will probably miscast."

"No you won't." Vendrick immediately drew his spellbook and thrust it into her hands. "Read that over; I'll find you something to mark pages with."

Vendrick took a moment to bandage Frelia's arm with a handkerchief before he set about ripping pages out of his notebook. Frelia scouted the prison for company, but only found corpses. Clarissa stopped shaking quite so much after commandeering lunch from one of the now-dead guards, but it all took too much time.

By the time they slipped back into the crypt, Frelia and Vendrick's own stomachs had begun growling.

"This place is awful," Clarissa whispered, her fingers curling into Vendrick's cloak hem as she tugged it more tightly around her. It dragged across the flagstones behind her, but Frelia figured it was the closest thing to a security blanket Clarissa was going to get.

Frelia spat in disgust. "There shouldn't be this many bodies in the crypt."

"They must be using them as experiment-fodder," Vendrick muttered. "Poor bastards."

"There is no peace," Frelia muttered, her hand curling around the hilt of her sword, "even in death."

Clarissa pressed her hand over her mouth. "I refuse to throw up; I finally ate something."

Vendrick's face was set into grim lines. "Is that from something, Frelia?"

"*Ja,* the prophecy of Heit Reiði. When Lady Midnight will crew the ship of the damned right into the Bay of Skjöldr."

"Well, don't jinx us." Clarissa shivered. "Also, where are we going once we get out of this accursed crypt?"

"To the left," Frelia said. "Stables are clear across the fort, though."

"What's the fastest way there?" Vendrick asked. "Don't tell me it's the mess."

"*Ja,* of course it is." Frelia grimaced. "We're going to have to take the long way around, through the outer ward."

Vendrick halted just before the door out of the crypt. Clarissa ran into him with a defiant squeak he ignored. "Frelia," Vendrick said, about as gently as one could in the middle of a rescue operation, "are we going to have to go through where your father fell?"

"There's only one fucking gate," Frelia muttered, pushing past both Caecillion siblings and out of the crypt.

Vendrick reattached the padlock to the outside of the crypt door, but Clarissa just stared at Frelia like she couldn't quite piece something together.

"Can I ask what happened?" Clarissa asked. "To the duke, I mean."

Frelia froze, and it felt like she'd been kicked in the ribs. "Do you not know your own history?"

Clarissa's smile was incalculably sad. "I know this is where Gaius della Luciana made his military name."

"That's not—" Vendrick began.

"He was eaten by a garmr," Frelia said sharply, and Vendrick's jaw snapped shut. "He gave me the Valerius Shield that morning, would hear nothing of how many of the stupid things I'd already killed, and charged into death like an idiot."

Silence fell as the padlock clicked shut again.

"I'm sorry," said Clarissa quietly.

"Why would he stop you from fighting darkbeasts?" Vendrick asked, not really to anyone. "That was what you were famous for."

"'Cause he was my Da." Frelia's chest suddenly ached like it hadn't in many years. "Now shut up, both of you; voices carry in here."

Though Vendrick was a trained assassin, and Frelia, a huntress, Clarissa was neither. She did her best, but her brother still grimaced at every misstep and loud noise as they slipped through the halls of Heit Reiði's keep. The further they went without encountering resistance, the more Frelia's brow furrowed. There should have been knights on duty, at the very least. She and Vendrick hadn't exactly popped by subtly.

It became readily apparent that no one was coming when they rounded on the door to the outer ward. There were voices filtering from behind it, the sounds of men and women at work and the occasional snap of astral energy.

"New moon's not until tomorrow," Vendrick muttered. "What are they doing?"

"They've prepped for this for months," Clarissa murmured. "I bet they're drawing the circle and... I don't know, whatever else they planned to do with the bodies."

"Bodies?"

Frelia and Vendrick both said it at once.

Clarissa's hands clenched around her borrowed spellbook. "These people are nightmares, Vendrick."

Vendrick's facial expression fell hard. "You said there's only one gate, correct, Frelia?"

"*Ja,* only other way out is to scale the bailey walls." Frelia flicked a glance to the door, and cursed Heit Reiði's layout for the millionth time just today.

"Well," said Vendrick, cracking his neck first one way, and then the other, "good thing I scored better than Athos in tactics."

Frelia cocked an eyebrow at him. "You got an idea?"

"Several," Vendrick said, "in fact."

CHAPTER TEN

FAUSTINE WAS THE FIRST one to show back up at the chapel, dressed in road-worthy clothes and with a travel bag slung over her shoulder. She'd never traveled so light before; she'd had to ask Christel how to figure out what to even bring.

They'd kindly walked her through what they usually considered essential, and Faustine had tried not to feel even worse than she already did about the whole 'stealing their blood so Markus could summon Muninn' thing. She really needed to figure out how to apologize.

She gave the still-burning pyre a wide berth as she hiked up the hill, slipping through the broken wall and into the chapel grounds. Students weren't normally allowed in here; it had been cordoned off the whole time Faustine had been at Silverwood.

It would have been majestic, once. It had all the parapets and swooping archways the rest of Silverwood did, only there was stained glass and finery, too. Unease coiled in Faustine's stomach as she approached, stepping gingerly over the rubble as she rounded on the building.

For there, curled up like a sleeping dog beneath the ruined ceiling, was the giant darkbeast that the Professor said was Thera Grimsdalr.

"Um," Faustine called over to the sleeping monster, "hello."

Its eyes opened, burning green around a more muted brown.

"My name is Faustine," she added, feeling a little stupid for talking to a darkbeast, but pressing on anyway. "I'm, um, going to be helping you get out of here."

The beast cocked its head, and just as Faustine was getting ready to say something else, it rumbled, "*Where... Frey...lia?*"

Faustine was so startled she tripped over a chunk of masonry. Darkbeasts couldn't speak; they were mindless siege weapons and wrecking balls, according to her father.

Well. What else was her father wrong about?

"You can *speak?*" Faustine squeaked out.

"*Ish,*" said the darkbeast. "*Where... friend?*"

Holy shit, maybe the Professor hadn't been telling her wishful thinking, after all.

"She and Headmaster Caecillion are going to rescue his sister," Faustine told the monster. It was hard to think of her with a human name like 'Thera,' but Faustine wanted to give her that dignity. "We're meeting up with them after she's safe and you and me and the others get where we're going."

"*O... thers?*" the darkbeast—*Thera,* Faustine reminded herself—asked.

Faustine opened her mouth to tell her about Christel and Professor Blightsen, but a sharp noise, followed by a curse, came from just outside the chapel.

Thera's head jerked up, her nose to the wind and sniffing. A moment later, a head of shaggy, golden hair poked into the chapel, and Faustine breathed in relief.

"Hi, Christel!" she called.

Relief broke across their face, and they waved. "I was hoping I wouldn't be the first one here," Christel said as they practically danced across the ruined floor. "Professor Blightsen said he needed to stop by the mess to get our rations before he'd meet us here, but that was an hour ago."

"*Blight... sen?*" Thera rumbled. "*Ed... mund?*"

Christel's head tilted to stare at the darkbeast like they couldn't figure out what to make of her. "Yeah, the white magic professor. Do you know him?"

"*Friend,*" Thera rumbled warmly.

"Would you believe me if I told you that Thera used to be a person, and one of Professor Valerius' friends?" Faustine asked. "Err, well, she's still a person, actually, but she used to be a human person?"

Thera began a kind of growling laugh, and after a moment, Christel said, "Yeah, I would."

"Also, I'm sure everyone needs to get their rations from the mess, Christel," Faustine said. "It doesn't surprise me that Professor Blightsen has been a while."

Christel made a face, and they bounced on their heels. "I dunno, it feels... off, somehow."

Christel had the Traust Bloodrune, and that gave them visions of the future and the uncanny ability to know what everyone else was feeling (although Faustine wasn't convinced that wasn't just inherent to *Christel*, not their bloodrune).

Thera was suddenly on her feet, looming overhead like a guardian statue. She sniffed the air hard and repeatedly, like a hunting dog picking up a trail, and then her eyes widened—all four of them.

"*Hide,*" the darkbeast rumbled, pawing at the ground beneath her.

"Sorry, sorry, sorry!" Faustine hissed, moving as quickly as her feet could carry her.

She fitted herself behind Thera's foreleg, trying her best not to look up, and across from her, Christel did the same. The darkbeast stood inert, its watchful, ruddy eyes staring at the only remaining entrance to the chapel.

For a long moment, Faustine held her breath, and waited.

Then Christel whispered, "What do you smell, Thera?"

The darkbeast didn't move. "*Ironfang.*"

Faustine froze. What was her *father* doing here? Didn't he have Ascalon to run back to, and Markus to do his bidding? Surely he didn't know Faustine was here? She was supposed to be reporting to the library, with the other kids going back home towards Caere.

"Can you see anything, Thera?" Faustine whispered up at her.

"*He... alone,*" Thera said after a moment. "*Walking... up... hill.*"

Faustine's stomach fell into her boots. Her father never went *anywhere* alone, not unless...

Oh no.

Faustine was moving before her brain gave the order. She had to do something about this, before her father did something irrevocable.

"Faustine!" Christel hissed, their blue eyes wide. "What are you *doing*? You can't let him see you!"

"He's going to do something to Muninn's corpse," Faustine said. "We have to stop him."

A moment later, you didn't need to be a darkbeast-wolf to smell the embers and ashes on the air. Faustine broke into a run, heading for the cemetery wall. She fitted herself to the edge of the hole in the wall, peeking around it to get a look at the hillside.

Ironfang was rooting around in the ashes of Muninn's pyre with his bare hands, like it wasn't blisteringly hot and an absolutely insane thing to do. He was muttering something that half-carried on the breeze, but it wasn't in Volsinii Standard, or High Volsinii, or any other language Faustine recognized.

"What's he doing?" whispered a voice from behind her.

Faustine clapped a hand over her mouth to keep from screaming. "Christel!" she hissed once she'd gotten her heart rate under control. "Don't scare me like that."

"Sorry," they said, sheepish. "But seriously—what is he doing?"

Faustine's stomach pitched and rolled like she was standing on the deck of a ship. "I think he's trying to put Muninn back together."

There was no other logical reason for why her father kept pulling blackened chunks of meat off the fire. He dug like a madman, heedless of the smears of ash and the heat and the cinders.

"I think he's looking for something," Christel said after a moment.

"That doesn't make sense," Faustine whispered back. "What could possibly...?"

She cut herself off when Ironfang barked a triumphant "Ha!"

He pulled a red, crystalline lump out of the pyre, and Faustine's throat seized. The one she'd seen before was only about the size of her palm, but this one was the size of someone's head. It shone a dull, ruddy red in the weak winter sunlight, and Ironfang cradled it to his broad chest like he'd found a newborn in the wreckage.

"What the hell is that?" Christel whispered.

Faustine had to manually unstick her tongue from the roof of her mouth before she could speak. "Its bloodstone. All darkbeasts have them, but..." She swallowed past the lump in her throat. "I don't know why my father..."

With a roar like thunder, the bloodstone began to shake in Ironfang's arms.

He held it tightly to his chest as the bloodstone began to rock itself back and forth. The crystalline lump grew darker, sanguine, more like a blood clot and less like a mineral pulled off a cavern wall.

Panic began to creep into the back of Faustine's mind. *You should stop him. You need to stop him. But you're a weak little girl with no talent for magic and carrying a dagger because that's the only weapon you have, and that's a monster wearing a man's face and where are Professor Valerius and Not-Headmaster Caecillion when you need them, and...*

The bloodstone cracked. Straight up the middle, like someone had struck it with a hammer and chisel.

Ironfang howled with laughter as he released the rocking thing. It dropped into the grass below, jumping and jerking in an erratic dance with no rhythm at all. Faustine clapped a hand to her mouth, feeling like she might be sick.

And then a jagged piece broke off the surface of the bloodstone. A tiny, taloned claw stuck itself out of the hole.

That's not a stone. The thought cut through Faustine's panic like a hot knife.

"Is that an egg?" she whispered between her fingers.

She was barely aware of Christel's hands yanking her towards the chapel. "We gotta move."

They had nearly made it back to Thera before the swarm hit.

CHAPTER ELEVEN

THE OPENING STRAINS OF the Grimsdalr War Song rang in Frelia's ears as she, Vendrick, and Clarissa huddled behind the door to the training ground. Its ghosts echoed off flagstones and slunk around corners, Cillian's voice clear as day in the back of Frelia's mind.

> *We battled our way through hell and back,*
> *And never counted costs.*
> *We battled our way through Helheim,*
> *Her river we did cross.*
> *And never once did we,*
> *Ever consider defeat;*
> *This is the end of days,*
> *my friends—It's Heit Reiði.*

Frelia shook her head. She wished she could tell his ghost off, but apparently, not even stabbing his memory was enough to free her entirely.

"Everyone clear?" Vendrick asked as he tugged a cloth over his mouth and nose.

"Clear enough," Frelia said through her own makeshift mask. "Let's get moving; I don't like standing around."

She pushed open the door and for a moment, her brain filled in the wide, walled courtyard that had served as the Kaldiri's training grounds, during the Tyrant's War. There was Egil and his lance over there, and Asvor and her sword over here.

Then Frelia blinked, and the expanse was filled with Volsinii red and a host of mages drawing something unholy on the ground.

Vendrick slid around her and opened fire with a swirling, choking cloud of grey magical miasma. At once, guardsmen and mages began to choke, coughing and spluttering as the thick stench overtook them. Clarissa followed up with an array of ghostly summoned knights, glittering and ethereal in the early afternoon. The three of them bolted across the outer ward amongst the chaos, and Frelia wished she had a shield to focus on.

They moved quickly, Frelia dispatching anyone smart enough to drag their collar over their nose. They paused just long enough for Clarissa to spit on the ritual circle and drag the ruined hem of her roughspun shirt through the bloody runes.

I'll break the enchantment with salt, she'd said at their little impromptu tactics meeting. *And then iron, just to make sure.*

Where do you plan to get those? Frelia had asked.

Clarissa had looked at her in surprise. *They're in the human body.*

As Clarissa worked to dispel the magic, Vendrick cast a second, choking Miasma across the next ward. In Frelia's mind, Cillian continued his war song.

> *Their eyes are green and verdant;*

And their hides as dark as night.
You'll never see them coming,
And they'll never step in light.
Their hearts are black as ice,
And you'll never bleed them
dry—
But just like you and me,
Every garmr can die.

Clarissa prised a scab off her arm, dug her finger into it, and, with the artistic flourish of a symphony's maestra, began raking lines through the bloody sigils inked into the floor. Frelia watched her work for a moment, and the faint, astral crackling in the air around her began to die off.

"That should do it!" Clarissa stumbled backwards in her haste to stand, and Vendrick stooped to catch her. "Let's move!"

There was only the gate ward left, now. Frelia grimaced as they passed the ballistae, as clean and oiled as the day she'd left them. She started to wonder if Athos' men knew about the hitch in the winch on the third one from the left, but caught herself mid-thought.

She had told Vendrick she could do this. She had to do this. She had to prove to herself that her ghosts did not own her, as much as she had to free Clarissa from the Unseen's clutches.

Vendrick cut into her half-formed thoughts. "How much further, Frelia?"

"Stables are up and to the left." She gestured aggressively towards them. "And that's the main gate, up ahead."

"How many horses are we stealing?" Clarissa asked.

"Two," Frelia barked. "You're probably going to collapse once the adrenaline stops."

Not much further now. If she could just hold it together—

"By order of the Imperator," came a cold voice, "Caecillion, Valerius, Caecillion the younger—*you will stand down.*"

Frelia whirled on the sound, drawing the Sword of Hana. Out of the corner of her eye, she saw Vendrick's hands immediately snap to casting position. But across their shared link, Clarissa's injured ribs burned as she raised her borrowed spellbook, and Frelia winced, too.

And there, standing in the main gate, was Orsina della Luciana, Athos del Priore, and a third, towering figure built like a bear.

"By order of the Count of Caecillion," Vendrick shouted back, "absolutely not!"

Beside Orsina, Athos flinched. "Vendrick, don't antagonize them!"

"Oh," said Vendrick, laughing a little, "now I recall—you championed appeasement."

An uneasy ripple fell across the gate ward, and Frelia's eye flicked across her surroundings. Every knight and Bloodrune Hunter in Heit Reiði not already dead or dying was closing in, at least a dozen. Frelia drew instinctively into a defensive position, her hand gripping her sword so tightly it was turning white. She forced herself to relax her grip before something wrested it from her fingers.

Orsina held up her hand in the Silverwood hand sign for 'halt.' She was dressed in the stylish leather armor of the Bloodrune Hunters, with a bandolier of alchemist's fire wrapped around her chest. She had the same grey eyes as the rest of her family, but blonde hair, which was currently attempting to escape from beneath her tricorn hat.

Orsina sighed, and made a battle sign Frelia didn't recognize. "I don't suppose you'll stop embarrassing your title, Caecillion, and come quietly?"

"Go to hell, Hunter!" Frelia shouted.

Over their link, Clarissa cringed with enough force that her scabs protested.

Vendrick studied Orsina with characteristic calculation. "You suppose correctly."

With a sharp twist of her wrist, Orsina finished the battle sign over her head, and Heit Reiði burst into chaos.

Vendrick and Clarissa fell back instinctively as Frelia burst forward. She tried not to think about how she'd done the same thing the last time she'd fought in Heit Reiði, and tried not to blink, for something deep in her knew that if she shut her eye, all she'd see were garmur.

We'll watch your back, Vendrick had told her earlier in their two-minute strategy meeting. *Focus on cleaving a path forward and irritating the hell out of them.*

Frelia could do that. She was good at raising hell.

And still, Cillian sang:

> *Set fire to their greasy hides,*
> *You'll never make a dent.*
> *Break their teeth out of their*
> *jaws,*
> *And you'll only end up rent.*
> *But blink onto their backs,*
> *And rip them open wide,*
> *Set fire from within,*
> *And the Goddesses provide.*

Dark Fire smashed across Athos' knights with the fury of a solar eclipse, and all around Frelia, ghostly imprints of both knights and disembodied weapons broke blows meant for her. *I'm a summoner,* Clarissa had said at their tiny strategy meeting. *You'll see ghostly assistance. Don't fight them; they're mine.*

Frelia was grateful for the ghostly polearms that lanced through the knights rushing her blind side; it made it so much easier to duel the ones in front of her, crossing blades. She needed to get to Orsina, to chop off her bloody head and punt it from the battlements.

But the Grand Huntress was still standing at the gate, hand on her hip, and that enormous bodyguard behind her. She hadn't so much as drawn her blade.

And still, Cillian's hoarse baritone sang a warning in her mind:

> *We battled our way through hell*
> *and back,*
> *And never counted costs.*

Frelia slashed and parried, weaving circles around Athos' knights as she thinned their numbers. But the Sword of Hana grew heavier with each swing, and not only was her own exhaustion weighing her down, Clarissa's was, too. Frelia's side burned with sympathetic fire when Clarissa dodged a poleaxe too late, and the ghostly knights around her flickered. Vendrick was probably dragging by now, what with all the grey magic he'd been casting. It would scar him further and leave all three of them injured at the end of this.

Frelia had to end this, quickly.

She raised her hand over her head, made the Silverwood hand sign for 'vanguard has a dumb idea,' and broke into a dead sprint towards Orsina and Athos.

"Valerius, the ever-predictable." Orsina sighed as though, *really*, she had never met anyone so dull. "Don't you grow tired of flinging yourself headlong into hell?"

"*We battled our way through Helheim*—" Frelia's singing was more of a shout, and almost in tune with Cillian's. "*—her river did we cross!*"

"I suppose that was a stupid question," Orsina amended.

The Huntress drew her rapier with a quick flourish, and Frelia slammed into the blade with her own a moment later. The clang rang out across the courtyard like a funeral bell, clear and iron.

Orsina was fast. She struck and parried almost as quickly as Ironfang, when Frelia had fought him in the Tyrant's War. She pushed Frelia on the defensive and no, *no*, this was not good.

Somewhere beneath Frelia's war instincts, her exhaustion, and her bloodrune's insistent buzzing, something felt very wrong. Like the sun had picked today to rise in the west.

"Del Priore," Orsina said over her shoulder, "kindly do your duty to the Crown."

Athos grimaced and drew his battleaxe from where it had been sheathed across his back. The massive poleaxe was going to make Frelia's life very difficult in about twenty seconds, if she didn't kill him quickly.

His voice was pained. "I'm sorry, Frelia."

She breathed, unwilling to shut her eye or show mercy. "I'm not."

She couldn't afford to be anything but Kaldiri.

And never once did we, sang Cillian, *Ever consider defeat—*

The Sword of Hana caught Athos' greataxe by the crook where the axe-head met the haft, and they pressed against each other, raw strength against raw strength. Frelia heaved, then disengaged to meet Orsina again.

She disliked battling the both of them, and unless her bloodrune activated, Frelia would lose a contest of brute strength. Clarissa's ghostly knights tried to close in, but they only clogged the duel and made things worse. Frelia was forced to step around them, to fall back, and it irritated her. Didn't Clarissa know to give the melee room to maneuver?

And why hadn't Orsina's giant bodyguard moved?

Sweat pooled at her brow as Frelia caught both Orsina's blade and Athos' greataxe, and she was forced even further back into the middle of the gate ward. She had never missed the Valerius Shield more than in this very moment. She could have bashed Orsina with it and finagled a way around Athos' guard.

And then Orsina said, "Well, as fun as this is—Drogari, if you would?"

The large man—Drogari—finally stepped forward, and Frelia realized at close range that his helmet was carved in the shape of a bear's head, complete with an open, fanged snout. She could just make out the edges of a very much human, bearded mouth beneath. It opened, as if to speak, but suddenly Frelia's bloodrune was screaming an absolute stitch in her side.

Something greenish and burning splattered across Frelia's face.

She screeched and disengaged, swiping at the gunk. It stung her face and where it caught her wrist beneath her glove, but she sloughed it away like cornstarch gravy. Athos shrieked in audible pain, and Frelia glanced up just in time to see Drogari vomiting another splattering of slime. Athos fell to his knees beneath the deluge, greataxe forgotten as he attempted to shove a finger down his throat. The slime must have gotten into the man's mouth, the poor bastard.

"Do us a favor and gut this dog, del Priore," Orsina said as she sheathed her sword. Then she added, almost as an afterthought, "Try not to eat her, though. That's what happened to the last Valerius to stand at the gates of Heit Reiði."

Black, bubbling, writhing ichor began climbing across Athos' chest, and Frelia's stomach fell into her boots. She backed away slowly, instinctively.

Orsina glanced to her ichor-spewing compatriot. "Drogari, get us out of this mess."

The man quick-cast a rune, and it swallowed him and Orsina with a weight like a dying star.

Athos clawed at his throat as eldritch energy began slithering up towards his eyes like sentient ink. "Run," he hissed brokenly.

Frelia fell back deep into the gate ward, saw Clarissa's ghostly knights swarm her out of the corner of her eye, saw Athos' knights rout in abject terror. She tightened her grip on the Sword of Hana, and began the Grimsdalr War Song again as Athos del Priore transformed into a garmr before her very eyes.

"This is the end of days, my friends,
It's Heit Reiði!"

"Frelia, fall back!" Clarissa shouted from across the way.

As if she would leave this to a ballista! Frelia just needed to see how tall Athos' beast was going to get. She made the Silverwood battle sign for 'kill it with fire' over her head, and somewhere behind her, Vendrick began to laugh.

It was quickly drowned out by a roar from the garmr that had once been Athos del Priore. Black hide was reaching across his face now, and muscle bubbled from his body like fungal growths. The monstrosity coalesced into something resembling a badger, although ten times the size.

Frelia's left hand slashed through the lines of the Grimsdalr Blink rune with the practice of a thousand battles. She completed it a millisecond before the garmr charged.

Astral energy shot her forward with the force of a cannonball, and the world crystalized around her for a moment before she shattered the frigid cocoon on the other side. She overshot the Athos-garmr by a handful of feet, and turned her head just in time to avoid smashing her face into the outer bailey wall.

Stars sparked across her vision as she fell, but Frelia drew a second blink rune on the back of her hand to hold it in place. The rune snapped her upwards a few hands' breadth from the ground, and this time, she smashed into the garmr's hindquarters sword-first.

The garmr screeched and shook itself, but the Sword of Hana held fast. Frelia scrabbled for tufts of its greasy, black fur as she hauled herself onto its rounded back. This was so much easier with a bloody axe; if the Unseen were going to start throwing these things at her again, Frelia would probably need to invest in a hatchet.

It was easier to think in practicum than it was to dwell on what this monster had been five minutes ago.

Over at the ballista line, Vendrick was fiddling with one of the massive, crossbow-like siege weapons, gesturing for Clarissa to help him load it. Frelia appreciated the foresight; getting at the chests of the four-legged ones was always excruciatingly difficult.

The Athos-garmr seemed to notice the Caecillion siblings at the same time Frelia did, and bolted towards them. Frelia redoubled her efforts to get to its head, dragging herself across its back like a climber with an ice pick.

Cillian picked up in her mind again.

> *The eldritch ones are even worse,*
> *They blot the sky like ink.*
> *Battle them at sea, my friends,*
> *You'll end up in the drink!*
> *They may not have a face,*
> *And we cannot speak their names,*
> *But they aren't impervious—*
> *They're terrified of flame!*

As if on cue, gouts of arcane fire blasted across the plaza. They smashed into the garmr's sides and clogged the air around Frelia with the stench of burning hair. She was forced to stop and stamp out the flames licking at the hem of her cloak. The garmr shook itself again, like a dog in rain, and Frelia lost her grip on the Sword of Hana. She fell, hard, onto the cobblestones below.

Her head was spinning as she stared up at the Athos-garmr's underbelly.

Across the outer ward, Clarissa flinched and her ghostly summons finally evaporated. Frelia's ribs screamed as she clambered back to her feet; Goddesses damn her if a few weren't broken. Above her, the garmr roared, and Frelia's eardrums didn't so much pop as erupt.

She knew from experience she couldn't outrun it. Without the Sword of Hana, she had only one option.

She bolted further beneath it.

Frelia moved with the garmr, twisting between its forelegs as it confusedly searched for her. If she were only a little taller, still had her blade, she could probably have gutted it from under here. Cillian or her Da could probably have managed it.

> "So run out the guns, my friends,
> We'll send them back to hell.
> The Soul Warriors have nothing
> On the stories that we'll—!"

Frelia cut herself off with a surprised yelp as a ballista bolt caught the garmr in the foreleg. The beast faltered, crashing down onto its injured leg, and Frelia just barely rolled out of the way of its crushing ribcage.

She wasted no time clambering back up its hind legs, keeping low to its hide as the garmr thrashed in pain. She forced her fingers deep into its greasy fur, hauled herself upwards while her shoulders and ribs burned. Up ahead, the Sword of Hana gleamed in the sunlight where it was lodged in the Athos-garmr's shoulder.

"We'll make them break their
oaths,
And we'll tear them open wide—
For just like all of us,
Every garmr will die!"

A veritable horde of ghostly knights began lining up on the garmr's injured side, and Frelia forced herself to climb faster. She yanked the Sword of Hana free and hopped back down the leg that was pinned to the cobblestones by the massive ballista bolt.

The moment her feet cleared the beast, the ghostly knights began to push.

Frelia could feel Clarissa's furious determination through the bloodrune link, and sweat broke out across her own brow as the mage strained against the garmr's weight. Frelia readied another blink rune, sparing the extra moment to actually aim this time.

The moment she could see its ribs, Frelia pulled sharply down with arcane energy.

She smashed through the crystallized version of the world again. But this time, Frelia drove the Sword of Hana straight into where the garmr's black heart should be. It roared in agony, and Frelia twisted her blade in its chest and yanked it back out with a spray of ichor. She drew back and stabbed again, widening the hole enough to shove her arm into it.

But the angle was wrong to break its ribs; she didn't have the leverage of gravity to do the work her own body could never.

"Frelia."

Her gaze snapped down to the plaza floor, some ten feet below, and there was Vendrick, poised to cast.

"We'll take it from here," he said.

Frelia grimaced and extricated her arm. She dropped to the ground a few moments later, her head swimming with Clarissa's exhaustion and the blink rune, ichor sloughing off her arm.

She positioned herself at Vendrick's back as the grey mage began to draw yet another rune in the air before him. Frelia glanced around the courtyard again, but found no Heit Reiði knights, no Orsina, no combatants.

They were alone.

Frelia felt Clarissa's entire body shudder as the grey magic ripped yet more energy from her. Thousands of spectral hands burst from the ground and climbed up the garmr's legs, stacking atop one another as they scrambled to reach its chest. Their ghostly fingers dug into its hide, and though the beast shrieked and thrashed, the hands had no form to shake, and no weight to paw off.

They piled into and around the hole Frelia had made in its chest, and with a terrible, fleshy rip, began breaking open the garmr's chest. Vendrick's eyes narrowed as he focused on the garmr that had once been Athos del Priore, as the summoned hands broke open its chest with the force of a thousand knights and he waited for an opening to light the beast's heart on fire.

And then he froze.

It wasn't long, and it wasn't enough to drop his half-drawn rune, but Frelia felt it at her back. She glanced around him to the garmr, and felt bile rise to her throat and threaten to paint the cobblestones.

Through the hole they had made in the garmr's chest, where its black heart and bloodstone should have been, there was instead a person. Like half-digested vomit, Athos del Priore's head and torso stood out against the garmr's viscera.

Frelia felt Clarissa heave through the bloodrune link, and her summons flickered like candles in the breeze.

"Athos?" Vendrick's voice shook.

"I don't think he can—" Frelia began.

"*Fucking kill me!*"

For the first time in her entire life, Frelia dropped her sword from outright shock.

"He's alive?" Clarissa called out raggedly.

Despair unlike any Frelia had ever felt ricocheted across the bloodrune bond, and it was all she could do to stoop and pick up her blade again. It was just like it had been at Silverwood, all the way across the continent.

There was no comfort to be had. Not with garmur afoot.

Was this how the Volsinii had made garmur, all along?

"Answer me," Vendrick ordered Athos, "and I shall grant you the mercy of a quick death."

Athos choked out a laugh. "You're a brutal bastard, Vendrick."

Vendrick's mouth tried to smile, but only got as far as twitching. "I daresay, you've known that thirty years."

Frelia had thought her stomach could fall no further, but somehow, it splattered against the cobblestones. Vendrick didn't talk much about the other Queenmakers, and she'd sort of figured it was out of respect for the dead Krakenguard. But thirty years meant that Vendrick had known Athos since they were both boys, running around playing knights and dragons with Princess Octavia while their parents deliberated in the next room over.

Frelia grimaced, and hoped Clarissa couldn't feel it.

"You were always on my side, though," Athos said.

Vendrick's face fell like a stone. "So why make me your enemy?"

Athos grimaced, as much as a disembodied... well, body could. "We can't win against these monsters, Vendrick. Not after her rebellion failed."

Athos jerked his head towards Frelia.

"Yes, we can." Vendrick closed some of the distance between him and the garmr carcass that had once been a very old friend. "That is my *entire* purpose of being."

"I know." Athos suddenly wasn't looking at him. "That's why they went after your sister."

"Well, I'm still here," Clarissa called over, "and you can all rot!"

"Who was that man?" Frelia demanded. "And why was Orsina della Luciana here?"

Vendrick didn't say anything, but squeezed Frelia's free hand.

"His name's Drogari." Athos coughed, and ichor splattered across his chest. "Don't know much about him; he doesn't talk much, keeps to himself. But he's Orsina's bodyguard, I think?"

"And she?" Vendrick pressed. "Why was she here?"

"The ritual." Athos coughed, and gestured with his head towards the outer ward they'd crossed with Miasma. "It was supposed to be for her."

"Ritual for what?" Vendrick asked. "An Ascension?"

"That's what they call it, yeah." This time when Athos coughed, it was accompanied by blood.

Not sticky, black garmr ichor, but red, human blood.

"They don't tell me much, but they're always here. Something about Heit Reiði sitting on ley lines," Athos added. "Sorry, you know I'm not a mage."

"Just describe what you've seen," Vendrick ordered.

Athos shut his eyes, and above him, the garmr's burning green ones shut too. "They drain a bunch of prisoners of blood and use it to draw that circle out there. And then, when the new moon rises..."

He coughed again, spewing blood down the garmr's exposed viscera and his own, still-human chest.

"...then someone stands in the circle and kills three more people, and when that Goddesses-forsaken ritual is done, the first person *eats the hearts of the dead ones.*"

Frelia pressed her hand to her mouth to stop the rising bile, but still, Athos wasn't done:

"And then they cut them, I guess to check if it worked. Because humans bleed red, and darkbeasts bleed black, but whatever the hell they do to people in that ritual makes them bleed green."

Athos shuddered.

"Disgusting, glowing green."

Frelia felt a twinge in her bloodrune connection, and glanced back to Clarissa. The mage wasn't looking at her, or Vendrick, or anyone. She had put herself physically out of line of sight of the garmr, so that even if her curiosity got the better of her, she would not see what Athos had become.

Frelia's heart would have broken for her, if it weren't already in pieces.

"Green like garmur eyes?" Frelia asked.

"...Yeah," said Athos after a moment.

Vendrick raised his hand to the level of his eyes. "Anything else, Athos?"

"I hope you can stop them, Vendrick." Athos sunk further into the garmr's insides, up to his collarbone. "I really do. I wasn't strong enough."

"You have my word," Vendrick promised. "And, well, would you prefer Dark Fire, or Nettles?"

Athos tried to smile, and the garmr head's lips pulled back over its jagged teeth, too. "Fire, always," he said. "Also... did you two figure your shit out, or something?"

Frelia and Vendrick could only laugh.

"Good," said Athos. "You were painful to watch, Vendrick."

"Well, I was going to give your love to your sisters..." Vendrick trailed off as he began to draw a rune.

When Athos was engulfed in Dark Fire a moment later, both he and the garmr died smiling.

CHAPTER TWELVE

ALL AROUND HER, FAUSTINE felt, deep in her bones, the intense crunch of darkbeast jaws snapping shut on human flesh.

The Silverwood Military Institute was swarming with darkbeasts. They spread across the campus like ink, blotting out paths and windows and soaking the weak, winter sunlight into their void-black hides. There was shouting and screaming and already, corpses. Faustine silently promised each one that she would light a candle for them, whoever they were. They didn't stop running long enough to check.

So far, the largest monster Faustine and Christel had seen was over towards the academic quad. It was thin, bipedal, and gangly, its limbs too long and jaws too wide. But the others were small, rat-like creatures, swirling around their larger sibling like water parting around stone. Faustine ducked around columns and into doorways to avoid their piercing green eyes.

She was suddenly grateful for Professor Valerius' unending sword drills and garmur-killing classes, because she was on the move instead of just hiding, sprinting instead of cowering.

They ran towards the mess hall, avoiding fighting as much as possible. They'd lost Thera amidst the chaos after the darkbeast told them she'd catch back up, and Faustine hoped no one tried to stab her in the meantime.

At least Professor Blightsen had been on the Kaldiri side in the war. He would know what to do, right?

She and Christel rounded the corner to the mess hall, only to stop dead at the sight of another big darkbeast between them and safety.

It was around the size of an adult moose, with the biggest set of antlers Faustine had ever seen. Its hollow green eyes stared her down, pinning her boots to the ground. It was much bigger than the rat-like things swarming the grounds, but not nearly so large as the bipedal one, or even Thera.

"You're not a mage, are you?" Faustine asked Christel, even though she knew the answer.

They shook their head. "You?"

"Not even a little bit."

The darkbeast snorted and pawed at the ground, and Faustine wondered if they could outrun this one, at least. She knew getting into a fight with an actual moose was a terrible idea, and couldn't imagine getting into a fight with a darkbeast-moose was any better. She drew her dagger anyway, dropping into middle guard and waiting.

A flash of mousy blonde caught Faustine's attention a moment before a heavy gust of wind sent the darkbeast careening into the side of Atticus Hall

"*Run!*" shouted Ellie, and Faustine had never been happier to see the class white mage in her life. "*Into the mess hall!*"

They burst through the double doors and the instant they were through, Siegmund lunged and slammed the door bar back into place. A huge thud came from the other side of the door a second later, but the bastion held.

"You guys okay?" Siegmund asked.

"For a given measure of 'okay,'" Faustine said, "sure."

"Where's Professor Blightsen?" Christel asked.

"Over here!"

The white magic professor was dressed in nondescript travelling clothes, except for his usual green jacket. His sleeves were pushed up to his elbows and he was casting magic over Professor Campagna's broken leg.

Before the winter ball, seeing the visible nub of bone sticking out of the Loremaster's leg would probably have made Faustine sick. Now, it just made her glad the woman was still alive enough to get it healed.

Is this what war is like? Faustine wondered, absently. It seemed like something Professor Valerius or Professor Corvinus would say.

"What do we do, Professor?" Christel called over to him.

Professor Blightsen made a face, but didn't break from healing Professor Campagna. "I'm trying to recall, besides 'throw Frelia and the Twins at them.'"

Faustine opened her mouth to say something back, but another voice beat her to it:

"Blightsen." Professor Serrana's bow was slung over her shoulder, and she had two quivers full of arrows. "We use the artillery."

Something in Professor Blightsen's expression snapped, and suddenly his eyes refocused. "That's a great idea, if someone can lure the Huntmaster out to the practice field."

There were cannons there, Faustine knew. The artillery practice field was on the very edge of Silverwood's campus, near the farm fields, and nobody bothered dragging heavy things like cannons back to the armory.

It was a good idea, only—"There's way too many of them, Professor," Faustine said. "We couldn't reload the cannons fast enough."

Still, anxiety pooled in her gut the longer she remained in place.

"We don't need to kill all of them." Professor Blightsen cut off the magic, and Loremaster Campagna gingerly set her foot back down on the floor. "We just need to off the Huntmaster—it'll be the one causing this. The rest will scatter without direction."

"And what," Professor Campagna said as she carefully got back to her feet, "do you propose we do with the swarm in the meantime?"

Professor Blightsen's smile was sad, and his voice was uneven as he said, "Set fire from within, and the Goddesses provide."

Faustine glanced over to the windows. They had been hastily boarded up with dining tables, but she could see swarms of the rat-like monsters skittering across the heavy glass and using their skulls as battering rams to break through.

"How are we supposed to lure a darkbeast anywhere?" she asked.

"I'm thinking on that," Professor Blightsen told her. "Humans can't outrun a g–*darkbeast* on foot."

So they would need cavalry. Faustine knew just who to ask.

"Siegmund!" she shouted as loudly as she possibly could over the chatter and the screaming and the monsters outside.

His head snapped towards her, even as he continued to press his bulk against the door. "Yeah?"

"Where's your wyvern?"

Understanding lit up his face. "She should still be in the stables!"

"We can get him there," Christel said firmly. "We just need swords."

"We are not using students to lure that thing anywhere!" Professor Serrana shouted over yet another thud from the moose outside.

But Professor Blightsen said, "Go now. Through the entrance hall." He gestured towards the opposite door. "Axemaster Ossani is out there with what we've been able to scavenge. Ask him for weapons."

"Go get that moose!" Professor Campagna said in a way that, for her, was encouraging.

"Oh, it's not the moose," Faustine said. "If it's the Huntmaster we're after, that'd be the gangly, two-legged one by the academic quad."

The professor's jaw dropped as Faustine, Christel, and Siegmund took off together through the side door.

Dust fell from the rafters as they skittered up the entrance hall. Axemaster Ossani was at the far door, pulling weapons off of—urp—corpses. These ones were in Imperial Watcher armor, which did lessen Faustine's guilt somewhat. At least they'd signed up for this, unlike everyone else.

"Cousin!" Siegmund shouted. "Professor Blightsen said to ask you for swords!"

Axemaster Ossani turned towards them, and Faustine saw a smear of blood across his forehead and his arm tied against his chest with a makeshift sling. "There are a few, but what are you kids doing?"

"Getting to the stables!" Siegmund called back. "We're going to lure the big one out to the artillery field!"

Faustine expected the Axemaster to argue about students being used as essentially bait, but he only nodded. "Good plan. I'd offer to help, but…"

He shook his bandaged arm, and then winced.

"That's okay," Faustine said. "We can do it."

They caught up to their professor and began sifting through his scavenged weapons. There weren't many, but they were able to find Christel a longsword and Siegmund a lance, so Faustine took a lance and tried not to be annoyed about it.

"Be safe, all of you," Professor Ossani said sternly. "Siegmund, your mum will kill me if anything happens to you."

"Don't worry about me, Cousin." Siegmund's smile was as broad as it had ever been. "We'll go home to Fairhunter together."

Professor Ossani nodded, and he tried to smile. "Make us proud, Violet Owls."

He pushed open the double doors that led towards the center of campus, stuck his head out, and then pulled back a moment later. "It's clear for now. Get moving."

Faustine took in huge gulps of air as they ran for the stables, her legs screaming as they navigated the familiar byways of Silverwood's campus and avoided what darkbeasts they could. They passed fleeing staff and students alike (and even a few of the Watchers, which was definitely treason), and even though Faustine knew what she was doing was helpful, it didn't seem it right then as she passed them by.

What horses remained in the stables were agitated, pawing at the ground in their stalls and whinnying loudly enough that you could hear it from across the road. Siegmund burst into the building and charged right through the row of horses, to the back of the stables where the wyverns lived.

"Valor!" he shouted, waving his hands before a great, black beast that was headbutting its stall door. "It's me!"

Valor the wyvern stilled and then made a keening noise that almost broke Faustine's heart. The wyvern's huge, triangular head came over the top of her stall door to nudge Siegmund's shoulder.

"I know, I know," Siegmund soothed, stroking the wyvern's scaly face just like you would a horse. "But we've got to get moving, so I promise I'll get you bacon as soon as I can. Come on!"

As he began saddling up, Christel appeared at Faustine's elbow with two more wyvern saddles. They shoved one into Faustine's arms and bundled the other more securely in their hands. "Come on, let's find the school ones."

Faustine drew in a deep breath and nodded unsteadily.

"I'm not letting him do this alone," Christel added.

Faustine hated wyverns. She hated how their reptilian hides were always cold, and she hated their carnivorous teeth. Horses might be able to take your fingers off with their blunt teeth, but an agitated wyvern could take your whole arm.

But Christel was right, damn it all. They couldn't let Siegmund do this alone. So Faustine rounded on one of the school wyverns and tried to mimic the Violet Owls' wyvern knight.

"Easy, now," she said to the beast. "We've got work to do."

She unlocked the stable door and the beast, mercifully, only stared at her with its beady, black eyes. Siegmund had to come and help her finish saddling the beast, costing them precious time. But soon enough, they were leading Valor and two of the school wyverns back out onto the quad.

Siegmund helped Faustine and Christel mount up, showing them the wing joints to avoid putting weight on, and where it was safe to step, before slinging himself onto his own wyvern's back with a cavalier's flourish.

"Let me take point," Siegmund said. "I don't think it's too proud to say I'm the best flier of the three of us?"

It wasn't, but–"It's huge," Faustine warned him, "sort of shaped like a person, and much, much faster than it looks like it should be."

"Got it!" Siegmund called back, and then they were off. "And I was at Garmur Killing one-oh-one, too!"

The school wyverns were familiar enough with Silverwood's campus not to run into any of the buildings, but Faustine could practically feel the beast's confusion as she steered it towards the academic quad instead of the open fields. She swallowed her fear as best she could, trying not to think about how high off the ground she was, or whether Professor Blightsen or Professor Serrana had made it to the artillery field yet. Whether they were still alive.

The thought came back to her, this time louder: *Is this what war is like?*

Siegmund led the charge into Iuvenlis Quad, and there was that skinny, bipedal one that she and Christel had only glimpsed earlier. It was glaring at them now, and at eye level, the unnatural, sickly green of its eyes was terrifying.

Faustine's wyvern tensed beneath her, and the Violet Owls barely had the time to scatter before the monster swiped at them. It screeched as its claws whipped through empty air, and Faustine felt something warm and wet burst from her ears. Siegmund darted towards the darkbeast's head, and his wyvern's claws raked at its eyes.

It screeched again and blindly swiped at the air in front of it, missing Christel by a margin so narrow it sliced into their wyvern's tail. Faustine cursed that no one had found a bow amongst the discarded weapons, but she had a cavalry weapon. She knew what came next.

Faustine drew in a deep breath, and then positioned herself in front of the darkbeast, at its eye level. It snatched at her with its gangly limbs, but her wyvern twisted them out of harm's way. She lashed out with the lance, scouring gouges in the darkbeast's greasy hide with the tip of her borrowed lance.

She swallowed down nausea as she and Siegmund took turns agitating it. The darkbeast howled again as Siegmund swooped through a broken window in Salonia Hall with an aerial maneuver that made Faustine queasy just looking at it, and finally, the darkbeast started to move.

She took off after it as Siegmund and Valor darted out of another window further ahead, and Christel was right behind her. They wound through campus and towards the artillery practice field at a frenzied pace. Faustine became faintly aware of a noise and looked about wildly for a moment before her gaze landed on Christel, their wyvern abreast with hers as they shouted something into the wind.

She pointed at her ears, and Christel grimaced.

That was when the darkbeast grabbed Valor's tail and yanked.

It whipped both wyvern and rider into the side of the dorms, and Faustine shot desperately forward. The darkbeast yanked Siegmund from Valor's back, breaking bones in the process, and held him aloft in its spindly fingers. Siegmund struggled against the beast, slamming his fists into its hand, its eye, its anything.

Faustine was a hair too slow to grab him before the darkbeast bit down on his head.

The crunch was horrifying, and Faustine felt it, deep in her bones. This was Siegmund Ossani, for the Goddesses' sake, the good-natured dumbass of the Violet Owls. And he was only in this position because Faustine had told him to be.

Bile threatened to choke her as the darkbeast crunched on what remained of Christel's best friend, and although they were probably screaming, Faustine couldn't hear them. Faustine put herself in the monster's sights and it snatched at her as she spurred her wyvern on.

She would finish what he started, and *then* she would cry.

Something shiny and metallic whizzed past her a moment later, and she stole a glance over her shoulder to find Christel with their hand poised to throw a knife, their face set into hard lines that didn't suit them.

Faustine kept the darkbeast's attention as they approached the practice field, as Christel landed and dismounted hurriedly, bolting towards the cannons. They dragged munitions from their crates and loaded the nearest cannon with practiced precision, and Faustine tried not to think about Siegmund.

She caught sight of Professor Blightsen standing near the other side of the field, making hand signs she was forced to fly closer to make out.

Veer right, he was saying, *and take cover.*

Faustine could do that. She sailed back toward the darkbeast, dodging its spindly arms and grasping fingers one last time, leading it towards the right hand side of the field.

And then the darkbeast's foot sunk into the snowy slush, and she understood. Faustine circled it again, forcing it to face the cannons just in time for an earth-shattering burst of artillery fire she felt in her ribs.

The first cannonball cracked into the darkbeast's chest with uncanny precision, and Faustine wished she could help, but knew better than to put herself in the line of fire. No wonder the professors always said cavalry needed both a long- and short-range weapon.

The second cannonball was a glancing blow off the darkbeast's jaw, and though it howled in pain, it did not fall. Faustine landed on the roof of the munitions shed, and the darkbeast tried to lumber towards her.

But then a third cannonball slammed into its chest, slightly off-center from the first. This time, Faustine could get her hands over her ears in time to block out some of its howl. Blood pulsed through her fingers anyway.

Christel was running now, torch in hand. Faustine swooped low, her hand outstretched, asking without words. The swordsman slowed, understanding crossing their face, and then they held the torch aloft.

Faustine's fingers wrapped around it with an air of finality, and she urged her wyvern forward.

The darkbeast startled backwards when Faustine came at it with fire, its greasy hide smoldering where the flames licked it. It swatted at her with flailing claws, but its wounds made it slow and predictable, as though it were underwater.

With a savage cry, Faustine jammed the torch into its exposed chest cavity, and the sudden, roaring flames nearly licked her eyebrows.

Finally, *finally,* she was able to land properly, to get off this accursed wyvern and have her feet hit solid ground again. Even slushy, uneven ground, like the practice field after last night's snow.

Tears began to fall as the darkbeast burned, and though Faustine couldn't hear Christel approach, she saw them in her periphery. For a moment, they just stared at the darkbeast as it screeched in silent—or, well, silent to Faustine—agony.

She didn't realize she'd moved until she bumped into Christel's side. They tore their gaze away from the burning monster to look at Faustine, and she saw the concern bloom across their eyes.

It was hard to say who moved first—Faustine, or Christel—but suddenly her head was pressed into the crook of Christel's bony shoulder, and her arms were tightening across their back. They were taller than she was, broader. Warmer. She pressed into them despite everything, despite herself.

Tears fell onto her face and mingled with her own before falling, lightless, to the ground.

CHAPTER THIRTEEN

BY THE TIME FRELIA, Vendrick, and Clarissa rolled into the nearest fishing hamlet, it was well past dinner. Vendrick settled up on a room with the innkeeper, the three of them ate a rushed meal, and then Clarissa took a key and disappeared to go sleep off what she called 'the mother of all hangovers.'

It was good to have his baby sister back, even if the haunted look in her jadeite green eyes was here to stay.

When Vendrick arrived back downstairs after warding their room, he found their table absent a head of black hair. Panic began mounting, somewhere deep in his chest, but a passing barmaid told him that the other woman he'd come in with had stepped outside, not too long ago.

He thanked her and headed to the main door. But when he pushed it open, the barroom gave way to an empty porch. Anxiety began to sing in the back of his mind, wondering if there were Bloodrune Hunters in town, or perhaps an Unseen agent, or—

"Vendrick," came a voice from his right.

He whirled on it, only to discover Frelia waving at him from the ground a few paces away from the door.

Relief and annoyance both bled into his voice: "Why do you always feel the need to disappear on me?"

"I told the server to tell you!" she spluttered.

Vendrick sighed, but exhaustion was already sapping his displeasure. "Also, why are you on the ground?"

"I got tired of standing."

"There's a perfectly good bar, you know." Vendrick took up beside her anyway, his joints cracking as he lowered himself to the ground.

"*Ja*, but there's people in there," Frelia said. "Also I think I have some bruised ribs from when I fell off the garmr and I wanted to sit with my back against something."

Vendrick grimaced, and resisted the urge to offer to heal her. He was capable of fixing fractures and bruises, but internal injuries were well beyond his pay grade. He was a grey mage, after all, built for destruction and devastation.

It was cold in the north this time of year, and Frelia burrowed into Vendrick's side as he settled in. The casual reality that he was allowed to just... leave her there still hadn't really sunk in yet.

Was it really just last night that they'd been dancing at the Silverwood winter ball?

"We'll have to find a healer tomorrow," Vendrick said. "I'm sure it'll be exorbitant, given that it's nearly Yule."

"*Ja*, well. Your sister definitely needs one, so call it her present." At the questioning look Vendrick shot her, Frelia added, "She's covered in cuts and bruises. I would not be surprised if something internal is broken."

Vendrick grimaced. "What else did you learn, while you were looking after her in the river?"

Frelia was the one who had brought up the fishing hamlet in the first place, but Clarissa had protested walking into civilization wearing nothing but prison rags and bruises. Frelia had suggested Clarissa jump in the river and borrow the swordswoman's spare clothes, and Vendrick had immediately volunteered to keep an eye on the horses, thank you much.

"She apologizes for taking up space," Frelia said, "and is pissed they cut off all her hair."

"I can imagine," Vendrick said, and they fell into exhausted silence together.

"Are you sure it's the real Clarissa?" Frelia suddenly asked.

"Yes," Vendrick said without hesitation. "That's why I asked her about the parties."

Frelia stared down at her hands—or more accurately, at the gloves he'd given her before they'd warped to Heit Reiði. They were buttery smooth, lined in soft grey fur, and stitched so beautifully, you couldn't tell at a glance where the seams even were. When Vendrick had given them to her, Frelia had flexed her fingers experimentally and the joints bent smoothly. Vendrick had hummed his approval and told her to make good use of them.

She hadn't asked about the fact that they were almost perfectly fitted to her hands, and so Vendrick hadn't felt the need to tell her they were supposed to have been a Yule present.

"So how many times did she have to use your reputation to get out of those parties?" Frelia finally asked.

"Only a handful." Vendrick didn't even have to lie. "Most involving della Trova."

They fell silent for another moment as a group of rowdy patrons left the inn, not even noticing the two old warriors sitting at their heels.

"I'm glad the bitch is dead," Frelia muttered, and she thumped against his side again. It shot lightning through his chest like an arrow.

As warmth suffused into both of them, Vendrick finally allowed himself a moment to breathe. The Bitterbane extract was starting to wear off, and it left a bone-deep weariness behind that wanted to drag his eyes closed and put him under for so long, he might wonder if he were actually just dead.

Then Frelia let out a huge breath and a withered laugh. "I can't believe that fucking worked."

Vendrick's returning laugh was quiet, unhurried, as he looped an arm around her shoulders and pulled her closer. "I can't either. We walked into—and out of—Heit Reiði."

Frelia's eye fell to where their knees rested against one another.

"Don't make me do that again," she said quietly.

Vendrick's heart twisted in his chest. "If it were fully up to me," he murmured back, "I wouldn't have asked you at all."

He knew what he'd been asking, and it made him sick to think she hadn't. Heit Reiði was near the Serpentbrook tributary, so really, what else would the Volsinii have renamed it? *Fort Elias, or something,* his many years of Volsinii history supplied, which was massively unhelpful at the moment.

"You're doing it again."

Vendrick glanced down at her, his brow furrowing at the exhaustion written across every line in her face. "Doing what?'

"Thinking so loudly I can hear you. What's the problem?"

Even as he wondered whether he was allowed to smooth over the furrowed lines of her face with his thumbs, something dark and anxious bloomed in his chest. He had known Athos del Priore for ages, grown up beside him, gone to Silverwood with him. It was horrific, to watch an old friend and fellow Queenmaker twisted by evil magic into something that should not have been.

Vendrick sighed. "I suppose I'm thinking about Athos."

Frelia nodded, her expression somehow even grimmer. "Did you know the Unseen could do that?"

"No, and I'm annoyed at myself."

Frelia snorted so hard, she groaned and clutched her bruised ribs.

"What?" Vendrick wasn't sure whether he needed to be defensive yet.

"That's the most 'you' thing I've ever heard." Frelia dropped into a Volsinii accent to approximate him: "'I'm annoyed I didn't know a thing I had no realistic way of knowing; the shame might kill me.'"

"One, rude," Vendrick said, but he laughed. "Two..." He glanced around, just to make sure they were alone. The nearest possible eavesdroppers were a mother and child hurrying down the hamlet street, so he dropped his voice and took his chances. "...I really did find human remains in Markus della Luciana's office. If I'd actually had time to think about it, I probably could have arrived at the conclusion without seeing it firsthand."

"*Ja,* well..." Frelia made a face as she watched the mother and child go. "Now you don't have to, and can think about other shit. Like what the hell they were Ascending Orsina della Luciana for."

"Yes, I don't like that either," Vendrick agreed. "Even without what della Trova told us, that ritual sounds like something I've heard of before. I've been trying to remember what the whole way here."

"I mean, it sounds like every evil ritual, ever." Frelia mimicked the cackling, old voice typically used for witches in operas: "'Bring to me the heart of a man, the wart of a toad, and some other gross shit, and I'll grant you a child.'"

"A *specific* ritual," Vendrick said, laughing. "I just can't think of which. I need reference books—for all three branches of magic, realistically."

Frelia cocked her head to study him. "Is there even evil white magic?"

"It depends on your definition of evil," Vendrick said, "but to use the conventional one, yes. Of course there is."

Frelia's nose wrinkled in confusion. Vendrick found it distressingly adorable. "White magic is mostly just healing, though."

"Oh, no, that's actually a common misconception. It's also necromancy. You'd think that would be grey magic, since that's the branch concerned with energy, but no." Vendrick sighed. "It's white magic—the one concerned with the balance of life and death, and all that."

Frelia considered this for a moment, staring into the rising night. "So necromancers are just bastardized clerics?"

That got a real laugh out of him. "I mean, at the technical level," Vendrick said, "they're actually inverse clerics. Sort of like how undertakers are inverse doctors."

Frelia laughed so hard she grabbed for her ribs again. It rumbled against Vendrick's chest and oh, that was nice. One half of his brain wanted to daydream a future where he felt that more often, but the other one was running down the rabbit hole of magical runes and theory and was reminded of something much, much worse that he still needed to ask about.

"And another thing," Vendrick said, his amusement dying as he spoke. "When were you going to tell me you can do blood magic?"

Frelia stiffened, but she didn't move. "I don't know. It's just for emergencies, like breaking your wounded friends out of prison."

"Emergencies," Vendrick repeated in disbelief.

He could understand necromancers, to some extent. Magical energy had to come from somewhere, and it wasn't a stretch to think it kinder to yank it out of the dead instead of the living. But blood magic was a bastardization of everything Vendrick had ever been taught or used. He could adjust the flow of his own energy into his runes like a painter switching to a different brush, but blood magic was like painting a landscape with a shovel. It might get the job done, but it cared nothing for the path it took to get there.

There was a reason it was the forbidden grey magic art after all.

"*Ja*, that's what I said," Frelia said, growing annoyed. "It's like leaving extra pickling jars at your hunter's lodge and bringing extra firewood indoors before a blizzard. "

"Blood magic is vile." Vendrick would not flinch; he refused. "And you're telling me your family treated it like extra kindling?"

"Of course not." Frelia puffed up like an angry mountain cat. "We treated it like a last resort for when things like garmur came knocking down our walls."

They stared each other down for a long, tense moment, and Vendrick knew he did not have the energy to fight her homeland.

"Besides," Frelia added, "it's not like I don't know the consequences. I'm exhausted—well, I was exhausted before I cast the bloodrune bond—and Clarissa probably genuinely does feel like she has the worst hangover of her life."

Fear ripped through him, sharp and virulent. Dammit, Vendrick knew he should have demanded more information before he'd let Frelia cast that spell earlier. "What did it do to my sister?"

"She'll be fine," Frelia insisted, "but she wasn't born with the Valerius Bloodrune. I'm sure it wasn't pleasant to have it grafted on for a bit."

Vendrick's mind whirled with questions that he did not have the energy, capacity, or reference notes to deal with. He settled for the most pressing one: "But is she hurt?"

"Not because of me," Frelia said with the kind of confidence he adored her for.

"I... can live with that." Vendrick sighed. "How about we make this a Tomorrow Frelia and Vendrick argument? Because frankly, I'm too tired to deal with it, right now.'

"Okay, but..." Frelia reached up and gently flicked his nose, her posture softening. "This is not the end of this."

Vendrick knew he had her—"That's fine. I'm the patient one."—for when he opened his arm to her again, she snuggled right up beneath it like a bird coming home to roost.

"So do you *have* those magic reference books somewhere?" Frelia asked from her reclaimed spot at his side.

"Of course I do," Vendrick said. "What kind of mage do you take me for?"

"The painfully academic kind, now answer the question."

"Painful?" said Vendrick. "What do you mean, painful?"

"I'm teasing!" Frelia said, exasperated. "Merciful Twilight, don't be so dense."

He flicked her nose in displeasure, but all he said was, "I have some books in the family villa, and the Silverwood library might have some in the restricted section. But we're certainly not going back to Silverwood—or to Ascalon, for that matter. Orsina will be reporting to Ironfang about Heit Reiði as soon as possible; we need to go to ground."

It fell between them like an axe.

"For what it's worth, I agree with you," Frelia said, annoyedly kicking at the ground. "But Silverwood was supposed to be safe. Where do we go if it isn't?"

They locked eyes for a moment, the Wolf of Kaldr and the Viper of Ascalon, and the weight of a thousand battles passed between them.

Then they said, together, "Tomorrow Frelia and Vendrick problem."

Just as Vendrick's shoulders were starting to relax again, Frelia said, "I wish we didn't have to share a room with your sister."

"Saints, Frelia!" Vendrick's face exploded in fire. "You can't just say that."

"Oh, don't tell me you're not thinking it, too." She tugged at his chin.

Vendrick had definitely not gotten used to this part. Casual proximity was one thing, but the reality that he was allowed to just kiss her was something else entirely. It was everything their seventeen-year-old selves had never been able to manage, and he still felt like a giddy teenager as she pulled him into it.

They fit together like they'd been made to. Vendrick could get used to the fact that her lips were far softer then the rest of her, her sharp tongue dulled. There was no beginning and no end in this moment, only the warmth of Frelia in his arms and the dizzying relief that they'd both survived another battle meant to kill them.

I love you danced on the tip of his tongue when they broke apart, but Vendrick knew better than to say that again.

Blurting it out had been an accident, last night. She was just being so dense that it had spilled out of him in frustrated amusement: *I love you, you fucking dorchya.*

He'd realized it sometime after Christel's Gyastfylnacht. That the dull ache he'd felt for most of his life was grief, actually, for the brief time where he'd experienced complete understanding at the hands of another.

Only she'd been on the wrong side, and he'd never been brave enough to kiss her anyway.

Frelia had frozen last night, which was to be expected, and it was why he'd originally resolved not to tell her. At least, not for a while. Long enough for her to stop running, stop fighting, stop having to work quite so hard to survive. And maybe actually decide to date him, while they were at it.

She hadn't said it back, though. *I am hell to love,* she'd said instead.

Vendrick wanted to make whoever made her believe that bleed.

"I can hear you thinking again." Frelia interrupted his spiraling thoughts about as gently as she did anything. "Now what's going on in there?"

Saints, he couldn't tell her this. It was enough of a struggle just to get her to sit still, and Vendrick didn't have the mental resources left to deal with a panic attack—his, or hers. He couldn't even think of a good way to lampshade it, either.

He might as well rip the bandage off. Some of it, anyway.

"We, um," he began, and then stopped. Swallowed against the lump in his throat. Started up again. "We didn't really discuss…"

Frelia cocked an eyebrow as she waited patiently for him to spit out whatever he was trying to say.

"...us," Vendrick finally landed on.

"Eh?" Frelia seemed genuinely at a loss. "What do you mean, us?"

She'd already kissed him for the Saints' sake. "Are we courting?" he asked.

Frelia blinked in surprise. "If you want to call it that, sure I guess."

It was like she'd dumped a bucket of frigid water over his head. "Well, you sound enthused."

She looked up at him then, and despite how fatigued she had to be, her amber eye was bright and clear. "I agreed to break your sister out of prison with you," she said after a moment. "Doesn't that... I don't know, prove my intentions enough?"

Oh. Well that was... fair, Vendrick supposed. Possibly very Kaldiri; he couldn't say for certain.

Still. He didn't gamble for a reason.

"That's not definitive enough, for me."

"Okay," said Frelia, and at least she didn't sound upset. "Then *ja,* we can call it courting, if you want. Seems kind of lofty, but..." She shrugged. "If what you mostly mean is exclusivity and support, then... *ja.* Your pain is my pain."

She smiled at him, then, and Vendrick realized, she wasn't being dismissive at all. She absolutely meant it. But still, it wasn't exactly a rousing endorsement.

"Is that what you want?" he asked, refusing to dread the answer.

"*Ja,*" she said at once. "I don't like sharing and I do like kissing you."

As if to prove her point, she tugged him down for another quick kiss that made his head spin a little.

"Sounds like exclusivity to me," she added as she pulled away again.

Vendrick stared at her for a moment in confused curiosity before he finally gave up and announced, "You baffle me, you know that?"

"That's fair," Frelia said through a yawn. "You confuse me, too, you *dorchya.*"

She said it with such warmth that Vendrick wondered how in Hypogia *dorchya* could ever be insulting. Even if it did mean, *I love you, but you're being an idiot.*

"You know..." Vendrick nudged her. "Maybe we should get to bed, love."

"Don't tell me what to do," Frelia said through another yawn.

Vendrick was gracious enough to let her struggle with her bruised rib until she looked to him for help. They headed upstairs together, and Frelia disappeared into the ladies' washroom. So their room at the inn was silent when Vendrick slipped into its imperfect darkness. He knew at once that Clarissa was not asleep; she snored abominably.

"Clarissa?" he whispered, just in case she'd developed the same habits he had, in war.

A soft "Harrumph!" came from one of the beds, and then Clarissa sat up, hair ruffled like a grumpy porcupine. "Hello, brother dear."

"What are you doing awake?" Vendrick asked as he pulled off his gloves. "I figured you would have crashed already."

"It's too quiet." Clarissa drew her knees up to her chest, and wrapped her arms around them. "Where have you been?"

She was nosy, curious—not accusatory. That was good. That was Clarissa.

"Frelia and I were downstairs, discussing some things," Vendrick said. "We'll all figure out what's next in the morning."

Clarissa eyed him warily, her eyes glinting like a cat's in the gloom. "So where is she?"

"Just down the hall, in the washroom."

Clarissa was quiet as Vendrick pulled off his cloak and splashed water on his face from the ceramic dish on the dresser. And *that* was not like Clarissa at all. He wanted to ask her a million questions but was trying not to overwhelm his exhausted little sister. It was bloody difficult, though, when his mind pulled itself in a million directions without any new information.

"So that's Frelia," Clarissa finally said, "huh?"

Vendrick paused his ablutions. "You met her at Gyastfylnacht."

"Yes, Vendy." Clarissa rolled her eyes, melodramatic in the midnight dimness. "I met her once for three days, and suddenly everything you ever told me about her made total sense."

"Excuse you," Vendrick said. "I very pointedly did not give you ammunition."

"I know." Clarissa's smile was tired. "It was mostly in what you didn't say."

"Which was what, exactly?"

Clarissa shot him a knowing look. "She's very pretty."

Now it was Vendrick's turn to roll his eyes. "Yes, *thank you,* Clary. Kindly boil down the largest thorn of my existence to 'she's pretty.'"

"Well, that was the problem, wasn't it?" Clarissa defended.

"The problem," said Vendrick shortly, "was that we got on like a house on fire, but she was supposed to be the Grand Duchess Valerius, I was supposed to be the Count of Caecillion, and then there was a war."

The Caecillion siblings stared each other down across the room for a long, tense moment.

Then Vendrick threw up his hands. "And she was pretty."

Clarissa cackled, triumphant.

"And why are you harassing me about this anyway?" Vendrick huffed.

Clarissa's smile suddenly vanished. "Because it's normal."

Vendrick had experienced plenty of guilt in his lifetime—for what he'd done in the Tyrant's War, for all the times he hadn't spared Clarissa their parents' ire when they were young, for any given black network mission that didn't go according to plan—but the heaviest thing by far was the fact that he hadn't recognized his sister's imposter immediately.

He should have known about the switch, should have known Clarissa anywhere. And she had suffered at the Unseen's hands because he was predictable and distracted and a lot of other words for bloody sloppy.

He could hear his father whispering in the back of his mind to go hang himself for being such a disgrace of a spymaster.

Vendrick shook his head, and collapsed onto the end of his and Frelia's bed. He rested his elbows on his knees and studied his little sister as best he could in the darkness.

"I'm sorry, Clary," he said, quietly. "I should have caught this much sooner than I did, and I—"

"None of this is your fault." Clarissa sliced through the air between them as though she could cut off his words at the root. "If you want to argue you're a spymaster and should have known better, then I'm a spymaster's lieutenant, and so should I."

She shrugged hugely, and Vendrick just barely made out the accompanying grimace. They would definitely have to find a healer tomorrow.

"But they fooled us both," she added, more quietly, now. "So I'll hear nothing of fault and guilt, alright?"

Her voice cracked on the last word, and Vendrick swore it echoed in the space between them.

Well, if she wasn't going to let him take responsibility, he could still be her older brother. Tomorrow they could deal with planning and her health and whatever else needed managed. Tonight, that could wait.

"Move over," he said.

Tears were shining in the corners of Clarissa's eyes. "What?"

"Did I stutter?" Vendrick shooed her towards the wall. "I said move over."

"Oh, we are far too old for this," Clarissa argued, but she complied anyway. "Also, I don't have any hair for you to braid."

"I'll manage."

Vendrick took up beside her, sitting atop the blanket while Clarissa cozied herself into the corner. Fetched between the literal wall and the one her big brother made, it was the exact way she had hidden from their parents when they were small and breakable and living at the family villa.

She was right that she didn't have enough hair to braid, which was normally what he did to calm her down. So Vendrick just scratched aimless runes into Clarissa's scalp until she relaxed into a fitful sleep.

He stayed beside his little sister until he passed out sitting straight up against the headboard, and Frelia's hunter-soft footsteps did not wake them.

CHAPTER FOURTEEN

To HEAR FOLKS TELL it after the fact, the death of the Huntmaster had an instant effect on the smaller darkbeasts. As soon as it was down, its smaller kin broke like a battle line of fresh recruits. Professor Serrana would say how easy it was to down the stupid things when they stood still, and Professor Ossani would say how he'd picked off a lot of the badger-things with throwing knives, even with his broken arm.

But those stories were of no comfort to Faustine at the time.

The attacking darkbeasts had cleared away from campus, sure—but so had Thera. There was no sign of the Darkbeast-woman at the Chapel, its nearby grounds, or out by the lake, and so Faustine, Christel, and Professor Blightsen were forced to leave without her, rather than make excuses as to why they were very clearly lingering.

We'll have to come back to look for her in the morning, the professor had said. *It's not safe to sleep near the dead ones.*

And so now Faustine sat on a log, swinging her legs for want of something else to do as Professor Blightsen rolled up his sleeves to examine her. He hadn't let them stop walking until they were deep in the forests behind Silverwood, the school well out of sight, and so it was pitch black. They were cold, tired, and without their darkbeast charge.

Fantastic. Today was just fantastic.

"How is your hearing?" Professor Blightsen asked.

"This one..." Faustine pointed to her left ear. "...is mostly okay. This one..." To her right ear. "...never came back."

He had done his best, after they'd felled the massive, skinny darkbeast out on the artillery field. The professor had rushed to heal her, but the damage had already set in. It was a testament to the professor's skill as a white mage that he had managed to salvage any of Faustine's hearing at all.

Over the course of the afternoon, Christel had withdrawn somewhere deep into themself, and despite how badly Faustine wanted to talk about Siegmund, or the bloodrune vial she'd stolen, or anything, she knew to give them space. Professor Blightsen evidently did, too, because he'd said nothing when Christel volunteered to go start a fire despite the fact that the professor could have magically conjured one after he was finished looking at Faustine's ears.

Is this what war feels like? The thought had been pounding in her head all afternoon. If it was, then Faustine didn't understand how so many of her professors were so... normal. She felt two steps away from crying, now that the world had grown still again.

"It gets easier."

Faustine glanced up at Professor Blightsen, and realized she'd missed something. "What, sorry?"

"Battle. It gets easier, though you'll never get used to it." At Faustine's confused expression, Professor Blightsen added, "I could see your eyes drifting."

Faustine ducked her head. "I'm okay, thanks."

"Faustine." Professor Blightsen set a gentle hand to her shoulder. "It's okay not to be okay."

That... didn't make any sense.

"I'm supposed to be trained for this," Faustine argued. "And it's my fault Siegmund is... is..."

She choked on a sob that refused to leave her throat.

"It's no one's fault but the garmr's," said Professor Blightsen firmly. "It's not as though you threw Siegmund at the monster."

"But I did," Faustine whispered. "It was my idea to have him and his wyvern lure them away."

"Siegmund knew the risks when he agreed to help." Professor Blightsen squeezed Faustine's shoulder again and let go. "That's what good soldiers do, Faustine. They protect those who can't protect themselves."

But there was one question that kept bouncing around in Faustine's head, whenever she wasn't wondering about the war thing. Something she had known intellectually before, but not viscerally.

"Is this what we did to Kaldr in the war?"

It was little more than a whisper, but Professor Blightsen froze over completely. He opened his mouth and then shut it several times, before finally settling on, "Yes. It was."

Hot shame burst into Faustine's face, despite the fact that she'd been born in the middle of the Tyrant's War and couldn't have done anything about it. How could anyone voluntarily set a darkbeast on people, even the enemy? Didn't they know what kind of horrible monster that made them; couldn't they feel the *crunch* when the beasts bit down?

What sort of person did it make Faustine that she was worrying about Thera still?

"So you understand now," Professor Blightsen continued quietly, "why it's so important to avoid war at any cost."

"Fire's going," Christel announced from across the way.

Professor Blightsen straightened. "Thank you, Christel."

They shrugged, said nothing, and turned back towards the makeshift camp. They were supposed to have gotten mounts and camping gear from the stables before setting out, but there had been no time after the darkbeasts had invaded. So their entire camp consisted of the two blankets the professor and Christel had in their packs, a well-loved pot, and mismatched travel cutlery.

"You should be good for the moment, Faustine," Professor Blightsen said. "Let's go stand by the fire where it's warm, eh?"

Faustine fell in behind him, grateful when the warmth of the fire slunk over her like sunrise over the cliffs back home. Christel was heaping snow into the pot to boil for water, their gaze both focused on their task, and somewhere far, far away.

"I've got some light rations in my pack," Christel said, distantly. "I don't think a handful of jerky is going to go very far even if we turn it into stew, though."

"Thankfully, food is the one thing I did manage to procure." Professor Blightsen pulled his travelling pack off his shoulder, set it on the ground, and began digging around. "Will one of you find me something flat to work on, please?"

Faustine set about looking for something suitable and returned a few minutes later with a piece of shale she'd found half-buried in the dirt by a couple of pines. Christel gestured for her to set it on the ground, and then shooed her away. They lugged the pot off the fire with a fistful of their cloak, and then dumped boiling water over the shale. The snow around it hissed and steamed.

"Wasn't that for dinner?" Faustine asked, gingerly. She didn't want to set off the torrent of rage that was probably building beneath the placid surface of Christel's face, but she was also gutted on their behalf for all the work they'd just wasted.

"I can make more," was all they said. "And now the stone's clean."

Professor Blightsen cleaned off his dagger in the snow, and then began pulling potatoes and carrots out of a small cloth bundle peeking out of the top of his pack. Faustine got to work peeling them with her own newly cleaned dagger, eager to be useful and give her hands something to do.

They worked in mostly comfortable silence for a while, Faustine cutting away potato peels and then burying them under as much dirt as she could manage, Professor Blightsen chopping them into rough quarters, and Christel throwing them into the pot to boil. But soon enough, they were out of potatoes, and Professor Blightsen was sprinkling salt into the water, and then there was nothing left but to wait as darkness fell and the world grew colder.

"Christel," Professor Blightsen said gently, "it's okay not to be okay."

"I know that," they said dully. "I'm just tired of everyone I care about dying."

Silence fell, broken only by the soft chirping of birds and insects in the forest.

There were rumors, Faustine knew, about why Christel had been enrolled at Silverwood. Some said their parents were murderers, or criminals, or spies that Not-Headmaster Caecillion worked with who needed a safe place to keep their child while they went on missions.

But Faustine knew the truth was a lot less complicated than all that. Christel was simply an orphan.

"Christel..." Faustine trailed off, because what could she possibly say? That she understood, when she didn't? That she empathized, when she couldn't?

"Do you want to talk about it?" Professor Blightsen asked, calm and gentle as ever.

"No," said Christel. "But I do want to know what the hell Ironfang was doing to Muninn's corpse."

Christel looked at Faustine then, and she startled. "What, you think I know?"

"You're the one from the beastminder family," Christel said. "You tell me."

"I don't know." Faustine pulled her knees up to her chest and rested her chin on them, staring into the fire even though watching a pot didn't make it boil. "They always kept me away from the darkbeasts, so I didn't know much more than normal people until Professor Valerius' classes."

Professor Blightsen had gone rigid. "What did you see the Imperator do?"

"Dunno." Christel sighed, and leaned forward to poke at the fire with a long stick. "He dug around Muninn's pyre with his bare hands for a while and found this..." They trailed off, putting their hands a foot apart in front of them and then shaping them around an invisible orb. "...red thing in there. Faustine said it was an egg."

"I was guessing!" she squeaked. "That's what it seemed like when a foot came out of it."

Professor Blightsen went very still. "A foot?"

"More like a claw," Faustine said. "A bird's foot."

"Do you think..." Christel trailed off. "No, never mind. It's a stupid idea."

Faustine's heart hurt. "Please tell me anyway?"

Christel harrumphed, and poked at the fire again. "Do you think your da was... I dunno... reviving Muninn, somehow?"

"No."

It wasn't Faustine who spoke, but Professor Blightsen. He wasn't looking at either of them, and in fact, had taken his glasses off to clean them on the hem of his shirt.

"Lord Muninn always has a twin, in myth," Professor Blightsen added, holding his glasses up to the light to check for smudges. "Lord Huginn. One governs memory, and the other governs..."

"Thought?" Christel interrupted suddenly.

Professor Blightsen squinted at Christel. "How'd you guess?"

"I saw it," Christel said quietly, "in one of my bloodrune visions. I watched the Imperator summon Muninn, but I saw the monster itself fighting people, too. But now I'm thinking I might have seen *two* giant raven-monsters, though. Not just one."

"Then my guess," the professor said quietly, "is that Ironfang was looking for Huginn, amongst Muninn's ashes."

"And found him," Christel pointed out dully.

Faustine vaguely remembered della Trova telling Markus about what Lord Muninn could do. About how he could make you relive fond memories and awful nightmares, but mostly, he just brought out things people had buried in their hearts.

Things like Faustine's anger at being treated like prey all her life. Like Professor Valerius' and Not-Headmaster Caecillion's obvious love for each other. Like Markus' bitterness at being passed over for Orsina for the Ascension ceremony the Unseen were putting together.

"What does Lord Huginn do?" Faustine suddenly piped up.

Professor Blightsen paused in the middle of putting his glasses back on. "What do you mean? Like in myth?"

"No, like..." Faustine blinked. "Well maybe yes, actually."

Christel shot her a look Faustine couldn't read in the rising darkness. But Professor Blightsen just glanced around and then said, quietly, "None of this leaves this circle, you understand?"

Faustine and Christel both nodded immediately.

Professor Blightsen sighed. "Lord Huginn belongs to Lady Daybreak, in the stories. He sits on her shoulder atop the golden throne, and whispers humanity's thoughts into her ear. Later, he becomes the Guardian of Konstantin Territory."

Reflexively, he glanced over his shoulder again, as if anyone were around to overhear.

Faustine's nose wrinkled. "Then... what did Lord Muninn do?"

"The same for Lady Twilight, atop the sapphire throne," Professor Blightsen said. "Only he whispers memories and becomes the Guardian of Traust Territory, instead."

Something tugged at the corner of Faustine's mind. *Why stop at Muninn?* Ironfang had sneered at Markus down in his laboratory. *Why not summon Huginn, too?* Plus other names Faustine couldn't remember but had a sinking feeling she knew where they'd come from.

"What about the other Kaldiri territories?" she asked, not bothering to hide her urgency. "Do they have Guardians?"

Professor Blightsen raised an eyebrow. "There was the Watcher, for the Northern Wilds. He was a hero from the Saints' time who, upon his death, became a mighty bear rather than join his ancestors in Helheim, so that he could guard the entrance to the afterlife.

"For Valerius Territory, there was the great wolf Freki, the Guardian of the mountains and Lady Midnight's companion before the garmur. The name 'Frelia' comes from Freki, actually; I'm sure that's why she's named that.

"And then lastly, for Einnaska Territory, there was the great wolf Geri, Freki's twin, Lady Midnight's other companion. He patrolled the land beside the sea, after Lady Midnight was sealed into Helheim."

Huginn, Muninn, Freki, Geri. Faustine's stomach twisted, and suddenly she was no longer hungry.

"I think that's what my father is after," she said, quietly. "He asked Markus why he didn't summon both of the ravens."

"Why didn't you say so earlier?" Christel asked.

Faustine flinched, even though they didn't sound particularly angry, just surprised. "I've only just put it together. But, Professor Blightsen, Muninn was a darkbeast, right? Wouldn't that mean these Guardians are, too?"

The white magic professor was silent for a very long moment.

"I've been thinking about that," he eventually said. "And I—"

A huge crash suddenly sounded from back the way they'd come, and everyone jerked to their feet.

"Get behind me, kids," Professor Blightsen said, raising his hands up to cast.

"You're a mage, professor," Christel said, already drawing their scavenged sword.

"Yeah, you belong on the back line," Faustine agreed, drawing her dagger (for she'd lost her lance in the chaos at the artillery field).

They pushed ahead of their professor, made sure to guard his front, and waited.

A second crash came from the same direction, and this time Faustine could see the top of a pine tree sway, and then start to fall a few seconds before the crash sounded.

"That has to be a darkbeast," Christel murmured. "Aren't they all supposed to be gone, now?"

Faustine grimaced. "Do you think one followed us out here?"

Heat bloomed on the back of Faustine's neck, and she glanced over her shoulder to see that Professor Blightsen had a fire rune three-quarters drawn in the air before him. He looked more serious than Faustine had ever seen him.

"*Found... you,*" rumbled an inhuman voice.

Four green eyes burned in the brush near the fallen trees. Faustine tensed, her fingers tightening on the knife, but she recognized that voice. "Thera?"

The scarred darkbeast came into view, blotting out the rising moonlight with her black hide and impossible size.

The heat at the back of Faustine's neck went out. "Don't startle us like that!" Professor Blightsen shouted.

The darkbeast who had once been a woman laughed that hoarse, bestial laugh, and sat back on her haunches. "*I... not... subtle.*"

"You never were," the professor said, and he sounded choked up.

CHAPTER FIFTEEN

FRELIA AND VENDRICK WERE up and moving before Clarissa, who grumpily told them to go on down to breakfast, she'd catch up. Frelia had the distinct impression it was to avoid having either of them see any more of her scars, but let herself be shooed out of the room alongside an embarrassed Vendrick, who really didn't want to stick around, anyhow.

"Excuse me, bartender," Vendrick said as they gathered cups of coffee and freshly baked meat pies at the bar. "Are there any healers in town?"

The innkeeper paused in counting out Vendrick's change. "There's an old cleric on the north end of town. She may not like your lot, though."

"Our lot?"

"He means Volsinii," Frelia said. "I can talk to her."

The bartender nodded to her. "What do you need a healer for?" he added, and Frelia shot him a look like he'd grown a second head.

She was about to let him have it when Vendrick swooped in. "We were couriers on our way to Serpentbrook Hold," he said. "By the time we arrived, however, it had been—well, attacked is, I think, the most appropriate word—by a darkbeast."

"A garmr?" The innkeeper blanched the approximate color of rancid milk. "This far from the Wilds?"

Oh, so Vendrick was spreading rumors, was he? She could help with that.

"*Ja,*" said Frelia. "Damn thing nearly ate our friend upstairs."

Vendrick squeezed her hand, beneath the bar, and Frelia felt her face warm over. As if she needed reassurance that she was playing along correctly. She knew what he was getting at.

"Trust that upstart in Skjöldr not to guard the place right." The innkeeper's expression soured. "How'd you get away?"

"She's a veteran of the Tyrant's War." Vendrick gestured to Frelia. "There's no one finer to handle a darkbeast."

It was kind of amazing, Frelia thought, how well Vendrick could weave a lie with the truth. And embarrass her. "He means we lit it on fire," she said, rolling her eye.

The innkeeper paused, and then began piling all their gold back onto the counter. "Keep this, then. Breakfast is on the house."

"Eh, thanks?" Frelia said. "You don't need to do that."

"I served under General Traust," the man said. "Trust me, yes I do."

Footsteps began on the stairs, and Frelia glanced over just in time to see Clarissa clamber gracelessly down the stairs. Frelia grabbed her half of the coffee and meat pies, and went to find a low table.

"How are you feeling, this morning?" Vendrick called over to his sister.

"Like I've been run over by a wyvern horde," Clarissa muttered.

Frelia set breakfast down on a table and dropped into a chair. A moment later, Clarissa lowered herself haltingly into the chair across from her, and nodded her thanks to Vendrick as he set down the other half of breakfast.

"There's apparently a healer on the north side of town," Vendrick said, claiming a chair between Frelia and Clarissa. "That's our first order of business this morning."

"Okay." Clarissa stared down at the faintly steaming meat pie. "I know I should eat, but I can't bring myself to."

"Small bites," Frelia said. "Like being hungover."

The corner of Clarissa's mouth tugged upward, and she broke off a small piece of pastry. "So after the healer," she asked, staring at the crumb between her thumb and forefinger, "then what?"

"A tailor," Vendrick said. "If nothing else, you'll need a cloak."

"While I do appreciate the spare clothes, Frelia dear," Clarissa said, "I think I'd prefer something that fits."

She flapped her arm at Frelia, the end of the sleeve whipping about like an old-fashioned mage's robe.

"Eat your breakfast," Frelia said, though she laughed, too. "Also, do you have the money for that, Vendrick? I'm a professor, in case you forgot."

He paused over his mug, even as Clarissa laughed, and it struck Frelia a moment later.

"Or, well," Frelia said, and her heart twisted with unexpected grief. "I was."

Clarissa's laughter cut off abruptly. "You didn't resign, did you?"

"We both did," Vendrick said.

Clarissa's froze in the middle of bringing a bite of pastry to her mouth. "Vendy, you didn't."

"I had to," was all he said.

"You love that role!" Clarissa protested. "And, at a guess, I'm betting you did as well, Frelia?"

Frelia didn't know what to say, so she shrugged and stared at the meat pie in her hands. It tasted like sweet gale and dill, just like the cooks at Castle Skjöldr and Valerius Lodge used to use, and that hurt, too.

Wasn't she supposed to be moving forward? This was ass-backward.

"Well I love having a living sister, living students, and living girlfriend more," Vendrick said. "They're evacuating Silverwood probably as we speak, and I—"

"Girlfriend?" Clarissa interrupted. Her eyes darted from Vendrick to Frelia and back again. "Are you two official?"

Vendrick turned a violent shade of red. "As of last night."

"Oh, so it *is* a Volsinii thing," Frelia muttered. At least his insistence on calling it courting made sense, now.

"Vendy, I'm so proud of you!" Clarissa squeaked, so loudly that several patrons looked over to their table in concern. She waved them off, saying, "My brother finally has a girlfriend!"

"You're awful," Vendrick muttered, even as the confused man across the way lifted his tankard in congratulations. "You don't need to announce it."

"Oh yes, I do!" Clarissa was beaming so hard it cracked a scab on her lip. "I've always wanted a sister!"

That was the moment Frelia decided, Clarissa might have been obnoxious, but her heart was in the right place. And that was more than a lot of folks Frelia had dealt with, over the years.

So Frelia put her hands on her hips and said, "Well we're not having sleepovers and talking about boys until we're holed up safe somewhere."

Even Vendrick laughed.

"Okay, fine," Clarissa said, like it was an enormous burden. "Tailor, healer—Vendrick, do you have the funds for that? I certainly don't."

"Of course I do." Vendrick, still pink around the ears, nodded over the rim of his coffee mug. "I was fairly certain we'd have to stop for clothes and healing at *some* point. We'll just be sleeping out in the open, for a while."

Frelia sighed into her breakfast. She *detested* night watches. "Bowyer next, if we can find one," she said. "Blacksmith if we can't. I can hunt for our dinners but I'll need something to shoot it with."

"Fair," said Vendrick, "but we are rapidly eating up our funding."

"Do you have a spell we could use to hunt instead, Vendy?" Clarissa asked.

He made a wishy-washy motion with his hand. "Not one that leaves behind meat I'd prefer to eat."

Clarissa grimaced, and Frelia snorted into her coffee.

"And then everything gets messy," Vendrick said, as though it hadn't been before. "We can't return to Silverwood, and, since Orsina will absolutely be reporting to Ironfang about what happened, we can't return to Ascalon—and therefore the family villa—either."

"Why not?" Clarissa asked. "He'll have to admit he ordered the unlawful imprisonment of a Volsinii citizen in order to complain about what we did at Serpentbrook Hold."

"Heit Reiði," Frelia said sharply.

Even as she said it, she wanted to kick herself. The memories were the same no matter what the fort was called. And again. Forward. Not backwards.

Clarissa recoiled. "What?"

"The fort's name," Frelia said, having already dug the grave. "It's Heit Reiði."

"Ironfang will also have ways around admitting that, Clarissa," Vendrick said. "He's been outspoken for years in support of the Unseen, and I wouldn't put it past him to pin Athos' untimely demise on me."

"Technically," Frelia said, "it was your fault."

"Technically," Vendrick argued, "it's Orsina and Drogari's fault. But moreover, I don't have the ability to turn someone into a darkbeast, anyway. That's been a della Luciana family secret for centuries."

Frelia took another slug of coffee to keep herself from reminding him the monsters were called garmur.

"That also reminds me..." Vendrick glanced reflexively over his shoulder, but the other patrons were back to their breakfast beers and meat pies, and the innkeeper was busily sweeping around the front door.

Then his eye fell back to Frelia and Clarissa. "I... let's say investigated Markus' laboratory at Silverwood before we left. Clary, I found something I want you to take a look at."

Clarissa pinched another bite of meat pie off her plate. "What kind of something?"

"A bloodstone." Vendrick dropped his voice to add, "A weird one."

"Oh, I love weird, probably unstable grey magic." Clarissa brought her hands together in mock glee. "I'm sure I'll have plenty of time to look at it on the road to... well, actually, if we can't go home and we can't go to Silverwood, where can we go?"

"Talis and Hazel's laboratory," Vendrick said. "We sent some students there for their own protection, alongside Edmund Blightsen anyhow."

Clarissa choked on the bite she'd just taken. "Talis isn't a fighter, Vendy; he's a scientist! And I doubt Hazel can guard the whole place herself."

"And what am I," Frelia asked, "a loose sled dog?"

"You're here, is what you are," Clarissa said. "Not, you know, guarding squishy children and scientists."

"We weren't exactly swimming in safe options, Clary," Vendrick shot back. "At least we know whose side they're on."

Clarissa set down her coffee cup. "So what happens if we lead Orsina della Luciana straight to them?"

"I gut the bitch," Frelia growled.

"Forgive me for not feeling better about our chances," Clarissa said. "What about the black network, Vendy? Where are they?"

"An excellent question," Vendrick said. "I left notes in the Silverwood dead drops, but Saints only know when those will get read. Frelia, do you have contacts somewhere that might assist? Old mercenary friends, perhaps?"

"Nobody who would hide us if we're wanted by the Imperium." Frelia gestured firmly for Clarissa to keep eating, and the younger Caecillion sibling took another sheepish bite. "Except Leon. But even if we went all the way to Duncregg, he may or may not even be there if the Cost Effectives are out on a job."

Vendrick wrinkled his nose. "I don't particularly want to go all the way out to the Free Cities, anyhow."

"Who's Leon?" Clarissa asked.

"Leon of the Titanheart," Frelia said. "He's an old friend, and also the Captain of the mercenary company I was with before Silverwood."

"That's an Islander clan, isn't it?"

Frelia nodded.

"Then," Clarissa added, "what about Irirangi? Would she offer us asylum?"

"Possibly," Vendrick admitted cautiously. "But it's the same problem as Duncregg. We'd be a long way from the continent and in no position to aid Talis, Blightsen, and the rest."

"*Ja.*" Frelia made a face. "We should go pick them up before they get themselves slaughtered by the Imperator or worse."

Silence hung over them for a moment like cobwebs from an ill-visited ceiling corner.

"I don't suppose you have any hidey-holes around here, Vendy?" Clarissa asked.

He shook his head, and Frelia said, "Might be an old Valerius hunting cabin still standing somewhere near the border, but that doesn't solve the Faustine, Edmund, and Christel problem."

"So we can't go to Silverwood," Clarissa surmised, "can't go to Ascalon, can't go to Duncregg, can't go to the Rippling Isles, can't stay in this fishing hamlet. We have no idea where our spies are, which means we only have so much money and nowhere to go to ground until I've recovered enough to fight."

Frelia slumped back in her chair. "'Bout sums it up, *ja*."

Vendrick pressed his thumbs into his temples. "Saints, what a mess."

They drank coffee in sullen silence for another moment.

"Vendy," Clarissa began, carefully setting her mug down, "you know who we haven't considered? Mum."

"Absolutely not." Vendrick straightened up at once. "Have you gone mad?"

"Think about it!" Clarissa began ticking things off on her fingers. "She's got the space, the funds, the embarrassment if she turns her own children away, and, if we get to her before Ironfang does, we have an ally."

"An *ally*," Vendrick repeated flatly. "Do I need to remind you this is the woman who divorced our father for what he did in the shadows? For what I continue to do?"

A warning buzz began to creep up the back of Frelia's neck.

"Mum's not unreasonable," Clarissa said. "I'm certain if we just explain the situation—"

"She'll clap us in irons," Vendrick interrupted. "Me especially, given that I'm apparently wanted."

"Wanted?" asked Clarissa. "Where'd you get 'wanted' from?"

"Orsina said 'come quietly,'" Frelia pointed out. "Also for what he did at Silverwood before we warped out, but that's another story."

"That's another thing, Clarissa," Vendrick said. "If Orsina seeks to arrest me, do you think Mum is going to just let us waltz right in and set up shop?"

"Yes," said Clarissa honestly, "if we can prove the warrant is unlawful. She's terribly predictable, Vendrick; you know that."

Vendrick pressed his thumb and forefingers more deeply into his temples. "Clary, why don't you tell the Kaldiri woman in the party who our mother is?"

The hairs on the back of Frelia's neck stood on end as Clarissa very sheepishly turned to her and said, "Governor Sulpicia 'Deadcut' Verona."

Frelia jerked away from the news so fast her chair crashed to the floor. "Fuck no," she barked, even as she scrambled back to her feet.

Forward motion or not, there were some things that simply could not be forgiven. One of them was the Winter War.

"Thank you," Vendrick muttered.

"Is this a fucking joke?" Frelia growled as she dragged her chair back upright. "*Deadcut?* You want me to go beg for scraps from the butcher of Traust Territory and the usurper governor of Einnaska Territory?"

"She's not that terrible?" Clarissa offered.

Frelia whirled on Vendrick. It was like being told the Tyrant's War would make them enemies all over again. "What did I tell you about keeping secrets?"

"That's, erm," said Clarissa, "not a secret?"

"It's not as if I get along with the woman, Frelia!" Vendrick threw up his hands. "If she weren't the bloody governor of New Ascalon, I'd be occasionally popping by to make sure she hadn't died in her sleep, or something, and that's about it."

"I think the last time Vendrick visited Mum was seven or eight years ago," Clarissa inputted. "And I know you two don't get on, Vendrick, but if you lay out everything logically in front of her, even she will have no choice but to believe you."

Vendrick shot his little sister a withering look. "I haven't any evidence, besides my word."

"You have me," Clarissa said. "Am I not proof enough?"

"Nothing is proof enough for our bloody mother."

"Well, what about just New Ascalon?" Clarissa said. "I'm sure you know the city better than anyone, Frelia."

"I knew Skjöldr." A muscle in Frelia's neck had begun to twitch as it held her jaw shut. "I haven't been back in years, since putting General Deadcut on the Coldiron throne is about as insulting as losing all my territory."

"Well, I don't see either of you coming up with any other ideas!" Clarissa threw up her hands the exact same way Vendrick just had. It was sort of uncanny. "How far *is* Talis and Hazel's laboratory from here, Vendrick?"

"A few weeks, I'd think," Vendrick said. "It's just..."

He trailed off, and Frelia glanced sharply to him.

"It's just what?" she pressed.

Vendrick shifted in his seat, discomforted. "It's, er, just east of here."

Frelia's gut clenched. East lay Valerius Territory, and there were very few places there that could support a settlement. The land was wild, forested and harsh, and most of their wealth had come in the form of pelts, scrimshaw, and sled dog sires and dams.

"Are you telling me," Frelia snarled, working to keep her voice low as she rose to her feet, "that this laboratory your Volsinii-ass friend built is in the ruins of my hometown?"

Vendrick had the decency to look ashamed, and Clarissa said, "He insisted it had to be in the cold?"

Frelia's eyes flicked from one Caecillion sibling to the other. From eyes too green to hair so dark to Clarissa's concern and Vendrick's carefully neutral mask.

"Go to the healer without me." Frelia threw over her shoulder, and headed for the inn door deaf to everything behind her.

CHAPTER SIXTEEN

THE FISHING HAMLET HAD a small, sad excuse for a tiltyard, so that's where Frelia went. She snuck over the fence to get to the open training ground space, and breathed in the ever-present smell of dirt and sweat.

It felt good to stretch her muscles and work through the sword fighting forms she'd used since practically birth. Her feet knew what to do, her arms knew how to manipulate the blade to strike exactly where she wanted—no less and no more.

It was a lot easier than navigating the battlefield she'd left behind at the inn.

Vendrick was a man made of secrets, and Frelia knew that. She knew, intellectually, that there were plenty of things he hadn't told her and likely never would. But somehow, Frelia had figured most of it consisted of Senatorial gossip and old state secrets. She had thought, apparently naïvely, that after a Gyastfylnacht and Thera, he would feel the need to keep fewer secrets from her.

Can't change the predator's nature, Frelia thought sourly.

Then she squashed the thought before it grew legs.

She became aware of eyes on her back, and turned just in time to see Vendrick inelegantly hopping the fence. His coat snagged on a post, and he took a moment to tug it free. Frelia refused to find the whole thing cute.

"Now what's happened?" she demanded.

Vendrick smiled—or tried to, anyway. "Nothing new." And then he dropped it, back to that damn neutral mask. "I just... thought we should talk."

Frelia's hands froze on the hilt of her sword. "*Ja,* when were you going to tell me that laboratory is in fucking Kjell? Or that your Mum is why I'm an only child?"

"Not like that, I assure you." There was an undercurrent of anger, there. "I've already had it with Clarissa."

Frelia stared at the Sword of Hana in her hands. Legend had it that her ancestor had cleaved it into Lord Muninn's side, before Muninn was Muninn, and turned out that the legend was even true. Vendrick had cut the ancient weapon free of the garmr's hide, and Frelia had used it to destroy him. They worked best in harmony like that.

The things that hurt us always come from closest by, she could almost hear her Aunt Brenn saying.

"I told you on that hillside, Vendrick," Frelia said, quietly. "No more lies. No more secrets."

"And I told you that if you think everything out of my mouth is a lie, this..." He just barely stumbled over his next word. "...relationship won't last."

Frelia met his gaze, and she saw anxiety worked into the lines of his face. Well. There was nothing to be done about that, right now, when the only way out was through.

"I understand why you didn't tell me about Thera right away," Frelia said, ticking things off on her fingers, "but you also didn't tell me the fort we needed to break into was Heit Reiði, that your Mum fought my da in the Winter War, and now I find out you didn't tell me you sent our students to fucking Kjell. What else am I supposed to think, Vendrick? They're lies of omission."

"In my defense," Vendrick said, holding up a hand as if to block a punch, "I didn't realize you didn't know we'd renamed it Serpentbrook Hold, as that name is ten years old at this point, and the Mitris' laboratory genuinely is the safest place I could think to put Faustine and Christel. We are working with the impossible, Frelia, and I couldn't let variables crater a plan that was full of holes to begin with."

Frelia stared at him for a long moment, but all she could read in his expression was anxiety. *Variables,* he said, when he really meant *free will.*

"Do you think I'm an idiot?" Frelia asked.

Vendrick looked taken aback. "Of course not."

"Then why treat me like one?" Frelia jammed the Sword of Hana into the tiltyard dirt and worked to keep from shouting. "Even if you had told me it was Heit Reiði, I still wouldn't have let you jailbreak Clarissa alone. And I still would have agreed to send everyone to Mitri, because those were the best options we had. But I would have been... fucking..."

She harrumphed and pulled loose hair out of her eye to give herself time to think.

"I could have braced for it if you'd just fucking told me what I was walking into!"

Vendrick winced. Just a little, but enough that Frelia saw it clearly. "I... couldn't risk your saying no. I'm sorry."

Part of her wanted to say *no, you're not, you're sorry you got caught,* but ultimately, Frelia realized she was working against the man's very nature, or maybe nurture. She had to make him *see.*

"If you have to manipulate me into doing what you want," Frelia said flatly, "then this isn't a relationship to begin with. It's not even a friendship. It's just convenient lies."

Vendrick's posture stiffened. "Trust me, if I wanted to manipulate you, you wouldn't notice."

"Again," Frelia barked, "do you think I'm stupid?"

"Again," said Vendrick, "no, but there's a lot more at stake than..."

He trailed off, but Frelia didn't let him find a nicer way to put it.

"Than my feelings? *Ja,* thanks, I'm aware." She glared at him, unable to stamp down the rage any longer. "I know the cost of letting those get in the way, Vendrick, so believe me when I tell you that I'd have said 'send them to Mitri fucking anyway.'"

They were nearly nose to nose now, Frelia's glare boring into Vendrick's eagle-eyed stare.

"I'm not made of glass," Frelia said. "I won't break at the mention of Kaldr. If I did, I wouldn't have survived after the Northern Rebellion."

For a moment, Vendrick looked like he wanted to argue. But then his gaze cut away, and he sighed instead.

"I know," he murmured. "I just... I suppose I just wanted to spare you pain."

"You can't."

He flinched. Outright, visibly flinched.

"So promise me you won't try, anymore," Frelia said, a little more gently. "Lay everything out to me, even the shit you think I don't want to hear, and let's plan like partners, Vendrick."

She held a hand out over his, asking without asking whether she was allowed to touch him right now.

He studied her for a moment, and then turned his hand to squeeze hers. "I can't promise that," he said.

Frelia jerked out of his grasp. "What the fuck? I'm not asking for the sky, here."

"The pain part!" Vendrick hurried to add. "I will never stop trying to spare you pain."

It was both sweet and frustrating. Frelia half-wanted to kiss him for it, and half-wanted to smack him upside the head.

"What I can promise," he added at her silence, "is that I will tell you the things I think will hurt, anyway. I'm probably going to be terrible at it, but I promise to try."

He took her hand again, and she let him.

"In return," he said, "I need you to promise not to blow up at the first sign of something you don't like."

"Fine." Now it was Frelia's turn to shut her eye and sigh. "I promise to try, anyway."

Vendrick's smile was small—"Good enough for government work, right?"—and he raised her hand up to press a kiss to the back of it.

It seared into the skin there like a brand, or maybe a weight.

"Also," he continued, "did you really not know my Mum was General Deadcut?"

"I knew your Mum was a general," Frelia said. "And I figured she'd fought in the Winter War somewhere, but I..."

General Verona had been the Butcher of Traust Territory. The Volsinii's ace-in-the-hole during the Winter War. Frelia had grown up hearing stories of the woman's overwhelming tactics and military discipline from her father and Countess Traust.

Shame she was never made a paladin, her da had usually said. *She'd have been a damn fine one.*

He had left unspoken, of course, that it would have meant Deadcut would have been on the Church's side—Kaldr's side—during the Tyrants' War.

How had a woman so rigid borne a son so devious? And moreover, what had she done to make him keep his distance?

"You really don't talk to her?" Frelia asked.

"Put it to you this way, love," Vendrick said. "When I was a boy, my father used to make me break into my own room to go to bed. And Saints forbid I give up and sleep in the hallway."

Given everything Frelia knew about the former Count of Caecillion, that wasn't surprising. He was where the spymastering came from, after all.

"It's why I'm now so good at lockpicking," Vendrick continued. "However, despite all her holier-than-thou posturing, guess who never stopped him?"

Frelia made a sympathetic noise in her throat.

"Guess who also tried to force Clarissa into axe-work," Vendrick said, as if she hadn't made a sound, "and arranged marriages, and threw up her hands at our general interest in the arcane?"

Vendrick laughed, but there was no mirth in it. "She lived in the same house as my father, but I don't think I ever saw them together except outside of it."

There was only one word for it, in Volsinii Standard. "She sounds like a coward."

"Tyrant," Vendrick corrected softly. "So trust me, Frelia, it will be a cold day in hell before I ask her for anything."

Frelia could live with that.

"Well aren't you two adorable!" came a voice from across the way.

Frelia glanced up to find Clarissa waving from the other side of the tiltyard fence. She had all three packs awkwardly slung across her shoulders, and a bright, cheerful smile.

"I told you to wait at the inn, Clary!" Vendrick called, releasing Frelia's hand back to her person.

"I got bored!" Clarissa called back. "Also I realized, I need a spellbook—I don't suppose either of you know if there's a mages' shop in town?"

"Probably not," Frelia said.

"The cleric might have some extra supplies she'd be willing to part with," Vendrick said, shaking his head as they headed back towards the fence.

"Fabulous," said Clarissa. "Shall we get on?"

"Like a king on fire," Vendrick said, and the way Clarissa cackled made Frelia figure there was a story, there.

CHAPTER SEVENTEEN

THE BLOOD ARCHIVES HAVE been stolen. Find them.

Ironfang stared dismally out the parlor window at the dark forest surrounding Norvegr, mentally turning over his options. The Sightless One might just as well have said Caecillion's black network had stolen the sun, for all the good the information did Ironfang. What was he supposed to do, exactly? Magically determine the culprit? Go back in time to stop it?

Never mind how desperately the Unseen needed those vials—Ironfang first needed to place the blame squarely where it belonged.

It was times like these that he missed Vittoro Caecillion. The man had been about as charming as a sea snake, but he'd been intelligent and paranoid and an excellent Spymaster. Ironfang missed having a mental springboard; none of his own children had ever come close to Vittoro's level of competence.

First there was Orsina, his eldest, a holy terror on the battlefield and an *un*holy terror everywhere else. She was too much like her late mother that way, and Ironfang was perfectly content to leave her to captain the Bloodrune Hunters, even if he couldn't yet publicly support her there.

She needed something to keep her busy, and Ironfang didn't have the time, energy, or patience to rein in her more brutal side. It was a relief she'd been born a woman, that way.

Then came Titus and Gaius, both slain in the Tyrant's War. That either had been sloppy enough to be felled in combat was half the reason Ironfang had been roped into commanding the Volsinii troops for the Northern Rebellion in the first place.

Then there was Galeria, married off and already the mother of four bloodrunes already. Two of them even came by it naturally. She fancied herself a businesswoman, when she was simply a glorified landlady.

Then Markus, his only living son, the little sycophant. He had always been running off to tattle on his siblings, as a child, so it was only natural that Ironfang had sent him out to Silverwood to keep an eye on Caecillion. If the man so much as breathed wrong, Markus had ensured that Ironfang knew.

And lastly there was little Faustine. Too young to be of any real use yet, although he did have plans. Ironfang had spent years impressing upon her the importance of the della Luciana family, and the ghastliness of its enemies, and still, the girl seemed to think she had a choice whom she served.

Swimming in options, he thought, *truly.* He supposed it was better than the alternative. Volsinii history was littered with the stories of Imperators whose children were as cunning and conniving as their fathers. Most of those fathers ended up in the Bay of Ascalon, or worse.

"Sir?" came a thin, reedy voice from over by the parlor doors. "You had wished to be informed when your associates arrived."

Ironfang's smile, at least, was genuine. "Send them in, would you kindly."

Orsina came striding in first, looking like she'd slapped makeup over a stone wall and called it a fresco. Though she was alone, Ironfang could sense the presence of her charge somewhere beyond the parlor door.

An unclean, frigid spirit in the air, no doubt making the house staff uncomfortable.

Lord Octavianus was a good sport about Ironfang effectively taking over his guest wing. The inherent prestige in hosting the Imperator likely helped.

"Ave, Imperator," Orsina said, sweeping into a low bow, "Long may he reign."

Ironfang's eyebrow rose. That was particularly stilted, even for his progeny. "Am I to understand things at Heit Reiði did not go according to plan, then?"

To her eternal credit, Orsina straightened up to meet his eye. "No," she said quietly, "they did not."

Markus chose that moment to come bumbling in on his older sister's heels. "Not only did the Ascension fail, "he said, gleeful and insignificant, "Caecillion and Valerius stole his sister right out from under her nose."

Orsina scowled. "You're intolerable, you know that, Markus?"

Ironfang's eyebrow was now stretching the limits of his forehead. "Valerius and Caecillion were at Silverwood during the new moon. How in Hypogia did they reach the Ivory Channel in a morning?"

Orsina threw up her hands. "I've no idea, but they did."

"He's got warp runes," Markus said. "I'm sure he used one of those."

Orsina made a disgusted, irritated noise that Ironfang allowed to echo in the room for a moment. Just long enough for both of his adult children to begin to realize they'd stepped in something he would not allow them to scrape off.

"So am I to understand," Ironfang said again, evenly, "you are not Hypogean, the Countess Caecillion is not dead, and Valerius and Caecillion are simply, what, off on their merry way?"

Silence, and then something cold and unwelcome slithered up Ironfang's brainstem.

Why do you keep such useless *tools to hand?* The Sightless One asked.

Ironfang wondered that himself, some days.

"That... roughly sums it up," Orsina said after a long moment. "Although I did leave them a darkbeast as a parting gift."

She never tried to dissemble, like Markus did, or cry, as Faustine did. She never whined, like Galeria, or persuaded him any which direction, as his late wife had. In that, Orsina was the most like Ironfang himself. She simply stood by her decisions and weathered the consequences.

He sighed, relieved not for the first time that Orsina had not been born a son, and began to pace.

"Remind me," Ironfang said, his voice as smooth and cold as the one in the back of his mind, "what is it you are?"

Orsina's head snapped up while Markus froze like he'd been caught with his hand in the cookie jar.

"A della Luciana," they said, in unwitting unison.

"And what does that mean?" Ironfang asked in a mock-educational tone.

Orsina and Markus exchanged a worried look, and Ironfang was almost starting to enjoy this.

"That what we do," Markus said, "we do for the family."

Ironfang said nothing.

"And when we fail," Orsina added, her shoulders tense in her leather, armored coat, "we fail the family."

Ironfang stopped pacing. He turned, slowly and deliberately, to face them. He let the silence stretch just long enough for Markus to begin surreptitiously itching the exposed skin of his wrist, and Orsina's facial expression to begin twitching.

They were expecting the hammer. It would be Ironfang's pleasure to bring it down.

"Here," said Ironfang, "is how you shall salvage this wretched state of affairs."

In the back of his mind, the Sightless One began to laugh.

"We have, in our possession, the Lord of Thought." Ironfang did not pause to let that sink in. "Orsina, you shall be in charge of his handling."

"Father, I must protest!" Markus said immediately. "Orsina's not even a beastminder."

"I am aware of your elder sister's skills, capabilities, and retinue," Ironfang snapped. "Which is why she will be entrusted with Lord Huginn's safety."

Orsina shot a smug look Markus' way, but Ironfang was not yet finished.

"She will also be entrusted with the recovery of the Blood Archives she was so lax in guarding."

The self-satisfaction instantly dropped, and Orsina turned corpse-pale. Ironfang didn't even need to add the *or else*—Orsina was filling that in herself.

She didn't argue that she'd been sent to Heit Reiði, nor did she list the names and ranks of those she'd left to guard the family villa in her stead. She simply said, stiffly, "How do you know about that?"

"The Sightless One sees all," Ironfang said, and he waited.

Predictably, his children refused to look at him or each other. Their discomfort was charming.

"Now," Ironfang continued, "I trust you've done the legwork on where they went?"

Orsina's lips pursed as she chose her words carefully. "I am working on it."

"You lost the archives?" Markus howled, incredulous. "After all the work I've done putting them together, you went and—!"

Ironfang stepped closer to the both of them, and Markus fell silent.

"I shall accept working theories, Orsina," he growled.

Markus scuttled backwards while Orsina reached for a sword that was not at her hip. Ironfang very pointedly followed the motion, and Orsina quickly withdrew her hand and folded them at her waist.

"We have been robbed of one Einnaska, two Nova, one Domitia, two Konstantin, two Grimsdalr, and the dregs of one Maximus vial." Orsina didn't even need to think to rattle them off. "The biggest questions, of course, are who wishes to steal these from us, and why?"

"Brilliant," said Ironfang sardonically, "next you'll be telling me della Trova is dead."

Orsina, wisely, said nothing.

"Well the answer to the first one is obvious," Markus said sullenly. "It has to be Caecillion and his black network."

Ironfang wished he'd thought to pour himself a drink before this meeting. "Which is," he said, "of course, why we're working to dismantle them."

Markus puffed up a bit like an under-feathered peacock and, ah, how delightful.

"Obviously." Orsina's voice dripped with disdain. "However, it wasn't the man himself, and it was not his sister, which leaves precious few folks capable of sneaking in and out of the family villa, cracking open the laboratory, and pilfering our vault."

Something in the way she said it snagged in Ironfang's mind like a coat on a bare tree limb.

"You think you know whom?" he asked.

Orsina's smile was not warm, it was triumphant. "It has to be the Mitris; he's been Caecillion's bloodrune investigator for years. And although he's a mage-scientist, *she's* a grey mage, and the black network presumably has plenty of muscle."

"Talis Mitri?" Markus scoffed. "Do you really think he's got the stones to steal from the Imperator himself?"

"If it wasn't him," Orsina said, "then whoever it was will still be heading to his laboratory with their prize."

An excellent point, not that Ironfang would be stroking her ego about it. "A laboratory which is... where?" he asked instead.

"Why, father." Orsina's smile was all canine teeth. "A little mountain town I burned a decade and a half ago."

Ironfang began to laugh and, belatedly, so did the Sightless One. *Circles in circles,* as the old Silverwood Tacticsmaster used to say.

"I'm certain Drogari would so love to see his old homestead," Ironfang said, wiping amused wetness from his eyes. "You may redeem yourself yet for your embarrassing performance at Heit Reiði and recall a place where you actually did your duty."

This time it was only Markus who laughed.

"You may go, Orsina," Ironfang cut in. "Take Drogari with you. I will send Lord Huginn to you after I am finished here."

Despite the armor, she curtseyed rigidly—"Imperator, sir."—and took her leave.

Ironfang turned to Markus then, his puffed-up, arrogant boy who was about as useful to him as the average straight razor. If only sons were so easily fixed or replaced when they grew dull.

He waited for Drogari's auric presence to recede in the hallway before continuing.

"With Silverwood deserted," Ironfang said, "I have a new task for you, Markus."

Markus stood up visibly straighter. "I shall do my utmost, father."

Ironfang knew he would, and that was always the problem, when one's utmost was mediocre.

"Though, first," Ironfang said. "What of Silverwood?"

"The whole place is deserted. Evacuated as plague protocol dictates." Markus' face contorted like he'd just eaten a lemon. "I hate to admit it, but it was very clever on Caecillion's part. The whole population's been scattered to the four winds. The Secundus boy is, of course, on his way back home to Ascalon, and the Traust child is likely wherever my dear younger sister has gotten off to."

"I'm not worried about locating your sister," Ironfang said. "She'll turn up wherever Caecillion and Valerius do."

"If I'm not finding Faustine or Caecillion," Markus began, his brow furrowing, "what am I doing?"

"I have need of your arcane training," Ironfang said. "You and I shall be investigating a certain hunting lodge in the northern forests."

Markus just looked expectant, and Ironfang sighed. What he wouldn't give to have Vittoro Caecillion back.

"The old Einnaska retreat," Ironfang clarified.

"Oh!" Markus' eyes widened as things practically snapped into place. "Wait, is anything still even there?"

"That," said Ironfang, "is what we shall be finding out. You recall that the late Hägen Einnaska was a white mage, yes?"

"Borderline cleric, really," Markus said dismissively. "He was nearly as insufferable as Blightsen. Why do you ask?"

"You are to accompany me to the Einnaska family retreat, where your..." Normally Ironfang would have said 'expertise' here, but he simply couldn't stomach it. "...training shall assist in scouring the place from top to toe for so much as a whisper of necromancy."

"You need *me?*" It came out of Markus as a sort of manic chuff. "I shall study up on my grey magic at once."

"No," said Ironfang exasperatedly, "you will not. It's white magic."

He left unspoken that if it had been grey, Vittoro, or even Vendrick, would have long ago discovered the information Ironfang hoped to find in a dead man's family annals.

The Einnaskas were a very old, very much bloodruned family, and the royal bloodline on top of that. If anyone were to be entrusted with the secrets of the Church of the Triad, it would be them.

"Well..." Markus looked like he wanted to belabor the point, but instinct told him otherwise. "What necromancy are we looking for?"

Ironfang smiled, and there was no warmth in it. "How to make a god."

Markus smiled back, a misshapen mirror.

It had always been the goal, ever since Ironfang had created his first darkbeast. They were stepping stones, a means to an end. And while building the mindless things was all well and good, they lacked that certain something that would transform them from flesh-hungry maws to intelligent beings like Lord Huginn or Lord Muninn or change them further still to something the Sightless One could inhabit.

And oh, the Sightless One certainly thought that was to his benefit.

Markus was rubbing his hands together gleefully. "And you think the old Einnaska ruins have it?"

"I think," said Ironfang, "that if they do not, the only places left to search will be Castle Skjöldr, and the old Church Library itself."

The Library at Mournheim was as much myth as legend. The literal place certainly existed, somewhere up in the mountains to the east of Kaldr. And the Church's clerics had, of course, once stockpiled all their teachings and trained their young acolytes there.

But that it was the holiest place in the Waking World? That all the High Kings and Clerics who had been buried there somehow guarded it still? That had to be superstitious, Kaldiri nonsense.

And if it wasn't, well, there was no harm in investigating the easier target first.

"I've always wanted to see Mournheim," Markus said.

Which was why Ironfang found a unique pleasure in crushing that hope. "From the Einnaska retreat, you will be going to Castle Skjöldr."

Markus' face fell, but Ironfang wasn't yet finished.

"I believe it's high time we called in our favors with Governor Verona," Ironfang said. "You will then, of course, do what you do best."

He looked pointedly at Markus, willing him to catch on.

And he did, eventually.

"Oh!" Markus began to laugh, a horrible, whining thing. "Oh I see. I suppose I am the only beastminder left in the family."

CHAPTER EIGHTEEN

FRELIA HAD LONG SINCE grown accustomed to life on the road. To the aching muscles and tweaked joints of endless marches and sleeping on the ground. It was one of the things she had missed least during her time at Silverwood.

And so when the snows kicked up somewhere around Skorraey and she mentioned stopping over with her da for the inn's famous mulled cider once upon a time, neither of the Volsinii had to be convinced further.

Frelia teased them about how balmy this time of year was in Valerius Territory, but it was mostly for show. She was looking forward to an actual bath, too; Frelia was so dirty her hair itched.

They were, unsurprisingly, the only visitors the inn had seen in months who weren't Imperial Watchers.

After soaking so long her fingers wrinkled, Frelia had just settled in to comb out her black hair in front of an honest-to-the-Goddesses *vanity* mirror when a knock came at the door. She snatched her eyepatch off the tabletop and tugged it into place, crossing the room in the process.

She pushed open her door to reveal a far cleaner version of the Clarissa who had disappeared into the bath after her. She must have trimmed her hair while she'd been bathing. It now resembled a sort of pixie cut, though it was still too severe for her round face.

"Why are you knocking?" Frelia removed herself from the doorframe. "This is your room, too."

Clarissa shrugged, wincing as it pulled at the bruises Frelia knew lay beneath her clothes. "Just wanted to give you the courtesy, in case you were changing clothes or something."

Frelia shrugged and went back to work.

Silence fell as Frelia began to work the knots out of her wet hair, and Clarissa settled onto the end of the bed near the vanity. The shoulders of Frelia's blouse dug in uncomfortably as she moved around the crown of her head, and she wondered whether this was one of the blouses she'd inherited from a mercenary mage sister.

"You said you've been here with your father, before?" Clarissa suddenly said.

"*Ja*, when I was a little one," Frelia said. "He would make a point to stop by the farm holdings and hunting villages on the way to and from Skjöldr for the moot."

She wondered, absently, if the innkeeper would remember him. Surely a Grand Duke showing up would have made enough of a mark in the man's memory to recall something?

Then again, maybe he'd tried to put it from his mind, the same way Frelia kept reminding herself she was supposed to.

"That's... where all your nobility would meet, right?" Clarissa asked, a little unsure. "Like our Senate?"

"*Ja*, every other summer."

It was why Frelia had never understood what the Senate had to argue about all the damned time. Kaldr had managed just fine without living on top of each other.

Silence fell again, this one more pronounced then before. Frelia was of half a mind to ask Clarissa what her problem was—for it had to be something, the woman was never silent like this—but then the comb slipped through her fingers and Frelia cursed, rough and low in Kaldiri.

Clarissa perked up at once. "Do you require assistance?"

"No." Frelia stooped to pick up the comb. "I require clothes that fit."

"Well, I can't help with that," Clarissa said, a touch apologetic, "but I can do your hair, if you like?"

Frelia scowled at her reflection. Her hair was half combed-through, and she didn't relish trying to braid it in this stupid shirt. Though now her eyepatch straps were crisscrossing everything and making a mess of the still-frizzy side, and she was too tired for this.

"Come on," Clarissa wheedled, "it'll be fun!"

Frelia cocked an eyebrow—"Hair is fun, to you?"—but held out the comb just the same.

"Of course!" Clarissa beamed, then took the comb. "Hair is the only part of fashion that's fun, honestly. Everything else has to be a certain way to talk to certain people, but hair..."

She tapped the crown of Frelia's head.

"Hair can *always* change."

Frelia figured that made a certain amount of sense, but—"What do you mean, has to be a certain way to talk to certain people?"

"Oh, you know." Clarissa waved dismissively with the comb. "Morning gowns versus evening ones, radical statements versus stoic ones, parlor clothes versus going-out clothes... it never ends, I swear."

Frelia's brow furrowed as Clarissa began to work through her still-wet hair. She was far gentler than Frelia was, even to herself. "Most of that can be combined."

"Maybe in Kaldr," Clarissa said, with enough deference that it didn't come off like an insult. "In Ascalon, you're lucky if your 'going out' clothes and your evening gowns overlap."

Frelia stared at Clarissa in the mirror, but the mage's focus was entirely on her work. "This is what happens when you don't have to worry about monsters and surviving the winter, isn't it?"

"Probably." Clarissa's lips pursed as she studied the back of Frelia's head. "Do you normally comb your hair with this on?"

She tapped one of the straps of the eyepatch.

"Oh." Frelia made a face. "No, I grabbed that when you knocked."

Clarissa nodded. "I can work around it."

"Don't be ridiculous." Frelia's hands were frozen on the vanity table. "It's in your way."

Clarissa gently set the polished wooden comb down beside Frelia's hands, and moved so that she was looking at Frelia herself, not her reflection in the mirror. "It's okay if you want to leave it," she said, gently. "I can work around it; I promise."

For a long, painful moment, Frelia's practicality warred with her discomfort. It wasn't that she was ashamed of the scar—it just meant she'd survived the thing meant to kill her—but that she hated the looks she got from people about it. Shame was one thing, but Frelia would not stand for pity.

But Clarissa had her own scars, and, well, some part of Frelia figured, maybe she'd understand. So Frelia reached up and tugged her eyepatch off. The sudden rush of air on her face was overwhelmingly cold.

"Thanks," Clarissa said, moving around to Frelia's back again. "I'll be quick."

Silence fell again as Clarissa got to work, and for once, Frelia couldn't stand it.

"Did Vendrick ever tell you how I got this?" Frelia pointed, probably unnecessarily, to her ruined eye.

"No, but I'm sure it's quite the story."

Frelia rolled her eyes—for the ruined one still moved, when it wasn't tamped down behind the eyepatch, even if it couldn't blink. "You don't need to lay it on so thick."

"I'm serious!" Clarissa protested. "It's not often I can get war stories out of my brother, but when I do, they're mad. And you're not nearly so cautious, so—"

"Hey!"

"What?" Clarissa batted her eyelashes, the picture of innocence. "My brother's paranoid; everyone knows it."

Frelia felt the urge to defend Vendrick in his absence. "He has every reason to be."

"Oh, so you are, too," Clarissa surmised. "That explains some things."

Frelia turned to glare at her. "I will put you *back* in prison."

Clarissa's eyes suddenly widened, and Frelia knew at once she'd said the wrong thing.

"You wouldn't," came a terrified whisper.

"You're right, I wouldn't," Frelia said firmly. "Sorry. I shouldn't have said that."

The silence grew tenser as Clarissa continued to work, still more gently than Frelia had any right to expect. The sudden stillness was a chasm opening up between them, and Frelia had no idea how to bridge the gap. She was so, *so* bad at this kind of thing; it was a miracle she had any friends at all.

Where was Vendrick when she needed him?

"I'm trying," Clarissa suddenly burst out, throwing the comb down.

Frelia recoiled. "What?"

"I know I'm a bother, alright?" There were tears streaking down Clarissa's face. "I *know*. I'm just your boyfriend's annoying little sister that you have to be nice to. But I'm really trying not to be difficult, and—"

"Stop it."

Clarissa cut herself off mid-sentence.

"I didn't say any of that," Frelia said carefully, rising to her feet. "I make jokes about shit I shouldn't; it's how I got this far." She tried to breathe evenly, tried not to sound angry, but it was a struggle the longer she stayed in her home territory. "But it's not how everyone does, and that's on me. So again, I'm sorry. And I will kill another garmr before I let the Unseen put you in prison again. Alright?"

Clarissa burst into genuine tears, leaving Frelia at a grimacing loss. She reached out after a moment, awkwardly, and patted Clarissa's shoulder a few times as though it were a homemade black powder explosive.

What would Edmund or Thera or, hell, Cillian, have said here? They were all so much better than her at this shit.

Clarissa suddenly latched onto her in the fiercest hug Frelia had maybe ever received, and Frelia let out a startled "Oof!"

"You promise?" Clarissa's voice was an urgent whisper.

Frelia did her best to squeeze back, tentatively patting Clarissa's back. "On the graves of my parents and brother, *ja.*"

"Saints, there's no need to be melodramatic," Clarissa mumbled without letting go. "No wonder you and Vendrick get on."

"Alright, alright." Frelia pushed Clarissa back to arm's length as gently as she could. "First of all, you be nice to your brother; he's been beside himself since he discovered your imposter."

Clarissa suddenly looked very small. "Really?"

"*Ja,* I had to stop him from warping into Heit Reiði without telling me the plan." Frelia paused. "Me, the vanguard. Had to tell him, *the Spymaster.*"

Clarissa clapped a stunned hand to her mouth.

"Second of all," Frelia said, "if you were a bother, I would just tell you. I am not subtle."

Clarissa laughed and hiccupped at the same time.

"So stop putting words in my mouth..." Frelia reached out and mussed Clarissa's hair. It was the most sisterly thing she could think to do. "...and let's get something to eat, *ja?*"

"Oh, but your hair's not finished!"

Frelia glanced back at her reflection in the mirror. Her inky black hair was combed stick-straight, and all she needed to do now was get it out of her eyes. "Braids take thirty seconds."

"But you have so much hair!" Clarissa protested. "I could do a whole crown!"

"You get one braid." At Clarissa's crestfallen expression, Frelia added, "Fine, maybe two. Just don't make me look too Volsinii."

"Oh, pish." Clarissa scrubbed her eyes clean, and got back to work.

***

That night, Frelia didn't sleep well.

She hadn't slept well any night since Heit Reiði, though. She would lay her head down, exhausted, and pray that tonight, *tonight,* maybe she'd be too tired to dream.

Somehow, she never was.

The morning of Hana Valerius' funeral was bitterly cold and brightly overcast like a slap in the face. Grand Duke Einar stood with his shoulders back and head high, while his children were over with the Grimsdalr kids while the mourners gathered. Diarmuid kept reminding Frelia and the twins to stand up straight and not cry (much, since all of them were barely old enough to swing a sword), and Kjeld was having his younger siblings guess which hand he held a stone in, and then bopping them in the forehead when they guessed wrong.

"Nearly time," said Margravine Herja Grimsdalr.

Einar had known Herja nearly as long as he'd known Hana—all of them, war veterans, Silverwood grads, and nobles' children. Herja's children had inherited her fiery red hair—and Cillian, by the way things were shaping up, her general demeanor—but even Herja was solemn, today.

"Jari has offered to light the pyre, if you like," Herja added. "Since we all know you about failed archery."

She was trying to joke with him, to yank him out of the numbness that had settled into his bones like the weight of a Kaldiri winter. Einar couldn't smile, not for this, but he appreciated it none the less.

"I will handle it," he said.

"What, with a flaming lance?" Herja shrugged. "Your—"

She cut herself off abruptly.

"You were going to say, 'your funeral,'" Einar said, "weren't you?"

Herja offered a dazzling, slightly apologetic smile, and this time Einar managed a weak laugh. "Hana is glaring at you from the Sapphire Fields."

"Good," said Herja, "she'll know I'm still hilarious."

Saints, Einar really was staring down an eternity without his wife. He felt groundless, weightless without her. Hana had been a lot of things—talented cavalrywoman, witch's daughter, doting mother—but most of all, she had been Einar's best friend.

Damn this fever, and damn that it hadn't taken him, too.

He knew that was the grief speaking. That tomorrow when her ashes washed ashore, he and his children would lay her remains to rest in a barrow, and then Einar would be Grand Duke Valerius again, tending to his people and trying to remember what it felt like to be warm.

At least Herja, Jari, and their brood were staying for a while. That would help brighten up the dark corners of Valerius Lodge, and maybe keep the ghosts at bay while Einar struggled to keep himself upright.

A shriek of laughter pierced the air. Both Herja and Einar glanced over at their children, only to find Diarmuid tickling his little sister while Thera kicked Kjeld in the shin. Tears were streaked across Frelia's face, broken up by the laughter she clearly didn't want to make as she struck her brother's chest with tiny fists.

"That's a Valerius if I've ever seen one," Herja said. "'I laughed, and I'm angry about it.'"

Einar punched her shoulder, the blow softened by her heavy overfurs.

They were quiet for a moment, watching as Hana's father and her sister finished laying her out on the pyre-boat, the latter fussing as she arranged Hana's hair and laid her lance beside her.

Einar glanced to Frelia, his little girl with her father's hair and mother's eyes. Her face was pinched in annoyance, her arms folded as she refused to play Kjeld's game any longer despite her own brother's wheedling.

"Herja," Einar said quietly, just as the silence was growing painful, "can you promise me something?"

"Like you have to ask." She rolled her eyes.

Einar took that as the go-ahead. "Promise me that you'll keep an eye on Frelia."

There was a pause.

"You mean if something happens to you," Herja said, "ja?"

"No, I mean in general," Einar said. "She has no sisters, no female cousins, and now, no mother. She has Brenn, but her aunt doesn't understand childbirth like you do."

A dreadful understanding filtered into Herja's green eyes, though she tried to play it off. "Is the great and terrible Warden of Kaldr afraid of explaining his daughter's monthly courses to her?"

Einar shot her a withering look. "She's going to see things, Herja," he reminded her. "Things I can't make any less terrifying."

For the bloodrune cared not for the age of its bearer. Its memories were indiscriminate, inscrutable—sometimes benign moments of families or peaceful afternoons, sometimes heart-pounding moments of battle and fury.

And sometimes, they were things you'd wish you'd never seen at all.

"For what it's worth," Herja said, *"Jari has never seen his mother giving birth, or something."*

Einar made an exasperated noise. *"Dammit Herja, would you* just—*"*

"Yes, Einar, you insufferable dorchya," she interrupted. *"I will watch over the girl. Saints know I always have."*

"Daaaaa!" came a tiny voice from across the field.

The Grand Duke and the Margravine glanced over to find a tiny, black-haired streak shooting up the hillside. Frelia slammed into her father's leg a moment later, and hid behind Einar's bulk while Diarmuid chased her up the hill.

"What is the meaning of this?" Einar thundered.

"Frelia's just oversensitive," Diarmuid protested.

"Am not!" shouted the burr attached to Einar's pant leg.

"Hush, both of you," Einar said. *"Now is not the time."*

"Diarmuid," said Herja reproachfully, *"if your sister says no, she means no."*

Diarmuid's lower lip wobbled, and Einar was painfully reminded of the fact that the boy wasn't much older than his sister. Diarmuid was also losing his mother too young.

"I just... wanted to help," the boy said.

"You can help by getting everyone to the shore," Einar said. *"It's time."*

He carefully unstuck Frelia's little fists from his leg, fighting her the whole time.

"Frelia, you don't want Cillian and Thera to beat you there," Herja said, *"do you?"*

Frelia kicked at a dirt clump. *"I don't care."*

Einar sighed. One day, her stubbornness would stare down Volsinii Knights and steer Valerius Territory true. But right now, parenting it was a Goddesses-damned nightmare.

Herja dropped to a crouch, but Einar missed what she said as a heavy hand clapped to his shoulder.

"Grand Duke Einar," rumbled the voice of the king, "I see we've arrived just in time."

"No time like the—"

Einar cut himself off, mid-sentence, for half of King Njal's face was caved in. Blood poured down his blond beard, collected in his collar, stained the front of his elegant mourning tunic.

Einar's eyes widened and he glanced about wildly. Arrows pierced Herja's back, all the way up her spine, and Diarmuid—sweet, tiny Diarmuid—was trying to hold in his intestines as they spilled over his hands.

Only Frelia remained unwounded, and she didn't seem to notice the death all around her. Einar tried to open his mouth, to tell her to run, but found he could not speak. His arms were heavy, his legs rooted to the ground.

Out across the lake, a specter rose. It was black as midnight, its arms too long and jaw too large as it opened its mouth to speak:

"Hverfa aptr."

Return.

Frelia sat up sharply, chest heaving in great, gasping breaths as she tried to right the world around her. She scrabbled for her hunting knife, slicing open her thumb as she drew it from beneath the pillow. But the pain was grounding, and as she wrapped her fingers around the knife's hilt, Frelia slowly came back to herself.

These weren't her memories. They were her da's, shared through the bloodrune. But Frelia had also been at her mother's funeral, and there had been no garmr there to ruin the day. So she was half stuck in memories that weren't hers, and half stuck in nightmares.

Of course she was. She was sleeping in the same woods, hills, and snowbanks that had haunted her for years.

She sat up, glaring at the smoldering embers of the fireplace as if that would make her warmer, and then glanced around. Clarissa snored softly on the other bed while, despite both Frelia and Clarissa's badgering, Vendrick was curled up on a spare cot the innkeeper had dragged in.

For a moment, Frelia just watched the rise and fall of his chest in the banked firelight. He was unnaturally still, in his sleep. Like he'd been awoken violently one too many times by garmr. (Although, given that he'd been on the Volsinii side, it was probably more likely just his knights.)

Both of the Caecillions were still asleep, though. Good. They hadn't noticed her night terrors. She didn't need them asking after what her bloodrune was shoving at her, right now. Not when she felt tense as a drawn bowstring the closer they drew to Kjell.

With her bleeding thumb wrapped in the hem of her shirt, Frelia fell back into the stiff inn sheets, and tried to close her eye.

Sleep did not return.

CHAPTER NINETEEN

FAUSTINE QUICKLY DISCOVERED THAT one of the worst things about extended travel by foot was that there was nowhere to go when you couldn't sleep.

So she stared up at the stars for the millionth time that night, finding the Great Archer and Saint Nova and telling herself their stories. (Or at least what she remembered of them, anyway.)

If she were at school, she could get up, perhaps do some light reading or wander down to the first-floor students' kitchen to make tea. Perhaps she would find an insomniac friend or two there, doing the same thing, and they could chat or play a round of Crowns versus Crooks.

But here in the wilderness, there was nowhere safe to go. No nook to curl up in, no tea to be made, and she didn't want to dump her problems in Christel or the professor's laps when they already had enough of their own.

And so Faustine found herself falling into the habit of talking to Thera, instead.

She would sit beside the darkbeast's forepaw and just... talk. About everything, about nothing. Sometimes Thera would rumble something back, but it was usually short and broken. Not so much a conversation and simply confirmation that the woman buried in the monster's heart was listening.

And so that night, Faustine curled around her knees as she sat hunched over beside the darkbeast—a girl and her demonic dog. "I wonder how the rest of the Violet Owls are doing," Faustine said.

She always felt like she was babbling, but Thera never seemed to mind.

"I hope Valente's okay—he has the Domitia Bloodrune."

"*Hunt... ter,*" Thera rumbled.

"Not Valente," Faustine said with a little laugh. "I know that's what his family's supposed to be and all, but he threw up twice trying to help the professor with Lord Muninn."

Thera's rumbling laugh was like the wind in the nearby trees.

"And I'm worried about Owen, too," Faustine added. "His family is from the far north, so Saints only know what he'll find on his way home. I think Johanna from the Iron Cranes and Wyvernmaster Gellir were going that way, too, but..."

Faustine stared at the tree line for a moment, as though it would make speaking any easier.

"I don't trust the Unseen," she whispered.

Beside her, the darkbeast shuddered.

"I'm sorry." Faustine reached out to pat Thera's scarred foreleg. "I know you don't, either."

"*War... time,*" Thera rumbled.

Faustine's brow furrowed. "Sorry?"

"*War... time,*" Thera said again. "*Makes... worry.*"

Faustine flinched. "That's what I've been wondering. Is... is this what war feels like?"

Thera nodded her great, shaggy head, and then laid it between her paws like a dog at rest.

"I wish you could tell me about it." Faustine shut her eyes, sighing. "Professor Blightsen likes pretending he doesn't know what the Tyrant's War was like."

She glanced over to their little camp, to where the professor was sleeping on a bedroll near the dying campfire. His back was turned to her, and so Faustine could only just make out the outline of the school medic in the darkness.

"*Ed... mund...*" Thera seemed to be looking for the words she needed. "*Too nice.*"

Faustine blinked. "What?"

"*Too... nice,*" Thera insisted. "*Won't... do... hard... thing.*"

Faustine started to ask what she meant, but movement from over by the fire caught her attention.

Her hand dove for her knife and her eyes raked the darkness. Professor Blightsen had cast some wards, but that didn't mean something—or more likely, some*one*—particularly enterprising couldn't have gotten past them.

Then the movement resolved into a familiar set of broad shoulders and golden hair, and Faustine relaxed her grip on the knife.

Her relief lasted only until Christel startled towards Faustine's bedroll.

They patted the blankets in the darkness, hissing, "*Faustine?*"

Oh.

Oh *no*.

"I'm here," she called, as loudly as she dared. She had no desire to wake up the professor, but also none to terrify Christel, either.

They probably dreamt of Siegmund, too.

Christel started at the sound, their hand snatching for the blade beside their bedroll. Faustine waved from her spot beside Thera's paw, an apology already on her lips.

Their eyes met, and then Christel's shoulders dropped with relief. They extracted themselves from the bedroll, pulled on their heavy boots, and padded over to the girl and her demon dog.

"I'm sorry," Faustine said softly as Christel drew closer. "I didn't mean to startle you."

Christel waved that away. "What are you doing?"

"Talking to Thera," Faustine said as though it were a perfectly normal thing to do.

Christel glanced to the darkbeast, and then a small smile tried to break through their melancholy. "Okay, let me try again. Why are you sitting here talking to Thera?"

Faustine glanced down to the forest floor. "I couldn't sleep."

Christel made a face—"Me neither."—and then plopped down, cross-legged, across from Faustine and Thera.

There had to be some kind of tactful way to bring it up. Some kind of 'sorry for your loss' that didn't feel so woefully inadequate, and that said Faustine understood, and didn't feel like a bump in the rug they were politely stepping around.

Then Christel said, "I keep seeing that fucking darkbeast, in my dreams." They paused. "No offense, Thera."

Thera grunted in acknowledgement while Faustine said, so quietly as to be nearly lost beneath the darkbeast's great voice, "Me, too."

Whenever she shut her eyes, Faustine could still feel the bone-deep *crunch* of the darkbeast's jaws around Siegmund's ribs. See the splatter of gore that had remained afterwards like the afterimage had been seared into her eyelids.

She felt like crying, but wasn't sure she still had tears left for it.

"It was supposed to get easier, when I went to Silverwood," Christel muttered.

Faustine broke eye contact with her boots to look at them. "What was?"

Christel stabbed at something in the dirt with their index finger. "Grief."

A fat tear rolled silently down Faustine's face, and look at that, she still had some left after all.

"No."

It wasn't Faustine who spoke, but Thera.

"Grief never... get... easier. We... grow around."

Christel just looked at the darkbeast for a long moment.

"Yeah," they finally said. "I bet you would know. Does your family bloodrune make you see shit, too?"

"All... do," Thera confirmed. *"Which... yours?"*

"Traust," Christel said.

Thera's large head was suddenly looming between them. *"Who is... parent...?"*

Christel's smile was rueful, sad. "Ulfhild."

Thera's eyes widened, until Faustine could only just see the bright green that outlined her brown irises.

"Did you know her?" Christel asked at Thera's silence. "Professor Valerius said she would have been her sister-in-law."

Thera's head thumped against the ground again, and suddenly, even the monster seemed tired. *"Friend."*

"I'm sorry." Christel reached out to scratch behind Thera's mangled ear. "I miss her, too."

Faustine wanted to say that she understood that pain, at least. That she missed the woman in her memory who had soft eyes and a spice cookie recipe that scented the whole first floor of the Villa della Luciana.

But just like before, there were no words for it in her throat.

"Wyvern... knight," Thera said, and the moment was gone. *"Like me."*

"You were a wyvern knight?" Faustine suddenly felt ashamed that she'd never thought to ask Thera what she'd been before this.

"Family... tradition," Thera said.

"There's so much I wish I knew," Christel said quietly. "Professor Valerius said it's my clan's job to remember, but I never even knew."

"Time... now?" Thera offered.

"You can barely talk." Christel hunched over their knees, now, broad frame folding into something deftly small. "And Professor Valerius told me legends I'd never heard before, but they felt... I don't know, right somehow?"

Thera's breath puffed out, and rustled their hair. *"Bloodrune... recall."*

"Yeah." Christel was quiet for a long moment, and then suddenly burst out, "Siegmund was a wyvern knight. Did we tell you that?"

It fell like a weight between the three of them, and no, Faustine would not be silent again. She at least had words for this.

"I'm sorry." Faustine squeezed her eyes shut tight. "I should never have asked him to—"

"Don't be stupid," Christel interrupted thickly. "He was the best wyvern knight we had."

But he'd also been Christel's best friend, and what was she supposed to say about that?

"Besides," Christel continued, "he wasn't going to sit back and *not* help. That's not how Siegmund was."

The loping, unsteady gait of that darkbeast still echoed in Faustine's mind. "I don't understand why we use darkbeasts in war," she said with a shudder. "They're absolutely vile—err, sorry Thera. I don't mean you."

Thera's hoarse laugh echoed softly in the quiet woods.

"That's why," Christel said flatly. "I mean, look at her."

"Should have... seen me... before." The darkbeast thumped her tail against the ground.

Christel snorted, but it didn't reach their eyes. "She's huge, and she's terrifying even when she's just sitting there. I have to remember there's a person in there so that I don't run screaming, you know?"

"Yeah," Faustine said quietly. "I know."

Even though Thera was about the sweetest-natured monstrosity Faustine had ever met. Her own family included.

"So I think it makes perfect sense why the Volsinii would use darkbeasts in combat." Christel thumbed at some dirt on their tunic. "It's just shitty. And honestly, it makes me twice as scared of Professor Valerius."

Thera burst into her roughest laughter yet.

"I want to learn the blink rune," Faustine suddenly said. "I'm not good at magic but that I would struggle through."

"Shit," said Christel, "me, too."

Thera's laughter abruptly gave way to a keening whine, and Faustine and Christel turned to her, alarmed.

"*Our rune...*" Thera managed after a moment.

"You know it?" Faustine didn't dare hope.

"*Family... secret.*"

Christel's brow furrowed. "Was Professor Vee a Grimsdalr somehow?"

"*Basically... sister,*" Thera said. "*Almost... married... twin.*"

Faustine suddenly thought of the winter ball, and of watching Headmaster Caecillion leading Professor Valerius through a waltz, and of seeing the both of them soften, just a little. How did Cillian Grimsdalr fit into that, she wondered?

A moment later she remembered what she'd done to Christel just before the winter ball, and suddenly her meager dinner threatened to come right back up her throat.

"I don't think the headmaster would have liked that much," Faustine managed after a moment.

"*After... that.*" Thera's lips twisted, as though the darkbeast were trying to smile. "*War... time.*"

And just like that, everything circled back around to war.

Circles in circles, as her father said, and Faustine mentally wrinkled her nose at him.

Everything's a cycle, Professor Valerius had said, and Faustine liked that one better. It felt less like some swooping bird of prey was trying to breathe down her neck, and more like something she could do anything about.

CHAPTER TWENTY

IT WAS SAID THAT before he'd been a Saint and a King, Randolf Einnaska had been a sea raider. Ironfang wondered why that meant he'd decided to build a retreat in the middle of the Saints-damned woods. But here they were.

Sea raiders, of course, had been frighteningly common in that era of history. Before Kaldr was Kaldr, and before the Volsinii Imperium had been much more than a handful of conglomerate city-states. They were brutal men—and women—who farmed in the summers and stole from distant kinsfolk in the winters.

It was hardly an auspicious start for a man who would become a saint, but so it went. Hana Valerius had been a warlord before she'd Ascended, after all, and Klaus Konstantin had been a mere village doctor.

Like a great many things Randolf Einnaska had founded, the Einnaska summer home, such as it was, was a blunt, squat thing in the hilly woodlands near the border of their territory. A striking lodge of wood and stone, it had clearly been made to weather blizzards and darkbeasts alike, and its vantage point atop a hill ensured an eye kept on all things.

Ironfang could appreciate that. The Villa della Luciana had been built high on a cliffside for the same reason.

They were coming around to the lodge, now, nearly up the massive hillside path leading to it. Weeds had grown between old flagstones, and Ironfang hoped to Hypogia that this wasn't a dead end waste of time.

Neither he nor the Sightless One had much patience left, after travelling with Markus all this way. And Ironfang, even less so after being reminded up and down of his 'Sacred Tasks' the whole trip into the woods. The Sightless One was more repetitive than an old drunk, and it irked him.

What Ironfang wouldn't give for a bit of peace and quiet!

"I'm surprised this is still standing," Markus said, as though he hadn't been chattering Ironfang and their escort's ears off all afternoon. "Though I suppose it's not much use as a defensive point in a war."

"Ah, but that's where you're wrong," Ironfang said, as though Markus being *correct* weren't stranger. "There is a reason we took Traust Territory first."

Markus' brow furrowed, even as his horse jostled him in an effort to step over something deep and pitted in the ground. "Is it not simply the closest point to Ascalon?"

"It is," Ironfang conceded. "However, the Traust family did not maintain nearly the same defenses as the Konstantins did. Slaughtering them in their stronghold was pitifully easy."

They tied up the horses in a nearby copse of trees, left their escort guard to keep an eye on them and make camp, and then father and son strode up the path to history together.

Ivy and mistletoe had long since overtaken the front door, long, green strands curling over dark, carved wood.

"Hold please," said Markus, pulling out his spellbook. "I can take care of these little nuisances."

Ironfang gestured for him to proceed, and the Sightless One was muttering in the back of his mind about *Elias' little sycophant.* Annoyed as the intrusion made him, Ironfang still fought the urge to agree.

Markus drew a rune in the air before him with quick, decisive strokes, his rose-gold magic nascent like ashes in the mountain air. He completed the rune, and then plant life began to rake itself away from the door as though by giant claws. It broke and twisted, falling away to reveal a heavy door carved with a starburst-like rune Ironfang would have recognized anywhere.

"The Einnaska Bloodrune," he said. "How quaint."

"The Kaldiri never were a subtle people," Markus agreed, sheathing his spellbook again. "After you, Father."

Plant life had invaded the foyer, as well, through cracks in window frames and lintels. It gave the austere interior a sort of rundown atmosphere, as though the hunting lodge had died alongside its host family and been decaying ever since. The light streaming in through cracks and windows dappled the air with dust motes and shadow.

"Search the upstairs," Ironfang said. "I shall take the main floor."

Markus dutifully trotted off, and Ironfang was left alone for the first time in weeks. The silence was glorious, even as he began to pick his way through overgrowth and discarded furniture. Terribly blue, all the décor was. Positively gauche.

To the immediate left was a kitchen, its cast irons rusted and woodpile empty. There were ashes in the oven, though, and Ironfang's metaphorical ears perked up.

Someone had been here. Recently, too, if the greying ash was anything to go by.

Beyond the kitchen was an unremarkable dining room, and beyond *that,* an equally unremarkable parlor.

Except.

Some of the furs and blankets were moth-eaten, but others looked perfectly serviceable. Most of those, however, had been bundled into what Ironfang could only think of as a nest. The bundle of furs and blankets were still laid out before yet another fireplace full of ashes.

"Curious," he murmured.

He nudged the pile with the toe of his boot, and when nothing immediately shouted or jumped out at him, Ironfang fell to a crouch. A quick search told him nothing useful had been left behind, but something about evidence of human activity in a place so clearly abandoned set his war instincts buzzing. It could have been a local hunter seeking shelter from the weather, but with the obvious door closed and no broken windows to speak of, Ironfang doubted it.

He breathed in softly and opened his divine senses.

The room instantly grew cold—*too* cold, even for winter in Kaldr—and a faint, bluish aura hovered over the blanket nest, as though it were radiating chill.

Well, well, came a familiar voice in the back of Ironfang's mind, *what have we here?*

"Excellent question, my Lord," Ironfang said, rising to his feet.

He began to case the room more methodically, his divine senses marking where the unnatural chill floated alongside objects as if to devour them whole. This drawer had been pulled open by that abnormal cold, that fire poker moved and set back upon its holder.

If I didn't know better, the Sightless One mused in the back of Ironfang's mind, *I would suspect death had walked here.*

Ironfang paused in the middle of pulling an urn off the mantle.

You mean your sister, my Lord? He asked the Sightless One.

Nothing so powerful. Ironfang could almost picture the Old One waving some ghastly appendage to dismiss the notion.

Then what? Ironfang asked, resuming his business with the urn.

The Sightless One was quiet for a moment. Ironfang always figured it enjoyed lording its ancient knowledge over its mortal host.

One of her children, I'd imagine, it said after a moment. *I do not understand her fascination with you pitiful creatures.*

The trail seemed too human to have been made by a garmr, but Ironfang knew better than to contradict the Old One in his head. He instead tilted the urn to examine its contents. Empty, but with a fine film of something that could have once, perhaps, been cremains.

He set the urn back atop the mantle and surveyed the crisscrossing bluish dust flitting about the room. There was no way, but still, he had to ask. *You believe a garmr did this, my Lord?*

Oh, no. Its laughter was a fetid rustle, in the back of Ironfang's mind. *Her* other *children.*

For a moment, Ironfang squinted at the wall, utterly perplexed, as though the Old One could see him. There was disdain in its voice, murder. *Lady Midnight's children are the garmur, are they not?*

I mean the human ones. The Sightless One sounded annoyed, now. Well, Ironfang supposed that made two of them. *The walking corpses—the smart ones.*

It couldn't mean draugur; their intelligence spanned a lurching gamut. But that left only one other option, and one Ironfang scarcely dared believe existed. It would be one of the few things on par with a Hypogean.

"A lich?" he asked.

Yes! The Sightless One sounded pleased with itself. *That's the mortal word.*

There hadn't been a known lich since the time of the first Imperatrix Nigella, and even *that* had faded into legend by this point. To become a lich was to sacrifice what made you human and put you in a sort of stasis between life and death. But it carried with it none of the benefits of an Ascension—a lich was still subject to his phylactery, after all. If it were destroyed, a lich could die like anyone else.

But the path to lichdom also required deep knowledge of white magic, and the skill to cast the most complicated of its runes. The Church of the Triad had long since forbidden the practice, and for once, Ironfang couldn't blame them. Liches were powerful beings the church would have little means of control over. An immortal mage would have little to fear from Goddesses determining his fate after death, after all.

An immortal warrior, too, for that matter.

But still. A *living* (such as it was) lich, here in the Einnaskas' old homestead? Something stank of treachery, and it gnawed at Ironfang's psyche.

A lich was an unknown. Possibly an asset, possibly an enemy. Too dangerous to be left alone on the playing field, in any capacity.

I quite agree, the Sightless One whispered from his hovel in Hypogia. *I could very much use a creature of walking death.*

The way the Old One said it made warmth creep into Ironfang's spine. It was *amused* at the breaking of its sisters' world order, and why shouldn't it be? They would be ash, by the time Ironfang's plans were through.

Where did someone with the required skills even find the information with which to become a lich in our lifetime? Ironfang half-wondered, half-asked the Sightless One.

It struck him between the eyes a moment later, as though the Sightless One had flicked a slug at his forehead.

"The Library at Mournheim," Ironfang said, aloud.

It would have to be. Nowhere else would have the stockpile of information, unless some academic simply pieced together enough bits of lore to make an educated guess. It would be a dangerous endeavor more likely to end him up in a hospital bed or a grave, but possibly viable for someone desperate enough.

If he hadn't seen the man die, Ironfang might have wondered if the lich were Vittoro Caecillion himself. The man had crafted the Ascension ritual based on the one to become a lich, and although he was a grey mage by trade, he had been magically quite gifted. Lichdom had largely fallen out of favor due to the Church of the Triad, and Vittoro had cared as little about that as Ironfang did.

"Father," came Markus' voice from the dining room, "I think I've found something."

Ironfang mentally bookmarked the Library at Mournheim as the next order of business, and then turned to face his son.

There was dust streaked across his sallow face, and his eyepatch was slightly askew, but Markus was clutching a slim, leatherbound tome with a manic sort of glee.

"Get into a fight with a curtain?" Ironfang asked drolly.

"Erm, no," Markus said. "But I found *this* under a floorboard beneath the master bed."

The thin, blue tendrils that the Sightless One had likened to death swirled around the book, weaving in and out of the pages in an ethereal aurora.

"It positively *reeks* of necromancy." Markus was grinning now. "And, unfortunately, is also written in Kaldiri."

Ironfang's eyebrow rose with scholarly disdain. "Do you not have a spell for that?"

He left unspoken that Vittoro and Vendrick certainly did.

"No," said Markus, "I—"

He cut himself off as Ironfang sighed deeply and began to tug off his right-hand glove.

My Lord, he called out to the Sightless One, *could you perhaps assist?*

Silence descended for so long a moment, Ironfang almost wondered if the Old One had fallen asleep.

And then something icy slithered down Ironfang's spine, and his bare hand rose of its own accord. It twisted in unfamiliar, looping sigils, and then with a single one of Ironfang's thick fingers, the Sightless One reached out to touch Markus' forehead.

The Watcher gasped and clutched at his stomach as though someone had landed a blow there. Through his divine senses, Ironfang watched as a sick, unnatural chill bled through Markus' brain, and into the eye beneath the patch.

"There," said Ironfang, taking his hand back and relieved to find it moved when prompted. "Try now."

With a violent, visible shiver, Markus slowly opened the leatherbound book. He squinted at it, confusion clear in his face. Then he seemed to realize why his eye ached, for he reached up with one hand to pull aside his eyepatch.

The Grimsdalr Bloodrune shone a livid red in his scarred cornea.

"Woe be upon ye," Markus read, slowly at first, and then picking up speed, *"for he who holds this tome holds the terrible truth of Saint Randolf."*

Markus laughed, incredulous, and Ironfang felt a rare stab of almost fondness for his son. If only Markus had Orsina's intuition, or Gaius' talent, Ironfang may not have needed to hold his hand so much.

"Read on," Ironfang said, and he set about following the ghostly imprints the lich had made.

"What is done cannot be undone," Markus began, his voice falling into a rhythm not unlike a bard settling in for a long tale, *"what is made cannot be unmade."*

That sounded very nearly like a Triad teaching. Curious.

"What is done may only be answered for, and what is made can only be destroyed."

What followed was a lot of gibberish that didn't rightly translate. Motifs of wolves and ravens, verses about monsters slumbering in the depths below and sky above, and a price. Always a price.

"What specific word is used?" suddenly slipped from Ironfang's mouth in a rasping, hollow voice that was not his.

Markus startled, glanced around the room as though expecting another person, and then looked down to the book again. "Price," he said again.

"The Kaldiri, boy," not-Ironfang's voice snarled.

Markus didn't look up from the tome. He never could meet the Sightless One's eye.

"Were-gild," Markus said a moment later. "Is that not that barbaric old dueling custom where the ancient Kaldiri paid for crimes committed in either blood or gold?"

"No," said the Sightless One through Ironfang's mouth. *"It's far older than that."*

Markus' brow furrowed. "My Lord?"

"It is a sacrifice of blood paid for blood." Ironfang's smile was too wide for the face it stretched. *"It is the price of a man's life and what it can purchase from what lies beyond.*

Such as, thought Ironfang as an idea began to take shape somewhere between his and the Sightless One's cognizance, *a monster.*

CHAPTER TWENTY-ONE

FAUSTINE HAD KNOWN THAT the northern territories were cold, in a general sense. She'd known that the people there wore furs, and used dogsleds to get around, and most of the famous northern recipes were heavy stews or something pickled.

But it was another thing to *experience* it. Since when could air hurt your face?

"Your scarf's slipping, Faustine," Christel said.

Faustine's hands immediately went to her face, where, sure enough, her woolen scarf was slipping down into the collar of her coat.

"Thanks," she said, tugging it back up over her nose again.

"How much further, Professor?" Christel asked, somehow managing not to sound like a whining child. Faustine felt like she should be taking notes.

"Not much more now," Professor Blightsen said. "It should be just over that ridge."

Darkbeast-Thera huffed, her breath coming in thick clouds. "*I... check?*"

The mental image of the darkbeasts swarming over the rise at Silverwood was burned into the back of Faustine's eyelids. "I don't think sending you alone is a good idea."

"Yeah, you might want to hide, honestly," said Christel. "At least until we've found the headmaster's friends."

Darkbeast-Thera bristled. "*No... hide.*"

"You're a giant monster, Thera," Professor Blightsen said gently. "I think the kids just don't want you to get shot at."

Christel and Faustine both nodded, and Darkbeast-Thera's mouth twisted. On a human, it would probably just look like she was thinking. On a monster, it looked ghastly.

"*Fine,*" she rumbled after a moment. "*I wait... in woods.*"

"Thanks, Thera," Professor Blightsen said. "We'll be back for you as soon as we can."

"*Better... be.*"

Thera scuttled off into the forest, and the rest of them waited for her to disappear from sight before heading down the last hill into town.

Kjell was a small, picturesque town made of gabled roofs, heavy wooden crossbeams, and rows of skinny trees that were currently midwinter bare. People scuttled back and forth about their business with purpose and didn't linger to talk to each other on the corner or in the shops. It struck Faustine as odd—didn't neighbors talk to each other?

"That... isn't right," Professor Blightsen muttered, and it only made Faustine feel worse.

He hurried down the hill, and Faustine and Christel had to run to keep up. They passed a few houses before a woman stuck her head out of an upper floor window. She looked old enough to be Professor Blightsen's mother, and spoke in quick, sharp Kaldiri.

The Professor sounded apologetic when he responded, and the hard lines of the woman's face softened a little. They said a few more things back and forth, and then Professor Blightsen said, in Volsinii Standard, "Come on, you two. She says the Mitri laboratory is clear across town."

He didn't wait for an answer before he started moving again.

"Why is everyone being so standoffish?" Faustine asked as she fell into step behind him. "Is it just that it's cold outside?"

"They're Kaldiri," Christel pointed out.

"Not only that..." Professor Blightsen trailed off, glancing over his shoulder as if expecting to be overheard. "...Apparently Bloodrune Hunters are staying in the woods and at the inn."

Faustine's stomach dropped. "Oh, Saints."

The lines of Orsina's Bloodrune Hunter armor were etched into Faustine's nightmares, and she didn't even have a bloodrune. They were just that horrible. Did they somehow know Christel was coming here? They would have to; there was no such thing as a coincidence, in her family, only carefully orchestrated opportunities.

Oh, Saints, Faustine felt sick.

If Orsina were here, that meant Father had sent her. But how had he even known where Faustine and Christel were going? Faustine hadn't even known where they were going until Professor Blightsen told them.

Another, worse thought occurred to her. Orsina usually did their father's bidding, unless it was Bloodrune Hunter related. Had she tracked them here after Christel's bloodrune?

No, no, no, this was not good. This was so, terribly not good.

"How could they know we were coming?" Christel asked, their blue eyes darting across the road.

"Supposedly," said the professor, "they're saying Mitri's wife owes them for a job, and they're not leaving until they're paid. But Mitri claims they've never worked with a Hunter in their lives."

Faustine's blood went cold. "What would a legitimate scientist need Bloodrune Hunters for?" She knew what Markus had used them for, of

course, but he wasn't exactly up to Alchemical Guild standards. "Can
we trust Sir Mitri?"

Professor Blightsen was quiet for a long moment. "Caecillion does,"
he finally said, "at least well enough. So be on your guard, I suppose, but
I doubt he's building monsters in the basement. It would be too hard to
hide, in Kjell."

They fell into silence as they hurried along the roads and Faustine
studied the small town with renewed interest. It was hard and compact,
built to weather winter storms and whatever else the world might throw
at it.

Just like Professor Valerius, Faustine couldn't help but think.

Faustine had nearly slipped twice on patches of ice by the time they'd
reached the Mitris' laboratory. Christel had nearly wrenched her arm out
of its socket both times in their haste to keep her upright.

The laboratory was a square building, built low to the ground and
out of heavy stone. Faustine knew that the actual laboratory would be
further below, in a basement (or several). Alchemical labs always were.
Supposedly it was better for the reagents, or so Alchemymaster Caelia
had said.

Professor Blightsen led them up to the heavy iron door and knocked.

For a long moment, all was silent as icy wind continued piling up
against them.

Then the door jerked open a little, and someone cautiously stuck
their head out. "I have already informed you I will not negotiate with
terrorists!"

Faustine blinked at the man. He had close-cropped, sandy blond hair,
and his waistcoat was mis-buttoned somewhere along the way to his
throat. His eyes were vividly blue and bloodshot, and if you'd asked
Faustine to costume the 'mad scientist' in an opera, he would look about
like this.

She wasn't sure whether that helped the case for the Not-Headmaster trusting him, or not.

"Oh," said the man. "You're not Bloodrune Hunters."

"Talis Mitri?" Professor Blightsen asked.

The man's eyes narrowed, instantly suspicious. "Who's asking?"

The professor held out a hand. "Edmund Blightsen. I believe you've received a message regarding me and a few Silverwood students?"

Sir Mitri's eyes refocused on them, and Faustine didn't like the gleam that entered his expression when he looked at Christel. Did Sir Mitri know they had a bloodrune? Was Christel safe, here?

She fought the urge to step in front of them.

"Might have," Mitri said. "I'm supposed to ask you, how's the weather been treating you?"

Professor Blightsen smiled, but it was tense and didn't suit him. "Perfectly balmy the whole way here."

Well *that* was a lie if Faustine had ever heard one. It had been bitterly cold the whole trip, and Faustine had finally understood the meaning of the phrase 'driving wind' while shouldering against it. And what did Sir Mitri mean, he was *supposed* to ask? If he was just trying to be polite, there were warmer places to do it.

"How fare the children?" Professor Blightsen asked.

Christel shifted from foot to foot. "Can't this wait until we're inside, Professor?"

Mitri's eyes gleamed again. "Withers just whelped her own litter of pups, actually."

The memory of the Not-Headmaster's voice chimed softly in the back of Faustine's mind. *Do me a favor, Clarissa, and remind me—what's that thing you gave me for my eighth birthday?*

Della Trova hadn't known the right answer, and Lord Caecillion had attacked her for it. Maybe... maybe this was Not-Headmaster

Caecillion's way of making sure people were who they said they were? If so, espionage sounded terribly dull in real life.

"I should like to see them," Professor Blightsen said, and he smiled genuinely, this time.

Sir Mitri finally removed himself from the doorframe. "Come along then, all of you. It's frigid out here."

The door opened into a small foyer lined with coat hooks and shoe racks. They fussed with boots and overcoats and all the while, Faustine couldn't help but look for proof Sir Mitri was trustworthy, one way or the other. Was this a resistance? Or was he just as bad as the Bloodrune Hunters?

They headed through the second door that led into what looked like the parlor in Atticus Hall and despite her misgivings, Faustine felt herself relax a little in the warmth. There were several sets of mismatched chairs clustered around worn-looking wooden tables, plus a comfortable-looking couch across from a roaring fire in a hearth that looked older than Faustine.

There were also *people* everywhere—chatting over mugs of something hot and steaming, lounging in comfortable-looking armchairs with their noses in books, and a few had glanced up at the noise from the foyer and looked startled to find people there. Faustine struggled to picture her family, so closed-off and paranoid, with so many staff working on their secret projects.

"Go about your business," Sir Mitri barked at the people staring without so much as breaking stride.

The other folks shrugged and went back to their conversations or books, and Faustine looked over at Christel. They wore a similarly confused expression, and only shrugged when she caught their eye.

Well, at least she wasn't the only one.

Sir Mitri led them through the parlor and into a side door that, apparently, led to a small kitchen. There was a pot of something bubbling on the stove that smelled strongly of cinnamon and cloves.

"You've caught us at a terrible time," Sir Mitri said. "We haven't had a moment of peace in weeks."

"So we've heard," Professor Blightsen said. "In town they're saying the Bloodrune Hunters are here because you haven't paid them?"

"Nonsense," Sir Mitri said. "They're here because I stole the Unseen's blood archives."

Professor Blightsen blinked at him once, twice, thrice, and Christel looked to Faustine like she had any more ideas than they did.

"What's a blood archive?" Faustine asked.

"A set of phylacteries with bloodrunes in them," Sir Mitri said brusquely. "The Unseen are quite put out about my taking them, last I heard."

"That shouldn't be possible." Professor Blightsen's jaw dropped. "A Bloodrune is..." He was practically stammering. "...is a most sacred relic passed down the Saints' family line!"

"Well, they've managed it," said Sir Mitri flatly.

Professor Blightsen looked like he couldn't figure out what to say, let alone how to shut his slack jaw.

"And quite frankly," Sir Mitri continued, "they should have kept a better eye on their research if they're going to be so put out about it. They let just any old Volsinii-looking man wander into their facilities wearing a laboratory coat!"

He shook his head as though *that* were the biggest problem, here.

"So," Sir Mitri continued, "we're now trapped in Kjell until the Bloodrune Hunters get bored—or, preferably, scared off. Wasn't there a darkbeast coming, or are you..." He looked them up and down. "...it?"

A terrible picture began to form in Faustine's mind.

"Hang on," she said slowly, "you think we're here to fight the Bloodrune Hunters for you?"

Sir Mitri's brow furrowed. "What else would you be doing on the posterior end of nowhere?"

Faustine and Christel both looked to Professor Blightsen, then, but he looked about as horrified as Faustine felt.

"You knew the codes," Professor Blightsen argued. "And you received Caecillion's last message, didn't you?"

"Sure," said Sir Mitri, folding his arms across his rumpled waistcoat, "but all Vendrick said was to expect guests from Silverwood. Given that *my* last message was a request for additional security, I suppose I sort of figured...?"

He trailed off at the blank looks he was getting.

"Vendrick never got that letter," Sir Mitri said tiredly, "did he?"

"I don't know," said Professor Blightsen, "but I'm beginning to doubt it. This was *supposed* to be a safe place to hide a semi-sentient darkbeast, a bloodruned child, and Ironfang's youngest daughter until Caecillion himself could collect them."

They stared at each other for a long moment as that sank in.

"Well, we can do something about it, since we're here," Christel eventually said. "Right?"

"Right." Faustine's tactics classes came back to her in fits and starts as she tried to think. "How many do they have, do you know?"

"Eight, I think," Sir Mitri said. "But now one of them is a Captain or something and there's also that damnable lancer-type."

Faustine froze. "What did you say?"

Clearly irritated, Sir Mitri repeated himself, but Faustine hadn't heard him wrong.

There was only one 'Captain type' whose lancer bodyguard would be strange enough to note. She had just hoped, beyond hope, that she was somehow wrong.

"Sir Mitri," said Faustine slowly, "is the captain a tall woman with blonde hair, and does the lancer wear a helmet that looks like a carved bear's head?"

The irritation left Sir Mitri in an instant. "Yes... how did you know?"

It was an effort to keep her voice calm and even, and not simply scream.

"That's my sister, Orsina," Faustine said. "And her bodyguard, Drogari."

Christel and Professor Blightsen were looking at her like they expected her to say something else, but thankfully, Sir Mitri understood.

His eyes went wide. "Oh, Saints."

"We can't fight Orsina," Faustine said, not really to anyone. "She's a holy terror. Maybe Professor Vee or the Headmaster could manage it, but..."

For a moment, the words just hung in the room, stagnant.

"Then we hide," Professor Blightsen said after a moment. "At least until they get here."

Sir Mitri seemed to be doing some kind of rough calculations in his head. "When will that be?"

Professor Blightsen's brow furrowed. "Do you have a map?"

That sent Sir Mitri poking his head into the main room and demanding one, and by then, the pot on the stove had begun to boil over. It turned out to be mulled cider, and so it was with her hands curled around a pleasantly warm ceramic mug that Faustine crowded around the kitchen table with Christel, Professor Blightsen, and Sir Mitri.

"They *were* here," the professor said, tapping an icon of a miniature fort that was halfway to New Ascalon from here, "but that was weeks ago. And since the weather has mostly held, they *should...*"

Professor Blightsen trailed off as his finger traced a major road towards Kjell that seemed to twist through the forest.

"...Oh," he added, a little lamely. "I forgot how often the main road does that."

Christel considered this over the lip of their own mug. "Didn't you say Professor Vee was from here?" At Professor Blightsen's nod, they added, "Then couldn't she bring them through the forest like you did?"

"Most likely," Professor Blightsen admitted, "but it's still—"

"Wait, Vee? As in, *Valerius?*"

Christel glanced at Sir Mitri, brow furrowing. "Yes, why?"

"Caecillion can't bring that savage here." Sir Mitri blanched. "She'll ruin everything."

"No she won't," said Faustine at once, feeling the driving urge to defend her swordmaster, but it was lost beneath Professor Blightsen's own spluttered defense.

"Frelia is about the only bloodruned person I would trust to go toe-to-toe with a Bloodrune Hunter and win," Professor Blightsen said. "Never mind that she and Caecillion are your best hope, right now. Frelia is brusque, certainly, but this isn't the time to be—"

At the withering look Sir Mitri gave him, Professor Blightsen fell silent.

"I have an archive of bloodrunes in my laboratory," Sir Mitri said slowly. "I will not have that hothead destroy it claiming sacrilege. I have worked too hard!"

"Too late to do anything about it now," Faustine pointed out, with no small amount of satisfaction. Sir Mitri was sounding like Madam della Trova had while giving Markus a stolen bloodrune, and Faustine didn't like it at all.

These were people's lives, their families—not just scratch marks on their bodies. There was a weight to what Sir Mitri had stolen, a price. He probably wasn't building darkbeasts, since he'd just come right out and admitted to the phylacteries, but that didn't mean she had to like him.

"And Frelia will likely be more concerned with the Bloodrune Hunters than whatever experiments you're currently running,"

Professor Blightsen added. "I truly don't think this is the thing to worry about right now."

"Can't you lot just do something about it?" Mitri asked, waving his hand vaguely towards the front door. "I know you're a mage, Blightsen, and the kids are Silverwood-trained."

Faustine fought the urge to splutter in shock. Sure, they'd offered, but you weren't supposed to just *say* that!

"A white mage," Professor Blightsen pointed out, "like you. And even if I weren't, I am not putting the students in harm's way unnecessarily. We need to wait for the Caecillions and Frelia. I'm certain he'll have an idea."

Sir Mitri froze, his mug midway to his mouth. "Caecillion*s*," he repeated, with emphasis on the plural. "As in, Vendrick *and* his sister?"

"That's why they went to Serpentbrook Hold," Professor Blightsen said, "yes."

For a moment, Sir Mitri looked like he'd just been told to swallow a sea slug.

Then he said, "Saints, not Clarissa, too!" and buried his head in his hands. "She'll turn this place into a circus."

"Probably just a tea party?" Faustine couldn't help but point out.

"That's worse." Sir Mitri fixed her with one watery eye from beneath his hands. "Surely you see how that's worse?"

That was the moment Faustine began to wonder whether coming here had been a giant mistake.

CHAPTER TWENTY-TWO

THE MAIN LEVEL OF the Mitri laboratory was apparently also his home, and so Sir Mitri had rustled up quilts and cots and pillows for his sudden guests. Professor Blightsen and Christel were sharing the guest room, while Faustine had a cot in a cozy little personal library.

They were just sitting down to dinner in the kitchen when one of the scientists burst through the door.

"Sir Mitri," she said, her voice high and tight, "they're *here.*"

Sir Mitri paused with his spoon midway to his mouth. "Who's here?"

"The Hunters," the woman hissed. "Decius is distracting them, but he won't be able to occupy them long."

Christel was immediately on their feet. "They can't find us here."

"Just go hide in the back rooms," Sir Mitri said, gesturing in the vague direction of the guest rooms. "I'm sure we can sort this out."

"Hide?" Professor Blightsen spluttered. "Are you mad? We need to run."

The stew Faustine had just been eating sank in her stomach like a stone. "Is there a back door?"

"Yes, to the firewood porch," the scientist said, pressing her back against the door she'd just come in through.

Sir Mitri seemed to consider this. "I suppose you could borrow the coats hung up back there and hide in the woods, so long as no one sees you leave town."

"We'll wait out the hunters there," Professor Blightsen said firmly. "And then you can send someone after us when it's safe, Mitri."

Sir Mitri looked like there was literally anything else he would rather do. "Well, how do you propose I distract them in the meantime?"

"Offer them tea," Faustine said. "A whole spread. Make a fuss about it."

Sir Mitri stared at her for a moment like she'd grown a second head, but then the scientist piped up, "Oh, that's a great idea!"

Sir Mitri harrumphed, and then shooed them out the side door to the kitchen.

Faustine, Christel, and Professor Blightsen hurried down the warren-like halls, looking for something that might signal a door to the outside. It took three tries to find it, and they hurriedly pulled on random coats and gloves in the back cloakroom. Christel snagged a lantern from the wall and fiddled with its flint and tinder for a moment. The lantern whooshed to life and shadows danced across the foyer and the hard lines of their face.

"Bring the tinderbox as well," Professor Blightsen said. "We're likely going to need it."

Christel nodded, pocketing the small metal box, and then the three of them burst back out into the night.

Faustine immediately noticed the snow was worse, now, thick and drifting.

"Dammit," Professor Blightsen muttered. "Stay close, both of you."

He looked scared to death, and Faustine understood that instinct. Orsina and her Hunters were terrifying even on a good day, and the snow was coming down in thick tufts, now. Faustine couldn't keep the chill out of her bones even bundled up in a sweater, thick socks, and a borrowed overcoat that was too big in the shoulders. It went against every survival instinct she had to go *outside* in this.

Then again, sitting around felt a lot like waiting to become prey, and that was worse.

Once on the main street, they found the town cold and quiet, all the shutters nailed closed and all the firewood piles empty since, presumably, the wood had been taken inside. Faustine got the very real sense that they should not be out in this, but already, she felt better to be moving and *doing* something.

She found herself grateful for the handful of assassin lessons she'd actually had, before everything had gone belly-up at Silverwood. She could just barely hear, in the back of her mind, Professor Olsen telling her how to balance her weight to avoid creaking floorboards and heavy footfalls as Faustine tried to find her footing in the snow.

The soft *whoosh* of enormous wings cut through the silent night.

Faustine froze, from the tips of her ears to the toes of her boots. Her eyes raked the snowy darkness, looking for whatever had made that sound, but she found nothing. She couldn't have even told you which direction the noise had come from.

"Faustine," Christel began, very quietly, "Professor Blightsen... you don't think the Grand Huntress brought Huginn, do you?"

Oh. Oh Saints. Faustine hadn't considered the idea that her father would let Orsina handle the enormous raven—she wasn't a beastminder, after all—but it *would* have been large enough to made that sound.

"Let's not stand still to find out," Professor Blightsen said firmly, and he took off at the fastest pace he could.

They didn't hear the wingbeats again as they moved through the silent city, but when they came to a crossroads that made the Professor squint, Faustine swore she heard something a street or two over.

She reached for Christel's arm, putting a finger to her lips. When she had their attention, she pointed to her good ear, and then made the

Silverwood hand sign for 'wait' with her free hand. Christel nodded, and stood frozen as the landscape, listening.

A moment later, Faustine heard it again. It was a soft, crunching sound from a few streets over. It was probably footsteps, and certainly not big enough to be from a darkbeast. The footsteps were even and unbothered by the snow, so it was probably someone who lived here.

And yet, Professor Blightsen made the Silverwood hand sign for 'wait' at the small of his back. He must have caught the unusual sound, too, and only then did Faustine realize—why would anyone who lived here be out in this? Weren't they the mad ones for trying?

The loudest crunches yet sounded from a single street over, and the professor gestured for Faustine and Christel to follow him down a side alley. They moved like specters in the snow—Christel and the professor better than Faustine—until they came to the corner of a building. Professor Blightsen pressed into the corner, making the Silverwood hand sign for 'halt' as he did. Faustine did, but not before she chanced a glance around the building.

An enormous shape took up most of the narrow road, and for a moment, Faustine's stomach seized at the idea of fighting a raven monster like she'd cut apart at Silverwood. But then her eyes readjusted, and she realized she was looking at the back of a man.

A man with an ornately carved bear helmet and very large shoulders.

Faustine jerked back around the corner of the building as fast as she could. Christel stared at her, their eyes wide and questioning.

"That's him," Faustine whispered. "That's Drogari."

Terror seized Faustine's throat and refused to let go. If Drogari where here, that meant Orsina could not be far. And Orsina was a Hunter, just like Professor Valerius and the Not-Headmaster, and Faustine, Christel, and Professor Blightsen were just prey, and dammit, she suddenly missed her swordsmaster something fierce.

To their credit, Christel didn't startle at the news so much as widen their eyes and reach to tap the professor's shoulder. Professor Blightsen startled, though, his hands clapping to his mouth and strangling a squeaky noise in its cradle.

Faustine felt like she might throw up. If the professor had seemed scared before, he was terrified, now.

"What do we do?" Christel asked, practically mouthing the words. "Fight?"

Professor Blightsen shook his head, firmly. "Run."

Faustine wanted to scream at how unhelpful that was. Wasn't that what they were already doing? Dammit, he was supposed to be the adult! The Magicmaster!

"Something is very wrong with that man," the Professor added, low and quiet. "His aura reads like death. Both of you, run. Split up if he follows you, and I will meet you at the stone circle in the woods."

"What are you—" Faustine began, but she cut herself off as the crunching footsteps picked up again.

"Go!" the Professor ordered, shoving at both Christel and Faustine's shoulders.

Faustine had just barely gotten her feet back under her when Drogari's glittering blue eyes appeared in the gloom over Professor Blightsen's head.

This was a terrible idea, Faustine thought, her mind racing even as her feet began to move. *Running was a bad idea, and hiding was a worse idea, and you're going to die here, because you're soft, and you're stupid, and you'll never—*

The thought died in its tracks as light burst across the road. Faustine chanced a glance over her shoulder just in time to see Professor Blightsen with a growing ball of fire between his hands. Drogari stood in stark silhouette as he reached for his lance.

"Don't look behind you," Christel ordered between gasping breaths. They were more sure on their feet, in the snow, but sounded no less winded.

Feeling like prey as she did so, Faustine turned away from the blooming fight, and focused on the alley ahead.

The city's streets twisted and turned, and more than once Faustine almost fell when her foot twisted in a crust of piling snow. Christel told her to keep to the powdery bits, and that helped some. Together they ricocheted through spiderweb-like streets until civilization gave way, quite suddenly, to forest.

Only when they'd found a large path in the woods did Faustine chance a look back. There was no sign they'd been followed, and the wind was kicking snow into their haphazard footprints.

"We'll be sitting ducks out here," Christel murmured, their voice going cold as the wind around them.

"We should find Thera," Faustine said. "She said she's hiding in the woods, and I'd rather have a darkbeast on my side than nothing. Do you know where the stone circle Professor Blightsen mentioned is?"

Christel shook their head.

"Thought not," Faustine said. "Can you sense her, like the professor does?"

Christel made a face but dutifully shut their eyes. If they weren't in the middle of a Saints-forsaken snowstorm, Faustine almost would have thought they were meditating.

"That way." Christel's eyes snapped open, and they pointed towards the deep forest. "I can feel that bone-grindy feeling the Professor talked about."

Faustine hurried to follow Christel's sure footsteps, pulling her cloak more tightly around her and, not even for the first time in the past few minutes, cursed Orsina and her hunters.

"Do you know how far?" she asked.

"Not really," Christel offered, a little apologetically. "All I can tell you is that the rumbling gets stronger when I lean this way."

Faustine considered this for a moment as they stepped awkwardly over a log half-buried in a snowdrift. "That's not a very helpful compass, is it?"

"Nah," Christel agreed. "It's more like a warning bell than anything."

Despite their earlier flight, that was when the lantern decided it'd had enough, thank you, and plunged the two Violet Owls into darkness. Faustine froze instinctually, her boots locking in place while her eyes readjusted.

"Shit," Christel said. "Do you have the tinderbox?"

"I thought you—" Faustine began, but she cut herself off.

Just around the bend, nearly out of sight, sat an enormous shape. It was nearly the size of the tree beside it, and almost imperceptible in the gloom.

This was a mistake, Faustine thought again, her mind racing to piece together what the thing could possibly be, other than a darkbeast the wrong shape to be Thera. *You're going to die here, eaten by a monster, because none of the adults here are competent enough to know how to handle an emergency and—*

"That can't be Thera," Christel whispered, "can it?"

The monster's head turned.

It moved jaggedly, like it had clockwork joints that hadn't been oiled properly. It hopped a few feet towards them, like the pigeons that roosted in Iuvenlis Quad in the spring, and tilted its head.

There were six acid-green, bioluminescent eyes set into its face.

"What can steal your soul," the raven asked in a voice that felt like winter wind, *"but cannot kill your flesh?"*

Faustine blinked at it, and Christel even said, "What?"

The raven-darkbeast repeated itself. *"What can steal your soul, but cannot kill your flesh?"*

It cocked its head expectantly, like Professor Campagna waiting for someone to pipe up with the right answer.

Faustine's jaw dropped. "Is it seriously asking us... *a riddle?*"

"Boredom," came a cool, Volsinii-accented voice from beyond where the darkbeast sat.

Faustine's stomach fell through her boots. She knew that voice. She had never heard it anything less than perfectly composed, even as a child. It commanded armies and ordered subordinates to their deaths and told Faustine to sit still and pay attention.

For a moment, it seemed like the darkbeast was choking on something, a rhythmic *hurr, churr, churr.*

Then Faustine realized, it was probably laughing.

"You know you're not meant to wander far from camp, Huginn," said the offcomer, and Faustine's spine stiffened further. "What if something happened to you?"

Another moment passed, and Orsina della Luciana stepped into the scattered moonlight.

CHAPTER TWENTY-THREE

WITH HER TRICORN HAT pulled low over her eyes and the bottles of alchemist's fire on the bandolier around her chest rattling together, the Bloodrune Hunter took self-assured steps towards them. Her leather armor blended into the darkness, but the sword at her side did not. It glittered ominously in the gloom, like unmoving ice.

"I suppose I can forgive you, just this once," Orsina said, her grey eyes fixed on where Faustine and Christel stood, still frozen in the dark. "It can be our little secret."

Hurr, churr, churr went the darkbeast.

"Having fun out here, sister?" Orsina asked.

Faustine swallowed against the lump in her throat. She knew she needed to say something, *do* something, but she felt stuck to the floor.

Christel's voice cut through Faustine's rising panic. "Who are you?"

"Well, sister?" Orsina's eyes turned to Faustine. "Won't you introduce us?"

Don't. Be. Prey, echoed in the back of Faustine's mind in an accent rough as the northern winds.

"Christel," Faustine managed, and Orsina's face twitched in displeasure, "this is my eldest sister, the Duchess Orsina della Luciana, grand mistress of the Bloodrune Hunters."

Faustine could feel Christel's horrified stare digging into her side, but she didn't break eye contact with Orsina. She couldn't.

"Orsina," Faustine added, "this is Christel Vilulf. They're a friend of mine from school, one of the other Violet Owls."

"Violet Owls," echoed Huginn, and it chortled again.

"You know, Father asked me to collect a few things on my way back home." Orsina airily inspected her gloved hand as though she could see her fingernails through it. "But it seems our dear, injured brother and Madam della Trova have both gone missing."

Oh Goddesses, she knows everything. Faustine's hands shook so hard, she made herself hold onto her cloak for want of something to do with them.

"Della Trova isn't missing," Faustine said, as coolly as she dared. "She was eaten by a darkbeast."

It punched a hole in the wounds left by Siegmund's death, but at least it was the truth.

"Who told you *that?*" Orsina scoffed, but Faustine could just see her blanch beneath that stylish hat.

"No one," Faustine lied. "I watched it happen."

Orsina stared at Faustine for another long moment and then said, "Do you think you're clever?"

Faustine opened her mouth, but Orsina kept right on.

"I hear you have something that belongs to us," she said. "I can't believe that after everything I've taught you, you *continue* to disobey our father."

"So what?" Christel put in sharply, and Faustine could have kissed them.

Orsina's eagle-eyed stare dropped to Christel. Faustine watched them flinch. "I shall deal with you in a moment." Orsina paused, and then added, almost conversationally, "Traust-child."

Faustine resisted the urge to shiver, and her hand moved to the dagger sheathed at her belt. Though she would be deluding herself if she thought she could actually swing it at Orsina.

"You were enrolled at Silverwood, Faustine," Orsina said after so long a moment it made Faustine's skin crawl, "so as to not make a nuisance of yourself to the family in the future. Don't forget that's all we girl-children are good for."

Faustine grit her jaw. Orsina was right; she was only worth something as a pawn to her family, to the Unseen. She was a bloodruneless girl who could bear some faceless man's children until one of them slid out with the bloodrune her father wanted. That bleak, loveless future spread out before her like a whitewashed wall between her and anything that mattered.

"Galeria and I have made the best of it without throwing tantrums," Orsina continued. "I don't see why you can't."

Faustine's smile was wry and tight, even as the warning scream Professor Valerius talked about began to sing in her stomach. "Because I'm not like you, Orsina."

"Too right." Orsina snorted, and Faustine got the sense that her actual meaning had gone right over her sister's head. "Now, are you going to come quietly, or do I have to make you?"

Faustine's hands tightened on her dagger and she grit her jaw. Beside her, Christel drew their longsword with a practiced flourish.

Orsina's eyes flicked between Christel, Faustine's hands, and their faces.

Then she laughed, and the darkbeast joined in again. That avian chirruping was starting to grate on Faustine's nerves.

"The gall!" Orsina said over her shoulder, as if sharing the punchline of some joke with the monster at her back.

She reached up to the bandolier of alchemist's fire wrapped around her chest and withdrew a small vial of greenish liquid.

"We've been working on our formula for alchemist's fire, you know," Orsina mused, turning the vial this way and that between her gloved fingers. "It's even stickier now."

Her eyes flicked up to meet Faustine's and then Christel's, the warning clear. *You will never clean this off, and you will scream the whole time it burns.*

"When is a sister not a sister?" Huginn cawed.

Faustine glanced to the raven—"When she's a Saints-damned bitch."—and lunged.

Orsina side-stepped, even as she flicked the vial towards Christel. The glass was immediately lost amidst the falling snow, and as Faustine blew past Orsina, Christel yelped and tried to scramble backwards. Their boot caught on something beneath the snow, and they fell, hard, a half-second before the vial of alchemist's fire exploded across their chest.

A scream erupted from their throat that would echo in Faustine's ears for a long, long time.

She skidded to a stop, tried to reorient herself to lunge again. She had to do something, had to steal the antidote from Orsina's pockets because you couldn't get rid of alchemist's fire with water. But something hard as iron and black as night clamped around her middle, and stars sparked in Faustine's vision alongside the whirling snow and Orsina's hateful stare.

"Wrong answer," churred a voice from behind her.

Faustine barely had enough time to realize it was a claw grasped around her middle before the beast took off. It felt like her stomach stayed on the ground, but the rest of her burst skyward as Huginn took off. The wind rushed past her face like tiny, icy knives, and the world was a kaleidoscope of snow and sky.

Orsina put her hands around her mouth to shout, "A sister is not a sister when she's a sister-*in-law!*"

But Huginn was not listening.

The wind tore at Faustine's clothes and screamed past her ear, but Huginn held fast as he rocketed away from his beastminder. His claw was clenched tight around Faustine's middle, and no matter how much she thrashed, it stayed firm.

Knife, she thought. *Need my stupid knife.*

She was right-handed, but the left one was closer to where Huginn's front and back talons encircled her. So she wormed that hand towards her waist, eyes watering as Huginn's claw scraped clean through her sleeve. Faustine grimaced as she kept dragging her hand down, bracing herself against the pain.

With one last heave, her hand came free. Faustine wrapped her gloved fingers around her knife hilt and pulled, slicing through the webbing of Huginn's foot as she did.

The darkbeast screeched, and for once Faustine was grateful she couldn't hear out of the one ear. It muffled the horrific noise as she twisted her hand and plunged the knife into a different part of Huginn's foot.

The darkbeast's scream was almost human as it kicked. Faustine's head swam, and the world was icy white around her, but she was dead if she didn't move. She stabbed again, this time catching her own side in the process. The pain was bright and hot, but apparently it did the trick. Huginn's claw started to give, and Faustine leaned all of her weight on the edge of its talon, pressing as much as she could.

And then, all at once, she was falling.

She barely had the time to tuck herself into a sort of fetal position before she crashed into the snowy ground.

Red spots swam in her vision, and Faustine gasped against her own lungs. Huginn's enraged caw pierced the sky, and Faustine rolled deeper into a snowbank just in time to avoid being swiped at again. The claw left an ichor-splattered rent in the snow.

Panic seized her as her lungs burned, but Faustine lay in the snowbank, unmoving. The raven-darkbeast's enormous shape was silhouetted against the whirling snow and scattered stars, and was... was it moving *away* from her?

Chest heaving in great gulps of air, Faustine dragged herself unsteadily to her elbows. She was no huntress. She had no idea where Huginn had dropped her, and no idea how to navigate a forest. How far had she been pulled, a mile? Two? A few hundred feet?

Faustine became aware of a sound in the middle distance. She had to turn her head to hear it, and she listened hard for an unearthly caw or Orsina's piercing voice.

More footsteps, Faustine thought, horrified.

They were more crunching footsteps, as sure and steady as Drogari's had been. *Was* it Drogari, coming back to Orsina and instead finding Faustine on the way? Was it Orsina, dragging Christel with her? Surely she would have doused them in the antidote, if she had what she wanted?

Dammit, Faustine was not prey!

She shook herself as if to loosen her panic, and stooped to pick up her knife. She had to go back and find a way to help Christel, and Professor Blightsen, too. She would save them. She not only owed it to Christel, but also Siegmund's ghost.

Faustine stumbled on something hidden beneath the snow, and went down hard. Her knee slammed into something that might have been ice and might have been a rock, and blood blossomed across her woolen pant leg.

Fantastic. This was just fantastic. Everyone was going to die and it was going to be all her fault.

Wait a minute.

Faustine was not prey. Not anymore. She needed to stop thinking like it. She wasn't a bug, and Orsina wasn't a boot, and Faustine was already taking steps to make sure Christel would be okay. She just needed to get to the town, and find—

"I'm sure you've got a good reason for wandering around alone in a blizzard?" a familiarly jagged voice asked.

Faustine's jaw dropped. "Professor?"

From beneath a heavily furred hood, Professor Valerius smiled. "Not anymore, remember?"

CHAPTER
TWENTY-FOUR

"Are you certain we shouldn't find shelter?" Clarissa asked for what was, conservatively, the hundredth time.

Frelia tugged her scarf down beneath her nose. She sniffed the air, and the clear, icy scent of winter dug into her face.

"We still have time," Frelia said, pulling the scarf over her nose again. "And seriously, Kjell isn't far."

She knew these woods better than she knew her own veins. Knew every bootleg path and game trail and all the places that small, furry things liked to hide. There wasn't anything useful for human-sized supplicants for miles—no caves, no barrows, no hunter's cabins. There *had* been some, even this close to Kjell, but Frelia doubted anyone had bothered restocking them in years.

"We're much better off finding the town than out here," Frelia added, kicking at a snowdrift for emphasis.

It toppled over, revealing an icy layer of hard-packed snow beneath it.

"Merciful Saints," Vendrick muttered. "Why is the north like this?"

All three of them were dressed in furs and woolen underclothes, because Frelia was a daughter of winter and knew how to deal with the snow. But even she found it freezing out here, when she stopped moving. The Volsinii had to be miserable.

"Sucks less when you're walking," Frelia offered.

"No offense," said Clarissa, as lightly as ever, "but I don't believe you."

Frelia and Vendrick both snorted as she checked the stars again.

Kjell had been built in such a way that the north star always shone between the spine and the dragon in the Thundering Peaks. Frelia could just make out the north star when the clouds moved. It wasn't quite between the two peaks that always loomed in her mind's eye, but it was close.

They would make it.

"How do you know where we're going?" Vendrick asked. "I haven't once seen you check a compass."

Frelia pointed to a bright star just before the clouds swallowed it again. "That's Hrafn, the north star. I'm following it."

Vendrick squinted, tracking the line of sight off Frelia's finger. "Oh," he said after a moment, "we call that Aurelia, after the legendary archer."

"Ours is named for the reunion of Huginn and Mu—" Frelia cut herself off as the world began to shake.

Or, no. Not the world.

Just her bones.

"Do either of you—" She started to ask, then stopped.

"Do we what?" Clarissa asked anyway.

Frelia harrumphed. She'd stepped in it, so may as well smear it around. "I was *going* to ask, do either of you feel that. But you're both runeless so you can't and I realized it's a stupid question."

Vendrick grew visibly paler in the moonlight. "You don't feel the rumbling, do you?"

"Let's not stick around to find out, *ja?*" Frelia took off in a sort of sled-dog-jog that was hampered by the snow. "I'm not fighting one of those bastards in a blizzard unless it's in my bloody way."

"Right behind you," Vendrick agreed, even as Clarissa said, "Good thinking!"

Out of the corner of her eye, Frelia could see Clarissa mimicking her awkward trot with the flair of a dancer, and Vendrick with the patience of a coiled snake.

The wind was picking up, kicking hair and snow into Frelia's eye, and she tried to navigate the forest cleanly while poking at her insides about the rumbling.

It always began deep in her bones, singing against the Valerius Bloodrune like a choir of angry hornets. But if she listened hard enough, she could sometimes pick out melodies, so to speak.

The garmr was close, whatever it was.

Frelia began to bounce on her heels, grateful to be moving for fear she might vomit if she weren't. It felt like her very soul had begun to vibrate, and if she didn't *move*, didn't *fight*, she was going to combust.

And then massive wings blotted out the snow.

"Is... that *Muninn?*" Clarissa sounded as horrified as Frelia felt, staring up at an impossibly-sized bird as it soared over the tree line.

"Can't be," Frelia called back. "I hacked apart his corpse and fed it to the flames."

Still, she drew the Sword of Hana, her left hand gearing up to cast. Had she told Vendrick and Clarissa how fast these bastards could move? She hoped so. He certainly knew, but she wasn't sure Clarissa did.

Skitr, Frelia missed the Valerius Shield. It would have protected her flank if she needed the Grimsdalr Blink rune, and she could have used it to smash into the raven, if it came to it.

Far overhead, the garmr cawed.

It was like weaponized panic, slamming into her from all sides. *Did you douse the fire before you left your last camp? Will Vendrick survive this one, will Clarissa? Are the students...?*

Frelia shook her head roughly. There would be time for worry later.

There was something in the garmr's claws—or, well, there *had* been. Frelia only realized it when the shape began to fall, dragging snow with it as it disappeared behind the tree line.

"*Move,*" she ordered.

Frelia pushed toward that uncomfortably familiar, teeth-grinding feeling in a zig-zag sort of thing that was absolutely crazy-making in the snow. But as she chased that buzzing feeling towards the garmr's dropped prey, she pulled up short at the figure pulling itself out of a snowdrift.

Even bundled in wool and furs, Frelia would recognize that curly hair and those grey eyes anywhere. "I'm sure you've got a good reason for wandering around alone in a blizzard?"

Faustine's jaw dropped. "*Professor?*"

"Not anymore, remember?" Frelia was faintly aware she was smiling. "Now, seriously, what are you doing out here? You know blizzards can freeze your eyelids shut?"

"No, we did not," Clarissa muttered.

Faustine practically tripped over her words in the haste to get them out. "There... there are Bloodrune Hunters! In the town! And they're after Sir Mitri's research and they kept sniffing around his laboratory, so Professor Blightsen said we should run, and then while we were trying to get out of town, we ran into Drogari, and then Orsina, and—"

"I beg your pardon?" Vendrick hissed.

"How'd they get here ahead of us?" Clarissa asked. "That doesn't make sense."

Frelia made a short, sharp gesture in the air to silence the chatter. There would be time for speculation later. "Where are Edmund and Christel now?"

The teenager was holding her arm in such a way that advertised it was injured. "Christel is back there, with Orsina and I think Lord Huginn. She just caught them with alchemist's fire; they need our help *now.*"

Faustine pointed over her shoulder, back the way she'd come. "And last we saw, Professor Blightsen was fighting Drogari."

"*Skitr!*" Frelia snarled. "Edmund won't last five minutes against that bastard."

"Faustine," Vendrick added, urgency underlining each syllable, "where is Grimsdalr?"

Faustine's jaw worked like she wanted to say something and couldn't find the words. "I don't know," she finally said. "We told her to wait in the woods and we would come get her when it was safe, but... well..."

All three Volsinii looked to Frelia then.

"What?" she barked. "I don't feel the rumbling right now."

"Alright," said Vendrick, and he began doing the thing he did best, "so this just became an extraction mission."

Frelia made a face. "I'd rather just kill them."

"I'm sure you would, love," Vendrick said, "but the rest of us are mages and teenagers. Faustine, is that bird the only darkbeast?"

"Yes, but..." Faustine trailed off.

"You said Huginn, *ja?*" Frelia asked. At Faustine's nod, Frelia added, "He's Muninn's twin, Vendrick. Expect just as hard a fight."

Vendrick looked like he wanted to say something a teacher would never say in front of a student. Frelia almost reminded him that he didn't have to hold himself so stiffly anymore, but then he spoke again.

"We should avoid confrontation at all costs, and preferably this blizzard as well," Vendrick said. "There aren't enough of us to do much else. Faustine, do you know the way back to Talis' laboratory?"

"Yes, but..." Faustine's glance slid helplessly to Frelia, and it took her a moment to realize what the teenager was trying to tell her.

This was already a fight.

"Vendrick, if we rely on stealth, we'll die screaming," Frelia said. "Garmur hunt by smell, remember? And I have no idea how the Bloodrune Hunters always find me, but they do."

Frelia didn't know how to impress on him that nothing was safe, not with garmur afoot. The Kaldiri couldn't control them like the Volsinii could, and he was fighting his own, now. There would be no avoiding the bloody slaughter of severed limbs and broken families unless they fought back.

Just like in Ar, and Mydalr, and Norvegr, during the war.

"They use blood magic to find folks," Faustine offered after a moment. "Or at least, I think they do."

Vendrick's face twisted in displeasure. "Of *course* it is."

"How about," Clarissa interjected, "we sneak in, but fight if we have to? That seems most logical to me."

Frelia made a face, but said, "Fine; we're wasting time standing here."

"We should move," Vendrick agreed. "Faustine, the laboratory?"

"Wait, wait, what about Christel?" Faustine said hurriedly. "They're not in town and they need our help!"

Vendrick caught Frelia's eye, and she could suddenly read his expression. She'd seen the same on her da, during the Siege of Heit Reiði, and on Hägen, at the Battle of Skjöldr. It was a commander who knew he would be ordering knights to their deaths or worse, if he gave the word.

It was painful, to see it in Vendrick's intelligent, green eyes, when so often he spent most of his time looking for the way around.

But he was still thinking like a Volsinii.

"Then we split up," Frelia said, quickly. "Faustine, take Clarissa and find Christel. Bring them back to town. Vendrick, come with me, we'll go straight to Kjell. With any luck, I'll have downed Drogari and you'll have lit any Bloodrune Hunters on fire by the time the kids and your sister get back. If anyone runs into Thera, they can keep her for now."

"We should absolutely not split up," Vendrick said. "Clarissa and Faustine have no idea how to navigate this forest and you have no idea where Talis' laboratory is."

Frelia shrugged. "There's only like three places it could be. Faustine, is it near the west end of town in an old military barracks?"

"Erm," said Faustine, "I don't think it's a barracks, but it *is* on the west end?"

"Eh, *ja,* I can get us there. Clarissa, which star is Hrafn?" Frelia paused, trying to remember the Volsinii name. "Or, what did you call it, Aurelia?"

"Oh, that one," said Clarissa immediately, pointing to the bright spot between the Thundering Peaks.

"Good," said Frelia. "Any other complaints, Vendrick?"

He still had that grim, commander's look about him, almost more so now that Vendrick realized he was losing.

But Vendrick was the Imperial Spymaster. His instinct would be to hunker down and wait for things to blow over, or to sneak through enemy lines with the precision of a surgeon's knife. But if they waited too long, or if Faustine was wrong and there were more garmur than just Huginn, no amount of sneaking around would matter. They had a chance—a *real* chance—to get in and get out, but not without fighting.

And Frelia was *not* a Spymaster.

He seemed to realize it, too. With a long-suffering sigh, Vendrick pressed his thumb and forefinger into his temples. "Shall we plan to meet up at the laboratory unless it's on fire, or something?"

"We were, um, heading for the woods to hide before Drogari and Orsina found us," Faustine offered.

"*Ja,*" Frelia confirmed. "Laboratory."

They started to move, but then Vendrick paused. "Faustine," he said, "why would Mitri suggest you run? His wife is a grey mage. She could have handled a few Hunters if it came to it."

Faustine blinked. "He's married?"

Frelia's stomach clenched even as Clarissa said, "Oh no."

Hazel Stonebreath, beyond being another Silverwood classmate, beyond being one of a handful of scientists who knew anything about the bloodrunes, beyond the fact that she was Vendrick's friend—Hazel had the Háski Bloodrune, and thus the Task of the Sundering.

"Small Duncreggan woman," Frelia offered stiffly, "green eyes, penchant for grey magic, always seems two steps shy of coming at you with a scalpel and forceps?"

Vendrick snorted, but didn't contradict her.

"I..." Faustine's brow furrowed. "We didn't meet anyone like that at the laboratory?"

"Shit." Frelia caught Vendrick's eye, but he looked about as lost as she felt. "Vendrick, you don't think—"

"Don't say it," Clarissa interrupted.

"Saying it won't make her any more or less dead," Vendrick muttered, even as he made the Silverwood hand sign for 'move out.'

CHAPTER
TWENTY-FIVE

Frelia's heart ached for Kjell.

The whole trek into town had felt hushed and uneasy, even without her bones rattling or the anxiety radiating from Vendrick. But the town proper felt even worse. The whole place was obviously shuttered up against the snow, and, slowly, the stillness in the air had begun to creep into Frelia's blood.

That's where the furrier was, her mind filled in despite her best efforts as they crept along the main thoroughfare in snow and silence, *and the carter, the tanner, the apple tree that bloomed in the summer...*

They reached the town square without the rumbling intensifying, and all the hair on the back of Frelia's neck began to stand on end.

"Something's wrong," she muttered, her hand resting on the hilt of the Sword of Hana. "Faustine said Edmund ought to be fighting Drogari around here somewh—"

The town alarm bell began to clang.

The sound was as baked into Frelia's memory as anything else about Kjell. The tolling of the iron bell was the warning for everything from raiders to garmur to blizzards, and it set her teeth on edge.

Swiftly, now, she could almost hear her father say. *Armor up.*

Up ahead, a door slammed open and a man staggered out, still doing up the clasps on his cloak. He stopped dead at the sight of Frelia and Vendrick, and his jaw worked in silence for a moment before he finally managed, "*Oi, you!*"

Frelia had not heard someone else speak Kaldiri in a very long time. She was grateful her eye was already watering from the cold.

"*That's the warning bell for a garmr heading towards the village!*" He was frantically tightening a belt across his chest, now. "*I don't know what you're doing here, but get to the pub! Auntie Brenna will keep an eye on you.*"

He pointed up the path, towards the same pub that had always been in Kjell.

"*What kind of garmr?*" Frelia shouted back, also in Kaldiri.

"*I don't fucking know!*" the man shouted back, as though it were an absurd question. "*The big kind?*"

"*Four legs or two?*" Frelia held up the requisite number of fingers. "*What's the bell saying?*"

The man stared at her for a moment like she'd lost her mind before saying, "*Two.*"

"*Helheim.*" Two legs meant a much smaller target to land on, and also that it couldn't, by some minor miracle, simply be Thera causing trouble somehow.

"What's he saying?" Vendrick asked.

"A garmr's heading this way," Frelia said. "He's telling us to take cover in the pub. I was asking what kind of garmr."

Vendrick nodded, his expression taut. "So what did he say?"

"Two legs. So I'll need you to light up its insides on fire after I crack open its chest." Frelia mimed the motion over her own sternum.

"Right." Vendrick nodded. "Did you have a hand sign for 'draw me the Grimsdalr Blink,' during the war?"

"No," Frelia admitted, "but we probably should have. That's—"

"Oi! You lot!" the man from before shouted again, this time in Volsinii Standard. "Are you deaf? Move! You can't fight a damn garmr!"

Frelia opened her mouth, but she was cut off by a voice from the belfry of what had once been the town's chapel:

"Oh yes, she can! That's General Valerius!"

Frelia squinted up at the man in the belfry. He had a bow and quiver slung across his chest and the shoulders to use them. "Where'd you serve?" she shouted up at him.

"Heit Reiði and the Northern Rebellion!" The sniper's relief was palpable. "Welcome home, Lady Frelia."

Frelia couldn't help but smile as she unslung her travelling pack from her shoulder. "Thurid?" she called up to the man, trying to remember his family name.

"Drífa!" There was a smile in his voice.

That was right; Thurid had died in the Siege at Heit Reiði.

"Well, shit," said the man who had, until a minute ago, been telling them to hole up. "Go dump your packs in the pub, I guess."

He gestured the same way he had before.

Frelia led the way, even as Vendrick undoubtedly mentally marked the street as they surrendered their deadweight to the innkeeper.

"We're much obliged," Vendrick told the woman absently, even as he reluctantly handed over his own travelling pack.

The innkeeper frowned, her face scrunching as she glanced over to Frelia. "*He's Volsinii?*" she asked, in Kaldiri.

"*He's with me,*" Frelia said firmly, and she turned back to face the street.

The wind was kicking snow across the thoroughfare in thick, swirling arcs. Frelia pulled her scarf more tightly over her nose and drew the Sword of Hana, while Vendrick drew back to hide in the eaves of the furrier's.

It started slowly, like a boiling pot, gradually rising to a level too loud to ignore. Frelia's teeth began to clatter, and she continued scanning the street for unnatural movement. Heat pricked at the back of her neck, and she chanced a sidelong glance to see Vendrick with Dark Fire bristling at his fingertips.

That was the moment she heard it scream.

Fuck, fuck, fuck, why did you look away? Frelia jerked her head back around just in time to see massive wings blotting out the snow. A monstrous raven dove through the snow, aiming for the belfry—the tallest thing in town—even as Drífa scrambled to get a shot lined up at the awkward angle.

Even if it *wasn't* Lord Huginn, it was still as big as Lord Muninn, and Frelia refused to live that nightmarish memory loop again. She began to draw the Grimsdalr Blink rune, its jagged lines like an open eye. Icy blue arcane energy dripped from her fingers, and the raven-garmr cocked its head to study her like it wanted something, even as arrows studded its shoulder and Dark Fire rushed to meet it.

The chirruping noise forced from its throat made Frelia want to scream.

She drew down sharply on the Grimsdalr Blink rune, completing it. Then came the familiar jerk behind her navel, and then the world crystallized around her. Frelia shot across the boulevard as though ripping through the fabric of reality itself, disappearing into that familiar, liminal space for the time it took to blink.

She reappeared over the raven-garmr's head, and fell upon it like a guillotine.

Frelia scoured a deep gash into its chest, dragging the sword with her as she fell. It caught on the raven's mantle, wrenching Frelia's arm and jerking her into an abrupt halt.

She was suddenly jerked upwards by the hood of her armored coat, suspended by the garmur's beak near the level of its eyes. It studied her as though Frelia were a particularly interesting bug or clump of dirt it had removed from its taloned foot, its head tilting. She held its gaze for a moment, terror raking at her insides and her wrenched shoulder burning.

It was like staring down Thera, before she'd known it was Thera.

How can we fight such creatures? They were many times their size, many times their strength and speed. They were soulless creatures who only existed to devour humanity and shit them back out again. And what could one, lone woman do against such monsters?

Then the war instincts kicked in.

Frelia slammed the Sword of Hana into its beak like a club, not so much trying to slice as maim. The raven-garmr screeched and released her, and Frelia landed hard on the belfry's thatched roof.

Why hadn't Vendrick cast something? Where *was* he? It was too dark to tell.

"Alright, you bastard," Frelia growled, breathless as she got to her feet again. "Are you Huginn?"

All six of the beast's green eyes fixed on her.

"When does your reflection walk free of the mirror?" the monster asked, in a voice that was clear, if bestial.

Frelia scowled. "When you're a twin, you fucking menace."

She swung at its leg, but Huginn—for it *had* to be Huginn, what with the riddles—made that chirruping noise and took off again.

What was it doing so far from Konstantin Territory? Had Orsina summoned it? Could the Bloodrune Hunters even do that?

"Though I swim, I am no fish," Huginn said from just too high overhead to swing at. *"Though maternal, I am no friend to you, and my children keep watch from the stars. What am I?"*

Frelia knew better than to answer it, but still. The Guardian of Konstantin Territory couldn't speak, as such. It could only tell you riddles. So if she wanted to know what the fuck was happening here, it would only be found in the answers to its unending questions.

"A bear," Frelia said, annoyed, even as she began to draw the Grimsdalr Blink rune again. "Wait, shit—Orsina della Luciana brought you?"

Huginn laughed, because that was all that chittering sound could be. Then it threw back its head and screeched, loudly enough that Frelia winced and covered her ears with her gloved hands.

Those burning, hollow eyes fell to Frelia.

"*When is a victory not a victory?*" Huginn asked, even as its wings buffeted Frelia atop the chapel.

"Oh, fuck off!" Frelia snarled, and she started to cast.

Huginn was fast, a streak of black lightning that would have been invisible in the night, if not for the snow. His first grasping claw missed her by a hair's breadth, and Frelia was forced to abandon her half-cast Grimsdalr Blink rune to dodge. The second claw caught the edge of her armored coat and ripped the hem, jerking her sideways with it.

Frelia's war instincts were screaming in her ears—*Get onto its back, you idiot; do you want to die?*—but she did her best to focus as the monstrous raven swiped at her again. She ducked under its massive claw, only to collide with the blink rune she'd been in the process of drawing.

The burst of miscast energy sent her flying across the rooftop, smashing her into the belfry a stone's throw from the sniper. Drífa scrabbled for her, his hands scratching uselessly at her shoulders for half a second before she plummeted toward the lower chapel roof. Frelia tried to catch herself by drawing another blink rune on her hand, but it was too short a drop. She hit the tiles hard enough to spark stars in her vision.

A voice came to her, then. It wasn't hers.

The fight is not over so long as you breathe.

Frelia dragged herself to her feet, clutching at her shoulder and eye raking the rooftop battlefield for her sword. She couldn't see the damn thing; where had it gone? The street below?

Vendrick's Dark Fire whizzed past the lip of the roof, trying and failing to find purchase in the garmr's hide even as Frelia sprinted away from Huginn's raking claws. An arrow from Drífa from the belfry clanged against Huginn's skull, just between all the eyes, but it fell, useless, its arrowhead shattered.

Frelia's brow furrowed. *That* was new. Dammit.

"Frelia!" shouted a blessedly familiar Volsinii accent. "Catch!"

An astral sword crystallized into being, several feet down the roof. Frelia immediately snapped towards it, hastening to snatch the translucent blade out of the snow.

She rolled beneath a buffeting wing, bracing for an oncoming migraine as she braced to draw the blink rune again. She raked the dark skyline for Huginn's shape, but it was missing from its previous perch.

A caw sounded from over by the belfry. Drífa already in its beak, Huginn threw back its head and cracked the poor man between its mandibles.

Even from down on the roof, Frelia felt the deep *crunch* of the garmr's jaws snapping shut on human flesh as it rebounded against her bloodrune. She flinched at the jagged pain spreading from her hip, at the way Huginn's churring laughter swept across the town as it glided to the ground.

Dammit, she needed to gut the bastard.

She made the Silverwood hand sign for 'kill it with fire,' and finished drawing the Grimsdalr Blink.

The air behind her navel jerked, and the world crystallized around her. She brought the Sword of Hana up to striking position, and then braced to slam into Huginn's exposed breast.

The usual *whump* never came.

Frelia tore out of the blink rune with no garmr at the end of it. She thrashed about in the air, looking for black hide to snag the blade in and slow her fall. But she only caught sight of black feathers smoldering with

Dark Fire a split second before she locked gazes with those hollow green eyes.

Time seemed to slow. Why did it keep staring at her like that? Was it the bloodrune? The lack of fear? Frelia still wasn't sure what went on in a legendary monster's head, but this one was staring at her less like prey and more like...

An *adversary.*

It was so wrong. Garmur weren't supposed to be intelligent. They weren't supposed to stare down their prey or make you relieve your worst fears and nightmares. They were just supposed to cower from flame and try to eat you.

But as Frelia tucked her head and moved to draw the Grimsdalr Blink on her free hand, the cutting edge of Huginn's raptor-like beak loomed just overhead.

And then, there was only darkness.

CHAPTER TWENTY-SIX

THE FOREST WAS GHASTLY at night, and Faustine couldn't shake the feeling that something was watching her.

She wished Christel were here. They would have been able to tell her if there were darkbeasts looming in the forests just off the path, and if the eyes Faustine felt on the back of her neck were real or not.

And then Faustine remembered the scream from when Orsina had doused them in alchemist's fire, and flinched.

She was going to get them back, Saints-dammit!

"It shouldn't be much farther now," Faustine said in an effort to drown out the scream in her mind. "Lord Huginn didn't carry me *that* far, I don't think."

Up ahead, the wind began to whine as it cut through the trees. Faustine only had a vague idea of where they were, but she had a feeling Orsina was still further ahead. She thought about stopping to investigate the strange whining, but then she smelled it.

Blood.

"Human," whispered Lady Caecillion, drawing arcane energy a pretty shade of lilac around her right hand. "Got to be."

Faustine didn't ask how she knew that, and instead swallowed hard against the growing lump in her throat. They pushed onward into a clearing where the snow was patchy and the wind died down in the trees. As they rounded a line of half-snowy lumps that were probably tents, Faustine's stomach dropped.

Dozens of green eyes stared back at her from the trees, around the tents, even a log being used as a makeshift table. At first, Faustine thought she was seeing a multitude of different, snake-like monsters.

And then the entire thing sat up.

It was sort of like a ball of yarn, if those were made of disgusting, stringy flesh instead of wool, and possessed locomotion. The giant lump of flesh rose slowly, assuredly, like it had nowhere it needed to be and was just now deciding noon was an appropriate time to get out of bed.

"What in Hypogia?" Lady Caecillion said, staring in consternation.

"Hide," Faustine whispered.

But she was too late.

The yarn-ball darkbeast had been staring at them with myriad eyes that rose up on eyestalks like a snail and swayed in the fierce wind.

It lashed out.

Faustine yelped and took off running as a tentacle (she didn't have a better word for it) smashed into the tent just behind her. It collapsed in on itself in a heap of ripped canvas and broken wood, and then the yarn-ball darkbeast was rotating one half of its eyes towards her and the other half towards Lady Caecillion. It readied another tentacle as Faustine began to sprint towards the tree line.

Shit, shit, shit, this was not good. This was so, fantastically not good. Faustine was armed with only a knife, and even though Lady Caecillion was a mage, she would have to stop moving in order to cast, wouldn't she?

Another tentacle lashed out, closer than the first. It clipped Faustine's cloak as it whipped by, smashing into a tree at the edge of the clearing. Faustine shrieked in terror and moved to draw her knife.

What good is a knife going to do against this thing? a voice in the back of her mind told her. *It's massive and angry and probably wants to eat you, and you don't have any fire and you can't try to cut it with a stupid knife, Faustine!*

She needed a real weapon; the Professor had always been right about that. But now Lady Caecillion was sprinting through the clearing too, zigzagging her way around tentacles and bits of broken crockery and the detritus of living people. There were even some cattle carcasses, butchered and skinless in the moonlight.

It wasn't until Faustine spotted a tricorn hat that she realized where she was—Orsina's base camp. It had to be.

The place was deserted, and looked like it had been abandoned in the middle of a meal or something. Had they been attacked? Were all the Bloodrune Hunters just in town?

But even as she thought it, Faustine knew. Deep in her stomach, she knew. She'd been in Markus' stupid laboratory enough to figure it out.

"Over here, you monstrous thing!" Lady Caecillion shouted.

All the yarn-ball darkbeast's eyes turned to face the mage woman, whose lilac magic was trailing from her fingertips as she furiously began to draw a rune Faustine didn't recognize.

All around her boots, mist began to rise out of the ice and snow. Ghostly hands began to claw their way out of the ground, and for a half-second, Faustine's chest seized in panic.

Then she remembered the Lady Caecillion was a summoner.

A ripple of ghostly hands drove across the camp, as translucent as the weapons the headmaster usually summoned. The hands clambered up the yarn-ball darkbeast's stringy hide, latching on wherever they could.

"Find something to light on fire!" Lady Caecillion ordered. "I'll hold it down as long as I can!"

For a brief moment, Faustine almost asked why the woman couldn't just cast a fire rune. Then she remembered mages could only cast one spell at a time, and began scrounging in the dirty snow for something useful.

The yarn-ball darkbeast roared, the sound like the fetid air of a grave—or, Faustine realized belatedly as she dug through someone's half-buried kitbag, a carcass. Orsina must have been building this monster out of the cattle, probably to sic on Kjell.

Faustine didn't know why her sister had abandoned it, or why she'd tried to build such a monstrosity, but it didn't matter. If it were a della Luciana darkbeast, it would respond to della Luciana darkbeast commands. And although Faustine hadn't been trained to beastmind like her older siblings, she'd picked up the basics by virtue of living with them and not being a complete idiot.

"I have an idea!" she told Lady Caecillion. "Get ready to cast something fiery!"

"While you do what, exactly?"

Faustine drew in a deep breath, and shouted at the top of her lungs: "HEEL!"

The order felt warm in her chest, like good wine or a hot coal pressed just beneath the surface of her ribcage.

And then the yarn-ball darkbeast did the most wonderful thing: it sat. As much as its anatomy allowed it to sit, anyway.

Faustine slowed her steps, her lungs burning in the frigid air. The darkbeast continued to stay there, immobile, its eyes following her again. The ghostly hands were still clinging to bits of the 'yarn,' and Faustine thanked the ever-loving Saints that Lady Caecillion hadn't dropped the spell first.

You need to run, a voice in the back of her mind told her. *You need to get to Christel and make sure nothing happens to them, because all you're good for is mucking things up.*

Faustine shook her head as though she could fling the thoughts away, and tried to remember the other basic darkbeast commands. They weren't all that different from dog commands, all in. There was sit, stay, down, come, heel, attack, and drop it. But Faustine didn't know what Orsina had bothered to teach this one.

"Down!" she called.

And it did, lowering its yarn-ball-like bulk further towards the forest floor. Faustine could make out the remains of a fire pit, beside it, and for a moment, hope flared in her heart. Lady Caecillion could light the fire and then Faustine could... could...

Could do what? she thought, a little angrily. *Hope it keeps standing still while you saw off tentacles with a knife?* Maybe it would be better to just burn the whole thing?

"Lady Caecillion," Faustine said, "now!"

There was no sudden burst of magic. No rush of heat or light or even so much as a curse. Faustine looked at the Headmaster's sister, only to find her chewing her bottom lip and staring at the darkbeast.

"So," said Lady Caecillion, a note of sheepish apology in her voice, "a bit of a confession. I don't have 'fire' memorized and I can't read my spellbook out here in the dark."

Faustine gawped at her for a moment, unable to string words together. "How do you not... know that one?" she finally managed.

"I have it," Lady Caecillion insisted, tapping the spellbook sheathed at her hip. "But I can't read in the dark."

Faustine turned back to the yarn-ball darkbeast, only to discover it was shaking.

Not moving—not exactly. For that, it would need to drag itself forward by the tentacles or the eyestalks and probably leave a smear of fleshy gunk behind. This was more like... shivering, except darkbeasts didn't feel cold, apparently.

"Are you..." Faustine trailed off, barely able to comprehend the idea. "...in pain?"

The darkbeast roared, although it didn't have a mouth Faustine could see. The sound felt dredged from the depths of the land itself, like something ancient was crying out for mercy.

Maybe Orsina had found this one, and started augmenting it? Oh, that would be worse than just making one. That would be so much worse.

Faustine opened her mouth to ask what hurt, but the darkbeast lashed out again. Its lower tentacles smashed free of the ghostly hands, reaching to drag towards the source of its pain.

"*STOP!*" Faustine shouted, but it didn't work, this time.

The yarn-ball darkbeast rounded on Lady Caecillion, its tentacles a frenzy of black streaks in the blizzarding gloom. Lady Caecillion was stuck in the middle of her summons, even as more ghostly hands shot up from the ground. They scrabbled at the yarn-ball darkbeast's oil-slick hide and fell just as fast as they tried to cling to it.

Faustine's knife wasn't going to do any good here, so she did the next best thing: she sprinted towards Lady Caecillion. If she couldn't move the yarn-ball, she could at least move the woman.

Unfortunately, the darkbeast had the same idea.

"Lady C, your right!" Faustine's voice echoed hoarsely across the ice.

The warning came too late.

For the second time in her life, Faustine flinched as a garmr laid waste to human flesh. The crunch echoed in Faustine's bones and, with a furious roar, she flung her dagger at it. The steel buried itself deeply into one of the darkbeast's eyes with a disgusting squelch. It reared in surprise, moving away from where Lady Caecillion had fallen into newly-crimson snow.

She wasn't moving.

Faustine rounded on the yarn-ball darkbeast, unarmed and unarmored and with fire singing in her chest.

"You will be still!"

The order rolled off her tongue smoothly, easily. Faustine had never been so confident in a thing she'd said in her life.

And then, unthinkably, the darkbeast lowered itself to the floor, rolling over like a kick ball to reveal a giant hole in its underside. (Did balls have an underside?)

It looked sort of like the octopus dissection Faustine had done with her tutor, once upon a time. A writhing mass of tentacles around an obvious, fleshy hole. On the octopus, the hole had been a beak that the creature had used to eat, but on this disgusting amalgamation of flesh and magic, it was a literal gap. Like Orsina had been piecing together a puzzle and stopped partway through.

Wait.

That was probably exactly what she'd done.

"Is that why you're lashing out?" Faustine demanded. "You're hurt and... unfinished?"

A dozen eyestalks bobbed, and it took Faustine a long moment to realize, the thing was nodding.

"Okay, okay, okay," Faustine murmured to herself, over and over again just to hear the comfort of a human voice.

Darkbeasts weren't supposed to be intelligent; that was one of the few things the Professor and the beastminders agreed on. If she didn't know any better, Faustine would almost say this thing wanted her to help it.

To kill it.

She looked to Lady Caecillion again, relieved to find the woman hauling herself weakly to sit up against a tree trunk. That was a good sign; she was still conscious and wasn't cold supposed to help with injuries?

But there was no way to help her if the yarn-ball darkbeast was just going to smash Faustine into the ground as soon as she tried, so...

"Alright you monster," Faustine growled. *"Heel,* dammit.*"*

It stayed where it was, and so she began to creep carefully towards the unfinished hole in its underside.

"Faustine..." Lady Caecillion's voice was a hissed warning that Faustine ignored.

The flesh inside the yarn-ball was already turning purple, like it should have been on a darkbeast, but the yarn ball-like strings of component parts were more clearly defined. The outside of the monster was black and greasy, like all darkbeast hides.

But inside?

Inside, there were ribcages and shoulder blades and skulls that still had skin and hair on them. This monster hadn't been built from cattle or forest animals at all.

It was built from people.

For a split-second, Faustine just stared in uncomprehending horror. The darkbeasts Markus had killed people for weren't very big, with the exception of Muninn. This thing would have taken way more people, like...

"Like the whole camp," Faustine whispered.

She felt like throwing up. Had Orsina murdered her own people to build this thing? Why? For what purpose? Was Christel in there?

Oh Saints, Orsina had better not have killed Christel and then stuck them in this horrible, twisted conglomeration. Faustine's logical brain tried to tell her Christel's bloodrune was more valuable than that, but she trusted absolutely nothing when it came to the Unseen, and especially when it came to her siblings.

The yarn-ball darkbeast moaned—outright, agonizingly moaned—and Faustine tightened her grip on her knife. She wasn't sure when she'd pulled it from the darkbeast's hide, only that she felt better with steel in her gloved fingers.

She would cut out this monster's heart. And then she would throw it on a fire. And then, she didn't know, maybe she could set the whole thing burning from the inside? It would take too long to burn not to draw more of them, but maybe it was far enough away from the town not to matter?

I wish Professor Valerius were here, that same voice in the back of her mind thought, *or Lady Caecillion could remember the rune for fire, or...*

"SHUT UP!" Faustine roared.

The voice in her mind was silenced.

She'd started to have a nagging feeling about all those anxious spirals she'd been having. She didn't usually panic like that, and the voice wasn't her inner voice. It was an obtrusive, external voice pretending to be hers.

And if Lord Muninn could make you relive your worst memories, then why couldn't Lord Huginn make you think your worst thoughts?

"Don't be prey," Faustine muttered, stalking towards the hole in the darkbeast's underbelly with careful footsteps that crunched the snow beneath them.

It was even worse, the closer she got. She could make out individuals woven into the purple darkbeast flesh, as though they'd been partially digested. Her fingers tightened around her knife again, and she pulled her scarf up over her nose and mouth at the encroaching smell. The cold was helping, but it couldn't mask the stench of meat and decay forever.

She was almost at the hollow in the creature, now. "Don't move," Faustine called out to it. "And don't try to eat me. Okay?"

The darkbeast rumbled, and a fetid breeze caught Faustine in the face and made her eyes water.

Great. If that's where the noise came from, she was probably standing at its mouth. *Fantastic,* that voice thought for her. *You're a stupid girl who's going to get herself killed by walking into the mouth of a darkbeast, and no one will even mourn you.*

Shut up, Huginn, Faustine told it, and then she stepped over the threshold.

Inside the monster's... what, belly? Mouth? (Faustine was just going to think of it as 'inside the yarn-ball.') It was warm and dark inside, like the hot springs in the Imperial Volsinii palace basement.

It took her eyes a moment to adjust to the darkness, and she stood in the monster's mouth unflinchingly. She did not focus on the faces screaming silently in the walls, and she did not try to offer comfort to Orsina's victims.

She toed across the squishy floor, breathing evenly through her scarf and thinking, over and over so that Huginn couldn't get a word in edgewise, *Don't be prey, don't be prey, don't be prey...*

There. She could just see the glint of daylight on something crystalline overhead. Trying not to think too hard on where she was putting her hands, Faustine began to climb towards it, squinting all the while.

This was the yarn-ball darkbeast's bloodstone heart. It had to be.

Faustine dug her clunky, leather boots into the fleshy wall to keep her balance, and carefully, as carefully as someone carrying boiling hot tea across the common room floor, she began to cut away the flesh around the bloodstone.

The monster groaned again, pushing disgusting wind past Faustine, but she held on, and kept prying. Despite how absurd it was, she tried to do as little damage as she could to the flesh around the bloodstone. It felt right, somehow, not to unduly hurt these poor folks who had been hurt enough.

Strand by slimy strand, Faustine worked the bloodstone free. Its surface was sticky and uneven beneath her gloved fingers, but there was a small, glowing rune set into the center of it, with arms that whirled and she'd seen before, down in Markus' laboratory.

The Grimsdalr Bloodrune. Thera's bloodrune.

Faustine teased the bloodstone free with a wet noise she didn't want to contemplate. For a moment, she hung there halfway up the inside of the yarn-ball, staring at her palm-sized prize.

And then the whole monster began to shake.

Faustine yelped and dropped to the floor, landing hard on her butt and rattling her teeth in her jaw. She scrambled to her feet as the walls began to convulse. Her window to the outside was shrinking, and Faustine dove for it.

She landed hard on her stomach, the walls of the monster pressing in all around her, and began to drag herself out by the arms. She dug her knife into the dirt for purchase, and tossed the Grimsdalr Bloodstone up ahead of her with the other.

It rolled to a stop against something enormous, black, and furry.

Panic seized Faustine as her eyes traveled up the monster's leg, and she tried to drown it out with what she knew about darkbeasts. *They hunt in packs, they're big and hungry, they're... they're...*

Wait, she knew this one.

"Thera?" Faustine shouted up at her.

"*What... happen?*" the monster rumbled.

"A lot!" Lady Caecillion's voice was thin and tight. "Help me up, would you?"

"*With... what... thumbs?*" Thera grumbled, but she still trundled off towards Lady Caecillion.

Faustine's arms shook with the effort it took to pull herself free of the collapsed yarn-ball darkbeast. She kicked and scrambled and then, with the same sort of wet pop that had freed the bloodstone, Faustine's boot came free of the monster's innards. She scrambled several feet forward in her sudden weightlessness, snatching for the bloodstone and rolling over to face what had become of the yarn-ball darkbeast.

It wasn't there.

What Faustine stared down instead was a mass grave. Dozens of mutilated bodies were piled atop one another, plus bits of cow carcasses and possibly a deer. The bloodstone must have been keeping it together like a lynchpin, and when she'd pulled it free, the whole thing had collapsed.

Numb with cold, and shock, and horror, Faustine could only stare at the terrible thing her sister had done, and weep.

CHAPTER TWENTY-SEVEN

VENDRICK DIDN'T PANIC, AS a general rule. He assessed, he strategized, and he cast the nastiest spells in his book, but he did not, would not, panic.

And so when Frelia disappeared down Lord Huginn's throat, Vendrick's stomach twisted and something cold as the wind began building in his chest, but Singularity pellets burst to life over his head. He yanked on his newly-conjured projectiles like a puppet master on the strings, and they came with him as he broke into a run.

Huginn soared overhead, and a wet, chirruping noise began to grate on Vendrick's soul. How dare the thing laugh after what it had done? It had no teeth, though, so what Vendrick did in the next—generously—thirty seconds would determine whether Frelia lived or died.

With a flick of his wrist, Vendrick sent the first of his Singularity pellets skyward. It blasted through Huginn's leg, and the arch-darkbeast cawed loudly enough to wake the dead. The raven-like creature was sagging in the air, now, and Vendrick moved to send his second pellet zipping after it.

Singularity won't down it, said a rough, feminine voice in the back of his mind. *You need to cut its chest open and you need fire to burn its insides.*

He would do it. He owed her that much. Fuck, where would she want to be buried, here in Kjell? At Silverwood? He didn't know.

A wave of anxiety so thick he thought he might vomit overtook him as hard and fast as nightfall in these mountains, and Vendrick forced himself to stay steady. He didn't have a long-range fire spell. Dark Fire was mid-range at best, and hardly accurate after a certain yardage. He'd have to bring the creature down first, cut open its throat.

Or... Vendrick's eye rose to the skyline. *...bring myself to it.*

He flung his remaining Singularity pellets at the darkbeast. One went wide, but the other scored a hit to the primary covert feathers on its enormous wing. Huginn shrieked again, and Vendrick grimaced as he yanked his spellbook out of its holster.

He began paging through his book, even as he fetched up against the nearest oil lamp still burning. Calm, calm, he needed to stay calm. He could break down later.

The first stroke of the rune he wanted was a looping arc, which meant it sat somewhere between Eidolon (and why did he still waste ink on that one? He never used it) and Miasma.

There. He paused his frantic page-turning on the rune for the Grimsdalr Blink.

You arrogant usurper, a little voice said in the back of his mind. *Are you sure you can even do it?*

Ah, here was the panic he'd been trying to stave off. That wasn't Frelia's voice—it was his own anxious thoughts trying to eat away at his resolve.

Are you really worthy of casting this stolen spell?

His hands stiffened on his spellbook. Since when had he had time to doubt like this? Vendrick didn't freeze up like this, even when faced with the Imperator himself.

He forced himself to loosen his grip, look back down at his spellbook. His hesitation would cost Frelia her life, and no, *no,* he would not allow any more mistakes. He would take out this bastard darkbeast in her name.

Mistakes like serving Ironfang? That damned voice asked. *Or letting Frelia walk away from you at the Battle for Skjöldr?*

Vendrick bit down on his molars as he began to draw the Grimsdalr Blink rune. The familiar rush of energetic magic erupted from his fingertips, painting the atmosphere vibrantly purple as he dragged his forefingers through the motions.

A moment later he felt the spell bite down, and he was no longer on the ground.

The world opened up in a kaleidoscope of crystalline light and sound, snow and sky melding into a hellish, white-washed nightscape. Just like when he'd first tested the rune, a migraine began to bloom between his eyes just in time for the spell to spit him back out again.

He landed hard on the chapel roof, and reached for the first rune that came to mind. Singularity ripped into the fabric of the open sky, and Huginn jerked around as though drawn to energy so like itself.

Vendrick had never been eye level with a darkbeast before. Even Thera had looked down or up at him, most of the time. But as those glowing green eyes bore down on him, Vendrick became acutely aware of how small, how breakable, he actually was.

Of how very little he could actually do, if Lord Huginn decided he was prey.

"*What glitters like gold,*" Lord Huginn chirped, "*but hangs heavy as a stone?*"

Vendrick blinked. Surely the Lord of Thought wasn't making a pun? Still, it was his only idea, so Vendrick said, "Guilt."

Hurr, churr churr, went the darkbeast, and it was as if the monster had cast something.

Despair unlike anything he'd ever felt rushed over Vendrick. His mind swirled with thoughts of *You should never have served Ironfang* and *what were you thinking, closing Silverwood?* And *Frelia is dead, because of you.* The collective weight of his failures was enough to cut his concentration, and his Singularity pellets fell, lightless, from the sky.

And for the first time in years, Vendrick Caecillion knew what it meant to lose.

He was standing at the gates of Skjöldr, watching Cillian's retreating warhorse bring him and Frelia further from Vendrick's grasp with every hoofbeat.

He was seated at Imperator Claudius' war council beside his father, listening to the Imperator Volsinii's insane plan to turn his own daughter into a siege weapon.

He was running along the trenches at Heit Reiði, blasting Miasma at the Kaldiri knights who had made it through the line of Gaius della Luciana's darkbeasts.

No, *no,* dammit! Vendrick was standing on a rooftop in the middle of the night with snow piling around his boots, and he owed it to the woman he loved to pull her body from the darkbeast's gullet and lay her to rest properly.

You should have stopped them at Skjöldr, said that little voice in his head. *Or gone to Grimsdalr Territory right then. Should have never let yourself be stationed at Heit Reiði in the first place. Should have done something to stop this.*

"What blinds like light and cuts like a sword?" Huginn croaked, its voice thick. *"Binds like rope, and is man's truest ward?"*

A single tear fell from acid green eyes, and Vendrick gritted his teeth.

"Truth," he rasped.

Vendrick had long since grown adept with weaving lies in with the truth, but the darkbeast was right. Truth could blind, and cut, and bind, and it would be the only way forward.

And the truth was that he had always tried to find the mythic third path. The option between the options. The grey in the binary of black and white. And he failed as often as he succeeded because, quite simply, there were times when binary choices were all there were.

Most of Vendrick's failings, he was realizing as he stood on this Saints-forsaken rooftop, were not because he'd done something, but because he *hadn't* done something.

There was no third way with darkbeasts. He could see that now, as he stared into Huginn's inhuman eyes. There was only predator and prey. Kill before you were killed.

Small wonder Frelia had always been so furious, but he *saw it,* now.

He had to do this her way. He was too used to being able to anticipate his opponents, too used to having all the good cards in a hand and waiting for the opportune moment. But there wasn't one, here; Vendrick would simply have to win in real time.

"*What can—*"

"Enough," Vendrick hissed.

And Huginn, the Lord of the Slain and Lady Twilight's Raven, fell silent.

"No more secrets," Vendrick murmured to himself, even as he dragged the back of his free hand over his eyes. "No more lies."

He didn't have a long-range fire spell, no. But that didn't mean he couldn't make one. The rune for 'truth' was part of the rune for 'Integrity,' which Vendrick used as part of his handful of white magic wards. The flayed edges of the Dark Fire rune could easily be dovetailed onto it, and he could combine *that* with the 'stability' part of Singularity...

Yes. Yes, it would work. So long as he could cast it correctly.

You're arrogant, said the voice in the back of his mind.

Vendrick laughed, just a little, as he began flipping through his spellbook. "I am," he told it, "a former Senator."

A snake!

"That is the nom de guerre."

A liar!

Vendrick began the first lines of his Dark Fire rune, smoldering purple in the frigid air before him. "Half-truther at best."

A murderer.

"And I would do it again." Vendrick was pulling the loose edges of the Dark Fire rune into the rune for 'truth,' now.

He finished the rune for 'stability' with a flourish worthy of a maestro, and then the very air between him and the monstrous raven began to vibrate.

Traitor!

The first knot of solidified fire burst into life over his head, ripping through reality like a Singularity pellet. The second tore into being on his right-hand side a moment before another clawed itself into reality on his left. The heat was scorching, melting the falling snow in its path and searing bright light into Vendrick's eyes.

"No," said Vendrick, as wind and fire buffeted him. "I may be many awful things, Lord Huginn, but I am not, and have never been, a traitor."

With both hands, he pulled on the fire-knots with arcane puppeteer's strings. The magic responded at once, speeding towards him as he wound up to throw.

Churr, hurr churr, said the darkbeast, and Vendrick didn't stop to consider that the sound was different.

He flung the fire-knots towards the raven, bracing against the rooftop. The first knot streaked across the skyline like a shooting star, burying itself in Huginn's breast and cratering a burning hole there. The second struck its wing slantwise, taking meat and feathers with it.

And as the third one hurtled forward to strike Lord Huginn between the eyes, the raven asked, *"What greets you in the morning and disappears by evening?"*

The fire-knot careened through its head, splattering purplish gore against a nearby wall even as Huginn's wings seized up and it began to plummet.

"Light," said Vendrick to the dying bird.

***

Cold rage burst in Frelia's blood as she struggled against the musculature holding her in place. Red spots began splattering across her vision as Huginn's throat closed in on all sides. Frelia couldn't breathe, couldn't move, couldn't get purchase in this thing's slimy innards.

She thought of her father, crushed between a garmr's teeth just before he died. Had he been cognizant, in this darkness? She hoped he hadn't. Life hadn't been kind to Da, but maybe death could afford a measure of it.

Her sword hilt pressed painfully into her gut, and Frelia wondered, distantly, if she could survive Huginn's stomach acid long enough to cut her way out, and then the drop streetside if she made it that far. Did garmur even have stomach acid? Saints, there was too much she didn't know about Lady Midnight's Children.

Dammit, she was Frelia Helm's Grace Valerius, and she needed to *breathe.*

With the last of her strength, Frelia jammed her hand into indiscriminate, slimy flesh. Huginn was saying something, and she felt a rumble well up from beneath her feet, but there was no sound. Frelia would have snorted if she could have afforded the air loss.

So she was in its vocal cords, was she? Served the bastard right.

Frelia jammed her hand further into Huginn's throat, and its disgusting, chirruping laugh followed. She shoved her boot into another wall of slimy flesh, twisted until her shoulder screamed and she could shove her other fist into the walls of its throat, too. Gagging followed, and Frelia pressed as hard as she could into Huginn's insides.

Light burst against her closed eyelids, and then she—or maybe Huginn—was falling.

Insulated as she was in the great beast's innards, the impact was something far off and distant. A moment later, the world stopped spinning. Spots were sparking in her vision, and she needed to *fucking breathe.*

A rush of cold air hit her face, and Frelia cracked open her eye. Instinct kicked in, and she sucked in a huge, foul-smelling breath of blessed air, and then began to claw herself out of Huginn's breast.

Her head was pounding, her body shaking. It would take a miracle to put enough force in her shaking hands to crack open the creature's chest at this range. *A miracle,* Frelia thought sourly, *or my bloodrune triggering.*

She felt the stirring of arcane energy somewhere beyond Huginn's chest wall, and then something clasped around her arm and heaved.

With slow, methodical precision, Frelia wormed her way free of the mire of viscera. She grasped fistfuls of feathers, her gloves coming away ashen, and all the while, that hand tugged insistently, grabbing for purchase in her armored coat.

With a squelch like a dying leech, Frelia was birthed from Huginn's insides only to be hit with a face full of the cold, clear air of her hometown. She scrubbed at her eyes and ears, becoming dimly aware of a quiet litany of curses, admonishments, and spellcraft.

"Merciful Saints, don't scare me like that!"

She felt herself bundled into an embrace, then—blood, ichor, garmr-viscera, and all.

And then something cold and wet touched her face, and Frelia startled. She blinked a few times before Vendrick's face came into focus, determined as ever as he wiped the grime away from Frelia's eye, nose, and mouth with a fistful of his cloak.

Frelia wanted to ask what he was doing, wanted to thank him, wanted anything to come out of her damn mouth, but her vocal cords were paralyzed and she just stared at him like an idiot.

His face was pinched, beneath his scarf, and his eyes gleaming with manic light. "Are you alright?" Vendrick asked, moving to clean the gunk out of her ears.

Was she? Frelia wasn't sure how to answer that question.

"I'm alive," she croaked, and winced when the bitter taste of garmr ichor stung her tongue.

Despite her parents' vestigial screaming in her ears about it, she scooped up a handful of snow—and then another, when the first immediately turned grey—and washed her mouth out as best she could with it.

"Good," said Vendrick. "Now stay that way, would you? You gave me a bloody heart attack."

He scraped snow across another corner of his cloak, something wet glittering on his face and turning to ice. He was also kneeling in bloody garmr innards, did he know that?

"Fire," Frelia rasped.

"What?"

"Light Huginn's insides on fire," Frelia managed, gesturing at the crevasse she'd opened in its breast.

"I'd see you breathing first," Vendrick said.

Beneath the battle-haze and exhaustion, Frelia almost smiled. "Finish the bastard off, Vendrick."

His eyes flicked across her face for a moment, and then, he managed a weary smile. Vendrick got to his feet, joints cracking, and offered her a hand up. For once, Frelia took it. She scooped up the Sword of Hana where it had fallen, and then planted her boots in the snow that had forged her.

Vendrick shooed her away from the dying garmr, and Frelia took a moment to scan the empty street. There were no signs of additional life, no footprints in the snow that weren't hers or Vendrick's, no sign of magic or clash of metal ringing off in the distance.

Where was Drogari? And more importantly, where was Edmund?

Frelia shook her head in an effort to center herself, and that was about the time that something sharp and arcane ripped into reality. She jerked towards the sudden blast of energy, only to stop midway through drawing her sword.

Vendrick was casting something she'd never seen before. It wasn't his Dark Fire—that didn't feel wrong, like this.

"What is that?" Frelia asked warily.

"How I downed Huginn, just now," Vendrick said as a void-like pit opened up in the air just over his head. "I combined Dark Fire with a bit of a ward and Singularity to create a sort of fire-knot thing that ripped through its chest."

Frelia blinked at him. It was one thing to know, intellectually, that Vendrick was a frightfully talented grey mage. It was another thing entirely to hear him say it so casually.

"You combined three separate runes?" she repeated. "In the middle of a battle?"

"Yes, the rune for 'truth' is part of that for 'Integrity,' which is almost always used in white magic wards. Combine that with the fiddly edges on Dark Fire and the 'stability' part of Singularity and you get..." He trailed off at the look on Frelia's face. "What?"

"Holy shit, Vendrick," she said with genuine admiration.

He reddened, just barely visible in the moonlight over the edge of his scarf. "It's just a bit of spellwork."

As if to prove his point, he flicked one of the fire-knots at Huginn's downed corpse. It sailed into the garmr's open chest cavity, quickly followed up by two more. A moment later, the acrid smell of torched garmr meat hit Frelia's already-assaulted nose.

But Frelia had been birthed by the frozen north, and she held it in her bones the way a canvas held oil paint. She was no stranger to garmur and their horrors, and she did not shiver in that frozen night.

"Come on," she said, feeling here and a million miles away all at once. "That stupid laboratory isn't far from here."

"Frelia, slow down!" Vendrick called after her as she started to trudge through the snow. "You are in *shock,* madam."

CHAPTER TWENTY-EIGHT

FAUSTINE HAD NEVER BEEN on a battlefield, before today. Not really. She heard the stories from her father and professors, read the tactics books, had seen the occasional body or two thanks to Markus' disgusting experiments. She had seen the plague pit memorials in Ascalon, those gilded statues of the dead piled higher than the Capitoline buildings.

None of that prepared her for this.

The remains of the yarn-ball darkbeast weren't a battlefield, no. If it were, the dead would have had stab wounds and grey magic burns and arrow wounds, maybe. If it were simply a battlefield, the dead would not be ripped to pieces and skinned like deer carcasses. They would not have been sewn back together with parts that did not belong to them, and they would not be lumped together in an unmanageable, ghastly pile of unidentifiable flesh.

This was not a battlefield. This was an atrocity.

"Faustine?" came a quiet, pained voice.

The teenager flinched, and then straightened up, scrubbing at her eyes. She sat back on her heels and looked towards Lady Caecillion. Right, she needed help. Faustine needed to cry like a child later.

"Sorry, sorry," Faustine said. "How can I help?"

"*Band...age...*" Thera rumbled from overhead. "*Use... cloak.*"

"Capital idea," Lady Caecillion said, and before Faustine could put her off it, the woman had unfastened her wool cloak and handed it to Faustine. "Be a dear and shred this, would you?"

Numbly, Faustine cleaned her dagger as best she could in the snow, and set about cutting strips of cloth to bandage Lady Caecillion's ruined legs. They were twisted up like tree roots, and Faustine had a terrible feeling she was going to end up losing them.

"Faustine?"

She jerked her head up, and found Lady Caecillion studying her with more concern than the woman really ought to have been, just then.

"Are you alright?" Lady Caecillion asked.

Faustine knew she wasn't supposed to admit it, but—Hypogia, how was she supposed to not? "I don't know why I'm surprised," she said quietly, feeling tears welling up again. "My family always does this sort of thing."

Lady Caecillion's jaw fell open. "You think your sister did this?"

"Yes." Faustine scrubbed at her eyes with her elbow. "Or at least, I think so. I don't know who else would bother trying to make a darkbeast out of..." She hiccupped a sob. "Out of..."

She trailed off.

"The whole town?" Lady Caecillion guessed.

Faustine nodded. "And her own people, I think. I saw some tricorn hats before it toppled over."

"Merciful Saints," Lady Caecillion muttered, hissing as Faustine set to work. "How did you kill it from in there?"

Faustine was quiet for a moment as she began wrapping strips of Lady Caecillion's cloak around her broken legs. "It was in pain," she finally said. "I think Orsina had just... given up partway through making it, and so that's why it had that giant hole."

Reflexively, Faustine looked over her shoulder to where the darkbeast had been, and grimaced.

"I cut that thing out of its insides," she added, pointing to the red, crystalline lump that still lay in the snow near the ashen fire pit.

Lady Caecillion squinted through the snow, and then she somehow, despite all the blood loss, went even paler. "You didn't touch that barehanded, did you?"

"Erm," said Faustine, "probably. Why?"

"Never touch unstable magical artifacts with your bare hands, Faustine." Lady Caecillion spoke with almost as much authority as the headmaster. "Take some cloth and wrap it up; we'll bring it with us but let's not risk anything else in the process."

"I guess I wasn't thinking of it like an unstable, magical artifact," Faustine admitted quietly. "I was thinking of it like the beating heart of a creature in pain."

They all stared at the red, misshapen lump in the snow for a moment. It breathed with arcane energy that practically left a small halo around it, and the rune inside looped and whorled like falling snow.

Faustine wished she knew which bloodrune it was.

"Are you ready to move?" she asked Lady Caecillion instead.

The countess' face pinched. "You'll have to carry me."

It took them approximately four tries to realize Faustine was never going to be able to piggyback Lady Caecillion all the way back to the Mitri laboratory.

"I don't see you helping," Faustine grumbled at Thera, who was practically chortling.

A moment later, the enormous darkbeast began to rise steadily on her haunches. Snow rolled from her back in waves, littering the half-melted runoff beneath her.

"Saints," Lady Caecillion swore, reflexively trying to scuttle as far from the rising monster as possible.

With as much gentleness as a darkbeast could muster, Thera bit into Lady Caecillion's travelling pack and hoisted her up like a mama dog scruffing an unruly puppy. Looking rather put out, Lady Caecillion flailed a bit in Thera's grasp, but she stayed firmly fixed in place.

"Well," she said after a moment. "I've been in less dignified straits. Let's get on with this."

Faustine scooped up the bloodstone with her hand in the shrapnel of Lady Caecillion's cloak, and didn't look back at the mass grave the Hunter camp had become.

***

Frelia and Vendrick had barely gotten the basic hellos out of the way when Faustine came bursting through the door to Talis' laboratory in a panic. The white mage immediately snapped into his physician role, barking orders about where to bring the patient and the alchemical reagents he'd need.

Dread pulsed in the back of Vendrick's mind, low and buzzing like a nest of hornets, as they brought Clarissa down to the alchemy laboratory itself. Part of him desperately wanted to find somewhere dark to curl up in, but the garmur, the blizzard, Clarissa wouldn't wait for him to pull himself together. He would just have to ride out the rising tide of screaming anxiety the way he always did.

Frelia's voice yanked him back to center. "Breathe, Vendrick. She'll be alright."

"She had damned well better," Vendrick muttered, going to wash his hands.

It was cool and dark as a cellar, down in the actual alchemy laboratory. Oaken cabinetry was nailed into the walls, and a drain had been dug out in the corner for the inevitable refuse. Slate-topped tables took up most of the available space, their surfaces long since stained with alchemy spills and small explosions.

They clustered around the largest one, where Clarissa lay unconscious and supine. Beside her, Faustine was explaining what had happened in the past hour, and Vendrick forced himself to breathe evenly, listen dispassionately.

Then Frelia said, "Dammit, why wouldn't Clarissa have just said she didn't have the Fire rune memorized?"

Vendrick knew, and his fingers twitched uselessly at his sides. "She wouldn't have wanted to be a burden."

"Worry about her magical education when she's stable," Talis said, rolling his sleeves up to his elbows as he rounded on the table. "All of you, hold her down."

They followed orders, and Vendrick's insides twisted with every strip of cloth Talis pulled away from Clarissa's mangled legs. Talis set to work cleaning the injuries with boiled water and antiseptics, muttering to himself all the while, while the rest of them held Clarissa steady as her body reflexively jerked and twitched in pain. Slowly—too slowly—the blood began to clot and congeal, and Clarissa's breathing came a little easier.

It didn't make Vendrick feel any better that the laboratory now smelled like death—or, no, that wasn't quite right. Death was too pedestrian a word for it.

Talis' medical lab smelled like the Saints-damned Tyrant's War.

"Shattered," said Talis after another minute or so, smearing even more clotting agents across Clarissa's wounds. "I can try to salvage something, but ultimately, it will be better to amputate. We can better control the recovery that way."

Frelia and Faustine took the news better than Vendrick did. Frelia nodded grimly, while Faustine's eyes widened in sympathetic pain.

"Why do you—" the teenager began, even as Vendrick cut in sharply, "Saints, Talis, I've seen you heal far worse than this."

Even as he said it, Vendrick realized what had felt so odd about this whole medical exam: Talis hadn't cast anything. Not even basic diagnostic or analgesic spells. He'd tipped alchemical potions down Clarissa's throat instead.

And that was not like Talis Mitri at all.

"I had assistants, during the war," Talis argued. "So unless you've gotten a lot better at white magic lately, I don't see a better option."

Suspicion began creeping into the edges of Vendrick's mind, and he wondered, not for the first time, whether something else had slipped in beneath his notice.

"What if we go find Edmund?" Frelia asked. "Is a damned cleric good enough for you, Mitri?"

Talis' eyelid twitched. "If he were here, certainly. But he ran with the Silverwood kids hours ago, and only the little della Luciana came back."

"I said 'find!'" Frelia defended. "He's probably hiding somewhere to avoid Drogari, if he didn't set the man on fire."

Talis visibly blanched. "If he ran into that brute, Valerius," he said, almost gently, "he's probably dead, and I'm the one who has to operate on Clarissa."

"Bullshit; Edmund survived the Tyrant's War just fine."

Vendrick's eyes narrowed as the argument began picking up speed. He knew a distraction when he heard one. "You're wearing your spellbook, Talis," he interrupted. "What do you need that you don't have?"

Talis' watery blue eyes landed on Vendrick and dug in, even as he reached for the yellowed leather cover of the book at his hip. "I'm a physician, Vendrick, not a miracle worker."

Vendrick resisted the urge to shake Talis by his mis-buttoned waistcoat. Proof. He needed proof before anything else. "That's not an answer."

"And furthermore," Talis continued, with heat and as though Vendrick hadn't spoken, "if you're just going to be a thorn in my side, I will perform the operation myself before this clotting agent stops working and we have to—"

But Frelia—clever, merciless, wonderful Frelia— was apparently growing as suspicious as Vendrick.

"Oi," she interrupted, "Mitri."

Vendrick turned just in time to catch the glint of glass in Frelia's hands before she whipped it towards Talis. With a startled yelp, he jerked away from the table. A second later, the beaker shattered against the table behind him.

"Professor!" Faustine gasped.

"What in Hypogia was that for?" Talis shouted.

Frelia folded her arms across her ichor-splattered clothes. "You didn't cast a ward."

Any white mage worth his salt would simply throw up a ward when faced with a projectile at that range. Hell, even Vendrick would, rather than attempt to rely on his physical attributes. That's what magic was for.

"Talis," Vendrick asked with quiet urgency, "how are your cosmos, this season?"

For a moment, Talis spluttered in inchoate fury. "The sky or the flower?" he finally managed. "Because the sky is just dark."

Vendrick breathed a little easier. That was, mercifully, the correct answer.

"Have you read the latest Aloysius novel?" Talis shot back, insulted.

"I did." The code tasted like ash in Vendrick's mouth. "But I found it wasn't for me."

Talis' incredulous glare dug into him now, accusatory. "Are you really worried I'm not me?"

"Not now," Vendrick pointed out. "So tell me, Talis, what are you waiting for?"

The puffed-up, senatorial fire left Talis, then, and Faustine took a startled step backwards. Talis looked down at Clarissa's twisted legs, damaged beyond physical repair, and then, inexplicably, to Frelia.

"Not if you're just going to let her stab me," Talis said.

Frelia's eye narrowed, and Vendrick snorted. "Bold of you to assume I 'let' Frelia do anything," he said. "She's a grown woman perfectly capable of directing herself." He met Talis' eye then, as hard and unflinching a stare as he'd ever used out on the Senate floor. "And you are wasting our time with this useless stalling. Answer the question—why are you not casting?"

Talis busied himself with collecting things from around his laboratory. "You have to understand," he said, his voice suddenly and painfully quiet. "We haven't seen any Caecillion agents in months, and you know Hazel wasn't well."

Wasn't. Vendrick hardened his heart and tucked that away for future questioning. Hazel had been "is," not "was" last Vendrick had heard from the pair.

Hypogia, no wonder Talis was trying to avoid casting magic—grief made the arcane behave strangely. Better not to risk caster and recipient, if you weren't certain of the outcome of a rune.

"Didn't he send you a message with one?" Frelia asked.

"I did, and at the very least," Vendrick agreed, "you should have seen Arquitius, Dorso, and Cento within the past few months."

Talis threw his hands up, not turning from a cabinet full of alchemical ingredients. "Vendrick, do you think I'd be asking for additional security if your network were still functional and you were still a Spymaster?"

Something cold slithered into Vendrick's collar, and it wasn't meltwater. "When did you send that letter?"

Talis waved his hands loosely, as though time were as ephemeral as heat, down here. "I don't know, a few months ago? It was slightly after the Bloodrune Hunters turned up."

Vendrick's eyes narrowed. He had a horrible feeling about where this was going. "Would Hazel know?"

Talis suddenly froze as though, all at once, reality smashed into him. The man doubled over, holding his stomach as if in physical pain.

"They went for her first," Talis whispered. "She was the grey mage; she was the priority target." He looked, a little helplessly, around the room, but not even Faustine came to his rescue. "We had planned to test whether or not Hazel's bloodrune could be removed later this month."

For the first time since they'd shown up at his door, Talis' voice broke.

"We had checked and triple-checked the formulae. They were as close to theoretically perfect as I could humanly make them, and I—"

"Removed?" Frelia glanced sharply to Vendrick, though Goddesses knew why. "What do you mean, removed?"

Something thick and dark tightened in Vendrick's gut, but he was too slow to head off the oncoming wreck.

"Exactly that," Talis said. "Taking a bloodrune out of a person."

"Is this a joke?" Frelia's accent was thicker than usual, rougher. "It was one thing when Markus della Luciana showed up with a stolen bloodrune. That, I understood. That, I could fight. But you all, *too?*"

Frelia shook, more than she had in the snowstorm outside. More than she had staring down darkbeasts as they roared.

More than Vendrick had ever seen.

"We're supposed to be the good ones, in this fight," Frelia hissed. "Does my whole family mean nothing to you people?"

"Sit down, Valerius," Talis mumbled.

"No." Frelia was in his face, now, an accusatory finger jabbing into Talis' ribs. "How dare you hasten the death of a thousand years of ancestors and culture and... and trade these things around like unwanted furniture!"

"Frelia, I need you to understand something," Vendrick said, so quietly Frelia jerked her head around to look at him. "After that, if you still wish to yell about it, we won't stop you."

She looked visibly taken aback, that he didn't rise to meet her anger with his own.

No more secrets; no more lies. She deserved to know.

"The Unseen," Vendrick said, softly but unflinchingly, "can both attain and remove bloodrunes at their leisure. That means both political clout, and, yes, removing a thousand years of culture from a person."

Frelia's hand went for her sword hilt, but she didn't draw it.

"The point," Vendrick continued, "of having Hazel and Talis researching addition and removal is so that the Unseen can no longer wield that power as a political bludgeon. Until now, however, only they have been able to manage addition or removal. Likely using whatever information their failures with Thera Grimsdalr and the others gave them."

Do you see? He wanted to say. *Do you see the impossible choices we've had to make?*

But that wasn't fair. There had never been a choice—not for Frelia.

"Saints, Vendrick," Talis said, and he began unbuttoning his shirtsleeve, "you've ruined my punchline."

And there, sitting on the pallid skin just below his elbow, was the broken-hearted Háski Bloodrune.

Faustine stared grimly at the tattoo-like mark while Frelia staggered against a nearby table, blanching in the wan alchemical light. Vendrick just wished he could have been surprised.

"You said you removed Hazel's." Vendrick pressed his thumb and forefinger into his temples, exasperated. "You failed to mention that you put it in yourself."

"I had to put it somewhere," Talis said. "They can't just sit ambiently in the air until we need them. They're *blood*runes. They live in blood."

It certainly looked as though it belonged in Talis' blood. The Háski rune had erupted, scabbed over, and faded to the tattoo-like mark Christel now had, and that was about the only point of reference Vendrick had. Despite how often he saw the person, he had never seen Frelia or Octavia's.

"Faustine," Vendrick said, his voice muted as he looked to the girl, "is this how they've been passing bloodrunes around? This..." He gestured uselessly at Talis' arm, looking for a word.

"I've been calling it a transfusion," Talis offered.

"Yes," Faustine offered quietly, "it is. I watched della Trova give Markus the Grimsdalr Bloodrune before Lord Muninn showed up."

Some of Talis' usual zeal came back into his eyes at that news. "I shall want to hear about that the moment this surgery is finished. Can they make phylacteries?"

"Erm, you mean the vials?" Faustine asked. "That's how they transport them around."

"Hypogia, I knew it!" Talis seemed to remember Clarissa was there, and, sheepishly, he began tugging his sleeve back down. "But, since I've had this, I haven't been able to cast a single spell. I've tried everything I can think of, but even the simplest runes won't spark."

All the surprise Vendrick had wished he could've had before, apparently, had simply been waiting for this moment.

The implications were staggering. It wasn't simply that Talis was emotionally compromised and worried about what his spells would do; he had no faith he could cast them at all. And since white magic was *built* upon faith, in the same way grey magic was built upon energy and black magic was built upon logic, that meant, effectively, Talis was as cut off from the arcane as if he'd never studied it at all.

"Is that possible?" Vendrick managed hoarsely. "A master of the arcane simply... no longer a master?"

His mind was reeling. No—*no*—it went against everything Vendrick had ever learned, every rule of magic and law of the universe. Mages could not be cut off from their magic. Once learned, it was always learned.

"You're a white mage, *ja?*" Frelia asked. At the nods she got, she added, "Are you trying to set it off with white magic, or grey?"

Vendrick turned to stare at her. "What does that matter?"

"Grey magic is what sets off the Háski rune," Frelia said. "Didn't you lot learn this as children?"

Talis waved her off—"I have no use for theology."—but Vendrick saw the tremble in those steady hands.

"Well, I've never heard of a Háski scion doing anything but blasting holes in things," Frelia harrumphed. "So I'm guessing that's why your magic isn't working. Helheim, we need Edmund fucking Blightsen, and I said that from the start."

Talis studied his patient on the lab-turned-surgical table with the gravity of an icon of a Saint. Clarissa's wounds were clotted, for now, but she'd need white magic healing soon—or, failing that, surgery.

Dammit, Talis was right. If he couldn't cast white magic, it would have to be amputation. Even Vendrick could see that, and his white magic amounted to healing bruises and superficial cuts.

"How long ago did this happen?" Talis asked Faustine after a moment.

"I dunno," Faustine said. "An hour maybe?"

Talis' face tightened, and he seemed to be running mental calculations. "Vendrick, if I give you this..." he held up his spellbook. "...can you cast Sleep, Rejuvenation, and Tissue Restoration?"

Vendrick's lips twisted as he considered. He had never been adroit with white magic, but with the rune diagram in front of him, and Clarissa's continued health on the line... he'd just have to make it work.

"You'll need to walk me through it," Vendrick admitted, "but yes. Probably."

Out of the corner of his eye, Vendrick saw Faustine wince.

Talis shut his eyes, drew in a deep breath, and then snapped them open again, his decision made. "If you can cast Rejuvenation now, we can spare Valerius half an hour to go look for Blightsen. If she isn't back by then, I will amputate. We cannot risk sepsis or worse, at a time like this."

That was... reasonable. Except for the part where Frelia was supposed to go alone.

"You have any better ideas?" Frelia said, and Vendrick realized, he'd said that last part out loud. "I sure as shit can't cast white magic, and I'm not taking a teenager back out in that blizzard either."

"Hey!" Faustine protested.

"You heard me," Frelia growled.

Vendrick flinched at the memory of Frelia's armored form disappearing into Huginn's raptor-like beak. He couldn't send Frelia back out into that, any more than he could consign his sister to a life of relying on others.

Dammit, he was the Count of Caecillion. He was supposed to look out for his baby sister, his Countess, and he'd sent her off into a blizzard expecting her to handle things like a soldier instead of a sheltered mage-woman.

Frelia's hands were suddenly on his face, holding him steady and leeching warmth into his bones. Warmth he had almost lost.

"Vendrick," she said, gently but firmly, "this is my hometown."

As if he needed incentive to feel worse at everything that had already happened here.

"I know every back-alley and game trail," Frelia continued. "I can get wherever I need to go and back again before a garmr so much as *smells* me. Wherever Edmund is, I will find him."

"And what happens if you're wrong?" Vendrick shut his eyes and tried to regulate his breathing. "You're swallowed by something again?"

It felt horribly personal to tell her he refused to live through that again, what with Talis and Faustine staring a hole in his side.

Frelia thumped the heel of her hand against her chest. Against the darkbeast ichor drying across her armor, against everything Vendrick feared to lose. "I'm the Wolf of Kaldr, Vendrick," she said. "I've got a few more Blink Runes in me if something tries."

She glanced at Talis, then, steel in her eye and grit in her words. "I will look for Edmund, and you, Mitri, will answer for this theft, when we're through."

"I'm certain you will try," Talis muttered. "Why don't you heal up Clarissa, while you're at it, Valerius?"

"You can't guarantee that," Vendrick tried, his fingers twitching at his sides like he could cast something to fix this. "It isn't safe to go out there."

Genuine anger flashed across Frelia's face, then. "Do you think me a dog, Vendrick, or a wolf?" she hissed. "Because only one of those can be commanded."

He fell back like she'd smacked him, and, without another word, Frelia tore back up the stairs to the parlor room, Faustine hot on her heels.

CHAPTER TWENTY-NINE

FAUSTINE'S HEART WAS STILL pounding in her chest as she burst into the main room of the Mitri laboratory. They drove into the parlor that just this afternoon had been full of easy chatter and comfortable sofas and was now in complete disarray, furniture dragged this way and that to barricade against the snow and monsters outside.

"You're not seriously going out there, are you?" Faustine called.

Professor Valerius didn't even slow down. "Of course I am. Clarissa is going to lose both legs unless I can track down Edmund now."

Faustine's stomach twisted with even more worry, somehow. "How are we going to do that?"

"You," said the professor, "will do nothing. I am going to track him. What road did you leave town through?"

"Erm, I don't know, offhand, but we went out the back door and what about Christel?" Faustine asked. "Shouldn't we search for them, as well?"

The professor shook her head. "We need to secure a base first, and Clarissa is more pressing. If I can find them both while I'm out there, I will, but I'm not optimistic."

Faustine's brow furrowed. "So why are you going into a blizzard for Professor Blightsen when—"

"*Because Edmund is a white mage!*"

Faustine flinched at the sudden volume. Her eyes started to water and no, *no,* she would not cry. Even if she was beyond frustrated that Professor Valerius was acting like this. The woman was supposed to be a war hero, for the Saints' sake.

Professor Valerius seemed to realize it too, for she shut her eye and breathed in sharply. When she spoke again, her voice was quieter, more measured. "Mitri is a healer who cannot cast white magic right now, and Vendrick can barely manage basic healing spells. If we are to have any hope of surviving more fights with garmur, Bloodrune Hunters, or anything else, we need a white mage. That's more important right now."

One of Professor Valerius' lectures came drifting through the back of Faustine's mind. Well, not even the lecture, really, but an aside when someone—probably Owen—had asked her about the Tyrant's War.

Being a general means doing the right thing by the most amount of people, and winning the war. It doesn't mean every decision you make will endear you to your house knights.

But surely that didn't mean leaving someone behind? Especially someone with a bloodrune the Unseen wanted, and when 'behind' meant leaving them with the Unseen?

"But what about their bloodrune?" Faustine protested.

"That's exactly why they won't kill Christel outright," Professor Valerius said firmly. "The same cannot be said of Edmund."

Faustine wanted to tear at her hair and demand the professor lead a charge into the snow and go rescue Christel. She would much rather Professor Vee gut Orsina than leave Christel alone with the witch one more instant. Because who knew how long it would be before Orsina did something awful and irreversible, like draining them of all their blood and putting their bloodrune in a neat little impersonal vial? Faustine wasn't nearly so certain Christel was safe just because the Unseen wanted their bloodrune.

And the Professor was a war hero, dammit. Why wasn't she being heroic?

"I need you to follow your orders, Faustine," the professor said, even more measured, now. "Normally, I think your people are full of shit, but I agree with them about one thing: military units are built on trust. They have to be. If you don't trust the guy next to you to watch your back, and the guy giving orders to see the whole battlefield, you will die."

"I know that," Faustine said stiffly. "Tacticsmaster Vitellus said that all the time."

"I don't think you do," the professor said. "You don't trust that I see that Orsina is stuck in this blizzard too, so she's not going anywhere until it passes, and neither is Christel."

All the color drained from Faustine's face.

"You don't trust that this is my home and I learned to hunt here, so if anyone is going out there to find Edmund right now, it will be me. And you clearly don't trust that I care about my students, even if you aren't literally my students anymore."

"That's not true!" Faustine protested.

Something flashed across the professor's face. "Look me in the eye and call me a liar, Faustine della Luciana."

Her family name was like a whipcrack across her face, bloody and virulent and cruel, and she flinched.

"Don't call me that," Faustine got out.

"Your name?" the professor clarified, an eyebrow in her hairline.

"Della Luciana." Faustine's fingers tightened at her sides. "I'm not like them. And I don't want to be."

Faustine was tired of being prey, tired of being afraid, tired of running from Markus and Orsina and their father.

"Father's a tyrant," she hissed, "and Orsina wishes she could be. But she can't, so she pretends to content herself hunting everyone with a bloodrune for the Unseen instead. Galeria is a viper who fancies herself a businesswoman, and Markus is a whiny, tattle-tailing asshole even father doesn't like. I'm sick of all of them! I want to help people, professor. Not kill them, and not leave them for dead."

"And how much do you think you'll be able to help if you're dead?" the professor challenged. "You're lucky Huginn didn't try to eat you."

"I mean..." Faustine shifted from foot to foot. "He did. When we ran into him. I'm sure Orsina is supposed to be beastminding him, but she's not as good as Gallus or even Markus."

The Professor just stared at her in horrified consternation. "You didn't try to answer a riddle, did you?"

"Um..." Faustine tried to think back. "I didn't mean to, but I think I did? And got it wrong."

Professor Valerius put her head in her hands and groaned.

"Why?" Faustine pressed, anxious all the way down to her guts. "Is that bad?"

"It's how he communicates," Professor Valerius said with an exhausted sigh. "But listen, I have to get going; Mitri said he'd give a half-hour and I'm eating into that time. What do you know about Drogari?"

Faustine shifted her weight, acutely aware of how quickly time was now passing. "He doesn't talk much, and he was assigned to Orsina within the past few years, I think? I haven't seen much of him, since I've, you know, been at Silverwood."

Professor Valerius nodded, her eye cold. "Anything else?"

"Um..." Faustine tried to think. "Professor Blightsen said something about Drogari read like death before he told us to run?"

The Professor's face suddenly went slack. "Say that again."

It wasn't a question.

"Professor Blightsen said there was something wrong with him, and he read like death," Faustine said dutifully. "I don't know what—"

"Not that," the professor growled. "His name."

Faustine was so bewildered that it stifled the urge to cry. "Drogari?"

And Professor Valerius, the mad darkbeast-killer of the Kaldiri army, Wolf of Kaldr, and rebel general, clapped her hand to her mouth in stunned horror.

"You lot say it funny," she said, after a moment, "so I didn't pick it up before."

Faustine tried not to panic at the woman's about-face. "What are you talking about?"

"Draugr," the professor whispered. "You lot call them revenants. Bodies of the dead returned to hunt the living by Lady Midnight herself."

Faustine's breathing went erratic as the world began to squeeze in all around them. "That can't be," she whispered. "They're a myth, aren't they?"

"Not from your da's lot, it's not," the professor said. "Shit, that explains Athos, too. Legend says draugur are garmur-minders."

"You don't think..." Faustine was starting to feel nauseous, and had to start again. "You don't think that's why they trusted Orsina with Lord Huginn... do you?"

"Has to be." The Professor seemed like she was speaking from somewhere far away.

Faustine managed a very small, very tiny, *"Shit."* before she realized something else that should have been impossible. "You're not... afraid, are you?"

That couldn't be. Professor Valerius wasn't afraid of anything.

"Of course I am," Professor Valerius said. "I'm not stupid."

It was as though she smashed a haymaker into Faustine's chest. She struggled to breathe as the world ceased making sense. "Then how do you stare down monsters and think 'I can take them?'"

"Because if I can't, people like you die horribly!"

This time, Faustine didn't flinch at the sudden volume. She just blinked, uncomprehending. "But you're the Wolf of Kaldr!" Faustine managed. "The fearless darkbeast-killer all the Volsinii hate. Why aren't you acting like the war hero you're supposed to be?"

The professor stiffened like a cat whose tail had been stepped on.

"War does not make heroes," the professor snarled. "It makes survivors, and it makes widows and orphans, but not heroes. The sooner you learn that, the sooner you'll understand why I call things as I do."

Professor Valerius shook herself like the dog they called her, and although that haunted look stayed on her face, she seemed to calm down.

"I have to get Edmund," she said. "If Drogari has turned him into an undead thrall, he'll never forgive me unless I end it."

So despite the sheer terror in her guts, the professor was... going out there anyway?

"That sounds heroic to me," Faustine said quietly.

"Then you know nothing, child." Professor Valerius suddenly smacked her forehead. "Okay, maybe I am stupid."

"What?"

"You're a child."

"No, I'm not." Faustine bristled. "I'm fifteen."

"That's a child," the professor said. "Now stay here and assist Vendrick and Mitri. If I'm not back in an hour, you'll know a garmr got me."

Faustine's jaw fell open as the woman turned to go. "*That's not funny!*" she called to the professor's retreating back.

"I wasn't trying to be!"

CHAPTER THIRTY

FROM THE FIREWOOD PORCH, Frelia retraced the most likely paths Edmund, Faustine, and Christel would have taken out of her hometown. She kept a weather eye out for footprints in the snow or flashes of magic down alleys or around corners, but Kjell was as still and silent as a grave, and the snow kept coming down.

Her teeth on edge, Frelia tightened her grip on the Sword of Hana, still sheathed at her side. Sure, it was snowing hard and sure, it was the middle of the night, but there should have been at least evidence someone lived here. Or, failing that, evidence of the fight Faustine had said she and Christel had run from.

Unless I was right about the undead thrall thing.

The thought sent a shiver down Frelia's spine. *No*, Edmund couldn't be dead. He was nice to a fault, but if he'd been baited into combat proper, he wouldn't have stopped midway through. He knew better than that, especially if he sensed undead. They were an abomination to the Church of the Triad, whether or not Edmund called himself a cleric or not.

Frelia squinted through the hazy snow for the chapel steeple, the closest thing to a landmark she'd find in the dark. Kjell wasn't that big of a town, even before the Volsinii had burned it to the ground in the Tyrant's War. Surely Edmund had to be around here somewhere?

The fight is not over so long as you breathe, her father's voice whispered in the back of her mind.

Dammit, this was why Leon had always insisted everyone take a battle buddy on patrol with them. It was too easy to get lost in your own head on mercenary missions. They weren't like war, with its large-scale battles, war songs, and generals shouting tactics. Mercenary missions were usually raids, like this, or clearing out something, fetching something. Guarding something.

A crunch of snow from a few streets over snagged her attention.

Frelia froze, from her ears to her boots. Her eye raked the snowy darkness, but still she found nothing. She couldn't have even told you which direction the noise had come from.

Vendrick may not be so paranoid after all, came a small voice in the back of her head, but she ignored it and kept moving.

There, again! A soft, crunching set of footsteps, louder now. Comfortable in its stride. It was someone who lived here, or at the very least, was used to snow like this.

Frelia moved to put her back to the nearest building, surefooted as a sled dog. A daughter of Kaldr, finally home again.

And then the footsteps rounded the corner and came to a halt at the end of the road.

The figure folded his arms across his broad chest, his lance secured against his back. There was no trace he'd been followed, but still, Frelia's hand tightened against the hilt of the Sword of Hana.

She knew that silhouette from Heit Reiði.

"There you are, you bastard," Frelia snarled, and her voice sounded almost normal as it rang out across the alley. "Where's Edmund?"

Drogari did not move.

"Oi, *zychnik,*" Frelia called. "I'm speaking to you!"

She took a careful step forward. Frelia didn't exactly want to get into vomit-range, but she wasn't spoiling for choice with ranged options, either.

Still, Drogari didn't so much as twitch.

Frelia slid the Sword of Hana from its sheath. "If you've done something to him, I will slaughter you where you stand and feed your guts to the sled dogs."

If she was right, and this wasn't a man but a draugr, then she was bluffing, here. The only way to actually kill a draugr was to cut off the head, throw it into a fire, and bury the ashes and body separately and with runesticks stuck through anything solid for good measure. Anything less would only slow them down.

"Garmr got your tongue?" Frelia taunted, and too late, her war instincts kicked in.

Drogari was a blur of motion, unmoving one moment and then a rush of fur-and-metal the next. She only just managed to catch his first strike at the tip of her blade, never mind counter or parry.

Frelia could handle a lancer, sure, but the question was always for how long. Lances had the advantage against swords, since they had the reach. Though she could mitigate that somewhat with Kjell's close-packed streets, if she could keep him moving.

Advantages go in circles and circles, as the old Silverwood Tacticsmaster used to say. It was why Frelia had detested that class.

Blood began to sing in her ears as Frelia ducked beneath Drogari's next swing and thrust forward with the Sword of Hana. It sank deep into his stomach, and Drogari let out a soft grunt. Black gunk splattered against Frelia's fur hat and began to sizzle, and she quickly swiped it off her head. She yanked out her sword and twisted, bringing it hard against his side.

Still, he said nothing.

Frelia chanced a glance up, only to find herself staring through the intricately carved bear helmet and into eyes that were glowing blue, and somehow familiar.

"Skitr." She cursed, disengaged, and struck again.

Drogari caught her sword this time on the haft of his lance, and, dammit, Frelia needed to push him back onto a side road or something. It would limit his range of motion, if she could manage not to get herself stabbed in the meantime.

Helheim. Where was Edmund?

Despite having been stabbed through the stomach and his side ripped open, Drogari seemed no worse for wear. Thick, black gunk dribbled from both wounds, and Frelia wondered whether draugr-vomit and draugr-blood were the same.

Was this how the Volsinii had been making garmur this whole time, what he'd done to Athos at Heit Reiði?

Worry later, Frelia told herself. *Fight now.*

Snow danced all around them as Frelia pushed Drogari deeper into the bowels of her half-rebuilt hometown. She was uncomfortably reminded of Skjöldr, of its twisting turns and broken logic, but she had to keep pushing, had to keep going, had to find a way to end this and get back to safety.

What else could she do?

Drogari was fast. Frelia had likely only landed those first two hits because she'd surprised him; he caught and riposted every subsequent slash with brutal force. Frelia found herself on the defensive for the first time in years, stuck grounded in *Pflug* and unable to attack, just parry and defend.

Damn it all, did she miss the Valerius Shield! She could have parried him, caught the lance in the wood and twisted him out of position, or just shield-bashed the bastard. She was caught on the back foot, and, apparently, insulting both Drogari's mother and combat skills didn't so much as make him blink.

So really, it was no surprise when his lance finally grazed Frelia's ribs; it probably should have happened sooner.

Her side burned with bright pain, and blood began pooling across the right side of her tunic. She cursed it, and him, and this entire mess, and brought a vicious strike up from the low, fool's stance. The tip of her longsword caught Drogari's chin and snapped his head back.

It gave her an idea.

She abandoned the duel and pressed too close for weapons, scrabbling for the lip of his helmet. She yanked, a pile of Kaldiri curses pooling in the snow at her feet. He thrashed like an unbroken horse, trying to throw her, but, after a minor power struggle, the bear-helmet came free.

For a moment, all Frelia could do was stare in numb shock.

It was a face she knew almost as well as her own, even if it was deathly blue. Ink-dark hair and a well-trimmed beard streaked through with grey. Wintry blue eyes that missed nothing. Heavy brows that furrowed most often with disappointment.

She was her father's spitting image, after all.

"*No.*"

The helmet slipped from Frelia's numb fingers and crashed to the icy cobblestones, her voice echoing in the mountains beyond them.

No...

No...

No...

It echoed through the streets of her hometown, loud as her war cry.

Drogari—Grand Duke Einar Winter's Heart Valerius—stared down his only daughter without a single spark of recognition in his eyes.

I can't beat my Da. Panic rose in Frelia's throat, savage as the ice itself. *He's got the advantage even without the lance.* He was so much bigger, so much stronger, so much more experienced, and Frelia?

Frelia was just a child scrabbling in the dirt for her practice sword.

Drogari was falling back deeper into the alley, readying his lance for another punishing blow. The world seemed to slow as Frelia bolted for somewhere, anywhere, it-didn't-matter-where. She just needed to get out of his range.

Behind her, her father's heavy footsteps followed.

She was a child again, running through the halls of Valerius Lodge. Maybe they were playing tag with the dogs, before her mother had died and her father had grown too solemn for such things. Maybe she'd mouthed off to the wrong dignitary and her reckoning was incoming.

Frelia's bloodrune burned, snapping against her side just beneath her fresh wound. Did her father still have his bloodrune? Was that why the Unseen had somehow cut him out of the belly of a garmr and stitched him back together? Frelia had seen him go down the garmr's throat, had felt the crunch of its jaws around his chest. Still felt it some nights through her bloodrune when the world was quiet and there was no one left to hear her scream.

She felt a rush of air behind her, and dropped to the ground just in time to see her father's golden lance smash into the side of a building overhead. Frelia stumbled as she got back to her feet, nearly tangling with a ghostly chain that linked her father to his weapon.

From down the road, he growled, "*Hverfa aptr.*"

Return.

Overhead, the lance was shaking where it had stuck into the wall, and it occurred to Frelia almost too late what was happening.

She flattened herself against the side of the building just as the lance yanked itself free, the ghostly chain shortening as the weapon snapped back to her father's hand. He snatched it from the air, hands wrapping around the hilt like it had never left him.

That was new. That was deadly. Frelia felt like she might vomit, if she didn't die impaled on a paladin's lance, first.

Her side screaming in agony, Frelia sheathed the Sword of Hana and pelted into the frigid night.

CHAPTER THIRTY-ONE

TRUE TO HIS WORD, Talis waited thirty minutes and, after confirming that Frelia hadn't yet returned to the laboratory, began surgery.

It was a tedious, grueling affair that involved bone saws and multiple iterations of the Sleep spell. More than once, Vendrick found himself caught between the twin urges to throw up and to master the Regeneration rune in an evening to spare them all this gore-splattered version of medicine.

Which was impossible, of course. But Vendrick still felt as though he could fix this, somehow, if only the magic would come to heel.

But Talis was an accomplished physician as well as healer. He didn't falter as he applied surgical instruments and alchemical medications, just kept his focus on Clarissa's wounds with his sleeves rolled up to his elbows and his hands stained with blood.

When it was finally through, Vendrick bandaged the stumps of his little sister's legs with gauze stuffed with ointments, white magic, and antiseptic. At his side, Talis was pulling a final needle out of his arm and blotting the bloody beads it left behind with gauze.

"That should do it," Talis said, and it sounded so final that it hurt Vendrick's heart.

"How'd it go?" he croaked, unable to take his eyes from her small, supine form. He wanted confirmation of what his eyes told him, what his mind hoped.

An exhausted smile broke across Talis' face. Vendrick could hear it, in the man's voice. "She's stable. Needs somewhere better to sleep it off than here, though, so she can have the bed. I just changed the sheets the other day."

Good old Talis, Vendrick thought, and relief threatened to bloom across his stomach. *The misanthropic healer who'd still give up his own bed for a sick woman.* The mental gymnastics seemed staggering, but also not Vendrick's purview.

"How do you plan on getting her up the stairs?" Vendrick asked.

Talis' face pinched as he remembered that both of them were academics by trade and preference. "Why don't you go see if your Kaldiri caricature is back?"

Vendrick's relief soured. "Talis, you will be civil."

"I am," Talis said, indignantly.

Vendrick sighed and, unwilling to get into the argument right now, headed for the stairs. He took them two at a time, jittery with anxiety and Saints-knew-what-else.

The parlor was almost unrecognizable, its windows boarded up and furniture barricaded against the door and low windows. In less than an hour, it had gone from a cozy lounge to siege-worthy. (Or, well, as siege-worthy as a place like this was going to get.)

Small wonder Talis thought the Kaldiri savage.

Vendrick shook the thought from his mind. "Faustine," he called to the girl, "what are you doing awake still?"

Faustine didn't turn from where she'd posted up near an exposed slit of window. "I can't sleep," she admitted. "How's your sister?"

"Stable and out of surgery," Vendrick said, automatically. "Talis wants her to rest somewhere besides a lab table, though. Has Frelia returned?"

"Not yet," Faustine said. "Although she said if she wasn't back in an hour, a darkbeast got her."

Vendrick froze. "How long has she been out there?"

Faustine finally tore her eyes away from the window. She looked as haggard as Vendrick felt. "I mean, not much longer than an hour, but..." She trailed off, probably at the look on Vendrick's face.

It was strange, having this conversation with a student. Vendrick almost never had the chance to speak to any of them, one on one, and certainly not this informally. The close, once-cheery parlor felt almost oppressive now, the weight of wood and Hazel's décor tunneling his vision.

Or, no, that was probably the oncoming panic attack.

Vendrick tried to breathe evenly. "Did she say anything else?"

His voice was so smooth you'd never even know he wanted to crawl out of his skin.

"Not really," Faustine said. "Unless you count not thinking Christel important enough to go look for."

It was out of his mouth before Vendrick had the presence of mind to stop it. "The Unseen won't hurt Christel; they need their bloodrune."

Faustine's face twisted—"That's what Professor Valerius said, too."—and then she turned back to the window, scrubbing at her eyes.

The part of Vendrick that had a knee-jerk reaction to crying wanted to ask what was wrong, was she injured or ill. The part of him that had just watched an old friend saw off his sister's broken legs knew better.

His instinct was to turn her away from the window, to shield her from the darkness beyond. He was the dark one, made for the dirty work that came along with running an empire.

But what would be the point? What was seen could not be unseen any more than what was done could be undone.

"That was very brave, by the way," Vendrick said, quietly. "What you did in the forest."

Faustine didn't look at him. "Don't you mean stupid?"

"Well," he admitted, "perhaps a bit of both, but they go hand-in-hand."

He suddenly understood, viscerally, why the Kaldiri needed a contradictory word like *dorchya*.

"So, well done," he added. "Let's hope you never have to do it again."

It was a foolish hope, and he knew it even as he said it, but there was something else tugging at Vendrick, now.

He was the darkness that lived in the edges of the Imperium. And Frelia was the bright edge of a swung blade, the moment before it plunged into your heart.

But Faustine?

Faustine was neither.

Faustine was some third thing, not yet fully actualized. She could still live most of her life in peace, if her elders could only make it so. And if they could not, she could still defend herself and others with the wisdom passed on to her.

Faustine, Vendrick realized in that moment, was the third way.

"I dunno, Headmaster. Given the way my family works, I doubt that yarn-ball thing is the worst monster we'll see." Faustine flinched as she said it and Vendrick, ever wary, caught it. "I don't... well, no, actually, never mind."

"'You don't' what?" Vendrick asked, not unkindly.

For a long moment, silence fell across the room.

"I don't know why I'm so upset," Faustine finally said, scrubbing at her eyes. "Not about the people my sister killed—I know why that's upsetting—but... that she did it at all."

At once, Vendrick understood.

"For the same reason," he said, not really knowing why, "every time I'm forced to interact with my mother, some small part of me thinks, 'perhaps this time will be different.'"

For a few seconds, Faustine remained quiet.

"It's never different," she eventually said. "Is it?"

"No," Vendrick confirmed around a lump in his throat. "Never."

They both glanced at the sliver of exposed windowpane, then, and Vendrick flinched at the memory of Huginn's black wings blotting out the snowy sky.

He knew it was a stupid idea, and he knew she would have a better time surviving out there than he would, and, hell, he knew she'd probably call him a *dorchya* for trying.

But Vendrick would not—could not—let another piece of his heart crack today.

"I need you to stay here and assist Mitri, Faustine," Vendrick said. "Do what he asks. Help him keep Clarissa stable."

"Why?" Faustine's brow furrowed. "Where will you be?"

Vendrick shut his eyes and drew in a deep breath. "Finding Frelia."

***

Saints, Vendrick hated snow. A son of Ascalon was not designed to live much further north than Silverwood, and even then, Vendrick mostly tolerated the winters there by staying indoors. Still, he hadn't trekked all the way here from Heit Reiði without learning a thing or two from Frelia.

So while he hated the silent, icy hellscape he found himself in, Vendrick knew how to manage it. Where to step, how to navigate in the heavy snowdrifts. He was hardly the tracker Frelia was, but Vendrick could follow her familiar footprints well enough.

He was so focused on that, however, that he nearly walked headlong into Huginn's smoldering corpse.

The fire-knots had burned out at some point, leaving behind a singed, gore-stained carcass. For a long, frozen moment, Vendrick just stared at the ruins of the second dead legendary figure in almost as many months.

It was hard to say he felt bad about it, exactly. His mother had been the religious one in the family. She would have shook with fury at the implications of downing not one—but two—of the Triad Goddesses' divine beasts. His father had been the cold, phlegmatic one. He likely would only have cared because it was Ironfang orchestrating the resurrections.

Still, Vendrick couldn't help but wonder—"Were you always a monster? Or did Ironfang make you that way?"

Lord Huginn was no longer chirruping. It was no longer telling riddles or rending the sky with those terrible, black wings. It had simply burned like any other creature, feathers curled in from the dense heat of the fire-knot rune, organic tissue charred.

Before long, this place would smell like a charnel house, if other darkbeasts didn't find Lord Huginn's corpse first.

Focus. Vendrick needed to focus.

Pausing in place, he surveyed the town. No one was peeking around boarded-up windows to see what was going on out in the street. No one was running up the road and demanding Vendrick's head for murdering a divine beast, either. No darkbeasts came snarling through nearby alleys or buildings to congregate around their dead Huntmaster. Hell, Vendrick couldn't even hear distant sounds of shouting somewhere towards the horizon, and he had no doubt that if Frelia had encountered Blightsen, there would have been.

No. The world was silent, and it was deeply wrong.

He kept moving, his path drawing him closer to the half-burned corpse. The stench was worse, up close. Not even the bitter, blue cold spared him the odor of decaying sewage, and some small, tired voice in the back of Vendrick's mind told him he deserved it.

And he probably did, but still. He was no longer looking for that fairy-tale third way. There was no space between right and prudent, anymore, no place for panicked inaction.

"Rest well, I suppose," Vendrick told the corpse. "And say hello to Octavia for me, would you?"

He paused just long enough to summon a Singularity pellet, and then set off down the boulevard, trailing Frelia's footsteps again. The magic zipped around the back of his head like an off-color halo, but in his bones, Vendrick knew it was for show.

There was nothing left in this town to kill with it.

Orsina della Luciana had burned Kjell near the ending of the Grimsdalr Rebellion. It had been a last-ditch effort to try to provoke Frelia and Cillian Grimsdalr into leaving their strongholds in his territory. To get them down to the mainland where Ironfang's armies would slaughter them without having to cross the Ivory Channel.

It hadn't worked, but Vendrick could only figure that was because Cillian had been holding Frelia back by the scruff of her neck.

Frelia.

Dammit, he needed to find her, to set something right for once. There was no third way between 'blizzards and monsters' and 'possibly making it out of here alive,' no matter how much he'd wanted there to be. She was right and always had been—garmur didn't care whether you wanted to fight them, or not.

He would find and secure the other wayward piece of his heart, even if it fucking killed him.

CHAPTER THIRTY-TWO

FRELIA'S BOOTS POUNDED ON the gritted cobblestones, lungs heaving as she tore through the streets of Kjell, her father's draugr on her heels. She needed angles, turns; a lack of straight lines would make it more difficult to throw the lance, to drag her back by the metaphorical scruff of her neck and literal impalement.

She glanced over her shoulder after that last turn, and found her father gearing up to throw. The lance whizzed past her again, and Frelia barely managed to get out of the way this time. The lance struck another wall, and Frelia realized it was nearly as tall as she was before her father yanked it back again.

Merciful Twilight, that's almost as fast as the Blink Rune!

Which, actually, gave her an idea.

She forced herself to run faster, and found herself on the road into the mountains. It was the same one she'd traveled as a girl to get to Grimsdalr Territory, or Silverwood, or Skjöldr itself. There would be a plain at the top, wide and open, and if Frelia's father were still half the paladin he'd been in life, he wouldn't be able to resist.

She burst sideways through the underbrush, almost colliding with an old tree and wasting precious time stepping around its gnarled roots. A moment later, her father's footsteps sounded from down the hillside, and Frelia pulled herself around the heavy trunk without stopping to think.

Footsteps pounded in her ears as she sprinted up the hill and headed for the place she'd sworn she'd never go back to, and Frelia didn't know whether they were hers or not. She didn't stop to check as she vaulted a snowbank and skidded on the ice.

It was around then that her bloodrune began to sing, somewhere deep in her gut. It sang of her ancestors buried in these forests, of the warriors who had died in these foothills, of the ice and snow that had molded the entire Valerius Clan into what it had been and would be until its dying breath.

And Frelia was as helpless as a misbehaving child to resist the pull of her blood towards home.

It had once been a proud manor of stone and heavy timber perched atop a hill, its roofs peaked to run off the snow and its approach swept and shoveled at all hours. But as she trotted through the brittle, knee-high snow, all that remained were a handful of ashen cross-beams and piles of stone.

The floor plan was wide open.

Frelia pushed through the deconstructed threshold, putting her back to a pile of rubble that had probably once been a nearby wall. Across the way, it looked like the mantle had survived, albeit without most of the chimney. And there, etched into the flagstones beneath her feet, was the Valerius Bloodrune. Whatever precious metals once inlaid there had long since been scavenged, but the claw-like outline remained, a ghostly outline in the snow.

Just like her, and just like him.

Saints, there would have been life here, once. A crackling fire, friends and family coming and going, children running through the halls, shrieking with laughter.

He emerged like a specter from the mists of Helheim, pushing through the ruined doorway and dragging thick lines in the snow behind him. He huffed, eyes raking the darkness, and Frelia tensed. She would have one shot at this.

Their eyes met—whiskey amber and wintery blue—and that was all the warning she got.

Frelia flattened herself against the rubble behind her. But apparently, her father had learned that trick; the lance grazed her stomach as it blew past her and smashed uselessly into the pile of rubble at her back.

Frelia felt blood drip to the ground as she wrapped her hands firmly around the lance hilt. The wound in her gut burned with hellfire to match the one at her side, but Frelia felt that pain from somewhere far away, as though someone else had been injured.

"Hverfa aptr!"

The lance nearly wrenched her arms out of their sockets as it hastened to obey its master. Frelia fought gravity's heavy hand as she got her feet under her and wrapped her legs around the lance. She was parallel with the haft now, clinging to it as the ghostly chain whipped back towards Einar at a speed almost as fast as the Grimsdalr Blink.

She was only granted a half-second of surprise in her father's blue eyes before her boots collided with his chest.

They toppled to the deserted ground, Einar struggling for breath as Frelia dug all her weight into his ribs. Her knees felt like they'd shattered on impact, and it was agony to move on them, to dig them into his sides and right herself. They struggled for control of the lance, her father's strength and bulk offset by his adult daughter sitting on his ribs.

Frelia finally wrested the damned thing free of her father's iron grip, and smashed the hilt up under his chin. She pressed down on the joint up near the lance-head and down by the ferrule, leaning all her weight onto it. Einar thrashed and struggled, kicking at her and sinking fists into the open wounds in her stomach and at her side. He snarled in

Kaldiri—scrambled, gibberish curses that made no sense and carried no weight of recognition.

Frelia barely felt any of it. Her father was gone, really gone, if he wasn't shouting *Frelia Helm's Grace Valerius, you will cease this shit this instant!*

She pressed harder into the lance, so hard her arms shook as she pinned him to the ground. Her breathing was ragged and heavy, while her bloodrune continued to burn like someone had drawn it with a white-hot fire poker.

Frelia was always supposed to hold out as long as she could, and then meet up with everyone else when she'd taken care of the biggest threat. Vanguard, then rearguard, always.

But a strange sort of inevitability had settled over Frelia as she stared down her father's face but saw no acknowledgement in his eyes.

She couldn't win against him; she never had. And this draugr was only wearing his face. It didn't care if it gutted her, if she bled. She would die here, bleeding and alone in what was left of her childhood home, but at least she could spare Vendrick, and Clarissa, and Faustine the horror of this fight.

That's what the Valerius were for, wasn't it? The attack dogs of Kaldr, the guardians, the first downed. Maybe she was meant to die here, amongst her ghosts and the people she'd failed to save.

She shut her eye and, unbidden, thought of Vendrick. Of his bright green eyes and sharp-ass cheekbones and smile that twisted her insides into knots. Their argument seemed so stupid, now—of course he wouldn't want her to land in this exact scenario—but there was nothing she could do about that. She'd warned him, hadn't she?

She was hell to love, and it killed people.

It had killed her father, still fighting her hold on his lance. If he hadn't handed her the family shield and fussed over her, and instead worried about his own damn hide, he wouldn't have gotten eaten at the fucking siege of Heit Reiði. And then maybe the Kaldiri wouldn't have lost Skjöldr, and maybe Hägen and Cillian might still live.

Maybe Cillian wouldn't have dragged her across the battlefield at Spirits' Fen before going to surrender to Princess Octavia and Ironfang by himself, if he hadn't loved her. Maybe Hägen wouldn't have stubbornly insisted on staying in Castle Skjöldr as its last defense, if he didn't love his people.

Maybe—

"Frelia, move!"

All around her, ghostly hands rose from the ground like mist. They pressed into Einar's arms and legs, loaned their impossible weight onto the lance. One nudged Frelia away from her father's chest, taking her place weighing down his fetid breath. Two more followed, gently nudging Frelia until she was on her feet, staring down at a pile of ghostly body parts weighing down a draugr.

The relief in hearing that voice, though, was like the thinnest, crackling ice of late spring.

In the empty threshold, Vendrick cut the rune he'd been casting and began drawing up the one for fire. But no, *no,* that wouldn't work. It would take Frelia too long to cut off Drogari's head with a blade, and there was no way she'd hold him down a second time if Vendrick's magic failed.

"Need a stick!" Frelia said, forcing herself to move and start looking for one.

Vendrick's eyes bore into her back. "A stick?" he called back, incredulous.

"Runestick," Frelia managed, eye wide as she cast her gaze about. "It'll hold."

No, a crossbeam wouldn't do. No, she'd waste too much time hacking at a tree branch. No, that fallen bough was too thin. Dammit, dammit, *dammit!*

Something cracked over near Vendrick, and Frelia looked over just in time to see him ripping a broken shard of the wooden threshold free. Vendrick held it up, a question in his eyes.

"*Ja,*" Frelia breathed, taking one step forward. "That will—"

With a roar, Drogari dragged himself free of Vendrick's summons. Shit, the break in his concentration must have weakened the magic. The draugr heaved himself upright, patting around for his lance as he did.

Instinctively, Frelia shot forward, drawing the Sword of Hana in the same motion she brought it up to parry. It met the ghostly lance with a bone-jarring metallic clatter, and Frelia glared up at the man who had taught her to swing a sword.

"Vendrick!" she called, her voice breaking. "Start carving!"

"Carving what?" he shouted back.

Fuck, that was right, he wouldn't know. Vendrick hadn't been raised in the snows and brought up knowing how to ward his dead.

"E-i," Frelia called back, spelling it out even as she moved to cut and parry again, "n-a-r."

She prayed he was listening, prayed he was doing what she asked.

"V-a-l—"

She cut herself off as the lance butt smacked into her wounded stomach, as the world heaved around her and Frelia struggled to disengage and drag her feet through the heavy snow.

"I've got it," Vendrick shouted back. "What's the rest of the ward?"

It wasn't a ward so much as a prayer. She wished she could give Vendrick the Kaldiri, but there was no way he could spell it. Frelia spat it out as her father pulled back to throw, and she shoved herself forward to keep him from taking aim at the mage behind her.

"Keep well," she managed, "until we meet again."

Silence fell across the ruins as Frelia and her father exchanged blows again, and Saints, this was worse than the garmr, worse than getting swallowed by Huginn, worse than whatever sacrilege Mitri had done.

This was Helheim, fierce and cold.

"Fall back, Frelia!"

She did, keeping her guard high and eyes locked on the draugr. Her father followed for the first few paces but quickly realized the opening she was giving him. The lines of his huge shoulders were taut as he drew back to throw.

"Vendrick...?" Frelia said.

He didn't so much respond as hold the hasty runestick out in front of her face.

Frelia snatched at it, dropping the Sword of Hana and forcing herself into a run. She jerked to the side, hoping to throw off her da's aim and praying Vendrick was doing the same, even as she brough up the runestick to middle guard as though it were a blade.

The snow fell around her still, crystalline and uncaring.

The darkness was thick and profound, Lady Midnight's time surely approaching if not already arrived.

The wind bit into her still, bone-deep and howling as if in tears.

But Frelia held winter in her bones the way a canvas held oil paint. She was no stranger to garmur and their horrors, to the undead and their masters, to the wrath of a blizzard and the demands of her family line.

She drove the runestick towards the draugr's heart with everything left in her, and the power sleeping in her blood erupted.

Her bloodrune seared into her side as if to cauterize the wound there—a sharp, stinging arcane light that burst like a dying star. The runestick was thrust into her father's chest like a real weapon, tearing into bone and rotted muscle. Her da buckled under the brutal force, and they tumbled to the ground in a heap of limbs and black hair.

Frelia's arms juddered as the runestick struck solid ground, and the draugr grew as still as the corpse it should have been.

Her vision wavered, the stars overhead going hazy through the falling snow. Her wounds were starting to claw at her now, as though every ounce of frigid fury had deserted her in the wake of the fight.

There were hands on her shoulders, long-fingered and familiar. "Come on," said a voice like shadowed silk near her ear. "We need to go."

And, heart breaking and sides heaving, Frelia ran.

She ran through the broken threshold, did not stop as more of Vendrick's summons held the runestick firm in Drogari's chest.

She ran through blood-soaked snow, past the desiccated remains of her history and family. Past the tree line and into the forest, away from her home as it lay buried in ghosts, and ice, and blood.

She ran.

She ran.

She *ran* from the past, left it breathless and struggling on the frozen ground, and did not look back, for fear that it still hounded her.

CHAPTER THIRTY-THREE

FRELIA'S LUNGS BURNED ALMOST as much as her side, and while she knew, somewhere, that the footsteps tailing her were Vendrick's, she felt the prey-driven urge to go to ground.

Her name, behind her on the wind. "*Frelia!*"

She kept running, skittering sideways at a half-fallen tree and recalibrating. He was nearly on her, now. And while Vendrick had no prayer of holding her if she really wanted to run, she needed him safe too.

"Frelia." His voice in her ear, low and demanding as his arm caught her around the waist. "Love, you're leaving a trail of blood."

She froze and, for a moment, just stood there, her back pressed against Vendrick's chest. The anxious rhythm of her breathing tried and failed to match pace with Vendrick's steadily lowering heartbeat.

"*Skitr,*" Frelia managed, hoarsely, coming a little more back to herself.

It was with Vendrick's arm fixed around her that Frelia finally stopped moving long enough to check their surroundings.

The trees were thinner, here, and snow was piled in high drifts of irregular lumps. Lines of sticks like skeletal hands protruded from small hillocks, while, here and there, short, rocky outcroppings poked through the snow. It wasn't until she spotted a stack of stones that the snow hadn't yet fully swamped that realization swallowed her whole.

Burial mounds.

She was standing on the bones of her dead.

"Frelia, I need to get a look at your injuries." Vendrick's voice was soothing, but urgent—worried. "Do you know a place to hole up around here, or do I need to make one?"

Frelia's jaw moved. She breathed. The words were on the tip of her tongue, pressing against the barrier of her teeth, but she couldn't get them out. She was supposed to be moving on, wasn't she?

How can you move on when the dead keep trying to claw you back?

"My love, we aren't safe standing here," Vendrick said, his voice as soft as the falling snow. "We need to move, but I need your help to navigate these woods."

She could feel herself start to hyperventilate, shallow breaths echoing in the empty forest. Could feel her heartbeat pounding in her throat and the desperate need to move, to fight, to do something. Could still hear those heavy footsteps chasing her in Kjell, in Valerius Lodge, in her memories.

Her bloodrune pulsed so hard she gasped at the pain, screwing her eye shut and trying to breathe evenly. But every breath was a struggle, a sharp, wrenching pain in her ribs.

"Easy, now." Vendrick's voice filtered from somewhere overhead as he squeezed her tightly. "I've got you."

For a brief moment, the world stilled. The pain receded, slowly and with claws still dug in. It was enough to breathe. Enough to work herself free of Vendrick's arms, brace against the wind and scrub the weakness from her eye.

She glanced around, trying to pick out landmarks or gravestones and dammit, she had no idea where in the barrows she was in all this whiteness. "Do you see the north star?" she asked.

Those brilliant, acid green eyes shot upward, and a moment later, Vendrick pointed skyward and said, "There."

Frelia followed his line of sight towards the glittering diamond she had always called Hrafn and he had always called Aurelia. Once marked, it was a simple matter to follow the star towards the shadow of the Dragon, the tallest mountain of the Thundering Peaks.

Frelia grew more aware of her bleeding side with every step, the pain filtering back to her as though a veil had been lifted. She cursed with every oath she knew, in both languages, and even a few in Te Kuo that she'd picked up from Leon at some point.

"Haven't heard that one in a while," Vendrick said lightly, likely to distract from the arm he was sliding around her shoulders to keep her upright. "I forget, is that the one that's supposedly laying a curse on every ancestor you've ever had, or just the male ones?"

"It's the one calling your mum's family raven-lickers," Frelia muttered. "I think."

She pulled them up short at yet another hillock with no defining characteristics in the snow. But Frelia checked the sky again and, no, this was right. Provided they could actually get in.

"Volsinii don't get weird about dead bodies, right?" she asked, even though she was pretty sure she knew the answer. "Just living ones?"

Vendrick's brow furrowed. She could hear it in his voice. "I beg pardon?"

Frelia patted around the hillside at the rough level of her waist until her bloody glove found the long-lined protrusion she was looking for.

"It's tradition," she said, a little distantly, as she began brushing snow off the side of the hill, "to go sleep beside your ancestors before you march to war. It's supposed to teach them your soul-scent, so they can find you if you get lost on the way to Solivallr."

With a tumbled deluge of snow, a stone door appeared out of the hillside.

"My da and Diarmuid did it, before the Winter War." Frelia slowly wrapped both hands around the enormous iron handle, ignoring how everything in her protested the motion. "He and I did, before the Tyrant's. We..."

She trailed off as Vendrick's hand curled around the handle, just above hers.

"Understood," he said softly, and they wrenched open the heavy door together.

The instant they crossed the threshold into the imperfect silence of the barrow, the temperature jumped a good twenty degrees. Already, Frelia could feel the exposed skin of her face relaxing, her fingers aching just that much less in her gloves.

She moved to close the door, only for Vendrick to catch her arm. "Hold a moment, please."

Violet, arcane light lit the room as Vendrick began to cast. Shadows danced across the inner crypt, illuminating the long, bunkbed like rows of coffins and burial shrouds. More than half of the spaces were empty; the reigning Duke or Duchess Valerius had always been buried in a separate barrow with their immediate family.

This barrow, nestled in the foot of the mountains underneath the north star, was for the bits of the family who hadn't married, or died young, or been found years upon years after a war and needed somewhere to be laid to rest properly. Some were even family friends or faithful servants with no barrows of their own but would not be allowed to languish in death. The runesticks atop the burial mound were more general than the one she'd told Vendrick to carve for her da, their warding wishes wide and sweeping. The insides of this place went deep into the mountain; she and Vendrick had barely scratched the surface of the antechamber.

Her Aunt Brenn was down there, somewhere. The swordmaster she'd learned from as a little girl, too. Many a Valerius seneschal, Captain of the House Knights, or midwife. Ancestors' siblings who had died too young to become aunts, uncles, fathers, or mothers.

"Come here." Dark Fire erupted in Vendrick's hand, bringing very little light with it, but blessed warmth. "Let me get a look at your side."

"Hang on," Frelia said, "there should be a brazier in here, somewhere. They all have one."

It took some time to find it, in the clinging dark, but Frelia eventually stumbled over the shallow bowl they'd used to make fire, that night she and her da had slept here. Vendrick's Dark Fire erupted in the ashes, growing faintly brighter as the fire began to burn true. Only after Vendrick had cased the barrow and cast a few other things did he finally settle down enough to crack open his spellbook and demand to see her wounds.

Frelia allowed herself to be fussed over and, although she'd never say so, was relieved to have the pain recede and dull, even if Vendrick's magic felt nearly as cold as the wind outside. Slowly, they thawed out together, risked poking their heads out of the barrow to find some sticks to burn. When all the housekeeping was as settled as it could be, Vendrick pulled the door to the barrow shut and sealed them into their macabre little pocket of warm darkness.

It wasn't until he had his back against one of the support pillars, Frelia's wounds patched and she herself in his lap, that the vice in Frelia's chest truly loosened.

She could just sit here pressed against Vendrick's chest forever, right? Listen to his breathing, make hers match it? Listen to his heart, and thank the Goddesses it was still beating?

Then a fresh wave of pain radiated from her side, and it occurred to Frelia that maybe it was the blood archives bothering her. All those thousands of years of Valerius history and trauma, burned into her side like a brand. Keening the loss of their kings and families, from just beneath her feet.

Or maybe it was just what she would add to those archives, one day.

"Since you're here," Frelia began, unsteadily, "I take it Mitri chopped Clarissa's legs?"

"Mmm." Vendrick's confirmation was faint. "She was through surgery and resting, when I went to find you."

They were quiet for a moment, and then Frelia finally said the thing that had been eating her the whole run to the barrows.

"My Da." It was barely more than a whisper. "That was my Da, Vendrick."

To his credit, Vendrick didn't say that was impossible. He only said, "I wondered."

Frelia's breath hitched as something thick caught in her voice. Vendrick wasn't supposed to believe her; he was supposed to argue it was logically impossible. He was supposed to push back so that she would have something to fight.

"Vendrick, I felt him die," Frelia tried.

He smoothed down her hair, seemingly uncaring of the sweat, blood, and grime still covering the both of them. Their cloaks were drying over on an empty crypt slot near the fire, to be used as blankets if either of them could manage sleep.

"I've felt the crunch of that garmr eating his bones in my bloodrune for years," Frelia added at Vendrick's silence, "like a broken arm that never set right."

"Merciful Saints…"

"But that was him." Frelia tried to breathe, but she was crying now, like the little girl she'd last been in these hills. Fantastic. "I'd know his lance style anywhere. He's a draugr, probably because of the Unseen. I don't even know how that's possible, since he, you know, *got* eaten."

She gestured uselessly at nothing.

"I can't leave him like that, Vendrick."

"Of course you can't," he agreed softly. "How does one normally become a draugr?"

"Not being buried right, or being cursed." Flashes of runesticks and Nithing poles stuck in her mind. "But there wasn't even... *enough* of him... to..."

Vendrick hushed her, gentling her rising panic with quiet strokes of her hair, and for a long moment—too long a moment—all words failed her.

"We will put things right," he murmured. "It simply won't be right this minute; neither of us is in any state to fight."

Frelia snorted, but the ghosts hadn't left her eye. "I'm not an idiot."

"I have never thought you unintelligent," Vendrick said. "You're simply Kaldiri. Your instinct is to attack problems head-on, and you do it well. But if I were the Unseen, I would be handing you more targets than you knew what to do with, to keep you occupied until I needed you."

That... would explain a lot. She had run right at Lord Muninn, at the winter ball, and even before that, in the academic quad in the early days of the semester. Helheim, if not for Vendrick actively warping her out, she likely would still be at Silverwood, buried up to her elbows in garmur until it finally killed her.

It would be wiser to choose her fights more carefully, the way Vendrick did. But still, Frelia couldn't help but ask, "Am I to fight the dead again?"

"If so," Vendrick murmured against the crown of her head, "then I'm right there with you."

It was too sweet, too soft, and didn't he know she was hell to love? Hadn't she warned him enough?

"While I was looking for you down in town, I kept thinking," Vendrick said. "You recall how Muninn made you relive terrible memories?"

At Frelia's nod, he added, "I think Huginn forces you to think your most terrible thoughts."

"Why?" Frelia grimaced and refused to let her mind wander across what awful things it might try to make Vendrick re-live. "You didn't get stuck in the same memory like I did, did you?"

"No." Vendrick suddenly found the shadows across the room fascinating. "I..." He harrumphed, and started over, his voice growing quiet. "Everything Huginn said was true, Frelia. I should have stopped you and Cillian from leaving the Battle for Skjöldr. I shouldn't have killed the Imperator and my father. I should have—"

"You did what?" Frelia's neck audibly cracked when she lifted her head to look at him.

"Ah, right." Vendrick visibly grimaced. "You don't know that story."

Frelia couldn't believe her ears. "I heard Imperator Claudius died during the Rebellion, obviously, but... that was you?"

Saints, and she'd struggled not to jump his bones before. Frelia had never been so proud of a Volsinii.

"It was." Vendrick nodded, his tongue darting out to wet his lips like it would help him tell the story. "I was at the meeting where they told us... shit, you don't know this part, either."

A knot began forming in Frelia's stomach, right beneath the wound he'd healed. "Where they told you what?"

Vendrick stared into the fire for a long moment.

"I suppose this is the right place, to exorcise some ghosts," he finally said. "And I was at the meeting where they told us that they planned to squash the Northern Rebellion with an 'experimental' darkbeast. One Ironfang would create with the Nova Bloodrune."

Frelia tried to think back down that family line. "Did he take it from Claudius?"

"No, worse." Vendrick drew in a sharp breath, and then he glanced down to meet Frelia's eye again. "He used Octavia as raw material."

Frelia's jaw fell open. "Imperator Claudius was willing to turn his own daughter into a monster?"

"Not to put too fine a point on it," Vendrick said, "but I don't think you realize how close you were to winning the Northern Rebellion."

Frelia could only stare at him in shock. "Apparently not."

"So I sat in that council room, silently, and listened to these men decide the fate of one of my dearest friends." Anger was trying to worm its way under Vendrick's porcelain mask now. "And I remember standing up, the Imperator asking if I had something to say, and then I remember Dark Fire everywhere."

He clapped a hand to the opposite shoulder. "Burned myself too, so that when I went running to the Imperial Watchers, the panic would seem genuine."

"*Skitr*," was all Frelia could think to say.

"And it worked," Vendrick said. "But then I learned this... plan of Claudius' was already in motion, not merely discussion. So I killed a fair number of the Volsinii top brass still in Ascalon, and it didn't even matter."

For years, Frelia had seen the huge, winged garmr from Spirits' Fen in her nightmares wrecking her and Cillian's house knights and painting the wetlands with blood.

"They turned her anyway," Frelia said.

It wasn't a question.

"Correct," Vendrick croaked. "Then presumably, you killed her there, and we got Ironfang on the throne instead of Octavia."

"I didn't kill her." Frelia felt, more so than saw, Vendrick's surprise as he tensed behind her. "Although now I wish I could say I did, if only to have spared her."

For the first time since they'd holed up in the barrow, Vendrick held Frelia at arm's length. He stared at her for a moment, calculations working behind his eyes. "Did Cillian Grimsdalr?"

Frelia shook her head. "Not that I know of. The winged garmr was still wrecking our knights when he dragged me to the medical tent and went to surrender."

Frelia could practically watch Vendrick's clockwork mind processing that information. How heavy must all those secrets be? At least as much as Cillian's irreverent ghost cracking jokes in her ear, surely.

"If you didn't kill that darkbeast," he said after a long moment. "and if Grimsdalr didn't... then who did?"

Frelia waited a moment, willing Vendrick to arrive at the most logical conclusion.

"Probably Ironfang," she eventually said at his silence. "I never saw the garmr go down, but I guess I always assumed it was dead since I actually woke up in our medical tents."

Vendrick's jaw dropped a little, like he remembered mid-shock that he was supposed to be stone-faced. "Don't assume that with the Unseen."

For a moment, neither of them said anything, and Vendrick's hands fell away from her person.

"And don't you know it's rude to talk about another family's dead in a barrow?" Frelia tried to joke.

He stared at her a moment longer, and then Vendrick started to laugh. He pressed a hand into his mouth to stifle the echo in the confined space, and it filled both her heart and her family's ancient barrow with confused warmth.

"My dearest apologies to the esteemed Valerius dead," Vendrick said, putting a melodramatic hand to his heart. "It shan't happen again, I assure you, my lady."

"Don't be a *dorchya,*" Frelia said.

"Rude," said Vendrick, though he smiled back at her. "You're a *dorchya.*"

Even if Vendrick couldn't pronounce the Kaldiri word quite right and probably never would, Frelia appreciated hearing it more than she could say.

"But your constancy is also part of what I love about you, so..." He reached out to tuck a wayward strand of hair behind her ear, and then left his hand there. "Maybe I'm the stupid one."

Frelia stared at him, her face overheating. "My what?"

"Constancy," Vendrick said again. "I don't know. It's like how you're Frelia Helm's Grace Valerius whether you're talking to me, your students, or the bloody Imperator."

Maybe it was just the late hour, or all the fighting, but Frelia had no idea what he meant. "As opposed to who?"

"As opposed to a version of yourself specifically crafted for that interaction," Vendrick said. "Like how Headmaster Caecillion is separate from Clarissa's Older Brother is separate from Ironfang's Spymaster is separate from Vittoro Caecillion's Son."

Frelia could not wrap her brain around that much subterfuge. She had always thought he used the mask thing as a metaphor, not something this literal. "That sounds exhausting."

"I never even thought about it until I met you." Vendrick shrugged. "It's just how things are, in Volsinii. But you..."

He tapped Frelia's nose as he took his hand back, and though she recoiled at the sudden contact, she smiled, too.

"You, love, kept cracking my masks. And I had far fewer of them, as a student, so you were the first person in a very long time to just see... me."

Frelia's brow furrowed, uncomprehending. "You were always you."

Vendrick laughed again, and this time his arms came around her waist and tugged. For a moment, Frelia and Vendrick both just held each other, evening out their breathing together in the depths of her family's graves. If she were anywhere else, she'd have called it nice.

But Frelia knew what mattered, here. Or at least, she had a good guess. It was hard to predict him, sometimes, and Frelia wasn't sure if that was a Volsinii thing, or a Vendrick thing.

Still.

She knew him. Knew what lived beneath that mask, when he felt safe enough to loosen it. That's what he'd just done, wasn't it?

"Thank you for coming to find me," Frelia said. "Even though you should know better."

"Frelia, love, we've been over this." Vendrick made an annoyed noise and looked down at her, subtle relief was breaking across his face. "Worrying is the only thing I do more naturally than breathing."

Frelia tugged at his collar. "Don't forget fuss."

The kiss was soft and tentative, half an apology and half a reminder of why it was worth having these awkward, difficult conversations in the first place. Embers smoldered in her belly, begging to be lit, and Frelia cursed the world for what felt like the millionth time.

"How could I forget fuss?" Vendrick murmured when they broke apart, his forehead pressed against hers and unwilling to let her retreat.

CHAPTER THIRTY-FOUR

VENDRICK HELD THEM THERE, his forehead pressed against hers, and tried to breathe. This was fine, right? She was fine—hale and whole and in his arms. Not to mention, he'd cast life detection and auric vigor while looking around the barrow. There was nothing here besides him, her, and a nest of her ghosts.

He knew that, but still. Apprehension was spiking in his stomach now, unwelcome and unwanted. *Your vitals are exposed,* his anxiety whispered. *Your skin and scars on display for the carving knife.*

It turned his stomach, even though his body was screaming that it wanted to feel her skin pressed against his, and properly this time. Learn her scars and know, in his bones, that she was safe, and she was his.

Mostly, he just wanted all the screaming anxiety to bloody stop. It had no business tearing at the roots of reality like this. Frelia did not want him dead any more than she wanted herself dead.

Vendrick had just lived too long amongst people who did.

She suddenly pulled back, her hand resting against his chest. "Your heart's beating like a rabbit's," Frelia said softly, dragging her thumb across his pectoral. "You okay in there?"

After all the chaos, he just wanted to hold her, wanted to know what it might feel like to set the great weight he carried down for a while, stretch his shoulders or something.

But he also wanted to never, ever, expose the soft, squishy underbelly of the Viper of Ascalon, and how in Hypogia was he supposed to reconcile that?

"Just anxious," he said, and it was even true. "I feel like we should be getting back to Talis' laboratory, but—"

"Not worth it right now," Frelia interrupted. "We'll leave when it's light, go chop my da's head off and burn it separate from his body on the way."

She sounded matter-of-fact, but Vendrick could feel the tension in her shoulders. Still, it begged the question, "Why would we do that?"

"It's the only way to reliably down a draugr for good," she said. "We'll just have to pray Faustine doesn't come looking for us in the meantime."

"I told Mitri not to let her try," Vendrick said. "For what that's worth."

"It's something," said Frelia, and she settled back against him again. "That kid's too brave for her own good."

"Too clever, too," Vendrick agreed. "Frankly, she's just like I was, at her age. Granted, I never got into as much trouble as she does..."

But that was why Faustine was a better person.

Silence fell softly over them, and Vendrick wondered if Frelia was having the same surreal notion he was. That this was the sort of conversation parents had.

Turned out she was. "Do you want children, Vendrick?"

Vendrick nearly choked. "Erm..."

"Not just, you know," Frelia continued, staring at the flames of Dark Fire that danced in the brazier, now, "feel like you're supposed to have a few to continue the family line, but actually want them?"

Vendrick's hand moved, almost without his knowledge, to rest on the bloodrune at her side. He'd never seen it before tonight and hadn't exactly had the time to study it properly with the wound bleeding just above it.

Still, the dark, tattoo-like mark was all she had inherited from her family line. All the bloodshed, the trauma, the pain. The joys, the memories, the heartsickness, too. It was everything the Unseen wanted in the world, the reason for the blood spilled and wars waged and hell wrought in the Waking World.

It been a sort of abstract, to him, until that moment, in the same way education and democracy were. Worthy goals, but not something you could reach out and touch, exactly.

But a bloodrune was ultimately something both grander and infinitely less profound. It was the same kind of thing as Frelia's black hair and amber eye, and yet it was duty, honor, family rolled into one mark on her skin.

The difference between them was, Frelia would sooner die than give that legacy up, and Vendrick couldn't comprehend a world where he cared that much for anything he'd inherited, let alone had anything precious enough to pass down.

"I don't know," he admitted after a long moment. "After the Tyrant's War, I was never in a position to seriously consider children. I suppose I always hoped Clarissa would handle the 'carrying on the family line' business; she's far better suited to it than me."

"That tracks, for you." Frelia spoke more quietly than he'd ever heard her. "I always resented the fact that it was supposed to be a mathematical certainty, but... I don't know. Having children always seemed to me like the ultimate act of hope."

Vendrick had no idea what to say to that. Oh, he could see what she meant—why bother bringing more people into a world you thought was irredeemable—but not a world where 'hope' factored into his choices, any more than he could picture one where he felt safe enough to procreate.

Shit, no wonder he'd never been able to picture himself as a father.

"And before you get ahead of yourself panicking," Frelia added, seemingly at his silence, "I refuse to bring a child into a world where they will be hunted for the power that sleeps in their blood, and where their mum will always be fighting."

She smiled at him then, with just a little mischief. "Their da, too."

Something in his heart melted, even as panic tried to blot it out. Saints, how could she plan a future so brazenly? Didn't it make her instincts scream in terror? Make the blood in her veins freeze, the bile in her stomach rise?

Make her fear that everything she wanted would only be used as ammunition against her at a later date?

"So don't worry, Vendrick." Frelia's voice was hoarse and soft, like a heavy quilt that hadn't yet been used this season. "This is all just... theoretical."

Something hot and acidic was creeping up Vendrick's throat, now. He pulled away to press a gloved fist against his lips and tried not to let his thoughts spiral out of his grasp as he stared at a crypt on the pitted wall, just over Frelia's shoulder.

Future. She was talking about a future. Their future, without the Unseen. A thing that hadn't seemed possible for a very long time. It was so hard to believe it could be true, and it hurt to hope even fractionally.

But Vendrick Caecillion, the Viper of Ascalon, the Spymaster, the jaded mage, tried anyway.

"I know you're a wolf, Frelia," he managed to get out around his hand. "Sometimes I simply wish I were, too."

"No."

She pulled herself out of his lap, spilling onto the packed earth floor and then meeting his gaze with a battlefield eye.

"No, you are a viper," she said, urgently, like it was deftly important he listen now. "*The* Viper of Ascalon. That is how you are strong. You are patient, you are keen-eyed, and you are most deadly at the exact moment you decide is best to show your teeth."

She made it sound so... virtuous. Like a snake could be something other than a slithering, deceitful creature who poisoned its prey in the dark.

"There's no shame in that."

"Shame has nothing to do with it," Vendrick said.

"Oh, yes it does," Frelia argued. "Shame runs your Imperium; it's all your lot worries about." She paused, as something else apparently occurred to her. "Shit, this goes deeper than just tonight, or the fight with Huginn or my da, doesn't it?"

Vendrick suddenly found it hard to swallow around the lump in his throat. "What do you mean?"

"You're panicking, *kjerliat,*" Frelia said, and what did that mean? "I wasn't seriously suggesting we continue my family line directly in front of my great aunt..." She paused, squinting at the crypt behind him. "...Iðuun."

"Merciful Saints, no." Vendrick half-turned to the crypt behind him. "With sincerest apologies to the honor of the esteemed Iðuun Valerius."

Frelia snorted, but she didn't let him derail the conversation. "I thought maybe you just needed to decompress, or something. Breathe easier, teach your body you're not in combat right now." She glanced back up, sharply, to meet his eye. "I didn't realize this would just make it worse."

You've been found out. Vendrick's voice failed him at the realization.

But how could she know anything of what went on in his mind? He'd never said.

"You were anxious but normal, until just now," Frelia continued. "Is it me, Vendrick? Is it children, is it how you fight?"

"No, it's not..." His fingers tightened against her knee, the nearest part of her he could reach, and he made an annoyed noise at himself.

Saints, he didn't know what to say, and that was somehow worse than everything else that had happened tonight.

Although if anyone would tell him to just be candid, it would be Frelia.

"I honestly don't know what to tell you," Vendrick eventually landed on. "Anxiety attacks don't always have a reason. Sometimes they just... are."

She studied him for another moment and then, the way she always did, went for the killing blow. "What happened to you, Vendrick? Not tonight, but, in general?"

"I became a Spymaster?" he offered, unsure of the answer she was looking for.

"To make you so anxious like this," Frelia clarified with a small, sad smile.

He couldn't answer that. Not really. It wasn't any one thing, but a culmination of a thousand smaller cuts that had forced him to seal shut all of his hollow places, never to be opened again.

But then Frelia Valerius, with her pretty amber eye and crooked smile and Goddesses-awful sense of humor, had shown back up in his life and blasted the entire structure to pieces. He had cut himself open on all the shattered bits of concrete, tried to piece them back together and dismally failed.

It hurt, to be open to the sky like this.

"I don't know," Vendrick finally managed. "I don't think anything specific did it."

"Then how could you... spymaster like this?" Frelia asked.

"The anxiety is why I'm good at it," Vendrick said, a little rueful. "I am constantly looking for chinks in the armor, exit strategies, places where things could go wrong. If I'm over-prepared for something, it just means I did my job."

Frelia nodded, at first hesitantly, and then with understanding. "So after the job," she said slowly, "how do you rest?"

"There is no after." Vendrick looked down at his gloves, at the wasteland of crisscrossing dark magic burns he knew to be just beneath them. "There is simply the next job."

Frelia's hands suddenly thumped atop both of his, and he glanced back up to find her staring at him intently, concern etched into every single line in her face.

"That's madness." Frelia was as deathly serious as he'd ever seen her. "Who taught you to think like that?"

Vendrick felt himself smile—constancy, always. "That's just life, Frelia," he said. "A series of ongoing crises that frequently overlap."

Something in her softened, then.

"It doesn't have to be," she said, and it was so quiet, Vendrick almost missed it beneath the crackling flames. "The crises will still be there in the morning, you know? And you'll still have a sword to face them, then."

"That presumes a lot," Vendrick couldn't help but argue. "Like my surviving the night or being at all capable with a sword."

"Well, I am," Frelia said, "and I'd bring down the sky for you."

Vendrick stared at her for a moment, suddenly struggling to breathe.

There was nothing to actively cut into, here; the general state of the world was not something one could swing a sword at. But it didn't stop her trying, metaphorically at least, from fighting on his behalf. From defending her *volchya*.

From putting herself between the terrors of the night and everyone she cared for.

Vendrick drew her into a hug as fierce as he dared, burying his nose in her hair and holding on so tightly his fingers ached like they had in the weather outside.

"I adore you," he mumbled.

Frelia was silent for a very long, very painful moment, even as she held him back.

"I hate Imperator Claudius, you know that?"

Vendrick tried not to feel hurt at the topic change. "I'm not surprised."

"Not just because of the Winter War," Frelia added hurriedly, "but because of every moment he stole from us."

Her hands were suddenly on his face, making him look at her, making him *see*.

"We could have had years, Vendrick." Her voice alit with none of the expected anger or malice, but a broken hollowness that echoed in Vendrick's heart, too. "Years of lazy summer afternoons and cozy winter nights right here in my own fucking territory. We could have made fun of stupid politicians and shared alchemy recipes, and gone to moot summers and annual galas, and probably could've had a handful of black-haired, green-eyed *kjerfitchken* that were way too good at magic too young, and I just..."

Her hands tightened against the sharp planes of his face, and Vendrick wondered, absently, how she didn't cut herself.

"I hate him."

Vendrick couldn't breathe. He curled his long, stained fingers around her smaller, calloused ones, but couldn't bring himself to remove her.

"I'm sorry." Frelia suddenly wasn't looking at him. "I know that's not helpful about the anxiety, I just..." She made a frustrated noise. "I feel like I could have done something sooner, if I weren't so busy killing fucking garmur instead."

He saw it, then, with sudden clarity that practically burned his retinas. The language of combat was what came most easily to her, but that wasn't all Frelia Helm's Grace Valerius was.

She was hope, too. His hope, anyway—battered, bloodied, and full of spiteful fire, but raw, and bright, and solidly, tangibly possible. As real as she was, in his arms.

"Did you really want all that," Vendrick finally got out, "with... me?"

Frelia blinked at him, confusion settling across the curves of her face. "Vendrick," she said softly, her fingers curling around his face as much as they could with his still clamped over them, "I have wanted you since I was seventeen. I just didn't know what it meant, then."

She offered a small, embarrassed smile that Vendrick had never seen before but wanted to hold in his hands and commit to memory.

"And I, you," he managed around something thick in his throat.

It took him a moment to work up the courage, but he did it.

So this time, it was he who put their lips together, he who bridged the gap between what had been and what was possible. His anxiety continued to pulse somewhere deep in his mind, but Vendrick did his best to tell it to shove off.

"We can obviously talk more later, too," Frelia added when they broke apart. "I have every confidence we'll figure things out when we're not fighting monsters for five fucking minutes."

"You may overestimate our downtime, love," Vendrick said, and Frelia laughed.

He had no idea how long they lay there in the soft, amber light, beneath their half-dried cloaks and moments stolen from a day meant to kill them. But he knew that Frelia fell asleep easily in his arms, and eventually his heart stopped pounding in his throat, and that he had no words for how much *I'd bring down the sky for you* echoed in his ears.

CHAPTER THIRTY-FIVE

FOR ONCE, FRELIA WAS the one to wake first. Trusting her instincts to know the time, she let herself bask in the warmth of Vendrick's arms for a few extra seconds before forcing herself to get up and see what the world had done in the meantime.

The light was blindingly bright, after the dying embers of a Dark Fire campfire, screaming off the snow like opera spotlights thrown in her eyes. But the snow had stopped coming down, at least, and there were no footprints that weren't hers or Vendrick's in their immediate surroundings. Once her eye adjusted, Frelia went to go find somewhere to take a piss that didn't hold any of her dead ancestors.

This deep in the woods, it was hard not to think about the hunting trips she'd taken with her da or the Grimsdalr twins. About the stories they'd told and ale they'd drunk around shoddy campfires, with a deer or elk strung up and field dressed just outside of the cozy circle of hot air.

She tried to hold that memory in her bones as she went about her business, and not the ones where her father was trying to kill her, and Thera was a giant monster, and Cillian was a blue corpse hanging from the gallows in Ascalon.

By the time she trundled back through the heavy snow to the main
barrow, Vendrick was up and stretching the undoubtedly bunched-up
muscles in his back and shoulders. She tragically didn't have the time to
admire the view.

"Morning," Frelia grunted.

Vendrick's face was a soft echo of his usual dour seriousness. "There
you are. Sleep well?"

Frelia started to say something, and then stopped as she realized, "I...
didn't have a single nightmare."

Vendrick paused in the motion of pulling his cloak over his shoulders.
"Is that uncommon?"

"*Ja,*" said Frelia. "Especially here in Kaldr."

He started to say something, and then stopped, apparently thinking
better of it. He crossed over to where Frelia lingered just inside the
threshold and gently tugged her into his arms. He held her against him
for a long moment, then stooped to kiss the crown of her hair before
letting go again.

"What about you?" Frelia felt herself turning red. "Did you actually
sleep?"

"Only as well as I ever do." Vendrick shrugged. "And actually, I had a
thought last night as I stared up at the ceiling."

"I'm sure you had many thoughts," Frelia teased. "What was this
one?"

Vendrick's spluttering laugh echoed through the barrow, and he
clamped a hand to his mouth to stifle it.

"Don't do that." Frelia tugged at his hand.

"Sorry." A blush began to creep up Vendrick's neck, just over his
collar. "I'm sure I shouldn't laugh in a burial mound."

Frelia stared at him for a moment before her still-tired brain realized
he'd misunderstood. "I meant stifle your laughter," she said. "I want to
hear it."

"Oh." Vendrick somehow turned redder, as though that were possible with skin so fair.

Frelia would never understand how easy it was to unbalance him, but she smiled anyway. She started to ask him if he was ready to haul ass back to Kjell in this snow, but her voice cut itself off as her eye fell on a familiar shape on the wall at the far end of the barrow.

She'd missed it, last night, in the wan light of the Dark Fire and relief to be alive and throbbing pain of her injuries. But Frelia would know that round shape anywhere.

It shone pale brown in the early morning sun, unpainted, and there were no arm straps, but that didn't matter. Frelia knew that its back had been reinforced with steel, and that, if it were in use, there would have been a small bloodstone inset into the shield boss, keeping eternal watch over the Valerius heir.

The urge to touch it was so strong it practically stung.

"Frelia?" Vendrick asked.

"Hang on," she murmured, her feet already carrying her down the length of the barrow.

Her bloodrune pulsed with hot pain for what felt like the thousandth time, but all Frelia could do was reach for her family shield.

It unracked smoothly from the wall, and the weight of it in her hands was strangely comforting. Like an old blanket brought back out for the spring. For a moment, she wondered what it could possibly be doing here. Surely Ironfang and his men hadn't bothered to burn her family home, only to lay this relic to rest in one of the only places it belonged?

Then Frelia turned it over and discovered there was no bloodstone, and she began to laugh.

She stared at the hole in amused disbelief, sliding her gloved fingers across the back of the shield as if to make sure she was really seeing this. Her fingers fell into the divot left for a bloodstone, and merciful Goddesses, she was really holding one of these.

"What's so funny, love?" Vendrick spoke softly from over her shoulder, but he still startled her.

Frelia held up the round shield, and it caught the light drifting in from the open door. She could see that the Liden wood wasn't unpainted, it simply never had been. There were no cracks or splinters in the wood from battles and training duels and times the stupid thing was merely dropped while in the saddle. There were no enarmes and no bloodstone, but she knew what she held.

The Valerius Shield, sort of. In her hands again after more than a decade apart.

"My family..." Frelia trailed off, not knowing where to begin. "We didn't just have one Valerius Shield. Linden shields don't last forever even with enchantments. There were several copies, but only one bloodstone. It would get passed from shield to shield, whenever one was too mangled to keep using."

She flipped the round shield over to expose its empty shield boss.

"This must be one of the duplicates."

Vendrick came around her side and looked like he wanted to lay a hand on the old wood but wasn't sure if he was allowed. "What's it doing here?"

"I don't know." Frelia stared at the too-perfect rim, imagining the notches she'd swear she would get to after just this next battle, so familiar it ached. "I had the one with the bloodstone, obviously, and that was lost at Spirits' Fen. But these would have been in the house when the Volsinii came to burn Kjell..."

Vendrick was quiet for a moment, doing that thing where he went looking for a logical solution. "Could one of your House Knights have brought it here for safekeeping before the town burned, perhaps?"

"Maybe." Frelia tried to consider that. "Someone like Knight-Captain Riis or my da's old Seneschal Stigandr would have known what this was, and where this barrow is."

It... really wasn't that far-fetched a thought, the more she considered it.

Without its bloodstone, though, any Valerius Shield was useless. Less than useless, even—an actual detriment. It would be too flimsy for use in combat, and too brittle to withstand the heavy blows it had historically saved its bearers from. There was no more use for a broken Valerius Shield in Ironfang's grand new Imperium than there was for its last rightful bearer.

But still, Frelia could not let it go. She wanted to thread her arm through the missing straps, secure its weight to her side where it belonged. She was an old hand with broken things; what was one more?

"Can you tell if there's any magic on it?" she asked.

"There's nothing," Vendrick said at once. "I would have told you if there were. I can tell it was made to hold enchantments, though."

Frelia squinted at the unfinished shield in her hands, as if it could tell her what it had witnessed since she'd last seen it in the family armory. Cautiously, she pulled her hand out of a glove and set her bare palm against the old wood. It was dry and faintly warm to the touch, just like the one she'd always carried.

She flipped it back over and studied the planes of the shield face. Her family legacy, her first and, now, only inheritance, just needed a coat of woad-blue paint.

"I could fight garmur properly, if this thing were whole," Frelia said, not really to Vendrick. "That's what it was built for. It can withstand blows both magical and mundane, and if you catch a sword on the rim, the hole will usually seal right back up once it's gone."

Frelia's fingers danced around the rim of the shield, considering. But the wind tore at her sails as her eye fell back to the shield boss.

"Except all of that would require a working bloodstone."

"Maybe Clarissa will have an idea," Vendrick said. "She's a far better enchanter than I am."

Frelia hugged the shield to her chest and tried not to hope. "You think?"

"Oh, absolutely. She'll want to make sure it can properly hold a bloodstone first, but..." he trailed off, and a small, embarrassed smile crossed his face. "But we will build a world where you can openly bear it again. I promise."

It echoed what he'd said when she'd trusted him with the Grimsdalr Blink.

Frelia stared at the wooden shield in her hands, unable to keep the mental image of her father, riding into battle against a horde of garmur without it, from her mind. Maybe if he'd just taken it with him, instead of handing it off to Frelia like an idiot, he might have survived, after all.

Then again, if he had, the bloodstone would probably have gotten eaten by a garmr along with him—and Frelia may have been, too.

"We should get going," she said, tightening her fingers around the rim of the shield for want of a way to sling it over her shoulder. "Get our packs from the pub and then see about Faustine and Mitri."

"True. We can figure out weird, possibly unstable magical artifacts later."

Frelia couldn't help it. She leaned over and kissed his cheek before setting back off towards the barrow door.

"Did you ever meet my Da?" she asked as they stepped into the bright light.

Vendrick recoiled in surprise, but he fell into step with her. "Er, he was at a lot of the same formal state functions my parents were, growing up. Minus those during the Winter War, of course. But personally? I think once." He paused. "No, twice."

"Twice?" said Frelia.

"Your father stormed into the dorms after certification exams, remember?" There was a touch of laughter in his voice now, despite everything, and it warmed the frigid mountain air. "There I was, minding my own business, coming to grab you before the black magic study session like usual, and then—merciful Saints, I was staring down a duke."

It took her a moment, but then Frelia found the mental image of a teenaged Vendrick standing awkwardly in the doorframe of her Silverwood dorm room while her da stared him down, arms folded across his broad chest as he leaned against her bookshelves.

"I'd forgotten about that." Frelia couldn't help but grin. "Didn't he say something like 'you're not one of the ones I know'?"

Vendrick winced. "I feared I might get stabbed for it."

"Nah," said Frelia, "he just always sounded vaguely disappointed."

Vendrick made a face as they retraced their own footsteps back towards Valerius Lodge. "That... explains a lot."

Frelia leaned over and nudged him, perhaps harder than she'd meant to, with her shoulder. "I don't remember a second time, though."

"That would be because you weren't there."

Frelia's brow came down hard. "When the hell did you see my Da without me around?"

"That same week," Vendrick said. "Said he got himself lost trying to find the headmaster's office and hey, aren't you Count Caecillion's boy, would you mind assisting me for a moment?"

"Pfft," said Frelia. "That *dorchya*. I bet he knew."

"Knew what?"

For such an intelligent man, Vendrick could be incredibly *dense*. It made Frelia roll her eye. "That I liked you, Vendrick. Da was irritating that way."

Vendrick stopped walking. "You did?"

"Merciful Twilight." Frelia smacked his shoulder lightly with the face of her shield. "I still can't believe Professor Terzah stuck me with you."

Vendrick snorted. "You'd think she would have known better, politically."

"Well, that," Frelia said, "but also, stop being dense. Do you have any idea how cute you were? It was distracting, honestly."

Vendrick blinked a few times like he had absolutely no idea what to say to that, and Frelia, despite everything, laughed.

It echoed, in the woods of her homeland.

"Did you just figure out Duke Einar Valerius was, in fact, the Kaldiri tactician for the Winter War?"

"I thought that was Countess Traust?" Vendrick asked, weakly.

"It was both," Frelia said. "Traust to get them into trouble, Valerius to get them out."

Vendrick's shit-eating grin was back. "I take it you didn't inherit that part?"

This time Vendrick dodged the incoming shield-bash, and the Valerius Shield whooshed past empty air.

"So, about that thought I had last night," he said. "Did you ever hold a wake for your father, Frelia?"

It took everything in her not to stop walking.

"A small one, *ja,*" she admitted after a moment. "After the fall of Skjöldr, since we didn't have time before. Cillian was..." Frelia stared at the path without seeing it. "Well, he got so drunk, I had to carry him up to bed pissing himself."

That, too, was so familiar it ached. Cillian had almost zero concept of self restraint on a good day.

"We didn't have the body, though," Frelia added, even if just to fill the silence. "I had to burn a lock of my hair, since it was all I could think of that I had from him."

"Well," said Vendrick slowly, "if you're going to be burning his head anyway—is there a reason we couldn't have one now?"

That time Frelia really did stop in the middle of the game trail. "What?"

"We can see if someone in Talis' laboratory knows how to make barrow bread," Vendrick added, "and we can burn the draugr's head."

Something in her chest was turning runny and squishy, like yogurt that had been left in the sun. Disbelief trickled into her voice. "How do you know about barrow bread?"

Vendrick shot her a look. "Do you really think I debated marrying into a Kaldiri family as a young man without doing the proper research?"

She snorted. "Alright, no. I bet you read way too much into everything."

"That is what I do." Vendrick smiled.

He paused in the middle of the path with her, then. Not quite in the past, not quite in the future. She couldn't look at him, and instead stared down at her soft, hunter's boots.

"I'm supposed to be moving forward, Vendrick," she muttered.

She felt as if she were standing on the precipice of something. As if one wrongfooted step would send her tumbling into an abyss—and him with her.

"You *are* moving forward," he finally said. "You're laying to rest the ghosts of your past, so that you can walk into the future, unburdened."

Frelia squinted up at him. "Is that from something?"

Vendrick turned faintly pink in the morning chill. "Erm, Imperator Aurelius the Ninth's *Musings on the Dreaming of the World.*"

Frelia blinked at him, uncomprehending. "Is that a book or something?"

"A very famous Volsinii poem." Vendrick laughed a little.

"Sure, because I know so many of those." Frelia rolled her eye. "And anyway, I don't have anything of my da's to burn though, so even if we burn the draugr head, it's not a wake proper..."

She trailed off and, in that instant, a thousand futures flashed before her eye, but all of them cycled around the same point. She looked down at the empty Valerius Shield, ready to be fitted with a bloodstone and sent off to war or burned to ashes in the wake of everything else she'd lost.

There would be no going back if she cast her family legacy into the fire. There would only be forward.

Vendrick's hands came down hard over hers, on the linden shield. "I don't think it's wise to burn that."

Frelia shook him off—"It's not yours to burn."—and started walking again.

"Correct, but..." Vendrick hastened to follow her, footsteps unsure in the ice. "But I would not mourn the burning of a single Caecillion family heirloom."

Frelia physically recoiled. "Really?"

He nodded, almost feverishly fast. "I would burn all my father's books, the house, the jewelry, all of it, and not miss a single thing. I've actually donated or gotten rid of most of my father's things already, to be right honest with you."

Frelia raised an eyebrow. "Okay...?"

"Point being, that's not how you feel about your father, or your family." The weight of it fell on them like an axe. "So I'd be prepared to bet money you'd regret burning Saint Hana's Shield—even a copy of it—a lot more than you'll regret keeping it."

Frelia shook as though the wind were half as biting this morning as it had been last night. "But how do I move forward standing on his bones, Vendrick?"

He didn't seem to have an answer to that, but apparently, didn't need one. They'd turned the corner and found the ruins of Valerius Lodge.

"Can you make me an astral hatchet?" Frelia asked as they ducked under the threshold. "Doing this with the Sword of Hana is going to take—"

She stopped, her mouth falling open.

Drogari's body was gone.

There was no draugr, no ichor, no evidence he'd been there at all, except a broken runestick and a mass of footprints in the snow. Frelia blinked a few times, as though that would change anything.

"*Helheim,*" Frelia swore at the same time Vendrick growled, "*Oh go hang yourself, draugr.*"

CHAPTER THIRTY-SIX

SIR MITRI HAD SAID Faustine wasn't allowed to go out in search of the professor and the Not-Headmaster last night—but he hadn't said anything about going this morning. Faustine was almost out the door, too, before she'd been spotted.

"And just where do you think you're going?"

Faustine cringed, midway through pulling on her boots. "To... go look for everyone who's missing. The snow's stopped."

She expected Sir Mitri to yell at her about sneaking out, or chastise her into submission, or anything Markus or another of the Silverwood Professors might do.

Instead, he just sighed, said, "We may as well start by asking around the pub," and went to go find his own boots.

So that was how Faustine came to be trotting down the road alongside the surly physician. The morning was rudely bright, after the past few weeks of grey cloud cover, and Sir Mitri complained bitterly about the cold, the snow, the bright sun, the *everything*. Faustine held her tongue as best she could; she knew better than to poke at an irate adult.

She tried to step lightly in the snow, but broke clean through the hard ice that had formed between layers of the powdery stuff more than once.

Sir Mitri grumbled to her about keeping up, and Faustine did her best to ignore him.

Why was he so grumpy, anyway?

They pushed through the door to the pub, and at once, the smoky warmth of a hearth fire hit Faustine, followed by the genial hubbub of people chatting comfortably. Somewhere off in a corner, someone was playing a sad-sounding song on an old fiddle that almost sounded familiar.

As her eyes adjusted from the searing daylight outside, Faustine began to make out shapes in the comparatively dim exterior. There were a handful of women everywhere from Faustine's age to her grandmother's, here. Some were mending overcoats or socks, and the others were all half-bent over tables where, normally, the pub's patrons would have sat.

Right now, though, Faustine had a bad feeling about the lumpy bundles sitting atop them.

"Pub's closed for the—oh, Mitri." The older woman standing behind the bar blinked a few times. "Didn't expect to see you here, this morning."

"Let him be, Brenna," called a woman sitting over by the fire. "He lives here, too."

Surprised, Faustine managed a soft, "I thought this town was deserted?"

The publican—Brenna—laughed, and her hand slid from the bar to find something behind it. "Because of a garmr and a couple of Bloodrune Hunters?" She made a rude, negatory noise Faustine had heard from Professor Vee, once or twice. "Nah, it'll take more than that to kill this town."

"Either of you want some coffee?" The woman at the fire asked.

"There isn't any left," someone else said. "But I can see about making another pot."

"Oh, there's no need to—" Faustine began hurriedly, but stopped when her eye fell on the table nearest the hearth fire (and, apparently, the coffee).

A woman lay on the table, unnaturally still. Her brown hair was in disarray and there was a waxen sheen to her skin. Her eyes were wide open to stare, unseeing, at the ceiling, and Faustine knew a corpse when she saw one.

She tried not to shudder.

"This your niece or something, Mitri?" the woman by the fire asked. "I don't recognize her."

"Something like that," Sir Mitri said. "She's a friend's charge."

"Volsinii," said the woman at the fireplace with the same kind of fond derision Professor Vee used. "Well, I'm Hild. Welcome to the *Samaesett*."

The Kaldiri no longer rolled as strangely across Faustine's ears as it once had, but that didn't mean she understood it any better. "The what?"

"Ehhh..." Hild made a wishy-washy motion with her hand. "Brenna, where's your granddaughter gotten off to?"

A little girl popped out from under an unoccupied table. "Here I am!"

Faustine couldn't help but smile.

"How would you explain *Samaesett* to your cousins, little one?" Hild asked.

"Oh, that's easy," the little girl said. "*Samaesett* is what you do when something bad happens. Like how sled dogs sleep in piles after hard runs, or hunters build a fire in the woods at night."

"It's a gathering," Brenna added, still working behind the bar. "Also why the pub is closed today."

Sir Mitri's eyebrow rose. "Then why are you all here?"

"*Samaesett,*" said another woman as she wrung out a dishrag, as if that explained everything.

Sir Mitri made an annoyed noise, but didn't say anything. "Well, we're looking for a few folks. Newcomers, like Faustine here."

Hild gestured broadly across the room. "You're welcome to check the bodies."

Sir Mitri made a face as the room went back to their work. The fiddler picked up that same, gloomy song again. If it weren't so terribly sad, Faustine would have guessed it was a cradlesong. It looped and lulled in that familiar kind of way.

Heart in her throat, Faustine moved towards the nearest occupied table. Surely her friends and teachers weren't here among the dead? That seemed so excruciatingly unfair.

As she approached the dead, Faustine realized, the women working weren't holding dishrags at all. They were washing lifeless faces clean of grit and grime, and clearing the blood out of old wounds. There was something businesslike but uncomfortably tender in the motions, like watching a mother help her toddler learn to clean himself.

"You're... washing them?" Faustine asked, her voice uneven.

"Of course," said Hild, like it was the most normal thing in the world. "Can't go to meet the Goddesses with dirt in your hair. We'll send her to Solivallr whole and clean."

She made it sound so normal. *Clean the house, brush the sled dogs... oh, and honor the dead.*

"Are you a mortician?" Faustine couldn't help but ask.

Hild glanced her way, and for the first time, Faustine saw clearly the bags under the woman's eyes, the hard lines in her face, the bangs that had been frizzed from one too many frustrated hands flung through them.

"No," said Hild, "we don't really have those here. We take care of our own in death, same way we always have in life."

Mercifully, there weren't a lot of bodies to sort through. When Faustine passed the last one—a child, which, also felt screamingly unfair—some of the worry in her chest loosened.

"I don't see them, Sir Mitri," Faustine said. "Do you?"

"No," he agreed, sounding a little distant.

"So who are you looking for, Volsinii?" someone asked without looking up from the body she was washing.

"Volsinii," said Brenna derisively.

Faustine tensed, waiting for the vitriol that always followed.

"She probably has a name, Ingun," Brenna added.

Stunned, it took Faustine a moment to say, "Oh, I'm Faustine."

"Well, same question, Faustine," the washerwoman—Ingun— said. "Who are you looking for?"

Sir Mitri looked expectantly at her, as if to say, *well?* And for the first time in her entire life, Faustine realized, an adult was looking to her for an answer.

"We're, um..." Faustine swallowed against the lump in her throat, and started over. "We're looking for a few people. I came into town with two of them—a professor and one of my friends, from school."

Faustine was surprised to see folks still listening to her, although by all accounts, she probably shouldn't have been. It was just so odd.

"Professor Blightsen is bald, and wears big glasses and a green coat," Faustine continued. "He's really nice, and he's a white mage. Christel is my age, um, about this tall..." She held her hand over her head at, roughly, where she had to look to speak with them. "...blond and with really blue eyes. They're a swordsman."

"Where did you lose them?" Brenna the publican asked.

"On the way out of town, yesterday," Faustine said, although it felt like much longer. "We ran into D—"

Belatedly, Faustine realized she probably shouldn't admit how much she knew about the Bloodrune Hunters, and tried to make it sound like she was just stammering.

"—D-uhh into that huge lancer that works with the Bloodrune Hunters, I think? And the professor told Christel and me to run so that he... could..." She trailed off as she realized the room had grown silent. Even the fiddler had stopped.

"They were here, yesterday afternoon," Brenna said. "The lancer, that is, along with that prissy blonde huntress."

Faustine had to hold back a shocked laugh.

"They paid up for all the Bloodrune Hunters who had been staying here and then took off with them." Brenna wiped down a bar top that was already gleaming. "I... think I saw your man, later that night. Green coat, cleric style?"

The publican caught Faustine's gaze across the crowded room and Faustine's guts buckled under the weight of the ages, there. She nodded, woodenly.

"Then he's beyond you now, *yishka*. The lancer took him, and Saints only know where they went."

Faustine's stomach twisted, but the townswomen weren't done.

"There *was*," came another voice, this one from a young woman with a quiver slung across her back, "a Bloodrune Hunter camp out in the woods. I ran into it a few times tracking reindeer. This morning, though..."

She shook her head, and Faustine couldn't help but ask, "You only found the remains of a yarn-ball darkbeast sort of thing?"

The game huntress blinked. "*Ja*, how'd you guess?"

It felt wrong, somehow, to admit to killing it in here. Too personal, too... close.

"I saw it last night, out in the woods," Faustine said, and it wasn't even a lie. "Christel and I were separated out there and I stumbled around for ages before anyone found me."

"Helheim," Hild interrupted, "are there more of those fucking things to burn?"

Sir Mitri spoke up for the first time in a while. "What do you mean, more?"

"There was the giant raven in the street earlier," Hild said. "Can't miss the damned thing."

Lord Huginn, Faustine realized, although she didn't say it. "You mean you've already started?" she asked instead.

"What do you take us for?" Brenna put her hands on her hips. "Loose sled dogs?"

Faustine couldn't help but laugh, even though it wasn't really all that funny. It was just too hard to picture these industrious women as anything approaching useless.

"This isn't the first garmur attack we've lived through," a tired-looking middle-aged woman said, "and it certainly won't be the last."

"Someone go tell Arnkel to send the young folks to the woods for... what did you call it?" Hild looked over at Faustine again. "A yarn-ball?"

Faustine shuffled, suddenly acutely aware of her Volsinii vowels and consonants. "That's what it looked like to me."

"I'll go," said a girl, springing to her feet and scattering needle and thread as she did. She couldn't have been much older than eight or ten.

"Bundle up first," said the woman she'd been sitting beside—her mother, presumably. "And Faustine, you're lucky to have escaped a darkbeast if you saw one in the woods."

It didn't sound accusatory. Mostly, it just sounded like a warning, a relief. "I know," Faustine said softly. "It scared me half to death."

"You're not likely to find your friend out in the woods at this point," the game huntress said, a touch of apology in her voice. "If they were out there all night, you're more likely to find them frozen-solid come spring."

More like, Faustine couldn't help but think, blackly, *I'll find them chained in the basement of my family home stuck with a mess of needles.*

They must have read Faustine's silence as something else, though, because Ingun the washerwoman said, "We'll still keep an eye out. Was there anyone else you were looking for? You said 'a few'."

Something was stuck in Faustine's throat, now. "Y-yes," she managed to say around it. "A grey mage man, who dresses all in black and purple, and a woman who—"

She never finished that sentence. The door, instead, banged open, and in strode two more figures.

"Ha!" said Professor Valerius, striding across the threshold like she owned the place. "Told you they'd be doing the *Samaesett*."

"Yes, dear," said the Not-Headmaster as he slammed the door shut behind him. "You're very Kaldiri."

Faustine gaped at the both of them for a moment, relief and shock building in her chest. She felt herself move before her brain gave the order, and then she had pulled her arms around the both of them in a huge, squeezing hug. Professor Valerius grunted as if in pain, but still threw her arm around Faustine's shoulders and squeezed, tightly. Not-Headmaster Caecillion awkwardly patted Faustine's opposite shoulder a few times, clearly out of his element.

"Are you okay, Professor?" Faustine managed around the lump in her throat. "And you, headmaster?"

"Call me Valerius," Professor Vee interrupted. "You've... earned it."

"Well, quit standing in the bloody door, all of you," Sir Mitri harrumphed. "It's frigid out there."

Both Profe—*Valerius*—and the Not-Headmaster laughed, rather than pointing out that the door was already shut, and then let go of Faustine.

It wasn't until Valerius pulled the hat off her head that someone said, with quiet shock, "Lady Frelia?"

Valerius' head jerked towards the noise, and her stern expression softened a little when it fell on the old woman behind the bar. "Auntie Brenna," said Valerius, her voice as warm as the fire, "I thought this might be your doing."

Brenna smiled back, showing a missing front tooth. "What good is a pub you never *Samaesett* in?"

Faustine was not the only one who snorted.

"Don't suppose—" Valerius began, only for Sir Mitri to cut her off.

"Where have you lot been?" he demanded.

"Oh, don't pretend like you care," Valerius snapped. "I don't have any patience for it this morning."

"You were supposed to be gone an hour, Vendrick," Sir Mitri said. "I could have used your help all bloody night."

The Not-Headmaster turned a deathly shade of pale. "You said you had Clarissa's situation under control before I left. Was that somehow untrue?"

Oh no, why were they arguing like this in public? "He did!" Faustine hastened to interject. "Er, does! She's sleeping so we came to look for Professor Blightsen and Christel."

"And?" Valerius asked.

Faustine shook her head. "It's... not good."

Both Valerius and the Not-Headmaster winced, but didn't get the chance to follow up, because old Auntie Brenna interrupted, "What were you saying, Lady Frelia? 'You don't suppose we' what?"

The professor suddenly seemed subdued, too. "I don't suppose any of you lot unpinned the draugr in the ruins of Valerius Lodge, did you?"

Unlike anything anyone had said all morning, at this news, the room erupted into chaos.

"No, no, no, no," Hild was muttering softly, clapping her hands to her mouth heedless of the dirt and blood on them.

"Did you say draugr?" Auntie Brenna shrieked.

Valerius sharply met her eye. "*Ja.*"

Auntie Brenna made a warding motion with her hands, as though it would be enough to keep something like Drogari from her door.

"Unless Arnkel did something?" Ingunn said, and her daughter was suddenly attached to her leg.

"I doubt it." Valerius made a face. "We shoved a runestick through his chest; nobody here would be stupid enough to undo that. Would they?"

She cast a critical eye across the room, and Faustine felt a bit like she was being put on the spot in class.

"Helheim, no," the fiddler said firmly.

"Thought not," Valerius said. "So the draugr somehow worked himself free. And if he hasn't fucked right off behind Orsina della Luciana..."

She trailed off, and Faustine's stomach clenched at the unmasked pain in the professor's face.

"...Well, Mitri, Faustine. We need to talk."

CHAPTER THIRTY-SEVEN

FRELIA MADE IT THREE steps into Mitri's laboratory before he started in on Auntie Brenna's *Samaesett* being an awkward waste of time. Her boots weren't even off when she slammed him into the wall beside the coat hooks by a fistful of his overcoat.

"Shut. Up," Frelia growled.

"Professor!" Faustine started to move as if to pry them apart, but Vendrick put out a hand to stop her.

Frelia felt acid green eyes on the back of her neck. A warning.

"You raven-licking brute," Mitri hissed. "Unhand me!"

"You steal your wife's bloodrune," she growled, "and have the audacity to complain that Brenna Grima is doing something about the hell you have brought on this town?

"Bloodrune Hunters don't just show up out of nowhere, Mitri! They are trackers. They are bloodhounds. They are looking for anyone they can use to fuel the Unseen's plans, and you are sitting poorly in their crosshairs!"

Whatever Mitri was going to say apparently died in his throat and he slumped against the wall, exhausted.

"First of all," he said hoarsely, "I didn't steal anything, least of all from Hazel. Second of all, we didn't have a choice. Hazel was already dying and... said she didn't want her bloodrune to go with her."

That, at least, Frelia could understand. The same sleepless horror crept up on her, too, whenever her mind wanted to dwell on the reality that she had no heirs. For a moment, silence fell across the cloakroom as she tried to formulate what to tell him.

"I did all of this for her, you know," Mitri suddenly burst out. "All of it. Everything. She was the one with the interest in these bloody things."

He shook the arm with the Háski rune.

"I told her we were better off leaving it in the past where it belonged, but she insisted it mattered. Gave me a lot of religious gibberish about tasks and her ancestors and—"

Realization crashed into Frelia so hard it left her breathless.

"And for Háski," she said, not really to anyone, "the Task of the Sundering: when rot threatens the body, it is by your hand it shall be struck down."

There was no Háski scion. Not really. Mitri might have the bloodrune, but he had no idea what their Sacred Task meant. Frelia knew the old tales, sure, but she didn't have the family's wisdom stretching back a thousand years.

Only Hazel had.

Mitri stared at her blankly. "How do you know that?"

"I was born to a bloodruned family." Frelia's fingers slackened on Mitri's overcoat, and he hastily put space between them, brushing invisible wrinkles from the heavy wool. "I know them all by heart."

"So then," Mitri began, an edge of caution in his tone, "do you know the bloodrunes? Can you read them?"

Frelia's brow furrowed. "Of course."

For a moment, Talis Mitri studied her the same way he would a patient. It was dissecting, exacting, and Frelia was not built to handle it today.

"Come with me," he demanded, and he didn't so much as take off his boots before shoving his way through the secondary door into the house proper.

"Hey!" Frelia snapped. When Mitri didn't stop, she glanced, a little helplessly, at Vendrick.

"Give me your sword," Vendrick said, although he sounded wary. "You should follow him, but I doubt you'll like what he tells you."

Frelia opened her mouth to argue, but Vendrick's face was set into that hard-lined spymaster mask that was at odds with the softness in his voice. "Just trust me. You wanted to know all our secrets, yes?"

Frelia grit her teeth. "Fine."

Disarmed and distinctly uncomfortable about it, Frelia chased the white-mage-that-was down the stairs into his laboratory. He bustled across the large room, sliding around tables with practiced ease while Frelia knocked her hip into the corner of one and winced.

"Oh good, there you are," Mitri was saying as he went. "I will have you know we went through hell to get these, so I don't want to hear a word about honors and pride and whatever else rattles around your head. These are the first and only thing we've ever stolen from Ironfang himself and it is worth every sacrifice."

Frelia blinked, still tracking his movements. "You stole something from Ironfang?"

"Oh, the stealing was the easy part," Mitri said. "The miracle was that Hazel was able to get them out of the Villa della Luciana without someone impaling her on the spot."

He reached the far wall, then, planting himself before an enormous wooden cabinet that Frelia had mentally mistaken for an armoire until then. Mitri paused, then, glancing over his shoulder.

"You're not armed, are you?"

Frelia refrained from mentioning that she was a war mage, and pointed to her empty sword belt.

"Capital," Mitri said, and then he threw open the doors.

A chill ran down her spine as Frelia stared down the little wooden rack of glass vials, neat and orderly like they should be in a medical laboratory.

"What are those?" Frelia croaked.

"Blood vials." Mitri tapped one, gently, with his index finger. "They're part of what we stole from Ironfang, along with some other artifacts."

As Frelia drew closer, she realized why Mitri had asked if she knew the Nine Bloodrunes. There were small, swirling shapes buried in each of the blood vials, and bile began crawling up her throat.

She saw Hägen in the jagged sunburst of the Einnaska Bloodrune. Octavia, in the weighted scales of Nova. Valente, in the bell-like outline of Domitia. Cillian and Thera, in the whirling arms of Grimsdalr. Brigitte, in the rose-like blossom of Konstantin.

Blood. All of it stolen, all of it sacred. Ripped from its rightful bearers to build monsters, if what Vendrick had found in Markus' laboratory was true. The bile in the back of her throat turned to ice.

There is no peace, the old poem went, *even in death.* The older Frelia got, the more she felt that truth in her bones.

"Artifacts?" Frelia ground out. "You're talking about human blood, you *zychnik.*"

"I am a physician," Mitri said. "Do you think I don't know the cost of human suffering?"

Frelia glared at him, feeling herself bare her teeth more so than ordering it consciously. "And what do you think bloodrunes are born from, exactly, garden parties?"

"I served in the medical tents during the Tyrants' War!" Mitri spluttered. "You have no idea the traumas I've seen. The ones I've fixed, and the ones that keep me up at night."

Frelia grit her teeth so hard, the tendons in her neck stood out. "You mean like a bunch of scattered limbs from half-eaten knights, and the stench of human blood in the air?"

Talis blanched as he seemed to remember, too late, who it was he was arguing with. What she'd done.

"You mean like people screaming for their loved ones," Frelia growled, "and silence in reply? Like Hägen desperately trying to sew up every half-dead knight he could get his hands on? Like combing battlefields for dead bodies only identifiable by a weapon or family ring?"

Silence fell across the laboratory, and Frelia struggled not to drown in her memories of the Tyrants' War.

"It was no less than you deserved," Mitri said, borderline petulantly.

Frelia didn't realize she'd snapped until she was face to face with him. "Are you seriously saying we deserved to get eaten by garmur?"

"I'm telling you that your actions have consequences," Mitri fired back.

"You Volsinii can only sip wine by the seaside because we Kaldiri are up here killing all the garmur before they've hit the border. You know that, right?" Frelia could strangle this pompous fop. "And leading that charge is what it means to have a bloodrune."

She gestured sharply to Mitri's arm, and he flinched at the motion.

"Your wife would have understood that, Free City-born or not," Frelia said. "Don't dishonor her memory."

Mitri's jaw opened and shut a few times, and then he cleared his throat and began again. "I was a boy when your people came to Maximus Territory."

Frelia's own ire fell away, just a little. Mitri could rot in Helheim for all she cared, but that wouldn't help them take down the Unseen, and if he had been in Maximus Territory when the Winter War had begun...

"Let me guess," Frelia said, much more quietly. "Reina Einnaska was leading the charge?"

Mitri nodded, a long-ago horror in his eyes.

Reina Einnaska had been Hägen's older sister, and set to inherit. She was everything an Einnaska Queen should have been: swift, decisive, merciless on the battlefield and in the council chambers. She was the power and fury that Hägen had lacked, but *he* had the compassion found wanting in Reina. Little Frelia had never been able to articulate why she'd avoided the Crown Princess at the moots and anywhere else, but Thera had said once it was because their bloodrunes clashed.

Then again, the Einnaska Bloodrune clashed with everyone's. It had been made to rule the rest. Orders given while it was active demanded obedience right out of your runed blood, if you had it. And even if you didn't, you'd still feel the pull of the Einnaska Orders, the desire to obey.

Frelia supposed it was a small mercy she'd never been Grand Duchess to that.

"What did she do?" Frelia asked, already dreading the answer.

"Told the entire Maximus garrison to drop their weapons," Mitri said, "and slaughtered them all once they did. We were left defenseless, and I, fatherless."

They stared at each other for a moment like duelists on a battlefield, circling for a weakness.

"My mum died well before the Winter War," Frelia said without really knowing why. "It's shit growing up without your parent."

"Yes, it is." Mitri rubbed at his eyes, and seemed to find something else in his chest to carry forward. "And I thought, then, that I would never see a need for such brutality as I saw in the Kaldiri that day. I became a healer because I abhor violence."

Frelia paused, and turned to look at Mitri—really look at him. "You judged us all," she said, slowly, "on Reina Einnaska? The Butcher of Eastborne?"

"How was I supposed to know the rest of you were any different? You're just as furiously blunt."

"Blunt, yes," Frelia argued. "Murderous, no."

"I know that now." The admission was pained, like it had been ripped from his chest unwillingly.

For his honesty, Frelia supposed she should at least try to meet him halfway. She gestured to the nondescript row of glass vials. "So are these why the Unseen are after you?"

Saints, it was like staring down a host of garmur all over again.

Mitri audibly swallowed against a lump in his throat. "It is."

Frelia stared at the little rack of desecration. "And you can actually work with these?"

"Yes."

"Can you make more of them from living folks?" Frelia pressed. "Like, could you make a Háski, or a Valerius, if you or I donated to the cause?"

"In theory, I could," Mitri said carefully. "But I haven't worked out the exact science, and I can't be certain that wouldn't mean the bloodrune would no longer live in your or my body."

Holy shit, the Unseen really were trying to erase the Bloodruned Families. Or, no, maybe they just wanted to kick them around to their sycophants like a mad king bestowing favors on whoever was willing to feed his delusions. Frelia struggled not to be sick all over the slate laboratory table.

"Valerius," Mitri said, quiet and urgent now, "these phylacteries are the key to unlocking the secrets the Unseen are using like a political weapon. I'm sure you find them distasteful, and I..." Mitri paused, swallowed, and then, to his credit, continued. "I'm certain I would in your place, as well. But for the greater good, you need to tolerate them."

"*Ja*, well." A tendon in Frelia's neck twitched. "Maybe I'm tired of being erased for the greater good."

She could suddenly smell blonde hair dye in the stagnant underground air, could smell her hometown burning, could see Cillian's brown eyes wide with horror as he stared her down in Muninn's illusion.

"Perhaps you should have thought of that before—" Mitri cut himself off, but it was too late.

Frelia whirled on him. "Before what, I chose the losing side?"

As if there had ever been a choice—for any of them.

He reached out and lay a hand on her arm. His grip still wasn't strong; she could have broken his fingers to free herself without much fuss. But something in his posture reeked of desperation and fear, and it stopped her cold.

"You know Vendrick is going to say we need to run," Mitri said after a moment. "Don't you?"

"*Ja,*" Frelia agreed. "No idea where he thinks we can go, though."

"I'm less worried about that part than I am about this." Mitri pointed, firmly, to the row of blood vials in his laboratory cabinet. "I know you know what lies there."

"Thousand years of family history, trauma, and duty," Frelia said, automatically.

Mitri nodded, his face suddenly grave. "So can I count on you to guard them well?"

Frelia glanced at the row of sacrilege again. Part of her desperately wanted to smash the vials into the floor and cover the mess with baking soda, but that wouldn't bring back her dead friends and missing allies and, hell, even the enemies.

"I'll do it for Hägen," she finally said. "For Octavia. For Valente. For Cillian, and Thera, and Brigitte. For Hazel." She glanced up to meet Mitri's eye and was stunned to find him crying. "Not for you."

Mitri smiled, but it was as broken hearted as his borrowed bloodrune. "Good enough for government work."

CHAPTER THIRTY-EIGHT

By the time Frelia and Mitri came stomping up the stairs from the laboratory, Faustine and one of the remaining scientists had a pot of porridge going on the potbellied stove, and Vendrick had brought Clarissa out to the kitchen. She still looked unwell, but color was coming back into her face and she looked determined to stay upright, and that was a good sign.

The woman had been disfigured by a darkbeast, undergone major surgery, and was already up, moving, and cognizant. White magic was impressive, sure, but that feat belied a constitution Vendrick took for granted in his younger sister.

Frelia wondered if he realized that.

"Good to see Talis standing," Vendrick greeted them.

"Thanks for disarming her first," Mitri told him.

Frelia rolled her eye. "I used to kick the shit out of the Grimsdalr Twins all the time. Good for working through issues."

"Please don't hurt him," Clarissa said. "I already feel like I've been headbutted off a cliff by an aurochs, and he's the only one with any real medical training."

"Bah," said Frelia. "He's lucky I'm hungry."

Bowls and spoons were passed around and, as they ate, their odd little party pieced together what had happened to everyone else overnight and, after that, for the past month. More than once, Frelia wished she could simply split herself in half or something and send her copies to defend somewhere else.

Faustine looked like something had been haunting her for weeks, and it made the part of Frelia that still wore the professor-hat deeply proud when the girl actually said it.

"Profe—er, Valerius?" Faustine said. "Lord Caecillion? Now what do we do?"

Frelia looked to Vendrick, wondering whether he wanted to break everything down, or if he wanted her to.

"After you, Frelia," he said.

Just like that, they went from sitting at a breakfast table to a war council.

"Good question," Frelia said. "Mitri, how many of your lot can fight?"

He looked taken aback, as though the question was absurd. "Maria can do some fire spells and Decius, the laboratory assistant, can probably summon ice with enough forethought."

Frelia stared at him in horror. "That's it?"

"We're scientists, Valerius," Mitri said. "Not warriors."

"And do you think the garmur care?"

Out of the corner of her eye, Frelia caught Faustine making an apologetic face, as though any of this were somehow her fault.

Dammit, so much for vanguard. "Well," Frelia muttered, looking down at her breakfast again, "we're not charging the Bloodrune Hunters' base camp, that's for damn certain."

"Frelia, dear," said Clarissa. "There's no need for that anyhow. The base camp is what did this."

She pointed to the bandaged stumps of her legs, as though anyone needed reminding. Vendrick visibly cringed, but Frelia was caught between a grimace and weary acceptance. And Saints, no wonder Vendrick kept spiraling. Frelia didn't like watching her friends get cut up and stitched back together, either.

"Hang on," Frelia said. "I thought the yarn-ball garmr is what did that."

"It was," Faustine said, a little unsteadily. "I'm pretty sure Orsina made the yarn-ball darkbeast out of the folks in her base camp."

Frelia stared at the teenager for a moment, trying to understand the kind of officer who would do that.

She gave up.

"Merciful Goddesses," Frelia muttered, "I hate the Bloodrune Hunters."

"Furthermore," Vendrick began slowly, as if gathering together the ingredients to make a complicated alchemical potion, "we have proof Blightsen has been taken by the Bloodrune Hunters, and all but visible proof that Christel has, as well. Drogari is loose somewhere, likely with Orsina della Luciana, and although they haven't yet recovered the research Talis stole, I doubt Her Grace will sit on her hands while we regroup."

Frelia made a face, unwilling to argue as the odds continued to stack poorly.

"At least Lord Huginn is dead," Clarissa said with false cheer, and then she and Vendrick exchanged a look Frelia couldn't read.

"I'm thinking it, too," Vendrick said, moodily poking at his porridge bowl with a spoon, but it was Clarissa who picked up the thread.

"We're in the same place we were before," she said. "We can't go to the Rippling Isles, can't go to Frelia's old mercenary friends, and have no idea what's going on with the black network. All of our friends are in the Imperium, and most of Frelia's are either out of reach or at Silverwood. Talis was supposed to be the safe option."

Vendrick made an annoyed noise at his bowl. "Believe me, I have been trying to come up with a bolt-hole all morning."

It fell like a dam across the room, and Frelia felt pressure spike behind her eyes.

"Couldn't we stay here?" Faustine piped up. "Now that Orsina's gotten through all of her, erm, raw materials?"

"You mean Valerius Territory," Frelia asked, "or this laboratory specifically?"

Faustine made a face. "Either, both?"

"No," said Frelia. "They know where we are, now, and there's nothing stopping your family from sending more Hunters and garmur up our way. We could run to one of the old Hunters' cabins, I guess, but they're technically public; anyone could show up at any point. They're just meant to get travelers and game hunters out of the snow."

Faustine deflated a bit, but Frelia, unfortunately, wasn't done.

"So maybe if we'd been in the territory all summer preparing for winter and went to ground up in the mountains. But as it stands, we're looking at a lot of needlessly cold, hungry nights if we try."

Clarissa sighed deeply. "She's right, Vendrick; we need somewhere to go to ground. Somewhere with thick walls where we can properly heal up, and I can build myself prosthetics, and you can figure out what's going on with the black network."

Clarissa smiled, but it was a sad, knowing sort of thing that looked out of place on her. "Somewhere like Silverwood," she added, as if to twist the knife.

Vendrick stared sullenly into his coffee. "Talis, when was the last time you saw the network, again?"

"They've been absent a while..." Mitri's eyes flicked up and over as he considered. "Last summer, I'd say?"

All eyes went to Vendrick.

"I definitely sent Orychoe and Cento last fall, and Dorso with the letter about the students," he murmured. "I wonder who sold them out."

"Likely whoever sold me out," Clarissa pointed out.

"Dammit," Frelia growled, "I hate enemies I can't punch."

"I'm starting to see why," Mitri said.

Frelia almost choked on the bite she'd just taken. The conversation paused while Faustine thumped her a few times on the back, and Frelia coughed her airway clear.

"Vendy," Clarissa said carefully, and the nickname wasn't even funny, at the moment, "it's going to have to be Mum, this time. You realize that, don't you?"

Frelia managed not to flinch, but only just. The blow was no less brutal a second time.

"Absolutely not," Vendrick growled. "Are you concussed?"

Mitri turned to Clarissa at once and held up two fingers. He moved them around her field of vision for a moment and then, apparently satisfied, he said, "She is not."

"Like I said the first time, Vendy." Clarissa waved Mitri off over Faustine's disbelieving laugh. "Mum's got the space, the funds, the embarrassment if she turns us away, and, if we get to her before Ironfang does, we have an ally."

Skjöldr did make the most sense, when Clarissa laid it out that way. It was fortified, a mercantile center, and, if Deadcut could be trusted, secured. And the Volsinii valued appearances above all else. It would be social suicide for even someone like Governor Deadcut to turn her own children away, if everyone was technically in good standing.

Though 'technically' was doing a lot of heavy lifting in that thought, and though she hated it with every fiber of her being, Frelia knew a losing battle when she saw one.

"I was going to say," Faustine managed, "they're friends, aren't they? My father and Governor Verona?"

"Yes," Clarissa admitted, with a meaningful look sent her brother's way. "But he was much closer with our father."

"I'm not saying I don't see the logic," Vendrick said. "Mum wouldn't turn us out without a damn good reason, and certainly Frelia knows the town and surrounding territories."

Frelia snorted, but there was no mirth in it.

"But that's assuming..." Vendrick trailed off, and eventually settled on, "...well, quite frankly, too much."

Silence, then, but for the quiet clinking of cutlery.

"I can't believe I'm saying this," Frelia ground out, "but—Vendrick, how likely do you think it is that we can convince Deadcut to let us stay there?"

She only just saw Mitri's jaw drop, out of the corner of her eye.

"I think he could do it," Clarissa said immediately.

"I asked your brother," Frelia said, not unkindly. She was vaguely reminded of telling Owen or Karina to shut up in class, and wondered where her Violet Owls had gotten off to, by now. If they were safe.

She hoped so.

"With everything I've been doing under the Imperator's nose?" Vendrick clarified. "Highly unlikely."

Frelia was once again struck with the reason why he kept so many secrets.

"You just need to prove the Unseen are a bigger threat than the status quo," Clarissa argued. "And you've already done that once."

She gestured to Frelia.

"I don't really count," Frelia said. "I figured it out on my own."

For what was perhaps the first time since she'd met him, Mitri looked at Frelia with something other than wary disdain. "You did?"

Frelia nodded, while Vendrick said, "She demanded to help with... oh, how did you put it... 'whatever had gotten me exiled to Silverwood'?"

"Exactly." Frelia nodded. "Though you could have told me it was Thera."

"Not then, I couldn't."

Clarissa made a face, but said, "Where is Thera, anyway?"

"I asked her to hide after she helped bring you here last night," Faustine said. "She said she'd be in the woods. We'll need to bring her with us, of course, but I don't know how to find her. She keeps finding us."

"Garmur hunt by smell," said Frelia tiredly. "It's probably that."

All of the Volsinii in the room flinched at the implication. How easily the monsters found them in their beds, how mundanely.

"Well then." Clarissa stared at her half-finished porridge. "Sounds like we don't have much reason to stay here, other than to wait around on more unwelcome guests."

"Other than my laboratory and my work?" Mitri huffed.

"Bring what you need," Vendrick told him. "You are definitely not staying here."

"Pack light," Frelia piped up. "Skjöldr is, I think, three weeks from here, when you're not stopping to resupply at every hunter's cabin on the way."

The silence that fell that time was deafening. As though, all at once, the Volsinii in the room had remembered just who was sitting there arguing about Lady Deadcut and the Winter War.

"A sled dog team could get us there easily enough," Frelia added, just to fill the silence. "They're bred for this kind of weather. You got a sled team, Mitri?"

Mitri wrinkled his nose.

"Of course not," Frelia muttered. "Vendrick, Clarissa, I don't suppose you've got several thousand gold lying around?"

"No," Vendrick admitted, "but given the way the town reacted to you in the pub earlier, I'd venture to guess you might simply be able to walk up to a kennel and ask for a team."

Frelia wrinkled her nose. "I don't like taking something for nothing."

"It's not nothing," Faustine said quietly. "You're giving them hope, for it."

Frelia couldn't help but reach over and muss the girl's hair.

"Beyond that," Vendrick said as though he, too, couldn't bring himself to shatter Faustine, "is there anything else we need to discuss?"

"I mean," said Frelia, "my shield still needs looked at and Mitri has no idea what having the Háski Bloodrune means."

"Of course he doesn't," Clarissa said briskly. "I say this with all love, Frelia dear, but the bloodruned families are a terribly secretive lot."

"And look what happens when we aren't!" Frelia gestured violently towards the front door, and her hometown beyond. "Bloodrune Hunters in our homes, Christel taken, Edmund taken, monsters slaughtering our people, garmur running amok..."

"Does Blightsen have a bloodrune?" Clarissa asked.

"No," said Frelia and Vendrick at once.

"But he was a cleric," Vendrick added. "And speaking of, I've been wondering—Lords Huginn and Muninn are Lady Daybreak and Lady Twilight's ravens, correct?"

"*Ja,*" Frelia said. "Guardians of Konstantin and Traust Territory, in legend. Why?"

"In all those stories," Vendrick said, choosing his words with even more care than he typically did, "is it ever said what they are?"

Frelia glanced between the Volsinii in the room, but they all wore the same blank expression she did, or nearabout. "What do you mean?" Frelia asked.

"You've always called them ravens," Vendrick continued, "but they're not. They're darkbeasts that look like ravens."

Frelia wanted to explode in defenses and Triad teachings and Saints only knew what else.

She wanted to, but she couldn't.

"I'm also starting to wonder." It came out so quietly she almost missed it, herself. "If Lord Muninn is a garmr, and if Lord Huginn is a garmr... why not Lord Geri? Why not Lord Freki? Why not even the Watcher himself?"

Frelia stabbed at her porridge again as a terrible, sinking feeling began to bloom in her stomach. As a girl in these mountains, it had been comforting to know that the Wolven Guardian of Valerius Territory would come if the need was dire enough.

But Freki had never showed, and Frelia had a Saints-awful feeling why. Either he had never been real—or he wasn't a friend to humanity.

"I'll be honest," Vendrick said after a moment, "I was sort of hoping you'd just call me an idiot and tell us that of course they're ravens, stop being so Volsinii."

"Not this time." Frelia tried to smile, but she couldn't manage it. "If Lady Daybreak and Lady Twilight's ravens are actually garmr... then what have I been killing this whole time?"

The idea was so awful it threatened to paint the kitchen tiles with what little breakfast Frelia had managed. *Zychnik*, they would call her, *Godkiller*. And they would be right to.

It was Clarissa who chanced an answer. "Darkbeasts are the monstrous children of Lady Midnight, right?"

"*Ja*," said Frelia. "But they're supposed to be stupid, hungry, and indifferent to suffering. I don't think Huginn or Muninn fit any of those categories—do you?"

"Not when you put it that way," Clarissa admitted. "But, what, do you think they're lesser gods or something?"

"Maybe?" Frelia shrugged, holding her free hand up in a gesture of surrender. "What else would you call it? They're too smart to be basic garmur and too monstrous to be the Goddesses, so…"

"If I might assist?" came a small voice.

All of the adults jumped at the sound of Faustine's voice.

"I don't know exactly what my father wants with the Guardian darkbeasts," Faustine admitted, "but I do know he wants all of them. He, um…" she looked reflexively over her shoulder, as though any of her siblings were there to harass her for what she was about to say. "…He was having Markus work on it. That's why he summoned Lord Muninn at Silverwood."

"Why Markus?" Clarissa wrinkled her nose. "Surely the Imperator could find someone halfway competent?"

"He's a beastminder," Faustine said. "The only one left in the family besides our father, technically."

Frelia pressed the heels of her hands into her eyes. "This is not helping the 'they were always garmur' theory."

"I agree, the evidence is damning," Vendrick said carefully. "However, I've also been wondering since I put down Lord Huginn whether he was always a darkbeast—or if something made him that way to bring him here."

"By 'something,'" Mitri asked, "do you mean Ironfang?"

Vendrick's smile was tight and tense. "Precisely."

"Ironfang doesn't have the power to twist the gods." Frelia's reaction was knee-jerk. "He definitely has the power to fuck life up for the rest of us, though. Mitri doesn't even know the Háski Sacred Task!"

In the sudden silence, Frelia realized, all eyes were on her.

"I beg pardon?" Vendrick asked.

"You're joking." Frelia's jaw nearly thumped against her collarbone. "You have to be joking. You lot swear by the Saints all the time."

"It's an expression," Vendrick defended. "I can't say I'm particularly devout, and I thought you knew that."

"'And for Valerius,'" Frelia quoted, exasperated, "'the Task of the Guardian. So long as you draw breath, the fight is yours to claim.' Cillian's was something about 'you shall be the bastion between the Waking World and the one beyond.'"

"What is that supposed to mean, exactly?" Mitri asked.

"It means I know my place in the Waking World," Frelia said. "A lot of the other Sacred Tasks have gone undone for a decade, and the Goddesses only know how fucked we are because of it. Maybe that's why the garmur have been running amok on the mainland, I don't know."

She threw up her hands at the looks she was getting.

"You're talking about this like it's... well, for lack of a more delicate word, real," Clarissa said.

Frelia blinked, and turned, very slowly, to look at Clarissa. "It is real."

"I think what Clarissa means," Vendrick said, although he had to be guessing, himself, "is that you speak of this as though there is a real, tangible task that your family is meant to be doing."

Frelia could only tilt her head like a confused dog. "There is."

"But 'being the bastion between the Waking World and the one beyond,' isn't a to-do list," Clarissa argued. "It's more of an ideal."

"Okay, yes, but also, no." Frelia harrumphed. "There's the stories that everyone knows, and then there's the tasks that you do in private. I can only tell you what my family did to uphold our Sacred Task, and I shouldn't even be doing that."

Frelia sighed. "But who's still around to cuff me on the ear?"

Giving up on breakfast, Frelia got to her feet and began to pace around the tight kitchen.

"The Valerius Task is that of the guardian," she said. "I'm meant to fight for Kaldr and her people. The fight is not over so long as I breathe."

"Right," said Vendrick, clearly still not following. "All the things that make you... well, you."

Frelia caught his eye, and she felt the sudden weight of every blow Drogari had landed. "It means," she said, "that I am literally meant to spill my blood in defense of others. Every time I am injured in battle, I am fulfilling the Valerius Sacred Task."

Something grim and terrible began to ooze into the atmosphere. Vendrick looked torn between physical pain and horrified understanding.

"So when you broke your arm last fall in Iuvenlis Quad," he said, slowly, the clockwork of his mind beginning to turn, "and when you hurt yourself fighting Muninn..."

"*Ja.*" Frelia nodded fervently, as though she could simply will them all to understand. "And when Dro—fuck, when *my da* wounded me earlier and when I bled in the Northern Rebellion and when I broke my finger fighting as a kid. Each one of them helps keep Lady Midnight in Helheim where she belongs."

Silence then, charged like the air before a thunderstorm.

"That's a heavy burden," Vendrick said, quietly.

Frelia shrugged. "What else am I supposed to do, stop?"

Vendrick seemed to consider his words more carefully than usual. "Not if you believe it's the right thing to do. I... well, I suppose I simply find it unfair that it falls to you."

"Of course it does." Frelia blinked, uncomprehending. "Ironfang gutted the Church of the Triad and the Bloodrune Hunters have been gutting the bloodruned families."

"So what happens," Faustine began, her voice small and clearly scared, "when there are no more of either?"

"The stories are clear on that," Frelia said. "The Bloodruned Saints sealed Lady Midnight into hell. And she stays there because the Sacred Tasks are what power the seal. Without the Sacred Tasks, she'd be free to destroy the Waking World. Which is somehow what your da wants, Faustine—isn't that the whole point of the Unseen?"

Clarissa's jaw fell open, and for the first time since Frelia had met her, the woman was struck speechless.

"Vendrick," she got out after a moment, "is that... possible? The seal thing, I mean."

Vendrick's fingers twitched where his hand rested on the kitchen table, as though he wanted to cast something or flip through a reference tome.

"It's not impossible," he said slowly. "If the caster set up a ritual to bind the warding runes, then there would have to be some sort of trigger. That's all a ritual is, arcanely speaking. And we know that some sort of cataclysm took place, because Frelia literally wears it on her skin."

Frelia smacked her hand to her side, where her bloodrune lay hidden beneath layers of fur and wool. "And traditionally, it took nine of these to seal Lady Midnight into Helheim, and it will take nine to keep her there."

"The Nova family have all been dead for years, though," Clarissa said.

The energy that powered Frelia's entire self faltered. "I know," she said, hoarsely. "So have the Konstantins, the Trausts, and the Einnaskas."

She didn't pause to let that sink in. Couldn't.

"So, at best, Valerius is doing her task..." Frelia began ticking families off on her fingers. "...Domitia is doing her task, and Háski was until recently. Maybe there's a Maximus somewhere doing his job, and maybe Thera can do hers in her current state. And if we're very lucky, Christel did theirs accidentally. But realistically, we're sitting at three of nine."

Frelia looked at Vendrick then, nine fingers splayed like damning evidence in a Senate trial.

"How long do you think this ritual could last like that?" she asked.

"At a third of its power?" Vendrick's eyes flicked up as he tried to think. "If nothing is actively throwing itself against the ward, it's probably going along just fine. However..."

Vendrick was suddenly on his feet, hands pressing into the kitchen table as if to keep himself steady.

"If Ironfang intends to pit himself against the ward," Vendrick said, slowly, "it would do him well to weaken it first."

With a sudden, vicious intensity, he kept speaking.

"No wonder the Unseen have been chasing bloodrunes across the Continent," Vendrick continued. "No wonder Orsina della Luciana was after Christel as well as Faustine, and likely you too, Frelia. He's trying to winnow out anyone who could stop him going after that seal."

Frelia's blood froze.

"Wait, I don't follow you," Clarissa said. "I get the bloodrunes bit, but what does Ironfang need these—what, Guardians you called them, Frelia?—for?"

"I don't follow either," Frelia said. "They're the Guardians of the Kaldiri Territories and the companions of the Goddesses, but what does he gain by summoning them here?"

"I don't know," Faustine suddenly spoke up, "But I just had a thought."

She paused as if waiting for, what, permission? Frelia could almost picture her with her hand raised.

"Go on," Vendrick said, and he sounded so much like his old, headmaster's self that it ached.

"If they're Guardians," Faustine began, "then what do they guard, professor?"

"The people of Kaldr," Frelia said, "and, presumably, the entrance to Helheim, in a more roundabout way."

"Okay, so then," Faustine began, the same way she'd structured her argumentative essays, "does my father need the Guardians themselves for something, or does he simply need them out of his way?"

No one seemed to be able to come up with a damn thing to say, but if Frelia knew Vendrick half as well as she ought to by now, those gears in his mind were skidding and trying to come up with a plan.

She could at least help get him unstuck.

"Helheim," Frelia swore, "it has to be Skjöldr. To hell with Deadcut."

"What are you on about?" Mitri asked.

Frelia reached for her spoon again, mostly because she knew food would not be nearly as easy to come by on the road. "Lord Muninn is dead," she said. "Lord Huginn is also dead. Lord Freki would have shown up here by now if he were going to; this is his home as much as it is mine. He's our Guardian, so if he's not guarding, I'd bet he's also dead—or worse."

She left unspoken by whose hand.

"So, Lord Geri is all that's left." Frelia glanced up to meet the eye of each and every person sitting in the kitchen. "And Geri the Greedy One is the Guardian of Einnaska Territory."

CHAPTER THIRTY-NINE

THEY SCATTERED, THEN, OFF to gather supplies and burn evidence and do whatever else needed to be done before abandoning ship. Vendrick went down into the laboratory itself with Mitri to collect the bloodrune vials and notes and Saints-knew-what-else, while Frelia busied herself with raiding the kitchen for provisions.

She also tried not to wince at how long everything was taking.

From the mounting pile of foodstuffs on the kitchen counter, she figured they could at least get to the next village over, with a few days' rations to spare.

"Professor?"

Frelia's head jerked up, and it took her a second to find Faustine, lingering in the doorframe on her blind side.

"Hey," Frelia said, her stomach twisting at the sight of the teenager. Their last conversation hadn't exactly ended on a good note. "What do you need?"

Faustine held up her travelling pack. "My things are packed, so... do you need any help?"

That was so like Faustine. Always so eager to prove herself worthy of others' esteem. Faustine was visibly anxious, too, uneasy and fidgeting with the strap of her traveling pack. It stung Frelia in some long-forgotten, sisterly way, but there wasn't much to be done about it.

Then again. *Ghosts can't sneak up on you, with a fire burning,* the sailors had always said.

"Eh, I'm almost done," Frelia said. "Take a seat or something."

Frelia felt eyes on her back as she continued bundling their provisions into rations, felt a weight in the air as she tried to finish up her business.

Realization struck Frelia as suddenly as cannon fire. She had lived through many a battle, and the high-strung confusion of the aftermath was normal to her. A Tuesday afternoon.

But Faustine was living through, what, her second major battle? Third? Of course she was sensitive to it. Of course she didn't know how to process it. This was a reality a child should never have to face, and yet—

"Have you heard about anything that happened at Silverwood after you left?" Faustine suddenly asked.

Frelia paused in the middle of tying up a package of potatoes. "No, we got Clarissa and then came straight here. Vendrick hasn't so much as seen a black network agent in weeks."

Faustine looked down at her boots, toying with the hem of her woolen sweater. She was avoiding Frelia's eye.

"The darkbeasts attacked us, after you left," she said, probably as loudly as she could manage, which was so quiet Frelia strained to hear her. "Just like you always said they would. Muninn's corpse flooded the whole campus with... ink."

Frelia grimaced at the memory of the Massacre at Kollavik. She knew exactly what Faustine was talking about. The exact shade of midnight that crested the horizon and blotted out the sun.

"Christel and I had been waiting for Professor Blightsen in the Chapel when Thera smelled my father out on the hillside," Faustine added.

Frelia flinched so hard that she knocked over the mug of lukewarm coffee she'd been in the process of finishing. "Then what happened?" she demanded, even as she glanced around for something to sop up the mess with.

"My father dug around Lord Muninn's pyre," Faustine said, and Frelia knew that tone of voice. Faustine was still on that hillside, still staring at the ashes of a dead garmr. "And... then he pulled Lord Huginn out of it, only he was an egg at first. And then when Christel, Siegmund, and I tried to lure the Huntmaster out to the cavalry field, it..."

She hiccupped a little sob, and began again.

"It..."

Frelia stopped searching for a cleaning rag. Faustine was shaking like the last fall leaf, and there was nothing Frelia could do to help but stand witness.

"It ate Siegmund," Faustine whispered.

For a moment, the only sound in the room was the steady *drip, drip* of Frelia's old coffee falling to the floor.

Siegmund Ossani was dead? The *lapphund* kid? The boy who had gone from 'thickset' to 'nearly grown man' in a semester? The bright spot amongst sword drills who lived to make his classmates laugh and his friends groan? The last time Frelia had seen him, he'd been lugging a stack of dead garmr meat over to the pyre and laughing with the rest of the Violet Owls.

I'll see you later, professor? he'd told her when she went to tell her students goodbye. *You'd better be back next semester; I still need to win one of our duels!*

"Goddesses rest his soul in Solivallr," Frelia finally said, and though her voice was thick, it didn't shake.

Faustine's head jerked up. "That's all you have to say?"

Frelia's brow furrowed. "Would you rather I whine at length about how bitterly unfair this is?"

"Yes! Isn't that the least we owe him?"

Frelia abandoned her search for a cleaning rag, and instead padded softly to stand at arms' length from Faustine. Too close to ignore, too far to hug or squeeze her hand.

She had no idea how to comfort the girl, except by giving her the truth and standing by her for whatever came after. It was the Kaldiri way.

Though... maybe it would be better delivered Volsinii-style.

"Every time you face a garmr," Frelia said, making an effort to stay calm and measured like Vendrick, or Magicmaster Marcellius, "that is what you risk. I tried to impress that on all of you during Garmur-Killing One-Oh-One. They are ever hungry, and they don't care who they eat."

"But we do!" Faustine shouted.

"*Ja,* we do. That's what separates us from the monsters." Frelia frowned as something else occurred to her. "Don't mistake this for a lack of grief, Faustine. He was *volchya.* My charge, my student, my responsibility. And I've failed him."

Her voice cracked on the penultimate word, and on the Kaldiri one.

"But right now, I don't have the luxury of mourning him," she added. "I have four people I need to keep alive—five, including myself—and the Wild Hunt is on our tail. So I will worry about our winter survival first, the possibility of encountering garmur second, and anything else, third."

Faustine opened her mouth to argue, but Frelia kept on.

"Don't think I've forgotten that Huginn almost ate you, Faustine. You're damned lucky we found you when we did, or you may have ended up frozen dead come morning."

Frelia winced internally at herself as tears welled up in Faustine's eyes. Dammit, Frelia sounded like her da, and that wasn't comforting at all. She needed to think like Cillian, carry herself like Clarissa.

Frelia sighed at herself and tried to recalibrate. "Look, Faustine—"

"You're the Wolf of Kaldr," Faustine interrupted. "The fearless darkbeast-killer all the Volsinii hate. I don't understand; why are we running away?"

For the first time in many years, Frelia realized she did know how to offer any kind of consolation that would matter.

"Do you know why they call me that?" she asked after a moment.

Faustine blinked. "Because you're a scary warrior from the north?"

Frelia laughed, just a little. "Sure, but there's a story."

Faustine tilted her head like a confused dog, processing this new information. "There is?"

"*Ja.*" Frelia picked up her search for a rag again. "If you want to hear it., that is."

"Of course," said Faustine, so quickly it reminded Frelia of Thera at the moot, begging the skálds for one more story.

"We were at Portus Felix," Frelia began and finally, she spotted a washrag hidden under the lip of the sink. "It was a few months after the Massacre at Kollavik, and we were starting to learn how to counter the garmur."

"How did you do it?" Faustine asked. "The Blink rune?"

"That and heavy artillery." Frelia started over towards the washrag in the sink. "The Grimsdalr Twins would set out on reconnaissance, and I would do the rest. What we couldn't handle, the cannons did."

She could still feel the rush of wind past her face, when she closed her eyes, the feeling of Cillian's solidly armored bulk at her back as he readied his warhorse to charge. The rib-breaking *boom* of firing cannons.

"Anyway, Portus Felix was unique in that it was the first major battle in Einnaska Territory. We were on edge, smarting from our losses at Fort Frostmaiden and every single one of us there would rather die than lose ground in the north."

Frelia's fingers curled around the wet dishrag, and she shut her eye.

"It didn't matter."

Faustine gasped softly, somewhere across the room, a quiet, "Oh no."

"*Ja,* thought that might jog your memory." Frelia moved towards her spilled coffee, now, and the bitter, nutty smell rose to greet her. "Titus della Luciana showed up with more garmur than we'd seen in one place yet that war."

Faustine's jaw fell open, horrified. "So what did you do?"

"Same thing we always did," Frelia said. "Cillian flung me at them, and I cut their chests open until I got a migraine."

She dropped to a crouch, her knees cracking, and began mopping up the mess on the floor.

"It was around then that we started to realize how fucked we were. Baron Konstantin was dead, and so was the Einnaska cousin who had been serving as our general. The town's governor was dead, and so were enough of our house knights to choke the streets in blood."

Frelia focused on the coffee stains and tried to push the memory of that terrible stench from her mind.

"I forget which of us realized it—me, Cillian, or Thera—but we figured out quickly that I was the highest-ranked person still alive. The Duchess Valerius."

Dammit, this was harder than Frelia had expected it to be. She found herself falling into her old Silverwood habits, trying to keep her distance from the old, worn-in grief by using it to teach.

"So here's what I was working with, by then: a handful of mages who knew fire magic, scattered around the city. No artillery with good line of sight. My own migraine. Cillian and Thera on the brink of arcane sickness from over-casting. Archers out of arrows, and demoralized knights who had been exhausted before losing half their numbers."

Faustine's face was falling with every additional detail, but Frelia kept talking.

"No reinforcements coming, and no end to the Volsinii knights and their blasted garmur no matter how many we felled." Frelia straightened up, and met Faustine's eye. "So what would you have done, in my place?"

"I'd have fought," said Faustine, like it was obvious.

Frelia shot her a look, and resisted the urge to laugh. *What a fifteen-year-old response,* Frelia thought. "Faustine, *how?*"

Faustine opened her mouth, then shut it again. Frelia could see the Violet Owl working through what she knew. The only thing that could reliably down garmur was fire, and Frelia, Cillian, and Thera were lagging. The rest of their fire-force had been scattered, to say nothing of the weather, terrain, or point in the battle. And even if they could link up with their other mages, someone was going to have to down the monsters first.

The slow realization dawned on Faustine, like a soft poison across her young face. "Did you... retreat?"

She whispered the word like it would bite.

"I did." Frelia felt bile rise in her throat. "Called for the Traust War Song, and fell back into the woods. It took hours, and we lost hundreds more."

Faustine blanched. "That's awful."

"*Ja,*" Frelia agreed, thumping the washrag back into the sink. "It was."

Faustine was quiet for a moment as Frelia wrung out the rag.

"Wait," said the teenager, "I don't follow—what does this have to do with you being called the Wolf of Kaldr?"

"Portus Felix is the battle that earned me my war name."

"But that doesn't make any sense!" Faustine burst out. "Wolves are fierce, and powerful, and territorial, and don't let go of a kill... and...!" She was stuttering, trying to make sense of it.

Frelia held up her hand, and Faustine stopped.

"Wolves are smart," Frelia said. "They are social creatures. They know their sires and dams, and teach their little ones how to hunt. They care for their pack mates even through injury and into old age. The Kaldiri word *volchya* is the catch all word for close family and friends—but it literally means wolfpack."

A smile began creeping across Frelia's face.

"Your da started calling me the Wolf of Kaldr because he thought it was ironic, I'm sure. Look at the mighty Duchess Valerius, she thinks herself a hero after losing ground in Einnaska Territory and fucking retreating."

Frelia could picture Ironfang's smug face as the news spread amongst his knights, as her new name began to unfurl. *See how they retreat and call it a glorious victory,* he would have said, laughing at the pitiful Kaldiri resistance.

Ironfang knew nothing.

"But to us Kaldiri," Frelia said, "a mother wolf is the ideal of loyalty. She is the backbone of her pack, and will sacrifice herself if it ensures her family's survival."

She met Faustine's eye, then, willing her to understand.

"But if it won't," Frelia said, very pointedly, "she will get them out, instead."

Faustine was quiet for a long moment.

"So you're not..." Faustine was staring at her hands, now, thinking hard. "...you're not the Wolf of Kaldr because you can fight..."

She looked up at her old swordmaster then, really looked at her. Frelia wondered what she saw. A tired veteran, a stern teacher, an older sister, a friend?

"...but because you can defend?"

Frelia's smile was the same as when Faustine stopped stutter-stepping into her first sword strike of a duel. "Exactly."

Faustine made a noise somewhere between a surprised squeak and a laugh, slumping against the back of her chair.

"A retreat is not always a loss," Frelia said. "A retreat is a chance to regroup. But we'll need your help to get that done. So can I count on you, Faustine?"

For a long moment, Faustine said nothing. She looked to be on the verge of tears, but she didn't seem upset so much as overwhelmed. And honestly, Frelia could understand that.

Her voice was small when she spoke, but Faustine did. "I'll try."

"Good enough for government work." Frelia reached out to clap Faustine heavily on the shoulder and found herself pulled into a hug instead.

She stiffened in surprise, and then reached around Faustine's shoulders to squeeze back. Maybe teaching wasn't so distant from mercenary work, after all.

CHAPTER FORTY

IF YOU'D ASKED HIM six months ago, Vendrick would have told you that he was perfectly fine with other people's dogs, but had no desire for any of his own.

Two weeks of brushing down the little menaces after a day's trek across the snow, and learning to tell them apart so that he knew which to shout at, and watching them roughhouse during breaks and snuggle to sleep with whoever would let them, and howl at everything (Saints, the howling!), and the malamutes were starting to grow on him. A bit like their fur on everything he owned, really.

It was strange, the things you could get used to when you had no choice.

Like bedding down in the old Hunters' cabins the Valerius family had maintained throughout their territory, once upon a time. Apparently, locals had kept up the tradition in the duchy's absence; the one they'd found to bed down that night had actually been stocked with firewood and jarred rations with neat labels written in sprawling Kaldiri runes.

It wasn't large; there were two rooms only because homes in this part of the north were built with a double-doored foyer to insulate the living quarters from the cold. There was a fireplace on the one end with a cast iron pot hanging in it, a couple of wooden chairs and a small table, and a nest of furs and blankets on the other side of the room. It would fit the five of them and a few of the dogs, and that was all it needed to do.

It was warmer with four walls around you than without them, Frelia had said, and Vendrick was inclined to agree. Even if he felt like the last time he'd been properly warm was, approximately, childhood on the Coast of Ascalon.

So that was how Vendrick came to be fussing with the fireplace inside while Frelia, Faustine, and Talis went to brush down the dogs and lay out hay for the ones that wouldn't sleep indoors.

Clarissa sat in one of the two straight-backed chairs clustered around a tiny table, deposited there after sitting in the sled all day. The unpainted Valerius Shield rested on the table before her, along with both the bloodstone Vendrick had stolen from Markus' laboratory, and the one Faustine had cut out of the so-called yarn-ball darkbeast's heart.

Frelia had told them that the one from Markus' laboratory was the Traust Bloodrune, which had made Faustine turn unhealthily pale, and the one from the yarn-ball darkbeast was a Grimsdalr Bloodrune. Vendrick had done the honors of informing Thera of the news, and the darkbeast had disappeared into the forest for several days afterwards. She always turned back up, though, as if she knew when she was needed and when she could simply be alone. He wondered whether it was a skill she could teach; Vendrick could certainly use it.

Vendrick and Clarissa worked in relatively peaceful silence, and it struck him as odd. He knew that, after Heit Reiði and Kjell, what Clary really needed was rest and medical attention, not a haul across the frigid north. Still, it wasn't in her to stay silent, like this. She had to be more exhausted than she let on.

"Hey, Vendrick," she suddenly said, "do you know—what makes a 'good' shield?"

He scraped his stiletto across the flint in his other hand, piling metal shavings atop the nest of tinder and kindling. "What do you mean?"

"I mean..." Clarissa seemed to consider the question. "I know what makes a spellbook 'good,' you know? The right weight for the paper, the right kind of ink, that sort of thing. It just occurred to me, I have no idea what makes a shield 'good,' other than, you know, the ability to block something coming at you."

Vendrick snorted, and tried to think back to his Silverwood lessons. He quickly gave up. "That's probably a question better directed at Frelia," he said. "I honestly don't remember, if I ever knew."

Clarissa smiled, but it was nowhere near as obnoxious as it should have been. "I never expected to need what I learned at Silverwood, either."

Vendrick paused in the middle of striking the flint. "You didn't?"

"No," Clarissa said, earnestly. "I was supposed to be happily married to some political pundit, remember? And maybe do some light commission work for household enchantments and stop by yours for Sunday dinner, possibly drag you to the opera. You were supposed to do all the cloak and dagger, and I..."

She suddenly hiccupped, and Vendrick glanced over his shoulder just in time to see her swiping at the tears running down her face.

"I don't even know what normal is, anymore."

For a moment, Vendrick was eighteen years old and sitting in his room at the Villa Caecillion again. *It's fine, it'll dry,* he'd said when Clarissa had shaken him awake and he'd peeled his face away from the spellbook he'd been updating for the Tyrant's War. But his sister had seen right through him. She had known why he was working at three in the morning, why his spellbook was tearstained and why no amount of research would mend his broken heart.

But then Vendrick blinked, and he was crouched in a wilderness cabin in the middle of the frozen north, and his sister was going through her own kind of hell on a march to war.

He should have recognized the imposter, known that Clarissa wasn't herself, from the moment she'd first appeared in time for the winter ball. Logic told him that he'd only had a few interactions to realize it, and that della Trova not only knew his little sister well, but also was a very good actress. Still, Vendrick couldn't shake the feeling that this was his fault.

Clarissa was breaking apart, right before his eyes, and it raked at the place Huginn had cracked open in him.

"I *am* sorry, Clary." Vendrick didn't know what else to say.

"For what?" she asked, trying and failing to sound dismissive.

"You're right, for what it's worth," Vendrick offered. "This isn't fair. There just... isn't much to be done about that."

She looked at him, then. His baby sister with eyes so much like his, trauma so much like his. "I go back and forth between wanting to pretend the last few months never happened," she said, "and wanting to make the bloody Unseen pay."

Vendrick's mouth quirked up, not quite into a smile. "And you say you weren't built for war."

"You weren't either," Clarissa said. "You should have been a career bureaucrat, making Octavia Nova's political rivals miserable with unending stacks of paperwork."

She held her hand about a foot off of the table, as if to indicate his to-do list.

Vendrick laughed, but there was no Frelia for that version of him, and he knew it. "You mean I should have been like Mum?"

"Mum is terrifying!" Clarissa argued. "And you could have still loomed in the background and worn mostly black, I don't see the problem."

Despite himself, Vendrick snorted.

Clarissa cast her eyes back down to the unfinished Valerius Shield. "I know I'm being ridiculous."

"You're not." Vendrick got to his feet, ignoring the way his joints cracked, and reached out to squeeze her shoulder. "You are, in fact, being perfectly reasonable."

"It doesn't feel that way." She set her hand over his and squeezed back.

"Frelia and I have been through war before," Vendrick said, taking his hand back. "Proper war, on the frontlines."

"Proper war," Clarissa scoffed. "That's an oxymoron."

A sad smile tugged at Vendrick's face. "The point is, we're used to this kind of thinking. Frelia would tell you she was born for it."

Clarissa shuddered. "What a ghastly thing to breed for."

Vendrick laid a few cautious fingertips across the face of the Valerius Shield. He couldn't shake the feeling that he wasn't supposed to touch it, even though Frelia had entrusted it to them while she took care of the sled dogs.

"She carries them with her," he said, quietly. "All her loved ones, that is. I'd almost say she's haunted by them."

"I don't understand the way she thinks at all," Clarissa admitted, "but she clearly loved her father, so he must have done something right. She was *gutted,* telling us about the draugr. I wanted to give her a hug."

But she hadn't, and their own father and his inflicted miseries fell like a weight between them.

"That fight was horrible," Vendrick muttered, turning back towards the fire.

Quiet fell across the cabin again, and this time, Vendrick managed to get the fire sparked properly before Clarissa said anything.

"Do you think my hands will look like yours, by the end of this?"

Vendrick didn't need to ask what she meant. Summoning, after all, was grey magic, too. Beneath her gloves, Clarissa's hands were still pink and smooth, with only the smallest of grey magic burns marring her elegant fingers.

"Most likely," Vendrick said. "Unless you decide to switch to black magic."

Clarissa wrinkled her nose. "Black magic is boring."

He grinned, wryly. "Then you know your answer."

The door to the hunter's cabin suddenly banged open, and Frelia appeared with malamute fur all down her front. "Alright, we should be—" She froze, mid-step, at the sight of them. "Vendrick, what did you say to your poor sister?"

Clarissa gave a watery laugh, and scrubbed at her face with her hands. "He didn't say anything. I made myself sad."

"Well, what are you doing that for?" Frelia's footfalls were sure and steady as she strode across the floor. "There's already enough shit in the world to make you cry without adding to the damn pile yourself."

Not for the first time, Vendrick wished he could just tell Frelia he loved her without causing a damn scene. It would have been helpful, right about now.

"Have I mentioned I like you, Frelia?" Clarissa said, instead, and Vendrick nearly choked. "Truly, you're the grim elder sister I never had."

"You know, I never had a sister either? I had Thera, I guess, but she and Cillian were their own thing." Frelia rolled her eye. "Twins."

Vendrick smiled. One day, he might regret how well his sister and his girlfriend got on, but for the moment, all he could really bring himself to feel was relief.

"Ask her what you asked me," Vendrick said, gesturing to the Valerius Shield.

"Oh, right!" Clarissa brightened. "What makes a shield 'good,' Frelia?"

"Preference, mostly," the shieldmaiden said. "You don't want something too heavy or too unwieldy for you to comfortably handle."

And then Frelia launched into an explanation of the weight of the wood and the runes carved into the back of the shield until Faustine and

Mitri came in with a few of the dogs and someone mentioned it was about time to think about dinner.

If this was their new normal, well, there were worse things.

CHAPTER FORTY-ONE

WHITBORNE WAS A TERRIBLY boring town, Ironfang had quickly surmised. He had originally intended to stay there only until he heard from Orsina, but after two weeks, he had been bored to tears and decided to push forward to the mountains. His daughter would simply have to catch up.

And so when she did, it wasn't at an inn, or a pub, or anywhere remotely civilized. It was out in the middle of the forest, as the Sightless One had likely intended, and she looked none too thrilled to be there.

"Ave, Imperator."

Only his progeny could make the traditional greeting sound so sarcastic.

Ironfang rose to his feet, setting aside his travel cutlery. "Hail, Grand Duchess della Luciana."

Orsina was looking worse for wear, streaked with road grime and favoring one arm. Ironfang wondered, absently, which of her Bloodrune Hunters she'd bullied into doing her hair this morning for the chignon, still, was perfect.

Orsina's face twisted into something that might have been a smile on someone else. "I come bearing gifts, father."

She dismounted, gesturing for one of her retinue to come forward. And there, seated behind her on the horse and looking even more banged-up, was a figure Ironfang was surprised—and delighted—to see.

The man was scrabbling around the pockets of his green coat, quite desperately looking for something. He pulled out quills and bits of detritus until he finally retrieved a miraculously unharmed pair of glasses from an inside pocket. He cleaned them furiously on the hem of his shirt, and then shoved them back on his face.

It was amusing to watch the man's gaze travel across his surroundings. Ironfang could see the exact moment he realized just whose presence he stood in.

"Oh Saints," the man whispered, his eyes wide as saucers behind their lenses.

It lasted a half-second before Orsina and one of her men wrestled him off the horse and into the dirt. Now, what was his name, again?

"Blightsen," Ironfang said, "is it not?"

"Yes." The man coughed, dragging himself upright as best he could with Orsina still holding him back. "Your, um, Majesty."

This was a pleasant change of pace. Ironfang had half-expected his eldest to return with news that everything had gone to shit. With a former cleric to hand, not only was the Library at Mournheim that much closer, there was even less of a need to have Orsina or Markus complete the ritual built from the notes recovered at the Einnaska hunting lodge.

A cleric might even enjoy the ride.

"The Traust Child has also been recovered," Orsina added, and although she sounded nonchalant, Ironfang's divine senses could read the adrenaline buzzing in her skull. "They are on their way to the family villa now—alongside Lord Huginn and a considerable guard contingent."

She was expecting praise, that much was obvious. And yet Ironfang was torn between asking why she herself hadn't escorted the Traust child and left the considerably less important cleric to her lessers and admitting that crack in the armor of the Imperator's rule in front of an audience.

He settled for, "Where I presume you'll be headed after this?"

Orsina blinked in surprise, but that was all. "Of course, Father."

Did she expect to follow you into the mountains? The Sightless One asked.

Ironfang only just resisted the urge to startle. It was bloody cold out here; no wonder he hadn't noticed the Old One creeping into his mind.

Likely, he told the Old One. *Someone will need to perform the communion, after all.*

The Sightless One's laugh was hoarse and inhuman. *Of course, of course...*

"Very well, then," Ironfang said, and then he turned his gaze to Blightsen. "As for you..."

He purposefully trailed off, curious where Blightsen's mind would take them first. We were the keepers of our own worst fears, after all. It was usually a much more effective strategy for getting what you wanted than breaking out the threats first thing.

"If you're going to threaten me," Blightsen eventually said, "would you kindly just get on with it?"

He straightened his spine to stare Ironfang down, and, for a moment, Ironfang saw a Krakenguard mage, instead of a disgrace.

"Very well," said Ironfang, and he went for the throat. "Your gods are dead, Blightsen."

The ex-cleric recoiled so violently he almost knocked into Orsina's leg. Evidently, it was not what he'd expected Ironfang to say.

"I don't know what you're talking about." Blightsen was no longer looking at him, but Ironfang's divine sense could see where to press. "The Goddesses' gaze is on us, always."

Orsina laughed, scathing and bright, but Ironfang was the picture of a patient father. "Yes, you do," he said. "I'd guess you feel their absence keenly."

He touched Blightsen's balding forehead, and the man flinched. Ironfang hadn't even put any violence in it.

"If the Goddesses were dead," Blightsen said, "we would all be murdering each other while the sun never rises. And I don't see an apocalypse incoming, do you?"

He suddenly froze, eyes going wide again. Realization seemed to be dripping into his skull from somewhere beyond the Waking World.

The ex-cleric knew the stories, of course. Ironfang did too. *Heit Reiði* would begin with the death of Lady Daybreak—one way or another—and the world would be plunged into an eternal winter without her warmth and light.

Ironfang's smile was patient and predatory as he gestured to the snow-covered ground. "Funny you should mention that."

All the color drained from Blightsen's face. "It's just some snow. You can't be serious."

Ironfang stopped pacing and, for a moment, considered simply looming. Blightsen was clearly a coward, even if he didn't want to be. But then, maybe Ironfang didn't need to play that up at all. Blightsen already knew that about himself, by the look of him.

So Ironfang dropped to his haunches instead.

"Can't I?" he asked.

Ironfang didn't know if Blightsen's swallow was audible to everyone else or not, but his divine sense certainly heard it.

"What do you want, Imperator, sir?" Blightsen asked. "I haven't been a cleric in years, and I don't have a bloodrune."

Ah, but a runeless vessel was exactly what Ironfang needed.

"What do you know," Ironfang asked, as calmly as he inquired after the weather, "about the Library at Mournheim?"

Ironfang didn't need his divine sense to see the chill that ran down Blightsen's spine, but it showed him anyway. The man blanched, even as he tried to avoid showing how terrified he was at the question.

"Nothing," Blightsen very obviously lied.

Ironfang resisted the urge to throttle him, and instead put on the warm, paternal tone again. "There's no need to play dumb, Blightsen. I know you were a talented cleric during the war."

Blightsen snorted. "You could have told my superiors that."

Oh, so not just a coward, but a jaded one, too. Excellent. Somewhere over Blightsen's shoulder, Orsina's face split into a rictus grin.

"You weren't meant for the brash Krakenguard," Ironfang said, "and merely patching up Valerius and the Grimsdalr Twins whenever their brazenness went too far—were you?"

Blightsen stared down at the ground, still and silent as the grave.

"All that potential," Ironfang continued, "completely wasted."

"Thanks, Ironfang." An undercurrent of iron entered Blightsen's voice, although he wasn't stupid enough to sound outright annoyed at the Imperator. "I hadn't noticed."

Ironfang laughed genuinely for the first time in months. Blightsen looked faintly horrified at the sound.

"Besides," Ironfang added, "you would've trained there as an acolyte, no?"

Blightsen's face twisted, and after another moment, he said, "I never had the chance. Tyrant's War."

Ironfang grinned. Now he was getting somewhere. "So you've never actually been to the holiest place in your little cult?"

"What's it matter?" Blightsen sounded tired. "There is no Church of the Triad anymore."

Orsina made a face that said the man had a point, and Ironfang ignored her.

"True," Ironfang agreed. "But what if I told you there was another god? One long since forgotten by the absent Triad and their followers."

Ironfang got the sense Blightsen would have been toeing the dirt if he weren't kneeling. "You can save it, if you've got a spiel about the Unseen," he said. "Caecillion's already told me more than I ever wanted to know about your lot."

Well, so much for that. Plan B it was.

"I know you're bluffing, Ironfang," Blightsen said. "This is just winter in Kaldr. And I'm not going to help you end the world."

Ironfang smiled, wide and cheerful, and leaned into Blightsen's personal space. "Oh yes," he said, "you are."

A violent, preternatural chill began to soak the air around him as Ironfang reached for Blightsen. He laid a single finger against the man's exposed forehead, just like the Sightless One had done to him all those years ago. Images of azure fields and greenish sunlight and creatures black as night began running from Ironfang's mind like water through a sieve.

And then Blightsen began to scream.

CHAPTER FORTY-TWO

IT HAD BEEN A long time since Frelia or Vendrick had set foot in the capital of what had once been the Kingdom of Kaldr.

It was called New Ascalon now, but according to Frelia, it was the same cramped, cobblestoned cluster of peaked gables and grey stone, with streets that had been built through organically-grown chaos. Vendrick was almost glad to know the layout was just as frustrating to the locals as it had been to him.

No matter the color of the banners snapping in the stiff breeze off the Ivory Channel, Frelia had said, the heart of the city didn't change.

Thera had peeled off towards the coast well before the town came into view, and when the rest of them finally limped through the outer walls, it was early midafternoon. Their ragtag little party entered through the eastern gate—something that Vendrick had expected to meet resistance for, and instead found Frelia relieved and nodding. Clarissa and Faustine sent confused looks his way, but both said nothing and he pretended not to notice.

He would grant Frelia the mercies he could.

They had to check the dogsleds at the edge of the city, and so Faustine and Talis kept hold of their furry charges on leashes while Clarissa settled onto Frelia's back in a way that was becoming irritatingly familiar for both of them. Although Clarissa was not a very large woman, Frelia's shoulders hadn't healed right from the fight in Kjell, though the wounds in her abdomen had. Vendrick could only presume it was comfortable for a grand total of no one.

The Imperial Watchers shot them questioning looks as they made their way towards Castle Skjöldr, but none said a word. They had nothing to comment upon, technically.

Even the shield on Faustine's back was just an unpainted round shield, after all.

"Can't wait to work on some bloody prosthetics," Clarissa muttered as Frelia began to lead the way through what had once been her people's city.

"*Ja,*" Frelia grunted. "Would be nice."

"Won't that hurt if you do it too soon?" Faustine asked.

"Yes," Talis warned immediately.

Clarissa rolled her eyes. "I'm not thick, Talis. I'm not about to shove metal into open wounds or anything. I do have plans though."

"You always do," said Vendrick, a little fondly.

And so that was how they hiked all the way up to the castle, one foot after the other, past the inner baileys and up steep stairs, only to be halted in the courtyard of what had once been called Castle Skjöldr. Vendrick felt a bit like he was treading on Hägen Einnaska's grave—and, for all he knew, perhaps was.

"Her Excellency is not receiving the public this afternoon," a thin, reedy steward informed them down his nose from the castle steps. "You will have to return on the third Tuesday of the month."

"We're not the public," Clarissa said at once. "Would you kindly inform Her Excellency that Vendrick and Clarissa have arrived? If she still wishes us to come back another day, then we will."

The steward glanced pointedly at Frelia, Faustine, and then Talis, so Vendrick added, somewhat sharply, "Vendrick, Clarissa, and *guests*."

He was already sick of dealing with his mother, and he hadn't even seen her yet.

The steward sniffed—"Wait here, would you kindly?"—and disappeared back up the stairs and into the keep.

The sled dogs began to shift in their harnesses, as if scenting the unease in the air. From her perch on Frelia's back, Clarissa was looking at him with more concern than Vendrick wanted to deal with, right then.

"Ready?" she asked.

"Absolutely not," he muttered.

A moment later, something warm and solid nudged him, and it took him a moment to realize Frelia was leaning into his side. "Like we said, just talk her ear off," she said. "You're good at it."

Vendrick snorted weakly, and he knew he was disassociating because he couldn't bring himself to reach back. It was as though an ocean suddenly stood between him and everyone else.

"It's… a bit sparse out here, for a castle," Talis said in what, for him, passed as an attempt to be conversational.

"Too hard to have a garden up here in the north most of the year," Frelia said. "Great place for sword drills, though."

Talis looked like he wanted to say something likely condescending, but Faustine cut him off with a sudden, "Greta, *heel!*"

The lead sled dog was apparently finished standing still, and had figured out how to slip her harness. It took Faustine, Talis, and Vendrick several minutes to chase her down and wrestle her back into it, but by then, the steward had returned.

He studied the now mud-and-dog-fur-encrusted party with incensed distaste, although he sounded defeated when he said, "Her Excellency has decided to make an exception, and will see you now. Kindly board your dogs with the kennelmaster and follow me."

He turned back to the castle doors without so much as waiting for them to move.

Inside, the castle foyer was utterly utilitarian. Vendrick couldn't help but notice Frelia flinch at the bare walls and stoic furniture. He leaned over to ask, "What is it?"

"There used to be tapestries and art on the walls." She kept pace behind the steward, even weighed down by Clarissa and staring grimly at the bare walls around them. "And a mosaic of the Einnaska Bloodrune in the floor."

She gestured, somewhat uselessly, at the center of the room. Even Talis had the good sense not to interject after that.

The castle steward led them through twisting hallways built out of heavy stone, and though many were as functional as the foyer, there was at least a crimson tapestry here, a still-life painting there, some dried flowers in a beige vase.

"I see mother's taste in décor hasn't changed much," Clarissa muttered. "Would it kill her to put out some fresh flowers, or something?"

"It's winter in Kaldr," Frelia pointed out.

Ahead of her, the steward flinched at her word choice.

Clarissa made a face, and Vendrick shook his head. "Mum's nothing if not predictable."

"Is that a good thing or a bad thing?" Faustine asked.

Anxiety was eating at Vendrick's stomach, now. "To be determined."

They arrived at a heavy set of double doors that made Frelia flinch again, and, not for the first time, Vendrick wished everything about Northern Volsinii post-Tyrant's War hadn't been specifically designed to hurt her and anyone else still calling themselves Kaldiri.

And then the steward inquired as to their names and titles.

Wary suspicion pricked at Vendrick's neck. "She's not in court, is she?"

"Of course she is," the steward harrumphed. "Where else would a governor be?"

"A private sitting room?" Clarissa sounded aghast. "We're her children, for the Saints' sake, not a foreign delegation."

The steward shrugged, as if it was no concern of his. "You requested an audience, did you not?"

Saints, this was not good. Vendrick still hadn't yet figured out exactly how he was supposed to inform his mother about the Unseen; he had absolutely zero idea how to drop it into a court setting like anything other than a homemade black powder explosive.

He tried to catch Clarissa's eye but instead snagged on Frelia's. She nodded to him, making the Silverwood hand sign for 'I've got your back' against the space between Clarissa's leg and her own ribs.

And for the first time since setting foot in New Ascalon, Vendrick's anxiety quieted some. He could do this. And, for the first time maybe ever, he didn't have to do it alone.

"Should I be first," Frelia asked, "or last?"

"Or buried in the middle?" Talis pointed out.

"You've been acquitted of your conduct in the Tyrant's War," Vendrick said for what felt like the millionth time. "There's no rule that says you're not allowed to petition your own governor."

Something in Frelia's face twitched, but she said nothing.

"Bury *me* in the middle," Faustine said. "Or, erm, better yet, I can wait out here?"

"No," said Vendrick. He would not allow them to be separated. "All in together."

He rattled off their names and titles for the steward, who solemnly nodded and then shooed Frelia away from the doors.

The man straightened up, cracked his neck first one way, then the other, and then pushed open the doors with a "Your Excellency, your guests have arrived."

Vendrick watched carefully as the others slipped inside ahead of him, listening for his own tolling bell.

"Presenting, His Lordship Vendrick, Count of Caecillion!"

Vendrick straightened his spine automatically, and strode through the double doors with the same projected self-assurance he'd used in the Senate.

He had, of course, been in the throne room of Castle Skjöldr before. There had been galas and political meetings, growing up, and he'd eventually made his way here after the Battle for Skjöldr. But he hadn't set foot in it since Deadcut had come to roost, and he realized, somewhat dismally, that of course the new décor would extend here, too.

For everything in the room—from the tapestries, to the tiling, to the fabric cushioning the benches and chairs—was a vibrant shade of Volsinii Crimson. High overhead, Vendrick could just make out the outlines of an elegant crystal chandelier that he knew on sight was an Atieus piece and thus not original to the castle. He knew the intended significance, knew Frelia felt it, too—

This is a Kaldiri stronghold no longer.

And there, sitting on the Coldiron throne at the end of the room, was the messenger.

Sulpicia "Deadcut" Verona was a steely-haired matron who had earned her military honors (as well as a bad leg) in the Winter War. Vendrick had inherited her height—even sitting down, Deadcut's presence was towering—and Clarissa had inherited her round face, although Deadcut's was usually pinched. She wore a silver-and-sapphire diadem that seemed to be the only thing still blue in the entire castle, and when her dark eyes flicked up to meet his, Vendrick instantly felt the insane urge to double-check his report card.

"When my steward informed me that *both* of my children had mysteriously appeared," Deadcut began, folding her hands primly in her lap, "I wondered, 'what news could they possibly bring? Their father is already dead.'"

A round of amused laughter filtered through the room.

"A small part of me wondered if, perhaps, one of you was finally getting married," Deadcut continued, her voice high and severe, "but now I see before me the Imperator's youngest daughter, a physician, and a Kaldiri, as well."

Frelia's whole being tightened, as though readying to launch herself at a darkbeast. And while Talis cast his eyes to his shoes, Faustine looked torn between running, hiding, and standing her ground.

"So do tell me," Deadcut said, her voice never rising, "why is my daughter coming before me on the back of our enemy?"

Frelia spoke before anyone else could. "Because when you get both your lower legs smashed up, it stings a little."

Vendrick winced, and a vein pulsed in Deadcut's temple. Somewhere near the double doors, someone laughed, and Vendrick figured it was probably local-born staff.

Deadcut's hands tightened in her lap. "Smashed by what?"

"I'm fine, Mum!" Clarissa hastily interjected. "Or, well, I will be. Once I've built myself some prosthetics. Which I am perfectly capable of, you know."

Vendrick had to manually unclench his jaw to speak. "By a darkbeast, Your Excell—"

"'Mother' will do just fine, thank you," Deadcut interrupted. "I didn't labor with you for thirty-six hours to be called *Your Excellency.*"

A vein pulsed in Vendrick's temple to mirror Deadcut's. "*Mother,*" he corrected himself. "We were engaged in—"

"I'm well aware of the goings-on in my territory," Deadcut interrupted. "What I fail to understand is how you managed to get yourselves tangled up with a darkbeast in the bloody first place."

Clarissa's expression fell so hard, Vendrick felt the need to put himself bodily between his sister and his mother. "Because that's what happens when they're in your way," he said. "Or have you forgotten the Battle of Prehl?"

Deadcut breathed in so sharply it echoed to the vaulted ceiling. "I would expect," she said crisply, "a maverick like Valerius to play hero. Not you, Vendrick."

Silence fell hard and heavy across the room.

"Oh yes," Deadcut added, "I marked that black hair the moment she stepped into this court. And even if my steward hadn't been so kind as to announce it, she's the spitting image of her father. Without the beard, of course."

Frelia snorted mirthlessly. "Forgive me for not curtseying," she said. "I'm carrying your family on my back."

Deadcut studied her for a long moment with eyes like hard chips of flint. And Vendrick suddenly wasn't sure which he dreaded more—what his girlfriend saw in his mother, or the reverse.

"For goodness' sake," Deadcut snapped, "someone bring my daughter a chair."

One of the Imperial Watchers on the perimeter hastened to drag a bench forward, and all eyes were on Frelia as she dropped to a crouch to allow Clarissa to maneuver herself gracelessly onto the wooden bench.

Frelia straightened up a moment later, rolling her shoulders and casting a glance about the room. She met the eye of anyone daring enough to try. Clarissa, meanwhile, crossed one truncated leg over the other and folded her hands elegantly in her lap, her mother's perfect mirror.

That both of her legs ended just above the knee was impossible to miss.

The silence was pervasive, now, but Vendrick knew how to work with silence. It had been his stock and trade since he'd been old enough to understand its weight. Frelia, apparently, did as well, for she held an imperious hand out to Faustine.

Without question, the girl unslung the shield from her back, and Frelia reclaimed the last vestiges of her family inheritance with a facial expression like a broken oath.

"Mother," Vendrick said, "humor us with a question, would you kindly?"

Deadcut's eyes narrowed. "What sort of question?"

Vendrick and Clarissa had kicked back and forth a few ideas as to what they could possibly ask their mother to confirm her identity, and continually landed on the same, painful memory. Frelia had snarled something so angry in Kaldiri the first time she heard it, she went to go hunt hares in the forest to let off steam. Even Talis hadn't blamed her.

"What happened on my eighth birthday?"

Deadcut's expression didn't move. "Why would you go and ask a thing like that?"

"Please humor him, Mother," Clarissa said, the picture of the pitiful supplicant. Perhaps she had learned a thing or two from della Trova, after all. "It's important."

Vendrick's mother never shrank, exactly. But she was suddenly less intimidating than she had been, a moment ago. Could it be shame, stooping her shoulders up on the Coldiron throne?

Impossible, Vendrick thought blackly. Their family didn't know the meaning of the word.

"On Vendrick's eighth birthday, I returned home from the Winter War..." To her credit, Deadcut continued to hold her children's gazes as she spoke. "...having completely forgotten. It didn't occur to me until I found Clarissa digging in the garden much later that night and was halfway through reprimanding her for such a thoughtless action."

Her gaze fell to the assembled courtiers, as if she were simply telling a story. Some of their faces were familiar, even expected. Just at a quick glance, Vendrick noted the Senators for Norvegr and Aelfisir, plus their spouses and some hangers-on. No one significant enough to pose a problem, but still, no one Vendrick would care to have listening in. Particularly since no one looked surprised by the story.

"Not thoughtless, as it turned out," Deadcut continued, her face and voice neutral, "but simply a five-year-old girl looking for a present for her older brother. A stone with a hole in it and an iridescent beetle, I believe she found."

Out of the corner of his eye, Vendrick saw Frelia grit her jaw so hard the tendons in her neck stood out. Before he'd even had the thought to reach out, Faustine was there, squeezing Frelia's arm in his stead.

"Never mind that, apparently," Deadcut continued, a note of acid in her voice, now, "their father had decided birthdays were not worth celebrating, in my absence. Is that what you wished to know?"

And there it was. Right down to the dig at their father, Saints rest his soul in hell. This was Vendrick's mother alright, Saints help them all.

But he would have been a career bureaucrat, in another life, and so he had long since learned how to make even pleasantries sound insulting. "Correct, thank you."

The crowd drew in a stunned, collective breath.

"What was the purpose of this?" Deadcut demanded.

Vendrick met her eye. "How much do you know of illusion magic, Mother?"

A few courtiers gasped, a little too perfectly on cue. Vendrick's eyes narrowed. Someone here knew what he was getting at, and for all his paranoia, Vendrick had been right.

The Unseen were here.

Deadcut raised an eyebrow. "Enough to adjourn the greater court for the afternoon."

The outcry was immediate, and nearly as stunned as Vendrick was. He kept his face carefully neutral as Senators and dignitaries complained, and it wasn't lost on him that Deadcut did the same.

When the uproar died down, however, Deadcut merely said, "Was I somehow unclear?"

The muttering followed the courtiers out the doors, until all that remained were Deadcut and a handful of Imperial Watchers. She remained silent until the last of the heavy wooden doors thumped shut, and then turned her tactical eye on Vendrick.

"Further," she said, "I know enough regarding illusion magic to wonder why you fear an imposter on the Coldiron throne, Vendrick."

Frelia made a choking noise that dovetailed into a low, muttered curse Vendrick could have sworn he recognized.

Don't be cruel, Mum, he wanted to say, but that was a bit like telling a fish not to swim. So instead, Vendrick folded his hands at the small of his back and said, "What do you know of the Unseen?"

Deadcut's facial expression gave nothing away. "That religious... let's call it a *group* that the Imperator has gotten into in his middle age?"

Vendrick nodded. "That's the one."

"They always struck me as rather like a cult," Deadcut said.

"It's not 'rather like,'" Frelia said, "it is a cult. A bloodrune-obsessed one."

Deadcut's mahogany gaze cut swiftly over to the swordswoman. "You say that quite confidently."

Frelia held the old general's gaze. "Lots of practice."

Deadcut burst into sudden laughter that silenced whatever anyone else might have said.

"Very well," she said. "Vendrick, you may proceed."

He couldn't help but look to Frelia. To her strength and constancy. To her squared shoulders and set jaw. To her family shield on her back, not yet whole but at least back where it belonged.

Oh, Saints, this was it. The moment of quite literal truth. The time when all his secrets and all his subterfuge would either be made redundant, or shatter entirely.

He couldn't help the wry smile that twisted his features. "Then I shall tell you a tale."

He began chronologically, with the Winter War. Deadcut's facial expression tightened as Vendrick explained the background maneuverings of Imperator Claudius, even as his loyal generals fought and died against the Kaldiri. The Imperial Watchers that remained shifted uncomfortably in their boots, and Vendrick took an extra moment to mark each of them as he spoke.

They wouldn't meet his eye.

"I did wonder where those darkbeasts at Prehl and Ice Crown came from," Deadcut inputted at one point. "I'd never heard of any coming below the Northern Wilds, and then, all of a sudden, Ironfang turns up with several battalion-breakers? How terribly convenient."

"That's a word for it." Frelia was staring at the Coldiron throne, and, at a guess, her stubborn Kaldiri pride was warring with the reality that trying to do anything about it would get her killed.

Vendrick was not a praying man, as a general rule, but he fervently hoped Frelia wouldn't do something stupid. The set of Talis' mouth told Vendrick that he was likely thinking something similar.

"Is there a problem, Valerius?" Deadcut inquired acidly.

"Why wouldn't there be?" Frelia fired back. "You're in Hägen Einnaska's seat."

Silence fell across the room, and Saints, this had been a terrible idea. Vendrick could work with silence, sure, but not outright hostility.

"Also," Frelia continued, trampling the silence beneath her boots, "in a kind world, this would be my home. Not yours. But the world isn't kind, and your son is in the middle of explaining why."

By some miracle, Deadcut's hackles lowered. "Continue, Vendrick."

He launched into explanations for why it was increasingly difficult to get legislation passed through the Senate and why Kaldr had lost the Tyrant's War. How the Unseen were collecting the full bloodrune array, and how much a target that made any remaining bloodrune-bearers. He even threw in Frelia's guesswork about the missing Sacred Tasks, just to appeal to the pious woman Deadcut had once been.

And then he told her of the cold war he had been fighting for over a decade, now.

For her part, Deadcut listened intently after her first outburst. At some point, she flagged her steward and requested blank parchment, upon which she began taking notes. Though she occasionally asked a clarifying question, she mostly just let Vendrick speak.

It was strange, to monologue so much in the presence of either of his parents. Uneasy. Like he was on the precipice of a cliff without a railing.

When Vendrick eventually arrived at the explanation of Heit Reiði, Clarissa chimed in with her own two copper. Clarissa's talk of torture and bloodletting between the ambush and the incarceration was enough to put even a grizzled general off her tea, but some of the Imperial Watchers actively chose to leave the room on 'patrol' rather than continue to listen. Vendrick figured they were also running off to report on what was happening, and his hands twitched uselessly as he watched them run.

Then there was all that had happened in Kjell. Talis led with explanations of his lab work and the Bloodrune Hunters, and then Vendrick took over with Lord Huginn and Orsina della Luciana's so-called yarn-ball darkbeast. Faustine spoke up then, despite her best attempts to hide behind Frelia's armored coat, and somehow, hearing tell of the scene in a fifteen-year-old's voice just made it all worse.

"...Which brings us to now," Faustine finished quietly. "And I do have proof of the yarn-ball darkbeast, at least. May I fetch it?"

Deadcut nodded gravely.

Faustine unslung her travelling pack and set it on the bench beside Clarissa. She rummaged through her belongings for a moment, and then came up with a wadded ball of cloth that was probably a spare blouse.

With the careful ease of a cook handling a hot cast iron, Faustine peeled away the cloth until a rocky-looking blood clot sat in her hands. It was lumpy and misshapen, while, deep in its crystalline heart, a whirling rune glowed fiercely red.

"This is the bloodstone I was talking about," Faustine added, somewhat unnecessarily. "That I had to cut from it."

Deadcut stared at the girl and the bloodstone for a long, petrifyingly silent moment.

"I was never fond of the Duchess della Luciana," Deadcut eventually said. "I always found her arrogant and rather exasperating."

Clarissa's voice teetered dangerously on the brink of hopeful. "So you believe us?"

Deadcut sighed, and it was only years of Senate service that kept Vendrick's face neutral. "You present a compelling narrative, to be sure," Deadcut said. "However, there is a distinct lack of evidence, that bloodstone notwithstanding."

"*I* am evidence!" Clarissa said. "My hair is above my ears, Mother!"

"You've proven that you were unlawfully incarcerated, and that someone—Valerius being the most likely candidate—has recently downed a darkbeast," Deadcut said. "But that these Unseen have orchestrated an entire conspiracy—involving the Imperator, no less—is where I find the evidence lacking. What you present is... well, quite frankly, a hideous condemnation of the entire Imperium."

"Thanks for noticing," Frelia deadpanned.

"*So* many people would have to be complicit..."

"And they are!" Clarissa flung her hands up, and then pointedly shot their mother a look when she added, "Or at least can't be bothered to look up."

They nearly had her. Vendrick could feel it in his bones. He just needed a little bit of oratory to push her over the edge.

"Governor Deadcut," Faustine suddenly said, and her voice was too young for the weight in it, "have you ever been on the wrong side of a darkbeast?"

Deadcut stiffened. "I fail to see what that has to do with this."

"They're awful, Your Excellency." Faustine picked at something on her coat sleeve. "When one screamed, I felt like everything good in the world had just... vanished. Like nothing would ever be good again. Do you know where else I've felt that?"

"Pray tell," said Deadcut.

"Home." Faustine met the old woman's eye, and Vendrick had never been prouder of a student. "The Villa della Luciana is a factory for the things, and they don't reproduce like normal animals. So far as I know, they have to be built."

Vendrick could almost smell the blood in the air, the darkbeast ichor. He could see Frelia, in his mind's eye, casting the Grimsdalr Blink rune to hurl headfirst through hell, could almost see himself casting fire in her wake. Could see Markus della Luciana hunched over that worktable in his oubliette of a lab, sewing together hunks of bloody, raw material.

"Built from what?" Deadcut asked, and Vendrick could've sworn there was unease in her tone, now.

"For the little ones? Animal meat, like deer or dogs or cattle. Plus one of these." Faustine gently shook the bloodstone in her hands, for good measure. "But for the big ones, Your Excellency? Like the ones you find in the wild?"

Faustine braced herself against the wooden bench, her fingers tightening around the bloodstone.

"If a beastminder made it," she added, shaking, now, "then it's made of people."

Deadcut's stern mask finally cracked. Stunned horror dropped her jaw, and for a moment, she looked so much like Clarissa, it was uncanny.

"I beg your pardon?" Deadcut whispered.

"When the yarn-ball darkbeast fell apart," Faustine continued, speaking through the horror audibly closing her throat, "it was like a mass grave had splattered all over the forest. And my sister's not even a good beastminder! As terrible as it is to say, that's probably why it wasn't a very good darkbeast. But I know what Markus is capable of, Your Excellency. I watched him make and summon Lord Muninn..."

Deadcut recoiled at the name, as though lashed.

"...Saw my father summon Lord Huginn at Silverwood..."

Deadcut flinched again, and Vendrick was as fascinated by the uncharacteristic motion as he was by the old magics.

"...And I have a very bad feeling," Faustine added, looking to Frelia, now, "they won't stop at those two."

"No..." Deadcut clapped a hand to her mouth as if to take back what she'd just said.

The old general was wavering and, like the duelist she was, Frelia went in for the kill.

"This is what the Volsinii have wrought, Deadcut." Frelia sounded just like how Vendrick remembered her from the war—tired, resolute, grim. "From the very moment you decided you could command hell."

Deadcut said nothing for so long a moment, Vendrick almost dared hope.

"I understand that you believe that," she finally said.

"What do they *have* on you?" Disgust and exasperation dripped from Frelia's words like meltwater from a glacier. "We know you're you from the terrible parenting skills, but why do you insist on keeping yourself removed from the truth?"

Vendrick scrambled to find something to smooth everything over.

But then Deadcut said, "I see a decade and a half without a duchy has done nothing to improve that famous Valerius diplomacy."

"*He* was the diplomatic option." Frelia stabbed a finger at Vendrick. "But you're a general, Deadcut. I know I'm the expert, here, but can you not see a losing battle when it strikes you across the face?"

Faustine gasped, clasping her hands to her mouth, while Vendrick and Clarissa both tensed, waiting for a retort swung with all the force that had once been behind Deadcut's two-handed axe.

But instead, the ghost of a smile tugged on the woman's wizened face. "If I didn't know any better," Deadcut said, "I'd swear I'm arguing with Einar Valerius himself."

"Bloodrunes are more than inherited power," Frelia said. "They're inherited memory and trauma, too. So who knows? You may be."

Vendrick filed that one away for further questioning. "This is not the Volsinii you or I bled for, Mother," he hastened to get out. "But it is the one who felled her homeland..." Vendrick gestured to Frelia. "...and it's going to fell ours, at the rate it's going."

Talis looked up then, his mouth half-open like he had something to add, but before he had the chance, the steward cleared his throat with excruciating emphasis from the end of the hall.

"Presenting," said the man, "His Lordship Markus, Lord of della Luciana and Prince of the Volsinii Imperium!"

CHAPTER FORTY-THREE

HEIT REIÐI HAD BEEN bad enough. Kjell had been bad enough. Castle Skjöldr as a general, swooping, concept had been bad enough.

But watching Markus della Luciana striding into the throne room like he wasn't the reason it was colored in blood and fire was the last straw.

"You," Frelia growled.

Markus froze abruptly mid-stride. His jaw fell open and then snapped shut again a few times as he stared at the party assembled before the Coldiron throne. That heavy eyepatch was still over his eye, and he wore the banded, circular iron armor of the Imperial Watchers.

"Afternoon, della Luciana," Vendrick greeted coolly.

Frelia didn't so much speak as snarl. "Burn in Helheim, *zychnik*."

Markus' eyebrows rose and he pointedly looked to Deadcut, even as the steward began to titter with his staff.

"Do come in, della Luciana," Deadcut said, and it was so absurdly polite Frelia had to strangle a laugh. "We were having a most interesting discussion before your arrival."

Vendrick flashed his mother a warning look she promptly ignored, and warning bells began to sing in the back of Frelia's mind. Just whose side was Deadcut on?

"I'm certain you were," Markus said. "However, I come with most distressing news."

"Let me guess," Frelia said flatly. "Some combination of Vendrick, Clarissa, Mitri, and myself are wanted by the Imperium for various crimes committed at Heit Reiði and Kjell?"

Markus stared at her a moment in abject shock before his face quickly morphed into his usual disdain. "I'm not at liberty to discuss it with anyone but Her Excellency."

Deadcut sighed, and despite all the meetings she'd sat through with Markus, Frelia refused to sympathize.

"Report, della Luciana," Deadcut said.

He blinked, visibly surprised, and looked around the room. "Right now?"

Deadcut's eyes narrowed. "Was I somehow unclear?"

"Err, no, Your Excellency." Markus reached into a pocket on his belt, withdrew a letter, and began to recite. "Hail, General Sulpicia Verona, Governor of Northern Volsinii. This letter serves to inform you of a most wanted fugitive of the Imperium—"

"I don't need to be read the formal letter," Deadcut interrupted acidly. "I have eyes and can do so later. A summary will do just fine for now."

Markus cut himself off mid-sentence and very stiffly put down the letter amidst general amusement. "In summary, Vendrick Caecillion is currently wanted for a laundry list of crimes against the Crown that I'm certain he could recite far better than I, including the murder of several Imperial Watchers posted at Silverwood and Serpentbrook Hold. My orders are to bring him, alive, to Ascalon."

Frelia's lips turned up in a snarl. So she'd been right all along. *And they say I don't understand the Volsinii.* The only thing she'd missed was the fact that Vendrick was the only one charged.

So what did Ironfang want from the rest of them?

"I see," said Deadcut. "And what evidence have you?"

"Why," said Markus, "His Majesty's word itself."

Helheim, if Ironfang himself were behind this, it was all over. Vendrick had been Ironfang's Spymaster; no one would blink if he said Vendrick did things without the crown's approval, and that was before you even got to his time at Silverwood.

Frelia glanced to Vendrick but, as usual, his face was a mask.

"Is this how the Imperium rewards loyalty?" Frelia snapped.

Markus didn't look at her, but out of the corner of her eye, Frelia saw Mitri wince.

"Vendrick," said Deadcut. "Would you kindly confirm if the letter in Markus' hand is, in fact, written by His Majesty? I'm certain you're familiar enough with his handwriting to know."

Vendrick held a gloved hand out, and Markus handed over the letter as though the spymaster might bite.

"It's his," said Vendrick after a moment. "But there's no royal seal."

Internally, Frelia cursed Markus blackly and in her mother tongue. She tried to catch Vendrick's eye but again, could read nothing from his expression. What did it mean, there was no seal? That it wasn't legitimate? That sounded like something the Imperium would care about.

"Now, della Luciana," Deadcut said, "before we get into next steps—what do you know of the Unseen?"

"My father seems to find their teachings a compelling substitute for the Church of the Triad." Markus shrugged. "Beyond that, I've little interest in them."

"Merciful Goddesses," Frelia muttered, "he's not just going to admit it, Deadcut."

Markus' eyebrows lifted. "Admit what?"

"My son," Deadcut said, "seems to believe that these Unseen are at the heart of a vast conspiracy."

Vendrick threw back his head and exhaled sharply while Clarissa outright smacked her palm into her forehead. Frelia's blood began to boil like she was staring down a garmr, but there were no monsters here.

Only men.

"With all due respect, Your Excellency," Markus said, "your son is a paranoid git."

"You're actively trying to arrest him," Mitri pointed out. "Does that not prove him right?"

Deadcut turned her piercing stare on Vendrick. "Good point."

Merciful Goddesses, they had been so close. Deadcut was teetering on the brink of listening, and even Frelia could see it. They were going to have to fight their way out of this—mercilessly and painfully, if the Watchers surrounding them were anything to go by—and it was all because they didn't have proof good enough for Deadcut.

Vendrick's word was not enough. Clarissa's word was not enough. Mitri's notes were not enough, and Faustine's bloodstone was not enough. Frelia's presence here at all was not enough.

Her hand fell to her sword, but when she looked at the old Silverwood Watcher Captain, Frelia realized what might be enough even for Deadcut Verona.

It had just walked through the door.

"Markus has the Grimsdalr Bloodrune under that eyepatch."

The entire room turned to stare at Frelia.

It would prove everything, all at once. Everything Vendrick had said about the Unseen and their obsession with bloodrunes, and everything Mitri had said he could do. And therefore, everything about the Unseen, their agenda, and the Imperator.

Markus della Luciana simply could not have a bloodrune if it all weren't true.

"I beg your bloody pardon, Valerius," Markus snapped. "What a ridiculous accusation!"

"Accusation," Faustine pointed out, "but not impossibility?"

The girl was still hiding behind Frelia's left flank, and so Frelia reached out to squeeze her shoulder what she hoped was encouragingly. *Yes,* she told Faustine mentally. *Hold onto that anger. You have always deserved better.*

A calculating gleam—the same one Vendrick and Clarissa had—fell across Deadcut's lined face. "Della Luciana the Elder—remove your eyepatch, would you kindly? We shall settle this at once."

"I beg pardon, Your Excellency!" Markus spluttered. "Do you allow your guests to demand you forgo your cane?"

"My cane is not currently the lynchpin in a conspiracy theory," Deadcut said primly. "Particularly since I cannot believe Elias della Luciana would ever allow for Vendrick's public arrest over what he did for the Crown."

Frelia's ears practically pricked up. From a Volsinii, that was almost as good as outright calling the warrant bullshit.

And finally, she saw Vendrick's face move. He was hiding a smile.

"Honestly," Deadcut added, "I find that more impossible to believe than the idea that some sort of cult has risen in the vacuum created by the loss of the Church of the Triad."

Frelia cackled. The more Markus tried to slither out of this, the more he dug his own grave. By all rights, if he had the bloodrune, he wasn't Markus della Luciana, since he was not of the Grimsdalr family line. But if he didn't have it, then why argue so much?

"It's indecent!" Markus protested.

"I can remove mine, too," Frelia said. "Then we're even."

Vendrick's eye fell on her then. Frelia had had the injury itself at the Battle of Skjöldr, but not the painful echo that lay scratched across her face now. Somehow, though, the idea of exposing it bothered Frelia less now than it ever had. Maybe it had something to do with the armor on her back, again.

So let them see her scars. She'd fucking earned them.

"A sensible proposal," Deadcut said. "Thank you, Valerius."

"I will most certainly not be doing anything of the sort!" Markus insisted.

Clarissa stifled a laugh almost as manic as Frelia's, and Mitri was starting to look like he was waiting for the punchline.

"Then we shall go nowhere, and you may explain to the Imperator why you came back empty-handed—provided your warrant is legitimate."

Deadcut settled against the back of the Coldiron throne to wait.

And they call Vendrick a spider, Frelia thought as she began untying the knots holding her eyepatch in place. Her other eye stared at Markus as her fingers worked, and when she tugged the eyepatch over her head, she dared him to speak.

She knew what they saw. Branching lightning scars were etched into her hairline, and the eye itself was clouded over, milky, and could no longer blink. As though someone had taken her vibrant, amber eye and replaced it with a ghost.

"Your turn," Frelia said into the silence. "You're at least as brave as the Wolf of Kaldr, aren't you, Markus?"

At her side, Faustine hastily choked off a laugh.

"You're indecent," Markus muttered, side-eyeing Frelia's wound as though it were infectious.

"Valerius would not have had to," Deadcut said over the outcry from Vendrick and Clarissa, "if you had acquiesced to a very simple request."

"It's not proper!" Markus protested. "And besides, only one of us has the clearance of the Imperator here, and it certainly isn't a disgraced Kaldiri and the former Imperial Spymaster."

"And what of the Senate?" Mitri asked. "If there's no royal seal on the warrant, there's no Speaker approval, either."

Markus started to bumble his outraged way through Volsinii law and precedent, but Frelia knew what she was looking at.

He was going to run. You could see it, in the white of his eye, like a cornered prey animal. Markus was going to talk his way out of this just like Vendrick always did, and then he was going to run. Frelia watched him open that treacherous mouth and all she saw was that same bloodstained, fiery red that haunted Hägen Einnaska's throne room.

She launched herself into Markus with all the force she could muster, dragging the mage knight off balance and scrabbling for his eyepatch. He grunted as he fumbled back, planting his feet firmly as he threw a bony elbow. He caught Frelia's solar plexus, and she spat up blood onto the back of Markus' shiny armor.

"*Cease this at once!*" Deadcut roared.

By then, Frelia had gotten enough purchase around the strap of Markus' eyepatch to yank. It snapped in her hands, and she shoved her fingers into Markus' hair to hold his head steady and make him stare, guilty, at the Coldiron throne.

"Deadcut," Frelia ground out, "is there a whirling spiral in his eye?"

The court fell into silence as Deadcut stared down a prince of the Volsinii Imperium.

"I've no idea," Deadcut said. "He's holding it shut."

"*Skitr,*" Frelia snarled. "You spineless little shit."

Faustine was suddenly moving—"Oh no you don't!"

The teenager grabbed for Markus' forehead, tugging none too gently at his eyelid. Markus tried to fight her off, but Frelia's hand was still secure in his hair and his shaking went nowhere. Faustine brought her other hand around to pull on Markus' lower lid.

"There!" she said. "Lady Deadcut?"

Deadcut looked at him for only a moment longer.

Then the governor drew herself up to her feet, her stolen crown glittering in the afternoon sun. "It would seem my son is not so paranoid as you would like me to believe, della Luciana."

For a moment, Markus gaped at Deadcut in shocked horror. In that space, Frelia wondered what he'd expected, Deadcut to lie?

Then he smashed an elbow into Frelia's face with a bone-jarring crunch. She dropped him as her hands flew to her bleeding nose, and Markus tore out of her grasp and towards the nearest door.

But there was Faustine, smashing her shoulder into Markus' back and slamming them both into the tiled floor with a desperately loud thud. Markus thrashed wildly as Faustine fought to wind a gloved hand through his long hair. She yanked on a fistful, and Markus' neck cracked audibly in the motion.

"You're not getting away this time," Faustine spat even as Clarissa shrieked, "Vendrick, paralyze him!"

His rune was entirely drawn but for the last stroke, and Frelia could feel the arcane energy as hot as fire. "I'll just hit Faustine," he warned.

"Don't worry about me!" Faustine grunted, even as she caught an elbow to the face.

"Well, this is damning evidence if I've ever seen it," Deadcut said dryly. She bid Vendrick onwards with the Silverwood hand sign for 'advance.'

Frelia rounded on the fighting siblings, dragging her bleeding nose along her shoulder. It left a crimson streak across her leather armor. She grabbed for Markus' shoulders at the same moment he went for Faustine again, and the resultant tangle had Frelia's arms looped around his armpits and hoisting him to his knees.

In the sudden stillness, Frelia's bones throbbed so painfully she wondered for a moment if Markus had cast something, after all.

"It's been bothering me," Frelia snarled to him. "Your da wanting Huginn and Muninn."

There was no reason to care about Lady Daybreak and Lady Twilight's ravens, after all, when you only worshipped Lady Midnight.

"Geri and Freki would make much more sense," Frelia added. "They were Lady Midnight's companions long before the garmur. But Freki would never answer a gutless *zychnik* like you, would he?"

"You're insane," was all Markus said.

"So you killed him," Frelia added as if he hadn't spoken, "and that's why he never showed up in Kjell. So that just leaves Geri the Greedy, the other Guardian, whom I'm betting you can't summon. Can you?"

Magic smashed squarely into Markus' chest, and he immediately flopped like a puppet whose strings had been cut. Frelia took the opportunity to rearrange her grip, hoisting him up so that she could see the whites of the bastard's eyes.

"Grunt once for yes," Frelia ordered, "and twice for no."

"Professor?" Faustine said warily, rising slowly to her feet.

But Frelia stared into Markus' wide, terrified eyes. Why would Ironfang send such a coward for such a monumental task? It didn't make sense.

Except for the one thing Markus was that Orsina and Ironfang were not.

"You're here, beastminder," Frelia said, her voice very low, "for the secrets of the Einnaska family—aren't you?"

In the stony silence of the throne room, Markus made a single, pained grunt.

CHAPTER FORTY-FOUR

IN THE END, IRONFANG nearly missed the place altogether.

It was built deep into the mountainside, grey stone slab-work within a greyer, stonier mountain. Truly, a work of art Ironfang was simply thrilled had been preserved. Despite the fact that this place had supposedly been owned and operated by the Church of the Triad, the front façade lacked any statues, stained glass, or general ecclesiastical nonsense. This was supposedly home to the holiest monastery in the land? It was barely worth Ironfang's notice, ordinarily.

Where are you, Little One? The Sightless One whispered. *I sense death all around you.*

This, Ironfang thought back to him, *is the Library at Mournheim.*

It had only taken a single round of visions thrust into his psyche. Blightsen had been curled in the fetal position for hours afterwards, and when Ironfang had raised a finger to repeat the process, Blightsen had blurted out everything he knew about the Library at Mournheim, like vomit at the feet of his Imperator. It had turned out to be little more than common knowledge, with one key exception.

Blightsen knew there was a pilgrim's path to get there.

So they had trudged up the mountainside with Blightsen dutifully leaving offerings at shrines hidden both on purpose and simply by the snow. He muttered prayers that the Sightless One chortled at, and then hauled himself onto the back of his horse again. The once-cleric asked a few questions as they ascended the mountain but mostly kept to himself. Ironfang found that to be, by far, the man's best quality.

Blightsen's rounded glasses fogged up as they crossed the stony grey threshold into a high-ceilinged foyer designed to let in as much light as daytime in the mountains physically allowed. They paused only long enough to tie up their horses out of the wind and snow and for Blightsen to clean off his glasses, before they pushed into the room beyond.

In the meager torchlight he carried, Ironfang could make out hundreds upon hundreds of books.

There were shelves lining the room, stretching further back than Ironfang could rightly see. Some held proper, bound books, and others, folios or leather-bound journals. Still other shelves were hexagonal, honeycomb-like things built into the walls to hold stacks of scrolls. All along the end caps were spaces for torches, and there were solid-looking tables and chairs placed every so often down the rows.

Merciful Saints, thought Ironfang, *this will take an eternity.*

The slivers of information Ironfang needed would be like needles in the proverbial haystack of this grand monument to bureaucratic bloat. How many books about the nature of the divine and the garmur could one church possibly need?

"This is amazing," Blightsen whispered, his breath puffing out in soft, white clouds.

"Yes, well." It was just a dusty room full of books. "Any ideas on where to start looking?"

"There should be a catalogue around here somewhere." Blightsen blinked like an owl in the dim torchlight. "It's a large reference index, usually on its own podium. Let's begin there, unless you happen to find what you need during the search?"

Well, at least someone in these mountains had been civilized. "I shall take the left side, then," Ironfang said, and he started down the rows.

It didn't take long for the frigid air to swallow Blightsen's footsteps, and for the only sound to be Ironfang's own breath. He couldn't tell if the Sightless One were piggybacking on his psyche at the moment or not, and the thought made his skin crawl. He wanted that blasted creature out of his head!

Hopefully Blightsen was as half-decent a cleric as Ironfang had pretended he was, because even if they found what Ironfang was looking for, someone needed to cast the white magic involved and it certainly wouldn't be him. He had never had the talent for—

Something moved.

Ironfang froze midway between the shelf he'd just passed and the one in front of it. There were hardly any living beings this far up the mountainside, and fewer still that would make their way this deep into a shelter with no food or water. Besides, bears and snowy foxes couldn't open doors, and it had been too large to be a bird.

So what had he seen?

Ironfang switched his torch to his off hand, and moved his right hand to the hilt of his sword. He stepped carefully, soundlessly, and inched towards the shadow he'd sworn he saw.

When nothing stirred in the tense, chilly air, he called out, "Blightsen?"

A faint "Over here!" came from somewhere far to Ironfang's right.

Taking a breath, Ironfang opened his divine senses. He was immediately struck by the same cool deadness he'd felt without them—the stagnant air and musty papers—and he had to scrutinize the rafters to find so much as a hint of life.

His mind was playing tricks on him, then. It had to be. If there were anything in here, surely—

There it was again!

This time Ironfang was certain he'd seen something move out of the corner of his eye. He whirled on the spot, but his eyes only raked a hexagonal shelf full of neatly stacked scrolls. The shadows that crossed over them came from the torch Ironfang carried, and nothing more.

"Imperator!"

It echoed across the hollowed-out space.

"Found the index!"

Cringing at the sound, Ironfang hustled over to the source of the single, living light in the room. He shut off his divine sense as he drew closer; it was too hard to look at someone's face with it. Instantly Blightsen came back into focus, hunched over an enormous tome chained to a podium.

"It looks like undeath and the undead are covered in section seven-hundred-forty, and divination should be in nine-hundred-and-two." Blightsen took a few steps away from the catalogue, squinting at the numbers engraved into a library shelf nearby. "We're only at two-hundred-forty, here, so..."

They raised their torches to the aisle, towards where the stacks stretched into eternity. Ironfang opened his mouth to say that he'd take the nine-hundreds section, but a force unlike anything in this world suddenly clamped down hard in his stomach.

And a voice that was not Ironfang's own snaked from his mouth: "I shall take the section on the undead."

No, *no,* dammit! This was the last thing Ironfang needed.

Blightsen glanced over with a furrowed brow. "Sir?"

Without his go-ahead, Ironfang felt his feet begin to move down the aisle. He was unsteady on his own two Goddesses-damned feet, as though the thing controlling him was not used to walking, or, perhaps, walking on two legs.

Why is this body so weak? came the Sightless One's half-muted thoughts. *My sisters grant these wretched things sight and understanding beyond the veil and this is the result? Pah. No wonder humanity is failing; it looks like I must do everything myself.*

It was an effort for Ironfang to push through the deluge of thoughts that weren't his, to shout proof of his cognizance across the void. *Have I offended, my Lord?*

You take too long, the Sightless One whispered back, and Ironfang wished he had control of his own throat to scream.

"Sir, are you alright?" Blightsen appeared at his elbow again, jogging to keep up with the old general's long-legged strides.

"You will address me as *my Lord.*" came the voice that did not belong to Ironfang, yet lived in his throat.

Blightsen's eyes widened, and he stumbled into one of the nearby shelves. "That's..." He swallowed, audibly, as he straightened himself. "...that's not how you address an Imperator."

Neither is sir, Ironfang wanted to say.

"Are you feeling alright?" Blightsen continued.

The Sightless One turned Ironfang's head to coolly study Blightsen. And then it broke his face into a wide smile that stretched his cheeks and felt like it may well burst off his face.

"*I am,*" whispered the Sightless One.

CHAPTER FORTY-FIVE

"Valerius, explain yourself." Deadcut demanded from the Coldiron throne. "What do you mean, he's here for the Einnaskas' secrets?"

Frelia snorted mirthlessly, her arms still wrapped around Markus' shoulders in a wrestling hold. She half-wondered just how many things they could drop in Deadcut's lap today. "Haven't you wondered why you can't get into parts of the basement?"

Markus made a snarling noise that probably would have been some demand or other, if he hadn't been paralyzed.

"Oh, *ja,*" Frelia told him, and though she wasn't enjoying this, exactly, there was a strange sort of amusement to it all. "I wouldn't claim to know all the secrets of Castle Skjöldr, but I know a hell of a lot more than the usurpers."

Purple, astral energy coalesced around Markus, then, thick and binding, just like Vendrick had used to hold Lucia della Trova during the fight with Muninn. The magic pulled insistently on Markus' wrists, and Frelia took a deep breath before loosening her grip.

But the instant before his wrists locked, something in the air around Markus shattered. Frelia caught a glimpse of a rose-gold rune bloom briefly on his neck as she was thrown backwards by the sudden force. She slammed into something hard and bony, felt arms come around her middle to catch her.

"Faustine, hold!" Vendrick barked from somewhere over Frelia's shoulder.

Frelia scrambled back to her feet, the world righting just in time to see Markus shoot another blast of arcane energy over his shoulder. Faustine ducked, though she kept running, and the bolt slammed into a nearby Imperial Watcher. He groaned and crumpled to the floor.

"Dammit, Markus!" Faustine howled, scrambling after him towards a side door. "You're not allowed to run this time!"

She was three steps behind her older brother as he dashed through the a threshold and into the castle beyond.

For a half second, the Volsinii in the room just stood there in shock. Then Mitri was moving to see to the injured Watcher, and Frelia had started advancing.

She would not give the Volsinii another instant to play their games.

"Out of the Coldiron throne," Frelia barked.

"I beg your pardon?" said Deadcut, affronted.

Frelia fixed her in a withering look. "Do you want to chase Markus through the castle, or cut him off at the pass?"

For the first time since she'd set foot in Castle Skjöldr, the world fell well and truly silent. The injured Imperial Watcher stopped groaning as Mitri hunkered down to tend to him. And Frelia's footsteps made no sound on the plush, crimson carpet as she moved across the flagstones.

Was the Einnaska Bloodrune still inlaid into the floor, under all that sanguine carpet? If Frelia ripped off the bandage, would the wound have festered there all along?

"Thought not," Frelia said into the mounting silence. "So get out of the Coldiron throne, Deadcut."

Or I will make you, was left unsaid.

The old woman's eyes flicked, for some unknowable reason, to Vendrick. For a moment, he looked genuinely surprised—but it was gone, quick as it came. He looked to Frelia, an unspoken question in his eyes.

He seemed to find his own answer.

"Do as she says, Mother," said Vendrick.

Frelia was in measure with the seat of ancestral Kaldiri power, now. Close enough to hear Deadcut's old bones crack as the woman turned to retrieve an elegant wooden cane from where it leaned on an armrest. That in hand, she began taking slow, pragmatic steps towards where Vendrick and Clarissa still stood.

"And why am I being shooed away like a street cat?" Deadcut demanded.

Frelia pivoted around her like a wyvern on the wing, then dropped to her knees before the Coldiron throne. She tried to remember what it was Hägen had said, before the Battle for Skjöldr.

We have to be better than the Volsinii, he had argued. *I would sooner us all die than unleash a monster!*

And if I wouldn't? Frelia had demanded, all eyes in the war room glued to her fury.

Hägen had met her eyes, then—the last night she'd had both of them. His had carried the strife of the station he had never wanted, and so, *so* much grief. *Then if I'm dead,* he had said quietly, *check under the Coldiron throne. And pray you can live with yourself afterward.*

The Coldiron throne had not been designed with comfort in mind. No, it had been hewn from harsh angles and stern warnings against tyranny and megalomania. Protective runes decorated the worked metal, although Deadcut clearly no longer painted back over them at the Summer Solstice. Frelia wondered if Deadcut even knew she was supposed to be.

Was that why the southlands were being overrun with Garmur, these days?

She dropped to her belly, squinting at the cobwebbed dust beneath the chair legs. When nothing materialized, Frelia shoved her hand into the darkness, pressing around with blind fingers for whatever Hägen had to have meant. The strap of the Valerius Shield dug painfully into her chest.

"What in Hypogia are you doing?" Deadcut demanded from somewhere down the hall.

"Mother," Vendrick began sharply. "If anyone has the right to—"

"Oh I'm well aware she's Kaldiri," Deadcut fired back. "But what I do not—"

Saints, they did not have time for this!

"Hägen," Frelia interrupted, and the bickering was instantly silenced, "denied how fucked we were at the Battle for Skjöldr, right up until he died."

The old hurts and the old salt came right back. And how could they not? Three floors below, on what would number amongst the worst days of her life, Frelia had argued with her closest friends about how best not to lose everything they'd ever loved.

And then they'd gone and done exactly that.

She felt it, then. A warmth beneath the throne that could only come from magic. She quickly splayed her fingers on the underside of the seat, laying her palm against the rune. Frelia wondered which it was.

I need a light, she thought, but the angle was completely wrong. Even with one of Vendrick's runelights, Frelia wouldn't have been able to make out a damn thing without unbolting the Coldiron throne from the ground and flipping it over.

It had to be obvious, then. Something any Einnaska—any Kaldiri—would know.

"Ech er seiða," Frelia said immediately.

Nothing moved.

Dammit. "Vendrick!" Frelia glanced over her shoulder. "Are you feeling any, I don't know, magic bullshit?"

Deadcut harrumphed, and Frelia could just make out Clarissa rolling her eyes at her mother's back.

"Your hand is on something," Vendrick confirmed. "I can't tell exactly what, though. It's very old magic, so it's probably aurally activated."

"And you can just tell that standing there?" Mitri asked.

Vendrick raised an eyebrow. "You can't?"

And there it was again, the absolute juggernaut that was Vendrick's talent for magic. It was good to have that on her side, this time, in no small part because Mitri looked affronted at the question.

"I'm also getting tinges of something," Clarissa said. "I agree, it's probably something aural. What did you say to it, Frelia?"

"Ech er seiða," Frelia said again, looking back to the throne in the interest of not wrenching her shoulder again before she'd need it. "It's the oldest words the Kaldiri ever put to paper."

This is war, the old Thane had warned. And then she'd made good on that threat.

"What about before that?" Vendrick asked.

"What do you—" Frelia started to ask, but then it smacked her in the forehead.

Language hadn't begun with runes; those had been created later. There were stories older than paper, than ink, than even Frelia's bloodrune.

"The war songs." Frelia pulled her hand out from beneath the throne and sat up. "I bet it needs one of the family war songs."

She had never more desperately wished for another Kaldiri to talk to as she squeezed her eye shut, trying to think of which one was most likely.

"My family's is for victory," she said, "so it wouldn't be that one. Grimsdalr is for feints, and this is basically the opposite of that. Traust is remembrance, and Konstantin is... is..."

Dammit, if only the ringing in her bones would let up!

"Scouting, wasn't it?" Clarissa put forward.

"Maybe...?" Frelia felt the loss of knowledge like a punch to the gut. Was moving forward really worth it, if she left everything of worth behind to do so?

Dammit, Edmund would have had an answer to that. Maybe a thought about which war song to try, too.

"What about Einnaska?"

Frelia's eye snapped open and found her mark on Deadcut. The old general had been difficult to read before, but now it was downright impossible.

Just like her son. And like her daughter tried very hard not to be.

"We are in their traditional home," Deadcut added at Frelia's silence. "It would make more sense than another family's, would it not?"

"That's for war, though," Frelia said.

From over by the downed Imperial Watcher, Mitri called, "Is that not what this is?"

Frelia sighed, drew in a deep breath, and then hoisted herself back onto her feet. She backed up a few paces to stare down Hägen's ancestral seat, and reached for words she hadn't so much as thought of in a decade.

> *"Boots on, boys, it's time to go—*
> *The war moon's risen and the*
> *river runs slow.*
> *Thought they'd catch us by*
> *surprise,*
> *But we're blue, until we die."*

For a moment, Frelia's raspy alto rang out in the silence of the throne room. And then she felt something tug at her bloodrune hard enough to make her stumble.

And the Coldiron throne began to move.

Inch by inch, it dragged itself back, bolts squealing in protest as it tried to wrench free of the floor.

"Keep at it!" Clarissa said. "I think you've got it."

Frelia drew in a breath and went on, stronger now:

> *"Boots on, girls, it's time to move—*
> *The war moon's risen and it's time to choose.*
> *Thought they'd catch us by surprise,*
> *But we're blue, until we die."*

With a terrible, screeching groan like a burning garmr, the rivets on the Kaldiri throne began ripping themselves free of the floor. The Coldiron throne caved in on itself, as though a giant had picked it up and was crumpling it between his massive hands.

And only when it was nearly doubled over did the rune on its underside burst.

It blasted astral energy like a shot from a cannon, and Frelia threw up her arm to cover her face like she actually wore the family shield. Vendrick's eyes narrowed against the blast, and Deadcut actually grasped for the edge of Clarissa's bench.

"Once more, Frelia," Vendrick urged. "I think you've nearly got it."

Frelia made a face and started the next verse—"*Boots on Cavalry, let's ride!*"—only to nearly forget the ancient lyrics as two more voices joined hers.

One was low, masculine, and Volsinii, and she knew it very well.

The other was resonant, feminine, and just as accented, and it came as even more of a shock.

But Vendrick and Clarissa had heard the Einnaska War Song across too many battlefields not to know how this verse ended.

> *"The war moon's risen and the*
> *river runs high.*
> *Do you hear the thunderous*
> *sound?*
> *The war king in his jagged*
> *crown!"*

The astral energy intensified, and then rushed backwards as though sucked into a whirlpool out in the sea.

In its wake, a yawning, spiraling staircase lay carved into the ground.

CHAPTER FORTY-SIX

FAUSTINE'S BREATH WAS COMING in short, pained bursts. She chased Markus through hallway after twisted hallway, following the red smear his Watcher's cloak left in the air behind him. She desperately wished she had something to throw at him besides her only dagger.

"Markus!" she shouted, as though it would do any good. "Get back here, you coward!"

His heavy hobnailed boots pounded the floor up ahead with no discernable change in rhythm.

Orsina, Galeria, and Markus had already been out of Silverwood by the time Faustine was born, but she'd grown up with Markus, sort of. He had lived at home during his early days of Imperial Watcher training, and had ended up as sort of a cross between another parent and an annoying older sibling.

Stuck in a cycle with Markus, the professor had told her once. Faustine would be absolutely useless in a fight against an archdarkbeast, and she knew that. This was just Kjell, all over again, only this time she didn't have Thera for help and people to save. She still only had a stupid knife that was somehow supposed to stop her stupid older brother.

Wait. That was Lord Huginn talking.

And Faustine had commanded the yarn-ball darkbeast, hadn't she? Who was to say she couldn't do it again, Markus? The last time had been sheer panic and racing thoughts, but Faustine clearly knew the basics of beastminding.

Faustine would break this toxic cycle even if it killed her.

Up ahead, Markus' red cloak veered sharply down a flight of stairs, and Faustine hastened to follow. She pushed her way through a sturdy door at the foot of the staircase only to find herself in an empty room.

Or, no, not empty. Not exactly.

Late afternoon sunlight was filtering through the high windows onto vacant shield and spear racks. It glittered across empty glass display cases and naked armor stands, and Faustine's heart suddenly gave a terrible, pained lurch.

This had been the Einnaska's armory, once. It had to have been, given where it was in relation to the throne room. Why had Governor Deadcut emptied it?

To cleanse it, of course, came a voice in her head that both sounded like her older siblings, and like no one she knew.

Now that she was standing still, Faustine's entire body felt like it was vibrating with adrenaline. And it occurred to her exactly who she'd find in here. *He who always hurt you, belittled you, and made you less than yourself.*

Heavy hands came around her wrists and yanked. Faustine's chin slammed into one of the empty display cases, and despite her thrashing, the grip on her arms was like iron.

"You little turncoat," Markus spat. "You've dragged yourself in with Caecillion's lot, have you?"

What is your weapon? Professor Valerius had asked the class at the start of the grappling unit, although they hadn't known that yet.

Ellie had put a tentative hand up and said, *Your... sword? Or lance, or whatever?*

No. The professor was grinning at some private joke. *You'd think so.*
But no.

So what is it? Siegmund had asked, his brow furrowing like the valleys
in his home territory. *If not your literal weapon?*

The professor had grinned, then, beautiful and terrible. *Your entire*
self.

Faustine pulled her heel off the ground and jammed it hard into
Markus' unarmored shin.

He howled and released her just enough for Faustine to duck under
the display case. She scrambled through cobwebs and dust, tumbling
over table legs and wood framing to spring back to her feet on the other
side.

She whirled on Markus, drawing her dagger and gripping it tight.

"I don't see why you haven't switched sides," Faustine said. "Our
family sucks, Markus. And it always has."

Surprise colored her brother's patrician features. "What in Hypogia
are you on about?"

"Father hasn't been the same since his Ascension," Faustine said, and
she willed her hands not to shake. "He's awful, Markus. And I know you
think so, too."

"Don't be melodramatic." Markus didn't so much as move to draw
his blade. "Our father is Hypogean. I don't expect a dumb little girl to
understand."

There was that word, again. The same one Faustine had heard
whispered in her father's study for years, the one Lucia della Trova had
apparently called him, too. Markus sounded so much like Orsina had,
in the forest outside Kjell, that Faustine wondered if either of them had
ever generated a thought for themselves.

"Of course you don't," Faustine said. "You never expected anything
from me except a scapegoat."

Markus suddenly bolted sideways, and Faustine stepped opposite him around the display case, like in a duel. They remained equidistant, separate.

Cycling.

"I expected you," Markus spat through gritted teeth, "to behave appropriately. To do your duty as befits a della Luciana. And you have repeatedly proven you are not worthy of even that."

He spat onto the empty glass case, but it was just a dehydrated dribble of scorn.

"Orsina and Galeria have made themselves useful for the family, and I fail to see why you can't."

Was he really so blind?

"You made me prey!"

Markus was so startled at the sudden volume that he stopped trying to round on her. Something deep and distant seemed to rumble in Faustine's stomach, and she felt unbalanced...

No. She felt free.

"And now you want me to make everyone else into that, too?" Faustine shook her head, disbelief thick in her throat. "I won't do it. It's wrong."

"You think father's plans are about right and wrong?" Markus spluttered like the question were absurd. "It's about fate. About destiny!"

Fate.

Faustine had never liked the idea that everything she had ever thought, hoped, dreamt, or done had been preordained by some celestial judge who clearly didn't give a shit about her suffering. Was that why Father had stopped worshipping deities whose presences he couldn't feel? Why all of Volsinii had?

Or was it just that if you could command the children of hell, eternal paradise no longer mattered?

Markus lunged again, this time to his right. Faustine hurriedly hopped left like a grounded bird, ungainly and awkward. The yawning space between them remained.

"Do you know why father kept you from Beastminder training?" Markus suddenly asked.

Faustine's shoulders tensed, a warning buzzing deep in her brain. Markus was a mage. He was standing at point-blank, but surely he could still cast something? The Not-Headmaster certainly could.

Why wasn't he trying to blast her apart with magic?

"Cat got your tongue?" Markus suddenly laughed, the sound sharp and mocking against the stony castle walls. "Then I shall tell you. We kept you from beastminder training because you simply do not have the steel to do it properly."

The world seemed to freeze all around her, and the determined, buoyant anger that had led Faustine here fell away. "What?"

"You're soft, Faustine," Markus said. "Pliant. A dumb little girl afraid of her own shadow. Did you actually decide to turn your colors, or were you simply swept along by your betters again?"

This was treason? It didn't feel like treason. Then again, Faustine supposed she had very little thumbnail for that kind of thing. All she knew was that what Orsina had done was wrong—inhumanly, terrifyingly wrong—and it was on their father's orders, and Professor Valerius and Not-Headmaster Caecillion were the only people who ever stood up to the Imperator. She knew she still saw Siegmund's kind face broken in half when she shut her eyes. Could still hear Christel's scream as Orsina's unnatural fire burned them. Could still feel the warm, hollow darkness of the yarn-ball darkbeast's innards, the sharpness of Huginn's claws clamp around her middle and yank.

"That's demonstrably not true," she said.

It was like Markus hadn't even heard her. "Has Caecillion told you what he's done?" he added. "The lives he's taken, lies he's told, treason he's committed already? Has Valerius told you how she ripped men apart with her bare hands and laughed while they burned in spellflame?"

Lord Caecillion, Faustine knew, had been the Viper of Ascalon. And therefore, she also knew that all the terrible things he'd done had been in service to the Crown. He had been a weapon in Ironfang's hands, then, just like Markus and Orsina. The only difference was that Lord Caecillion had the good sense to leave.

And Professor Valerius was honest and dependable. She cared about the Violet Owls so much she kept them safe from Markus, from their parents, from their bullies. She ran headfirst into battle against legendary monsters so that other people didn't have to. She would never laugh while someone died horribly.

"I don't believe you." The words were sour on Faustine's tongue.

"The truth doesn't care if you believe it," Markus said. "Your hero is a monster, Faustine."

And he lunged across the display cases.

War does not make heroes, echoed in the back of Faustine's mind as she scrambled backwards. *It makes survivors and orphans, but not heroes.*

Glass shattered around them as Markus grabbed onto Faustine's hair. She thrashed again in his grip, dagger uselessly scouring a line down his Imperial Watcher armor.

"And I will show you firsthand," Markus snarled.

***

Ironfang pounded at the walls of this mental prison, but the Sightless One wouldn't budge. He wanted control of his limbs again, dammit, of his mind. Ironfang had no idea if this were a permanent change or not, and beyond that, he needed to warn Blightsen that there was—

Your humanity is showing, the Sightless One interrupted Ironfang's pounding. *There is nothing here but death.*

So the Sightless One kept saying, but Ironfang saw no skeletal remains of dead clerics—or of anything else, for that matter. Did the Old One mean the books? Ironfang supposed paper was death, in a manner of speaking, but the Triad and their forgotten brother worked magic far more visceral than pen and ink.

The Sightless One passed the four hundred stacks, the five hundred stacks, and Ironfang definitely could feel eyes on his neck, now. The hairs on his forearms rose beneath his sleeves.

My... Lord... He forced out, practically spewing the words inside the prison of his mind. *You... are... danger...*

"I feel them," said the Sightless One, quietly.

Blightsen squeaked, tripping over the hem of his cloak. *How low you've sunk, Elias,* the Sightless One told him, *that this is your assistant.*

"Feel what, sir?" Blightsen asked.

"Eyes," whispered the Sightless One as it turned Ironfang's head this way and that.

His eyes fell on the far wall, distant between lonely stretches of bookcases. It was almost lost in the gloom, a dark, looming precipice beyond human sight.

"It has been a long time," the Sightless One mused through Ironfang's throat, "since I have felt."

Blightsen shuffled for a moment on his feet. "You're... not Ironfang, are you?"

The Sightless One was already moving Ironfang deeper into the gloom.

Ironfang threw his consciousness against the Sightless One's grip again, but the Old One held on tightly. Ironfang felt himself slowly being swallowed by the god's vast, void-like consciousness, a dying star swallowed by the vacuum of the night sky itself.

"I am," the Sightless One said, "a god."

He was getting more comfortable with Ironfang's stride, with his human appendages and tactile senses. He was passing the six-hundreds now, holding the torch aloft like it was normal. Ironfang could feel himself drowning in the Sightless One's cognizance, struggling to keep his head above water.

Struggling to stay himself.

"There are no gods," Blightsen said. "Only Goddesses."

The Sightless One cocked Ironfang's head again, and Ironfang took advantage of the momentary distraction to throw himself against its psychic hold again. The Sightless One held him back like an adult preventing a child from swinging at his knees.

"And do you think their eyes are on you now?" the Sightless One asked Blightsen.

"Of course not," Blightsen said, and Ironfang could feel the Sightless One's surprise like a slimy creature on his neck. "I wouldn't be here if they were."

The Sightless One began to laugh, driving a nail into Ironfang's psyche.

"The Kaldiri are cursed," Blightsen added. "Even half-breeds like me. If we weren't, why are we the ones the garmur always eat?"

The Sightless One's amusement was plainer than Ironfang had ever seen it. "And what do you know of my sister's children?" it asked.

Blightsen tensed, but didn't question the epithet. *Smarter than we give him credit for,* Ironfang thought. He wondered what the once-cleric knew, what he sensed.

"I know the smell on the wind when they're sitting on the horizon," Blightsen said. "I know fourteen ways to sew up a bite wound—seven more, if it's broken something internal—and eight different tinctures that might—yes, *might*—prevent the ichor from starting an infection."

He stopped walking then, the seven-hundreds plaque glittering just over his head.

"And I know what happens," he added, even more quietly, "when they get to run, unchecked, through a populated city."

Ironfang rescinded his previous thought. No, Blightsen was not smarter than he seemed—for who would blame the Imperator to his face for the garmur? Let alone a god.

The real question was whether Blightsen was Kaldiri brash, or Kaldiri stupid.

"What are you really here for?" Blightsen asked. "If you're really the Unseen's god, in there, then it's not just for the books."

The Sightless One's laugh was a wheeze in the still, frigid air. "You will see."

He kept lurching towards the nine-hundreds stacks, and Ironfang slammed into the walls of his mental prison again. *Unhand me!* he demanded.

You have your purpose, the Sightless One reminded him. *But do not forget that once you serve it, you are—*

The instant Ironfang's heavy boot crossed the threshold to the nine-hundreds, something hard and sharp pierced his stomach. White hot pain tore through his and the Sightless One's cognizance alike, and Ironfang wasn't sure whether he clapped his hands to his abdomen, or the Sightless One did.

Either way, he felt the socket of a spearhead embedded deep in his stomach as his body crumpled to the floor. There to be silver in there; nothing else could make the Sightless One scream so.

Blightsen was beside him in moments, wadding up some of Ironfang's cloak and pressing it firmly into his gut.

Ironfang felt every single motion like a film had been cleared from his eyes. Even as pain laced through his stomach, he pushed away Blightsen's ceaseless fretting and sat up. His arms went for his screaming abdomen, and Ironfang found that his fingers bent to his will, and pressed against the wound in his stomach, and felt the warmth of his Hypogean blood.

And for the first time since Ironfang could remember, his mind fell silent.

"Cease your prattling," Ironfang growled, and his voice was his again.

Blightsen's lips set into a firm line as understanding filtered across his face. "I suppose I don't have to take a look at—"

"Know your place." The general rose shakily to his feet, eyes fixed on Blightsen. "What did you do?"

"Me?" Blightsen was visibly taken aback. "Nothing, I didn't fling a Spearhead spell at you."

Ironfang kept his hand pressed against his stomach. Already, icy shards of something metallic were seeping into his insides and burning into viscera.

Silver. Only silver could wound him, now. A Spearpoint ward, then.

"Who goes there?"

It was a voice like a fetid grave, and it sent icy claws into every one of Ironfang's vertebrae.

Somewhere, Blightsen found the courage to raise his torch higher, until the shadows licked the library's far wall.

A tall figure stood shrouded in a heavy, white coat nearly identical to the green one Blightsen wore. Ironfang's hand shot for the hilt of his sword, his gut wound protesting the movement. He should have sensed this man when he'd opened his divine senses, should have seen some inkling of his existence before walking right into him.

But there he was, and Ironfang's pain was suddenly blinding.

"Brother?" Blightsen asked.

"Leave here at once!" roared the impossible cleric.

Blightsen shrunk back, but Ironfang drew himself up to his full height. "You will state your name before your Imperator," he said in the imperious tone that had defrocked many a cleric. "And remove your hood and badge of office."

Something glinted beneath the cleric's heavy hood—eyes, maybe, shifting between Blightsen and Ironfang. "I don't think so," said the man, and his voice was heavily accented. Kaldiri.

Ironfang supposed that made sense. There were very few mad enough to live in an abandoned monastery high in the mountains. It would only be someone comfortable with blizzards, elk hunting, and Saints-knew-what-else who could survive up here.

"Brother," Blightsen tried again, "the Church has been gone a long time."

There was sorrow in Blightsen's voice, but he kept it light. Probably lighter than he wanted to, but there was the Imperator beside him. Perhaps the garmur comments hadn't been so thought-out, after all.

"Brother," said the impossible cleric, and Blightsen stiffened, "what makes you think I don't know?"

Blightsen crept forward as though despite himself. "Are you from Skj—New Ascalon?"

The other cleric tensed. "It doesn't matter."

"Yes, it does," Blightsen insisted gently. "Your accent sounds familiar. I was just wondering if you grew up near—"

Blightsen cut himself off as the other cleric's hand snapped up to cast. Rich, blue light dripped from the man's fingers as he began to draw slowly, unhurriedly.

"You will leave at once," the other cleric commanded, "or I will finish this rune."

Even as his stomach protested, Ironfang moved to draw his blade.

Blightsen burst out, "Are these your wards?"

Both Ironfang and the impossible cleric stared at the man, uncomprehending.

"They're very well made," Blightsen continued, and Ironfang could almost hear him coaching a Silverwood student. "I can see why nothing has bothered you in here."

The other cleric said nothing.

"But the war is over, Brother," Blightsen added, far more gently than Ironfang would have spoken to someone actively threatening him. "And the world is not what it was. Please stand down, so that the Imperator can work. We won't disturb you."

The cleric's eyes flashed again beneath his hood, and a deep, warning bell began tolling in the back of Ironfang's mind.

"Edmund Blightsen," said the cleric.

It wasn't a question.

"Yes, that's me." Blightsen's brow furrowed as he squinted at the lanky figure half-hidden in shadow. "Have we met?"

Silence fell.

Then,

"No." The cleric, inexplicably, released his half-finished spell. "Find what you came for, make notes, and go. You may not take anything from this place."

"Thank you, Brother cleric," said Blightsen, though he was very obviously confused. "May the—"

Ironfang had had enough of this farce.

"I don't think you understand how this works," Ironfang hissed. "You are in violation of Imperial law, which states that all the Church of the Triad's assets are forfeit and its clerics, unlicensed to practice."

"I have no interest in the laws of petty men," said the cleric.

Blightsen cringed. "Hermit or not, you live in the Imperium."

The cleric's glinting eyes turned sharply to Ironfang.

"Kneel before your Imperator," Ironfang said, "and I may yet let you live."

The cleric burst into spluttering laughter that sent fire bursting into Ironfang's blood, and made Blightsen seize.

"You'll *let* me live?" the cleric managed between laughs. "Now who doesn't understand how things work?"

The cleric threw his head back laughing, and suddenly Ironfang realized why those eyes glinted—they were luminescent, beneath his hood. Icy blue and glowing.

Undead.

The cleric drew a rune so fast, Ironfang's Hypogean sight couldn't even track it. The library shook as though struck by the hand of a giant, and Ironfang grabbed for the nearest sturdy object, stumbling as the bookshelf, too, shook. Paper rained down on them, and Ironfang instinctively curled to cover his neck from falling tomes. His stomach screamed with the protective movement.

Vittoro had been right; it was so cold in the Library at Mournheim, they would have to warm their inkpots between their fingers. Which meant that if it got even colder due to Hypogean interference, Ironfang would've had no idea.

This was no cleric at all.

"You're a lich," Ironfang snapped.

The cleric-who-wasn't froze, and all around them, the earthquake stopped. The sudden silence and stillness was deafening.

"This is your lair," Ironfang added dryly, "is it not?"

The lich opened his mouth to speak, but Blightsen beat him to it:

"*Hägen?*"

CHAPTER FORTY-SEVEN

FRELIA LED THE WAY down the sepulchral staircase. Vendrick was right behind her, and Clarissa tailed him, piggybacking on one of her ghostly summons. And bringing up the rearguard, as she always had, was Deadcut Verona herself.

If Frelia was right—if Hägen was right—then at the end of this staircase lay not only the Guardian of Einnaska Territory and legend immemorial, but a monster.

A garmr.

Skitr.

"Valerius, where in Hypogia are we going?" Deadcut demanded.

She was struggling to keep up with how quickly Frelia flew down the stairs, and Vendrick looked torn between his ire and his self-preservation instinct.

"Mother," he finally said, "you're a general. Certainly you can recognize hell?"

Frelia had no air in her lungs to answer, let alone laugh. She took the staircase turns at a breakneck pace until the air around them began to cool. The darkness grew all-encompassing, despite the runelight

Vendrick conjured, and their breath had begun to turn to frost down in the forgotten bowels of Castle Skjöldr.

And all the while, Frelia was trying to piece together something she was on the very cusp of understanding, but couldn't force the pieces into any kind of framework that made sense.

Because there was only one frame she could see, and for it to be true, it would mean Hägen had been right all along.

But no, dammit, she wasn't like Hägen. She did not crack under the weight of command. She would not crumple when faced with obliteration, the way he had.

Almost without conscious thought, she glanced over to Vendrick, and found his face set in grimly determined lines. Behind him, Clarissa was a panicking, softer-edged mirror of her older brother's expression. Deadcut's expression lay somewhere in between her children's, severe but not terrified yet.

Before long, Vendrick's blueish-white runelight slid over a heavy door.

Frelia had only seen it once before, a very long time ago. It held back what Frelia had argued with Hägen about unleashing, to keep the Battle for Skjöldr from turning into a siege. Or worse—a massacre.

The door itself was a plain slab of heavy stone, taller than Frelia and stout enough to pass a carriage through. A short row of Kaldiri runes had been chiseled into the face and, beneath that, a ring-like hole just about the size of a human head.

"What in Hypogia...?" Deadcut murmured, and even she sounded subdued. "What does it say?"

Frelia didn't even need to read it. "And for Einnaska, the Task of the Tyrant. Yours shall be the iron will by which the world is shaped."

"Is that a Sacred Task?" Clarissa called down from the stairs.

"Yes."

It came not from Frelia, but Deadcut.

"Frelia," said Vendrick, his voice low and urgent, "the magic signature coming from this room is so unstable I can feel it out here, through what is presumably lead."

He rapped a knuckle on the door, and the dark, cavern-like hallway swallowed the sound almost before the echo formed.

"*Ja,*" said Frelia. "That's what Hägen said, too. Only he called it an aura."

"Same thing," Vendrick said. "Wait, you've been here before?"

"Once." Frelia's facial expression tightened, and it pulled on the scars around her sightless eye. "The long way around."

She felt Vendrick's eyes on her now, his desperate need to ask her when, and how, and why. All Frelia could offer him back was dread-borne answers he wouldn't like.

"Valerius." Urgency bled into Deadcut's voice. "We had no idea this was down here. I demand to know what is going on."

Frelia looked to Deadcut again with smoldering fury seething from her every pore. "I already told you," the Kaldiri said. "The Guardian of Einnaska Territory. The Greedy One. Lady Midnight's Wolf—Geri—sleeps here."

She held out a gloved hand, imperious. "Now give me the crown."

It wrenched something in Frelia's insides, to demand of a Volsinii what should have been hers by right of blood.

It doesn't matter now, she reminded herself. *Hägen is dead and so are his dreams and it is never going to matter.*

"I beg your pardon!" Deadcut spluttered, a hand going to the sapphire-and-silver circlet resting at her forehead. "You go too far."

"One, it's not even the real crown," Frelia snapped. "Two, what do you think goes here?"

She tapped the circular ring beneath the Kaldiri inscription on the door.

"Mum," Clarissa said, her ghostly mount clambering down the last few stairs to the floor, "don't be obtuse."

For a moment, Deadcut's dark eyes flicked between Frelia and the door, and Frelia tensed.

"Step aside, then." Deadcut limped forward, her free hand reaching for the circlet at her brow.

Frelia rolled her eye but slid sideways to let Deadcut through. The old woman thrust her cane into Vendrick's hand, and he reflexively caught it with a scowl.

"Here goes nothing," Deadcut said, slipping the silver circlet carefully off her head, "I suppose."

And she pressed the circlet into the ring-like hole in the door.

For a moment, all was silent. Frelia tensed, waiting for the rumbling to start up in her bones.

Instead, something gargantuan cracked behind the large stone door, and the center seam began to separate. Late afternoon sunlight flooded the corridor, blinding after so long in the catacomb-like darkness. Despite the furious, frenetic energy that had brought them here, Frelia suddenly had the tangible sense that she'd just unleashed something best left forgotten.

Like the real crown, like the family barrows, like Cillian's laughter and her own grief.

The room beyond the sealed door was half-submerged in water, a cavern craggy and vast. The far wall, such as it was, lay open to the churning sea, and the smell of the salt air stung her eye almost as much as the sudden light did. The rest of the room was unremarkable, a wasteland of grit and rocky shore, except for one thing:

The wall just beyond the doorway was encased in a sheet of ice.

Immense as a glacier, pitted and with a dusting of snow, the ice was translucent enough to see inside, but only just. The shape frozen deep within was murky and black, with four pinpricks of green lightning that cut through their prison like angry stars in the firmament.

"There he is," said Frelia tiredly, flinging her arms out as if to embrace the turbid beast. "Geri, the Greedy One, forever frozen in a wall of ice to keep his hunger at bay."

We must be better, Hägen had said as they'd sloshed through the waterline across the room. *We cannot loose this!*

Deadcut's mouth fell open, and she looked to Frelia with unmasked horror. Frelia wished she had anything useful to tell her, but then Vendrick burst out, "Why am I not surprised it has luminescent green eyes?"

Something down here was tugging on Frelia's bones, as though her body was waking up from a long sleep and trying to recall how its parts moved.

Rumbling. Only far more subdued than usual.

"I guess that answers one thing." Frelia led the short walk to the ice wall, towards those hollow, green eyes that still burned like hellfire, and that tugging sensation. "Lords Huginn and Muninn must have always been garmur, too."

Her boots came to rest on the cold stone just before the ice wall, and Frelia stared up at the frozen shape with dread piling in her stomach. She still couldn't see clearly through the ice, but it didn't matter, now that she had all the other pieces.

"And if Lady Daybreak and Lady Twilight's ravens are actually monsters," Frelia said quietly, "then of course the Guardians of my territory and Hägen's are."

It was a sick, cosmic joke. It was everything that was supposed to have defended Skjöldr and nothing that they could ever use to do it.

"It's starting to make sense, why Hägen didn't want to free this thing." Frelia reached out and laid the tips of her gloved fingers against the pitted ice.

Nothing around her so much as breathed.

"I was for it," Frelia said. "The twins were for it. Edmund abstained from voting, but Hägen overruled us. He refused to break Geri's slumber for the Battle for Skjöldr. He said we had to be better than the attacking Volsinii, that we had to win without waking the monsters of our past."

Frelia dragged her fingers down the ice, leaving something like a claw mark of frigid, translucent frost.

"He must have known what this thing really was from the start, but he couldn't just fucking say that."

Frelia turned to Deadcut, and was surprised to find tears on the woman's face. "I may understand his hesitance," Deadcut said.

"We had a weapon he refused to let us use!" With a sudden burst of helpless fury, Frelia slammed the side of her fist into the ice. It landed with a solid whump, and she may as well have punched a mountain, for what changed. "He hemmed and hawed about how there would be no putting Geri back, once we'd broken the ice, and instead he let us all die."

Frelia's gloved fist shook against the ice, and she didn't know whether it was fury, shame, or the Rumbling itself. "I would have killed for a 'Geri' to loose on Ironfang at Spirits' Fen, you know that? And your lot loosed one instead."

Vendrick's eyes widened as realization struck him, but he was too slow to hold off the tidal wave of grief.

"No wonder the Unseen want these damned things dead," Frelia got out. "They're some of the only creatures with the spine left to stand in their way."

Frelia was only distantly aware of her boots on the ground. That her voice echoed in the cavernous room and out across the Ivory Channel. That there would be no hiding from whatever lay outside, when it came to that.

There never had been.

Skitr, she suddenly understood, with frightening clarity, the choice Hägen had stared down and stubbornly refused to make.

Do we loose the fucking garmr, and sacrifice what makes us human? Or do we die, fully and annihilated, but at least we die whole?

"But if we exchange its spine for ours," Frelia added, and the sudden silence around her was deafening, "then what do we become?"

She met Clarissa's wide, wet eyes, but, for once, couldn't meet Vendrick's. He had shut his eyes as if in physical pain, his hand resting on the spine of his spellbook.

"Perhaps, to Hägen Einnaska," Deadcut began, quiet, "it was simply never an option. He would rather press on, lightless, until the work was done."

Vendrick viscerally flinched, acid green eyes snapping open, and Frelia wondered what the hell she'd missed.

"Perhaps..." Deadcut breathed so shakily, Frelia could see it, in the old woman's shoulders. "Well." She looked up again, and something new was spreading across her wizened face. "Perhaps he argued that divine beasts had no place in human warfare. They had already been created to destroy humanity; did we really wish to assist them in that endeavor?"

The words were old, worn in. Like she'd said them many times before.

"Could we come back from that," Deadcut added, "if we did?"

"Father did mention you were a coward at heart during the Winter War," came a greasy voice Frelia wanted to smother.

All heads snapped towards the sea, where Markus della Luciana was dragging his little sister through the surf by the scruff of her neck. They'd come the long way around.

"There you are, you fucking *zychnik,*" Frelia snarled.

"How did you even find this place?" Clarissa asked.

"Why, the same way Valerius did, I presume." Markus' grin was visible even clear across the grotto. "I simply followed the rumbling."

Somehow, despite the fact that Markus had stolen Cillian's bloodrune like it was something as mundane as gold, it was hearing Markus so flippantly dismiss knowledge Frelia had watched her friends die for want of that made her blood boil.

"Help?" Faustine croaked, and Frelia's hand went for her sword.

"Ah, ah," said Markus, wagging a finger. "None of that now."

And he dragged them onto the shore, Frelia could just make out the barest hint of his rose-gold magic skittering across the hand holding Faustine's neck.

What would be worse—Markus getting at Geri, or Faustine getting herself killed? Frelia could gut Markus, sure, but there was no guarantee that she could get Faustine out of the line of fire first. And if they let Markus advance, sure, there was a decent chance Geri would berserk his way out of his glacial prison, maddened by centuries of hunger and isolation. But there was also just as much a chance that Markus could beastmind the Guardian of Einnaska Territory like he had Muninn or any of his wartime pets.

And then they'd end up fighting anyway.

Frelia could not handle Faustine's grey, terrified eyes joining Cillian's warm brown ones in her nightmares.

"*Zychnik,*" Frelia growled, but she released her vice grip on her sword.

"You've said that repeatedly," Markus noted, as though it were a bit of trivia over tea. "What does it mean?"

"Faithless." Frelia grit her teeth. "Heretic. Goddessless."

"Ah..." Markus drew out the word in mock-understanding. "See, now that's where you're wrong, Valerius."

He snatched the dagger out of Faustine's belt, and the girl thrashed in his grip, squawking in protest.

"I," said Markus, "am the furthest thing from faithless."

Faustine's face twisted, like she'd just caught a whiff of Markus' unwashed laundry or something, and Frelia felt the absurd urge to laugh. But disgust wasn't fear of her older brother.

Disgust was good.

Vendrick's hands twitched like he was itching to cast something. "Let her go, Markus."

"Easy there, Vendrick." Markus' smile was wide and threatening. "You're going to make me jumpy."

The rose-gold magic in his hand bloomed, even as Markus dragged Faustine closer to Geri's glacial prison. The teenager flinched at the sudden flare of arcane energy, and Frelia cursed that her bow had been broken on the way to Kjell. It was what she got for buying one from a smithy, instead of a bowyer.

"You too, Clarissa," Markus added. "Get down from there."

Clarissa glanced to Vendrick, eyebrows raised in an unspoken question. Frelia could practically see the cogs working in his skull, trying to determine a way to spring Faustine without setting off Markus.

He didn't seem to have any better ideas than Frelia did.

After a long moment, Vendrick sighed and made the Silverwood hand sign for 'fall back.'

Clarissa moved her fingers with the elegance of a pianist, and then the ghostly knight knelt down. Clarissa slid herself off its shoulders to sit, cross-legged and aggrieved, on the floor.

"There's a good girl," said Markus.

Frelia's snarl was nearly as loud as Clarissa's sharp "Shut up, you fop."

"So, you're here, della Luciana," said Deadcut suddenly. "Now what's your grand strategy?"

Mania gleamed in Markus' good eye. "I'm so glad you asked, Your Excellency."

The knife in his hand was a flash of silver light as he ripped it across the exposed skin of Faustine's arm. "Blood of the innocent," he said, flicking the edge of the knife towards the ice wall, "forcefully taken."

Without removing his grip on Faustine's nape, Markus hauled them both toward Deadcut. The old woman reached for an axe that was not at her hip, staring down the rogue Imperial Watcher like he'd personally insulted everything she held dear.

And maybe he had.

"Flesh of the wise," Markus added, snatching for Deadcut's gnarled hand, "deceitfully thrown."

They struggled for a moment, but Deadcut was not the warrior she'd once been. She broke off a nascent shriek as Markus' silver dagger sliced through her thumb. The digit fell, lightless and bloody, to the floor, even as Deadcut's uninjured hand flew to clamp down on the wound.

"Faustine." Markus eyed the severed thumb with distaste. "Pick it up."

Faustine's neck jerked like she was trying to turn her head, but Markus' grip wouldn't allow it.

"Now," he growled, squeezing.

Faustine looked at Frelia with wild panic, but she had nothing for the girl but her own choked fury. Dammit, Frelia needed to get out of Markus' line of sight! Then she would be getting somewhere.

"Do as he says, Faustine." Vendrick's voice was full of soft menace, leaving unspoken *for now.*

Faustine shakily lowered herself into a crouch, clearly trying to avoid looking directly at Deadcut's severed finger. Markus allowed her to move, leaning to give Faustine full range of movement without taking his hand off her neck.

"Here, you bastard." Faustine held the severed digit over her shoulder.

"May you choke on it," Deadcut added, pressing the stump of her finger into the folds of her gown.

Markus laughed. "To the wall, Faustine. Toss it."

Faustine drew in a deep breath, and then half-heartedly tossed the finger towards the ice wall. But instead of thumping against the ice and falling back to the floor, Deadcut's manicured thumb stuck against the ice, and then slowly began to recede.

As though consumed.

"Markus, what the fu—" Frelia began, just in time to feel a sharp tug on her braid.

"Pain of the conquered," said Markus over Frelia's inadvertent yelp, "aurally driven."

Frelia was in line with Markus' periphery, now, and the Watcher was rounding on Vendrick while still clutching Faustine's neck. Frelia tensed, primed to spring the instant she had an opening.

"Soul of the blackened..."

Vendrick had the fastest draw of any mage Frelia had ever seen. He could speak while drawing a completely different rune, and he could tie together runes off the cuff and create an effect that actually worked.

But even Vendrick wasn't fast enough to get ahead of Markus, this time.

"...*unwillingly given!*"

And Markus dropped Faustine to drive his shoulder into Vendrick's solar plexus.

Frelia snapped forward, still deciding whether to grab for Vendrick, yank Faustine out of harm's way, or pound Markus' head into the glacier until his brains came out of his ears.

She wouldn't get the chance to do any of it.

The moment Vendrick's shoulder hit the ice, an earsplitting crack echoed across the cavern. And then something black as ink and greasy as sin snaked around his middle, and pulled Vendrick bodily into the ice.

CHAPTER FORTY-EIGHT

IRONFANG JERKED HIS HEAD around so fast the muscles in his neck cracked. Blightsen didn't even notice; he was staring at the lich, tears running down his face like he'd turned on a faucet.

"Hägen," Blightsen murmured, "is this where you've been all this time?"

The lich took off running down the bookcase rows.

Ironfang tried to give chase, but his body fought him on every jarring step. He ached to yank the silvered spearpoint out of his stomach; it burned like hellfire. But he had no idea whether this silence in his head would hold, and that was more precious than even his own blood. This reprieve had to be related to the lich's wards, though. And if the lich were, apparently, Hägen Einnaska, they would be damn solid white magic.

It was the one thing the laughably soft last king of Kaldr had been good at.

"*Hägen!*" Blightsen shouted. "Hägen, stop! We can talk this out!"

Ironfang's vision was a pain-filled blur, but he caught the lich-king shaking its head.

"No," said the lich, "we can't."

He drew a smear of a rune in the air across his chest, and Ironfang wasn't sure he'd have recognized it even if his Ascended sight were working properly. But Blightsen certainly did; he nearly dropped his torch in his haste to cast a disruption. But Hägen was faster, disappearing from view a half-second before Blightsen's own rusty orange magic crashed into empty space.

And then there was only silence.

Blightsen stared at the space where his friend had just stood, fat tears rolling down his too-kind face. Ironfang forced himself back upright, scrubbing at his eyes as though he could physically clear the sheen of pain off of them.

"When," he began acidly, "were you going to bother telling me you knew there was a living lich?"

Blightsen didn't look at him. "When you asked."

"I am asking now."

"I told him not to do it." Blightsen wiped his nose on his sleeve. "But Hägen swore Kaldr needed him and he could do it ethically, and, well, he kind of did."

Ironfang snorted, and the silver embedded in his stomach throbbed through a fresh wave of pain. "How in Hypogia does one become a lich ethically?"

Blightsen finally glanced Ironfang's way. "By asking warriors dying in the infirmary if they want to serve Kaldr one last time."

It spoke to an almost cynical understanding of Kaldiri pride. *Perhaps,* Ironfang thought, *Hägen Einnaska wasn't a complete fool after all.*

"They fell on their own swords, for him," Blightsen added, not really to Ironfang. "Hägen was—*is?*—like that."

Blightsen didn't offer any aid as Ironfang pulled himself back onto his feet. "What did he cast, just now?" Ironfang demanded.

Blightsen only shook his head. "The Grimsdalr Blink. I... don't think he'll be back, though."

Ironfang shot him an oh-come-now look. Even he knew that was a short range teleport at best.

Blightsen didn't buckle. "If Hägen were going to be right back, he would be here, already. The legends must be true."

"Legends?"

Blightsen sighed heavily. "That the blink doesn't turn you invisible—it punts you into Helheim and back."

Well. That explained a lot about Spirits' Fen.

One arm curled around his aching stomach, Ironfang began limping up the aisle towards the back of the room that Einnaska had been so intently guarding.

"So I guess you'll tell the Sightless One you found a lich," Blightsen said quietly, trailing Ironfang again.

Ironfang waited until he was well past the shelf he'd first crumpled in front of before he said, "We will tell him nothing."

Blightsen startled—Ironfang could see it, in the torchlit shadows. "But if he can possess you, how are you supposed to—"

"He isn't currently present."

And how glorious it was, to be in possession of his own mind again, wholly and utterly. Usually Ironfang could feel the Sightless One lurking in his hindbrain, a window Ironfang was never completely certain was in use. But the curtains were drawn now, so to speak. Ironfang didn't care, so long as he could revel in this silence.

"We will tell the Sightless One nothing of what we saw past this ward," Ironfang ordered. "It was leftover by the church, understood?"

Blightsen's confusion turned into a slow nod of understanding. "It's the wards, isn't it? That's why you're dragging."

Ironfang continued to limp towards the end of this enormous room. "And you can tell, can you?"

Blightsen's voice was too light, too steady. "Do you think you're the first man to try to ascend to godhood?"

Ironfang turned to look at the small, bespectacled man. Blightsen's face was full of gentle angles, and although he didn't speak, he may as well have just admitted that all the stories were true.

"Which of your superiors was Hypogean?" Ironfang asked.

"None," said Blightsen. "But that doesn't mean our forefathers and -mothers didn't try."

Ironfang did some quick mental calculations. The first successful Ascension ceremony had been Hector Secundus', given that neither Vittoro Caecillion nor Ironfang had wanted to be the first test subject. Hector had survived and had tithed substantially to the Unseen ever since. Ironfang still kept a close eye on the Senator, but so far, the man appeared as content to simply play the senatorial long game as he had before.

That had been around the time Gaius was graduating from Silverwood, which put it around 1232. But Ironfang's father had been researching a means of Ascension long before that, and had nearly managed it in Ironfang's youth.

It had taken Ironfang many years to learn that it hadn't been any mistake on his father's part that had rendered the ritual a failure. No spellwork was so complex as to make its runes ineffable. It was simply that humanity had never been meant to understand them in the first place. Every foray made into the arcane was fraught with the sublime.

His father simply had failed to plan for that.

Ironfang would have shivered at the memory of his first meeting with the Sightless One, except that, apparently, the clerics had been doing it to themselves, too.

And so he laughed. They had been so close to understanding.

Blightsen stiffened. "I don't see what's so funny."

"You don't find the hypocrisy amusing?" Ironfang asked. "The Hypogean ritual is only a few steps away from that of the lich. Which your clergy *so* detested."

Ironfang was still chortling as they rounded on a heavy stone slab built into the back of the room. "The Sightless One would be howling if the bastard were still listening in."

Blightsen's eyes narrowed. "I thought you worshipped the Sightless One?"

Ironfang couldn't help it. He threw back his head and laughed, spearpoint burning.

"Oh, no," he managed after a moment. "You have it backwards. I mean to usurp him. And for that, I need to know how to make a god."

He came to rest at the edge of the altar Einnaska had been so hellbent on protecting. At first, it seemed like mere Church detritus, a heavy stone slab with a tattered blue altar cloth. But as Blightsen drew closer with the torch, Ironfang could see there was something sitting on it.

A reddish, fleshy lump not unlike the one Ironfang had swallowed out in the Konstantin forest sat in the center of a ring of runes. It was as fresh-looking as if it had been hacked off a living being moments ago.

Blightsen's face paled. "Don't touch that."

"Nonsense, it's only organ meat." Ironfang drew a dagger from his belt. "Could be part of a heart, or perhaps a lung?"

He reached out with the flat of his blade, but Blightsen caught his wrist in a surprisingly strong grip. "You don't want to do that."

"Don't I?" Ironfang yanked his arm free.

"No," Blightsen said firmly, and if not for the abject terror in the man's face, Ironfang would've flogged him for the impertinence, "I promise, you don't."

Blightsen pointed to the runes inscribed in the pitted stone, traced them from a foot away with his fingers. The line work was complex, and looked even older than the rest of the library. It whirled around the altar before coming to a twisting, geometric point beneath the lump of flesh.

And all of it said some gibberish about *morning, return, health, unending.*

"This is a surgery altar." Blightsen was turning faintly green. "They've been outlawed since at least Queen Hulda's reign."

Ironfang had no idea when that was, offhand, but figured it was likely ancient. "What does it do?"

"Keeps a patient alive far longer than he should be," Blightsen said, "at the cost of the practitioner's own life energy."

Ironfang glanced back to the lump of flesh sitting in the dead center of the runes, fighting the urge to grin. He had been right. "So who do you think Einnaska was so dutifully hiding?"

Blightsen shook his head. "I don't want to guess."

Coward. Just like Ironfang had figured.

Ironfang edged closer to the surgery altar. He squinted at the viscera and opened his divine sense again. Bright, blinding light stabbed at his eyelids, and Ironfang immediately squeezed them shut again. There could be no mistaking it then—Daybreak.

This had to be what was left of Lady Daybreak.

Soft laughter that didn't quite belong to him burbled in Ironfang's throat.

"Sir?" Blightsen pressed.

Ironfang reached out, and touched the fleshy lump with the tip of his pointer finger.

Every window in the place shattered inward. Ice and glass rained down on them, and Ironfang quickly threw a hand over his head to protect from the falling glass. The temperature dropped considerably, something Ironfang hadn't previously thought possible, and he cupped his other hand over the little, fleshy lump on the altar.

A cold, fetid presence slunk into the back of Ironfang's mind again, but he had the vessel he needed. Everything was falling into place.

What is the meaning of this? the Sightless One thundered. *What did you do to me?*

Nothing, my Lord, Ironfang told him, stowing his knife.

He plucked the heart of Lady Daybreak up from the surgery altar, and turned to face Blightsen. The man was turning faintly green, and Ironfang wondered, not for the first time, just how someone so squeamish had become a healer.

"So, now what?" Blightsen asked. "You kill me?"

"In a manner," Ironfang said, and then his hand shot out.

He grabbed Blightsen's chin and yanked, prying open the man's mouth with Hypogean strength. Blightsen struggled against him, burbling something that may or may not have been words, but Ironfang's grip—and his will—was iron.

"I should think a cleric would rejoice at the chance for communion with the Lady Daybreak," Ironfang said. "Say a prayer, or something."

And with his free hand, he shoved the fleshy lump down Blightsen's throat.

Blightsen choked and spluttered until his choking gasps turned into shrieks of pain. Ironfang removed his hands then, shaking spittle from the leather. Blightsen doubled over, pressing a hand into his chest as though Ironfang had dropped a burning coal into his esophagus.

"There, there," said Ironfang mock-paternally. "You're a cleric; it won't kill you."

Blightsen stared up at him with watery, agonized eyes.

"I'm sure it hurts, though," Ironfang added, almost as an afterthought.

In the back of his mind, the Sightless One began to cackle.

CHAPTER FORTY-NINE

ONE OF THE FIRST things Vendrick had been taught as a child growing up alongside the Bay of Ascalon was to never swim in a riptide. They broke even the strongest swimmers, and oftentimes were too dangerous to mount a rescue into. Vendrick had, of course, tested that theory himself, much to his nanny's terror and, later, his own punishment.

That was about how being dragged into the glacier felt. That frictionless suction of impossible strength.

Air. Vendrick needed bloody air.

He was dragged deeper into the glacier, somehow still thrashing. towards the lightning green eyes buried in its core. The black fingers held him too strongly for Vendrick to get his stiletto out of his sleeve, and casting was impossible without being able to move his hands.

His lungs burned, and a heavy presence pressed into his mind. It gave a garbled order in a language Vendrick almost didn't understand.

Sleep.

At once, he was no longer gasping for air deep in the ice beneath Castle Skjöldr. He stood instead, shivering, knee-deep in a river. There was no tang of salt air, here, no unstable magic, and as he took in his surroundings, he could have sworn the endless wheat fields were growing in blue.

And the light here was all wrong—seasick, acrid green, like alchemical smoke.

"Well, well," came a voice that sent rime down Vendrick's spine, "what have we here?"

Warily, Vendrick rose to his feet, flicking his wrist. The stiletto concealed in his sleeve slipped into his hand as he laid eyes on his father for the first time in many years.

Vendrick could ignore it most days, unless he was looking in a mirror. The late Count Vittoro Caecillion had been Imperator Claudius' Spymaster before Vendrick had been Ironfang's, and Vendrick had been told his whole life how much he resembled the man.

It was even worse than Vendrick remembered, now that he was older and thus closer to the age at which his father had died.

Vittoro had the same sharp cheekbones and green eyes as Vendrick did, although he also kept a meticulous goatee. His dark hair had been streaked with grey when he'd died, but there were no burn marks crawling up his neck, no sign of the grey magic that had killed him.

There was no sign of the struggle at all.

"What in Hypogia?" said Vendrick, incredulous.

Vittoro pulled that smug, insouciant smile that still haunted Vendrick's nightmares, and disdain dripped from every word. "How else do you suppose I found you?"

Vendrick wasn't used to dealing with his father anymore. The banal dismissal dug into him like an arrowhead, snapping the breath from his lungs.

"Your own fault, really," Vittoro continued, folding his hands behind his back and beginning to pace the unnatural riverbank. "What were you thinking, sleeping on the border to Hypogia? I'd tell you that woman will be the death of you, but..." He laughed, and the sound was a razors in Vendrick's ears. "Well, it's a bit late for that warning, isn't it?"

It took Vendrick a moment to realize what he meant.

It's tradition, Frelia had said, *to sleep beside your ancestors before you march to war, so they can find you again if you fall.*

But while her ancestors were largely a source of comfort, Vendrick's were not. His were the iron chains by which his future had been bound, gagged, and thrown into the sea.

Saints, he was never going to believe the line about 'superstitious Kaldiri nonsense' again, no matter what logic told him.

"Now, pay attention," snapped Vittoro, and sheer anxiety chased the chill running through Vendrick's spine.

He was a child again, being lectured in his father's study about this slight or that transgression. He was small, powerless, helpless, buried in hawthorn switches and belt buckles, hunger gnawing at his insides and exhaustion settling into his bones.

"You've certainly taken your dear time getting here," Vittoro said. "How hard is it to put yourself in a life-threatening situation, Vendrick? You're a grey mage, for god's sake."

God? It struck against Vendrick's Spymaster instinct, somewhere distant.

Vendrick shook his head as though it would clear away the helpless little boy screaming in his ears. "You think I'm dead?"

"Of course you are. How else could you land in Hypogia?" Vittoro dismissed his son's concerns with a flick of his wrist. "Or, I suppose, as your dear Frelia would say—you're in Helheim."

Fury suddenly burned in Vendrick's stomach. "You will keep her name out of your filthy mouth."

"Or you'll what..." The full force of his father's unconcerned amusement suddenly pinned Vendrick's boots into the river mud. "...kill me again?"

For a moment, that look froze adult Vendrick as much as it ever had his child self. Saints, this was a nightmare. How in blazes was he supposed to break out of the realm of the dead? Was it even possible? Was he dead? There was no way he was actually dead, right?

He needed to get back. Frelia needed his help, Faustine did. Clarissa and, hell, even his mum did. Markus could not be allowed to win, not after everything Vendrick had stopped, everything he'd done.

Dammit, Vendrick needed to think! Clear away the panic and remember what he was, who he could be.

Where his loyalty lay.

"Now that you're finally here," Vittoro added, "we can begin. Come on, then; I haven't all day."

Vendrick's child-self had never disobeyed an order in his life. Not directly, anyway. There had always been Clarissa's safety to consider, and the family name and reputation. It was what Volsinii did, after all. Make rules, and enforce them.

Rules, Vendrick thought, *like life and death.*

It was a great effort to pull himself away from the disassociated spiral, to raise the hand holding the stiletto, to snap his wrist and let it fly. But no more than it had been to stare down Lord Huginn and tie together three disparate runes in a blizzard.

The knife buried itself in Vittoro's chest with a satisfying thunk, and it was as if he'd shattered reality. Vendrick was suddenly six foot two again, tired, aching, definitely his adult self. He was out of knives, though, and his magic felt miles away, uncallable. But the laces of his boots doubled as garotte wire, and he'd suffocated bigger opponents.

He would take out Vittoro, and then he would fucking *think.*

"Picked up a new trick, have you?" Vittoro pulled the knife from his chest with the same amount of effort it took Vendrick to do up his shirt buttons in the morning. No blood stained the blade. "As though it grants you any merit."

Worthless. That was the word Vittoro Caecillion had always used to describe his son, just ahead of talentless, guileless, and altogether too soft.

But Vendrick saw now, what Vittoro had always meant was lacking cruelty. Lacking malice. Lacking whatever it was that had made Vittoro support the Unseen and offer up his own children as sacrifice to his ambition.

And the core of what made Vendrick himself, despite everything his father had done to make him a hollow, calloused shell, was simply too stubborn to let him win.

"Is that why you still trained me?" Vendrick's slow grin was sharp, pointed. The one he'd learned from the best. "Taught me everything you knew?"

Vittoro rolled his eyes. Green eyes, calculating eyes. Caecillion eyes.

"You're an arrogant fool," Vittoro snapped, just like Huginn had. "You cannot be bothered to look around the precipice you stand upon."

"Precipice of what?" Vendrick's mocking laugh echoed his father's. "Death?"

"Oh, you know very well what Markus della Luciana has done," Vittoro snapped. "I trust you to recognize a summoning ritual when you see it."

Vendrick's blood ran cold, even as he stood in the frigid waters of the River Gjöll. For that was where this had to be, if Vendrick were to take his father at face value.

The border between the living and the dead.

But Markus hadn't been using grey magic—Vendrick would've smelled that a mile off. So if he hadn't been summoning Geri, down in that cavern beneath Castle Skjöldr...

What had he done instead?

"I will not allow you to prevent the grand rebirth of the universe," Vittoro added. "Geri the Greedy One must walk again, and you will not stop it."

Vendrick couldn't stop the harsh laugh that escaped him, and he echoed that crackling, icy accent that he would rend heaven to return to: "I'd rather find out if the dead can die again."

It was a supreme effort to unstick his boots from the mud, to move against the roaring current of the river, but Vendrick did it. Pushing forward, always, whatever the cost.

It was what Frelia had always done, wasn't it?

"He can't hurt you, Caecillion!" called a new voice from further up the riverbank. "The dead can't affect change!"

Vendrick and his father both turned sharply, only to find a redheaded cavalier pelting towards them as though spurred by the Wild Hunt itself. His ghostly mount was a shadow of the one he'd used in life, but Vendrick would know that silhouette anywhere. It was always retreating, in his dreams.

Shock gripped Vendrick's throat as he tried to speak, caught between *"Cillian Grimsdalr?"* and *"He can't... hurt me?"*

"Nonsense," Vittoro snapped. "A knife is still a knife, in Hypogia."

He flicked it towards the river again, and Vendrick was forced to duck or be impaled. The stiletto splashed somewhere unhelpful, and yet too close for comfort.

The very notion was absurd, impossible. All Vittoro Caecillion had ever done to his children was hurt them, particularly Vendrick. But Vendrick also knew that if his father was annoyed with the interference, then that's what he needed to facilitate.

"Nonsense is what I do best," Grimsdalr said with a grin, and he glanced over his shoulder to Vendrick. "You need to leave, Caecillion. Go back across the river while you still can."

"Don't even think about it," snapped Vittoro. "You will come here, Vendrick."

The order echoed across a hundred thousand hours of grey magic training and alchemy practice and stealth missions. Vendrick's eyes snapped from where his father stood, to Frelia's best friend, and back again.

Clarissa's your volchya, Frelia had said, all those eons ago at Silverwood. *Of course I'll help.*

Cillian was Frelia's *volchya.* She had trusted him with her life and, more importantly, with the future of the country and the people she so loved. To this day, she mourned how he had dragged her to a Healers' Tent during the Battle for Spirits' Fen and gone to surrender alone.

When Vittoro Caecillion had died, all Vendrick had truly worried about were funeral costs and the deluge of clutter.

"So what happens," Vendrick said slowly, "if I cross the river towards you and my father, Grimsdalr?"

Cillian's eyes widened, and then he seemed to remember whom he was talking to. "You've probably never heard Frelia use it, but the polite way to say someone's died in Kaldiri is to say they've crossed the Gjöll."

It was a ridiculous thought. How could something so monumental as life and death be so boringly simple? A few more steps, and everything he'd fought for would have been for nothing? It didn't make sense.

No, no, he had just promised himself to listen to the superstitious Kaldiri nonsense no matter what logic told him.

"How is this a question?" Vittoro said acidly. "Vendrick Caecillion, you have a duty to fulfill and the Sightless One is not a patient god."

There it was again. A god, singular. Male.

"You are one, insignificant stich in a tapestry that has been woven since before you were born." Vittoro was lecturing, now, gaining steam. "Our family has been the backbone of imperial rule since the time of the bloody Saints, and this is not negotiable. You cannot teach an old dog new tricks."

Dogs can be commanded, Vendrick thought. *Wolves cannot.*

"So come *here,*" Vittoro said, "and live up to our family's legacy, for once in your incompetent life."

A slow, irritated smile began to spread across Vendrick's face. "So if Grimsdalr is wrong, why haven't you come out here to drag me home yourself?"

Vittoro looked incensed, but Grimsdalr threw back his head and laughed.

"And how did you find me anyway, Grimsdalr?" Vendrick couldn't help but ask.

The cavalier's grin grew a touch more genuine. "You think I can't track Frelia's soul-scent just because she's not technically a Grimsdalr?"

Volchya.

Vendrick made his choice.

He unstuck his feet from the muddy riverbed, and took one, slogging step backwards.

"You will listen to your father," Vittoro snapped, and for the first time in his life, Vendrick did not feel the driving compulsion to obey.

He could see now why the malamutes were so willful; this was sort of fun. "No," said Vendrick, laughing now himself. "I will not."

He dragged himself further away from the man, towards the riverbank at his back and the land of the living. The water was sluggish and stagnant, and a kaleidoscope like the Blink rune had opened up all around him, pressing in on all sides and squeezing.

"There, you've got it!" Grimsdalr shouted. "I can feel the magic working!"

Vendrick began to feel the crushing weight of a ton of ice pressing against him. He was here, but not here. Somehow aware of his physical body, stuck in the ice beneath Castle Skjöldr, and this... indeterminant form, here in the mud on the river of the dead.

"Alright, Grimsdalr," he called over, "I'm sure you know—how did I get here?"

"The way I see it," Grimsdalr said, still atop his ghostly mount and holding it steady like a sled dog itching to bolt, "Markus tried to kill you, but he was sloppy about it."

Vendrick laughed, and even Vittoro grimaced. "Oh, Vendrick's been half-dead since he was twelve," the old man muttered. "How could Markus not properly finish him off?"

"So while you're just hanging around, Caecillion," Grimsdalr added, "can you tell Frelia something, for me?"

Vendrick stopped moving.

The burning in his lungs faded.

For a moment, he was neither the boy Vittoro had terrorized, nor the man who had killed him.

He was just a teenage boy at Silverwood, making friends with his Kaldiri counterparts and wondering why he was supposed to hate them.

"Of course," Vendrick called back.

"Heit Reiði is coming," Grimsdalr said, as serious as Vendrick had ever seen him. "It may even already be here."

Something sunk in Vendrick's stomach like a stone. The end of the world, the death of the Goddesses, Lady Midnight's wrath was... here?

"Oh no you don't," Vittoro was saying. "I will not have you ruining everything!"

Vendrick ignored him, keeping his eye locked on Grimsdalr. "Because of Geri?"

"Partly." Grimsdalr nodded, as unapologetic in death as he'd been in life. "He and his monster-siblings are supposed to form the Wild Hunt—and are stuck without Lord Muninn." He laughed, a sound as fierce as the winds of the north. "Damned raven is incensed about it; it's hilarious."

Vendrick puffed a short, little laugh, even as his father began to bluster about decorum. But he wasn't attacking Vendrick or Cillian.

And that meant the latter was probably right. Or at least, close enough for government work.

The dead can't affect change. The idea pounded in the back of Vendrick's mind, curling like ivy up a garden wall.

"But, uh, make no mistake, the End of Days is coming," Grimsdalr added. "It's just not happening like it should. The eternal winter is beginning, but Lady Daybreak isn't dead."

Vendrick was tying hopeless threads together and trying to come up with an answer. The world couldn't end, dammit. He had worked too long and too hard for some swooping, mythological nightmare to blot out the sun and make all his struggles for nothing.

"Don't think you can stop it." Vittoro's voice was derision incarnate. "All things in their time, Grimsdalr, all times in their place. Is that not the most basic of the Triad's tenets?"

"It is," Grimsdalr conceded. "But that just means we have to rewrite the ending. New time, new place."

"Rewrite it?" Vendrick knew he'd been spending too much time with Frelia, because he felt the strangest urge to clean out his ears. "Like some playwright throwing out a first draft?"

"*Ja!*" Grimsdalr's grin was predatory, now—the general's, not the statesman's. "Exactly like that."

"You will not listen to a word this madman says," Vittoro snapped. "Do you hear me, Vendrick?"

Vendrick, pointedly, took a step further back in the River Gjöll. The weight on his shoulders was growing unbearable, and he struggled to breathe. *Then again,* he thought grimly, *if the way out of the land of the dead was easy, everyone would do it.*

"Say I believe you, Grimsdalr!" Vendrick managed. "How do you propose we do anything about it?"

"Find Lady Daybreak," Grimsdalr said hurriedly, as though he, too, could sense the crushing weight of dark ice all around Vendrick. "Don't let the Wild Hunt kill her!"

"So, what, you're telling me to break into Hypogia again?" A place Vendrick still wasn't certain how he'd gotten into the first time, but certainly couldn't go through alone.

"No need; someone's just broken the seal keeping Lady Daybreak in place."

Vendrick froze as the implications hit him like a secondary strike. "I thought..." He struggled to remember the exact phrasing. "Is Lady Daybreak not sitting on the golden throne somewhere off in the distance?"

He waved towards the rolling, sapphire fields.

"Oh, no." Vittoro's voice was gleeful, and it sent shivers up Vendrick's beleaguered spine. "There never was a golden throne."

Vendrick was struggling to process this, and he could charitably be called irreligious on a good day.

"You want to know why the Old Ones are drawn to humanity, Caecillion?" Grimsdalr added.

It echoed of what Vendrick had said over della Trova's corpse, even as Cillian's twin had cracked the woman's bones between her teeth. "We're a food source," Vendrick said hoarsely.

"What? No. Well, I mean, that too. But!" Cillian made a truly hideous face. "It's that we can affect change."

Vendrick couldn't help it; his mouth fell open at the theory.

But Grimsdalr wasn't done: "They're all static, playing their parts in an opera that's been going since time began. And the dead are the same—we're stuck here. But the living..." Grimsdalr stabbed a stout finger into the air between them. "You can change. You can forget your lines, say 'screw this play, this is stupid,' jump off the front of the stage, and go beat up the director!"

Vendrick wasn't sure whether to laugh or cry. "Are you..."

He couldn't get the words out.

Are you suggesting I have a future beyond all this? Beyond this tacit war with the Unseen, beyond the shadows and subterfuge, beyond the man whose face was so much like his own? A place in some sort of grand, cosmic play that wasn't a tragedy that ended in death and sorrow and silence?

That he could dredge up his future from beneath the Bay of Ascalon, unchain it, ungag it, and set it free?

"*Ja*," Grimsdalr said, as though he understood. "You just have to keep living, alright?"

Vendrick couldn't help the wetness leaking from his eyes. "Then I press on, lightless, until the work is done."

Grimsdalr nodded, apparently satisfied. His face was set in determined lines as he pulled on the reins of his undead warhorse. "Give Markus hell for me," he added with a wink. "I'll keep your da busy here."

"I'm very much obliged." Vendrick's grin felt lopsided. Like he couldn't fully bring himself to rights. "Oh, and I'm certain Frelia would like for me to tell you—you're a *dorchya*."

Beneath Cillian's unrepentant laughter and Vittoro's howling protests, Vendrick forced another step backward, toward the life he could build with this new theory. He stumbled in the heavy muck, landing on his backside in the frigid, rushing water. And the twofold pressure of water in Hypogia and ice in the Waking World dragged him down, *down*, to where all of his ghosts could never follow.

***

Professor Valerius stared in horrified disbelief at the hairline fissure in the ice of Geri's prison, and Faustine fought the rising wave of bile in her throat with a hand clapped to her mouth. She could still see the fuzzy outline of the Not-Headmaster, a slightly lighter black than the monstrous shape in the further distance.

"Markus," she managed to get out around it, "what have you done?"

But Markus just laughed. The sound was brittle and vile, and Faustine stared at her brother in horror.

"What—" she began, but cut herself off when Professor Valerius tackled Markus with the force of a charging bear.

He hit the floor with a startled *oof,* and the professor grabbed for his hair.

"Undo it," she snarled, slamming Markus' forehead into the stone floor, "now."

Blood trickled down his nose, and the professor slammed his head up into the glacier wall, and still, he laughed. Faustine winced—even if Markus deserved it, she would never be able to tank another's pain the way everyone else seemed to be able to.

"It's not supposed to break," the professor snarled. "The whole point of Lord Geri's prison is that it's not supposed to break. So how did you break it, you fucking *zychnik?*"

Faithless. A horrible feeling began piling in Faustine's stomach as she realized—there were many kinds of faith. Markus' and their father's was to the Sightless One.

"He can't do anything if you scramble his brains," Deadcut pointed out. "Much as I'd like to look the other way, I think we'll be needing those."

Markus's laugh was tinged with mania, now. The professor drew back her arm again, taking Markus' skull with her.

"Wait." Faustine's hand was gentle on the professor's arm.

Professor Valerius' head whipped around to stare at Faustine, and it took everything in her not to break under scrutiny. Markus was alone, here, in a way he'd never been at Silverwood or the family villa. There were no Imperial Watchers, here, none of their father's friends or their relatives.

Markus, Faustine was slowly realizing, was prey.

Professor Valerius stared at Faustine for a long moment, even as she dug an elbow into Markus to pin him to the ground. Faustine wondered what the swordmaster saw in her, then. A child still?

"I have an idea," she said.

Markus thrashed and the professor switched her grip to grab him by the shoulders. She slammed his whole upper body against the ice wall, pushing his bare skin of his face against the unnatural ice.

"Go for it," Professor Valerius said.

That same mad laugh trickled out of Markus' mouth again, and it grated on Faustine like... well, like everything Markus did.

"What happens if you break Geri out?" Faustine asked, without preamble. "Do you think our father will love you then?"

"None of your concern, you—"

The crack of Faustine's palm on the back of Markus' head echoed in the chamber.

"That's not what I asked." Faustine waited for some sense of satisfaction or balancing of karmic debt to settle over her.

Markus stared at her in sideways disbelief. "You little brat."

"Not very fun when you can't hit back," the professor said with grim amusement, "is it?"

No, it wasn't. For all the times Markus or her father had smacked her unbidden, Faustine found that reciprocating didn't make her feel any better. It just made her hand hurt.

"Try again," Faustine said, a growing numbness in her heart. "What's next, Markus? And what did you do to the headmaster?"

"Is this your idea of an interrogation?" Markus asked. "Caecillion, you are not."

A burst of arcane energy came from somewhere behind Faustine, and she turned just in time to see Lady Clarissa's ghost knight rush towards them.

"Well," Lady Clarissa said mock-cheerfully, "I'm one."

The ghost knight slammed its hands onto Markus' shoulders overtop the professor's. The swordswoman shuddered when the ghost entered her physical space, as though she stood in a great wind. She hastily skittered sideways, shaking herself like one of the malamutes.

Markus struggled against the illusory knight as though it were just as solid as the professor.

"And I'm not asking," Lady Clarissa added. "I'm simply telling you."

Even sitting cross-legged on the floor, Clarissa Caecillion radiated poise and authority. It was completely different from the way the Not-Headmaster did, or even the professor, but it was undeniable and Faustine felt the absurd need to stand up straighter.

"You will answer your sister," Lady Clarissa said, "and you will answer Frelia. What have you done to my brother, you little weasel?"

Markus flinched as the ghost-knight holding him down squeezed.

"I sacrificed Caecillion to the Sightless One," he managed, "in return for the Guardian of Einnaska Territory."

Faustine's stomach fell through her boots, and she felt unsteady on her feet. Like her bones were grinding together, and her blood was boiling.

Why, *why*? What did Markus gain from that? What did the Sightless One want with the Not-Headmaster? Was he just to be raw material, like Orsina had needed for the yarn-ball darkbeast?

There had to be something Markus wasn't telling them, but what could it be?

"Oh, I *knew* I recognized this madness."

All eyes in the room went to Lady Deadcut.

She held her injured hand in a tight fistful of her dress, crimson blooming across the starched fabric on her stomach. "Let me guess," she added, her voice remarkably level. "This is all to do with the so-called Sightless One and his grand designs for the universe?"

Faustine's jaw fell open. "How do you know about any of that?"

Deadcut didn't take her eyes off Markus. "Because my children's father was equally as mad."

"Vittoro Caecillion," Markus said, "was never mad."

"Oh yes, he was," Deadcut said calmly. "I protected my children from that lunatic until he was an active danger, at which point I ruined my entire family's reputation and divorced him."

Faustine knew the stories, alright. The only thing more terrifying than the Viper of Ascalon had been his father, or so they said. The Viper of Ascalon would be perfectly polite to your face, but at least if he killed you, it was liable to be a short affair. The Not-Headmaster was frightening, sure, but there was a person under there, a man.

Not so, with his father.

"For all the good that did Vendrick and me," Lady Clarissa muttered.

Deadcut's sharp eyes fell to her daughter. "Your father was the Count of Caecillion," she snapped. "Do you think a lesser—if wealthy—family has any sway over what happens to his heirs?"

"And how'd that work out for you?" Markus sneered.

"About as well as your own political career," Lady Deadcut said.

The parts of Markus' face not shoved against the ice drew together in offended shock. Faustine snorted so hard she had to wipe her nose.

"I was nothing but the Countess Caecillion, and I gave that up before it buried me." Lady Deadcut took slow, measured steps toward Markus. "But not before I learned enough to bury Vittoro and Elias."

Lady Deadcut stopped beside Faustine and the professor, and let go of her dress. She brought her injured hand into Markus' line of sight, and Faustine's blood froze in her veins.

There was a ruddy, bleeding nub where her thumb had once been—and it was growing back.

"What the fuck?" growled the professor. "Since when did you—"

The bone-grinding feeling got louder, and the professor and Deadcut both seemed to sense it. They glanced at the ice wall a half-second before something deep and dark moved inside it.

"Get clear!" Professor Valerius shouted, already moving away from Markus and Lady Clarissa's ghost knight. She shoved a hand into Lady Deadcut's shoulder and the old woman stumbled back, even as Markus thrashed furiously against the ghostly knight while it dragged him along the floor.

Panic seized Faustine as the rumbling in her blood grew louder. She took off for the far wall, nearly tripping over Lady Clarissa.

"Keep moving!" the mage woman said, gesturing for Faustine to follow the professor's line of egress.

Faustine dropped to a weightlifter's crouch. "You're coming with me!"

It was no graceful fireman's carry or piggyback, but Faustine managed to drag Lady Clarissa far enough out of the way that, when the dark thing in the ice wall moved again and her body vibrated so hard she felt tendons twist, Professor Valerius was able to scoop an arm under Lady Clarissa's armpit and help them along. Which was good; it felt like something deep in Faustine's stomach was on fire.

"What is that awful feeling?" Faustine asked, breathlessly.

Professor Vee opened her mouth to say something, but a wordless howl cut her off.

Faustine glanced over her shoulder just in time to see the glacier wall shatter into a million iridescent pieces. A dark shape tumbled out of the wreckage, and Faustine's heart seized in her chest.

And then the diaphanous mass unfolded itself into a familiar figure with two arms, two legs, a mage's coat, and blazingly green eyes.

"Don't move," said the Not-Headmaster.

His hands were at the level of his eyes.

CHAPTER FIFTY

FURY SANG IN VENDRICK's bones as his boots connected hard with the stony cavern floor. His gaze darted around the room—marking Frelia and Faustine intact, Clarissa uninjured but furious, and his mother visibly discomforted by whatever wound she held to her stomach, and Markus...

Markus was staring at him like he'd grown a second head.

The Imperial Watcher was sprawled across the floor, incredulous to the point that he lay there unmoving. "You're meant to be dead."

An honest-to-the-Goddesses growl escaped Vendrick's throat as he stalked forward. "I got better."

Vendrick's mind was a tangled mess of furious thought-threads and growing rage. He couldn't have drawn a rune even if he'd wanted to; Vendrick couldn't think straight enough to remember any of them, let alone do anything with it.

"We swore an oath, you gutless filth." Vendrick was rounding on Markus now. "We swore, at the start of the Tyrant's War, to uphold justice and meritocracy. To put an end to the stagnant hypocrisy of the Senate."

There was little point, but Vendrick snatched Markus by the loose fabric of his lowered hood anyway.

"You looked our Lady dead in the eyes and said you swore."

Vendrick cracked the heel of his hand into Markus' rigid nose. The crunch of wet bone breaking echoed in the cavern, and a quiet, Kaldiri murmur that might have been praise slipped between Vendrick's ears.

"So what the fuck," Vendrick hissed, "are you doing that my father approves of?"

Silence dug into them, then. A weight.

Markus' eyes were watering, even as blood trickled lazily from his nose. "What do you mean, your father?"

"He was waiting at the Gjöll for me." Vendrick's fist tightened in the fabric of Markus' hood. "Didn't you call him?"

"What are you on about?" Markus demanded.

"I 'spoke' with him and Cillian Grimsdalr, just now."

Vendrick expected the various, surprised gasps from behind him. What he did not expect, however, was Markus' jaw to drop like he was genuinely surprised.

"You were in Hypogia?" Markus shrieked. "Are you serious?"

This time it was Vendrick's turn to furrow his brow. "Did you not complete your ritual on purpose?"

"I have been trying to cross the veil for years!" Markus whined. "And I don't so much as get a toe into the River Gjöll. And you're telling me, I just... accidentally...?" He made a strangled noise as words, evidently, failed him.

"Have you finally lost it?" Vendrick asked. "Because it sounds to me like you're implying that you actually sent me to the mythical land of the dead while thinking you were summoning a darkbeast?"

Frelia burst into laughter. All eyes in the room went to her as she doubled over, eye watering as she tried to speak.

"You... slept in the barrow, Vendrick," she called over to him amidst her laughter. "They fucking found you!"

"Believe it or not," he said, "they did mention that."

The ghosts of his friends and ancestors and everything else suddenly pressed down on him, and Vendrick wondered, absently, if this was how Frelia felt walking into Castle Skjöldr, teaching at Silverwood, living in her own mind.

Shit, at least his ghosts had the courtesy to wait for him in death where they belonged.

"So what did it look like, in there?" Frelia asked.

Vendrick looked away from Markus for the first time since he'd stumbled back into the cavern. Over his shoulder, Frelia stood resolute as always, looking like she was torn between coming over to assist and letting him fight his own battles.

"Green skies, sapphire hills, and the light was all wrong," Vendrick said. "And I'm starting to see how this happened. You do know that wasn't really a summoning ritual, yes?"

"Of course it was!" Markus harrumphed.

"Summoning is grey magic." Vendrick's voice dripped with academic disdain. "What you performed was white."

All the color drained from Markus' face and Vendrick knew he'd nailed his target.

"None of what you do is summoning, is it?" Part of Vendrick wanted to laugh, but a larger part wanted to scream. "It's all necromancy!"

How had he never seen it? All the stories about the Lady of the Dead, and the grisly trophies down in Markus' laboratory, and somehow the idea that darkbeasts were undead had gone right over Vendrick's head. No wonder their blood was black. No wonder you had to burn them. No wonder the rules for killing a draugr properly were effectively the same.

Darkbeasts were simply not creatures of the Waking World. It was everything Frelia had ever said, and Vendrick had been a rational, logical Volsinii discounting Kaldiri superstition again.

He'd have torn his own hair out if he'd had a free hand.

Markus was desperately trying not to make eye contact with anyone in the room, and failing. "I don't have to answer to the likes of you."

"No," Frelia said, her eyes narrowing, "just your ghosts later. I hope they eat you, *zychnik*."

Vendrick pulled up short. *There is no peace,* the old prophecy supposedly went, *even in death.*

"Frelia..." Finally, his anger began to recede, and something else occurred to him. "Cillian Grimsdalr asked me to tell you something."

Her face went slack, and Vendrick couldn't read her expression.

"But, first..." Saints, this was mad, but, well, so was he. "Lady Midnight is the Goddess who will end the world, correct?"

"*Ja.* Mother of Garmur and—"

Frelia cut herself off with a pained grunt, pressing her hand to the side of her abdomen where Vendrick knew her bloodrune lay.

"I'm sure I already know the answers," she ground out, "but does anyone else feel that?"

Vendrick had half a second to worry about the rumbling before a roar like thunder came from out over the water. He released his grip on Markus' collar and brought his hands up to casting position, eyes raking the dark water for signs of unnatural movement.

"Can..." Faustine swallowed audibly. "Can darkbeasts swim?"

"Not easily." Frelia drew her sword with a quick, rasping noise, and then glanced, strangely, to Deadcut. "Well, Verona? What about you?"

"I feel it," said Vendrick's mother, quietly. "And so far as I know, there's nothing that big in the Ivory Channel except—"

A ragged chunk of midnight cut through the water at the other side of the grotto, dragging itself towards the shore with scythe-like claws. Saltwater sloughed off its greasy hide, revealing lacerations and burn marks unending. For a moment, Vendrick was staring into four brown eyes, ringed in burning green.

He had approximately half a second to feel relieved before Thera's massive jaws loomed, wide, overhead.

***

"Thera!" the professor shouted. "What the fuck are you doing?"

Faustine's heart was in her throat as everything all around them ceased to move. No, *no*, this couldn't be happening! Thera was a good darkbeast!

Right?

The monster that had once been a woman rumbled, low and menacing. Faustine flinched instinctively, but a moment later her brain connected it to the sounds she'd heard the malamutes make on the trek here.

Thera wanted something, and was worried someone was going to take it.

"Easy!" Faustine called to the darkbeast. "No one's going to hurt you."

She felt Lady Deadcut's eyes dig into her side, but Faustine kept going.

"What is it you want?" Faustine took a few tentative steps towards where her brother and the Not-Headmaster had been arguing.

Thera growled again, low and resonant.

"You can't eat Lord Caecillion," Faustine said. "And you really shouldn't eat Markus." Faustine thought on that for a moment, then added, "Yet."

"You worthless brat," Markus snapped.

Voices rose in her defense, but the loudest of all was that of Faustine herself.

"Thera," she roared, "heel!"

The darkbeast, inexplicably, snapped her jaw shut and sat back on her haunches, looking for all the world like Greta or Hrafn when they finally heeded whomever was driving.

Faustine couldn't resist. "Remind me again how I'd make a terrible beastminder, Markus?"

"You think yourself important because you can shout a few dog commands?" Markus laughed, but it was colored at the edges with something desperate. "Any idiot can make a hound sit."

"Well apparently," said Faustine, "I don't even need the family secrets to do it."

Whatever Markus had been expecting, clearly that wasn't it. He laughed, the sound sharp and mocking against the stony walls of the grotto.

"There is no secret," he said, "and I'll give you that one for free."

Faustine's eyes narrowed. "There has to be. Nobody can do it but us."

Markus rolled his eyes. "Just practice."

No, that couldn't be. If practice was all there were to it, then any idiot could walk up to a darkbeast and tell it to sit, stay, and beg. There would be no need for 'the Della Luciana Beastminders,' except perhaps to make them.

"If there's no secret to it," Faustine asked, "why were Titus and Gaius so much better at it than you?"

Somewhere to Faustine's side, the professor snorted.

"They're hell's children," Markus said flatly. "Who knows why they follow whom they do?"

It struck her suddenly, sharp and clear as a winter morning. *Markus has no respect for anyone other than himself.*

Faustine started to laugh, incredulous. Suddenly, she understood everything. Why the yarn-ball darkbeast had listened to her, out in the forest, and why Thera did, too. Why Markus always summoned small beasts he could easily overpower, until Lord Muninn forced his hand.

"What in Hypogia is so funny?" Markus snapped.

"There is a secret to beastminding." Faustine's grin was borderline manic. "And you'll never know what it is."

She looked up to Thera again, caught the darkbeast's inhuman gaze.

"Thera," Faustine called, "could you throw Markus into the sea, please?"

A deep rumbling echoed in the cavern a half second before a sopping wet paw batted at Markus like an oversized chew toy. He was thrown sideways with a yelp, landing face-first in the surf.

It was almost worth getting dragged down here by the scruff of her neck to see the disgruntled look on Markus' face. Incredulous laughter surrounded her, and Faustine felt, inexplicably, warm.

"Oh, she doesn't count," Markus growled, dragging his sopping wet hair out of his eyes. "There's something else in there."

Faustine opened her mouth to argue at the same time Lady Clarissa shrieked, "What is *that*?"

And a long, inky black foreleg began to drag itself out of the shattered ice wall.

CHAPTER FIFTY-ONE

WHEN FRELIA HAD BEEN very young, the malamutes her family used to traverse their territory had seemed enormous. It wasn't until she saw a wolf with her own two eyes that she realized, an eighty-pound dog was not only *not large*, it was downright *small* compared to a living, breathing adult wolf.

The creature dragging itself out of the broken glacier was to a wolf what that wolf had been to her family's sled dogs.

Its withers brushed the ceiling of its prison as it dragged itself free with long, inky dark forelegs. Claws like scythes clacked against the ground as it moved, and its jaws could have comfortably fitted a carriage between them and bitten down.

And then the enormous canid opened its eyes—six burning, hollow green eyes— and there was intelligence in there.

"Arch-garmr," Frelia hissed, just before a massive paw snapped towards Faustine.

The teenager yelped and scuttled sideways, and Frelia ran towards the monster the same way she always had—sword drawn and aim steady.

But this was Lord Geri. The wolf, the Guardian, the Greedy One. She had hoped—beyond hoped, even, *prayed*—that Lords Huginn and Muninn had been somehow corrupted by Ironfang and his men.

But Geri was the same as they had been.

How could Castle Skjöldr have been built by the King of the Saints to house a nightmare from his own legends? Saint Randolf Einnaska would have known what living atop a garmr would do to his descendants, and wouldn't have consigned them to a long history of iron rule and physical misery.

Except that would explain why Hägen was so different, Frelia realized as she stared down yet another garmr. *He didn't have the family bloodrune.*

"Markus." came Vendrick's voice, and Frelia was grateful she didn't have to be the one to ask, "What. Did. You. Do?"

For once in his life, Markus had the good sense to answer straight. "It's... as I said." He was staring at Geri, eyes wide and fearful. "I sacrificed Caecillion in return for the Guardian of Einnaska Territory."

"Demonstrably," said Deadcut, "you did not!"

Whatever Markus might have said drowned in the garmr's scream.

It was like no garmr call Frelia had ever heard before. Harmonics and sub-harmonics piled atop one another until the garmr's growl was no longer recognizable as such. It was a gut-deep wail of pain, grief, all-consuming hunger, and if the Geri of the old tales was in there, he was a long way off.

Frelia grimaced and clapped her free hand to her ear. A bolt of arcane energy zipped overhead and crashed into Geri's open maw, but Vendrick may as well have stabbed it with a toothpick for all the good it did.

Frelia pulled up short to start drawing the Grimsdalr Blink anyway.

She drew the first jagged slash as Thera's roar joined Geri's, and the second as her eardrums popped at the sonic assault. Frelia drew the next looping line, and the next, as not four, but eight garmr paws began picking up speed. She fell back, pivoting around the half-done rune to fix her trajectory.

The last thing she saw before dragging the sharp, final line down the center of the open eye was Thera, sized as a malamute to a wolf, running headlong towards Geri.

The world snapped into a chaotic, crystalline tunnel. Light and sound refracted and reflected in a spectrum not meant for human eyes and ears. They pressed on Frelia just like Huginn's throat had in Kjell, but instead of being swallowed by darkness, she was being swallowed by light.

She crashed into the Waking World swordpoint-first, stomach-droppingly far to thump onto Geri's back. The garmr rumbled that eldritch roar again, and Frelia drove the Sword of Hana deeper into its back.

No jagged line of purplish flesh appeared. No ichor rose to greet her. And as Geri reared onto his hind legs, both Frelia and the Sword of Hana went sliding down his back as though they hadn't been there at all.

Frelia slammed hard into the grotto floor, her shoulder crying out and leg screaming. The pain was dizzying, but still she rose, unsteady but readying the Sword of Hana for another go. The instant her weight fell on her left leg, bright, blistering pain shot all the way up through her hipbone. Frelia stumbled sideways into a nearby stalagmite.

Fuck.

"Professor!" Faustine shouted. "You need to fall back!"

Like hell.

Another round of Dark Fire blossomed up Geri's right flank, singeing the greasy black fur and littering the grotto with the stench of burning hide. Thera was right behind it, snarling, jaws going wide. She clamped down on the meat of the bigger garmr's withers, and shook her head as if to break his neck.

And then the most beautiful, fucked-up thing happened: the Grimsdalr Bloodrune activated.

Frelia had only a half-second to register the smell of ozone and the gooseflesh-feeling of astral energy coalescing before Geri's enraged howl drowned everything out.

In the cacophony, there was no sound of tearing flesh as Thera ripped a hunk of meat from the garmr's bones. There was no time to process the smell of garmr ichor in the air, or even Frelia's own blood as it trickled from her ears.

There was only an enraged, finally injured garmr, and an idea.

Frelia sheathed the Sword of Hana, waiting for the instant the garmr's shrieking stopped. She weathered the sonic storm even as, all around her, the Volsinii pressed their hands to their ears in horrified wonder.

Geri managed to throw Thera, slamming her into the grotto wall, and the dogfight began again in unnatural quiet.

"Vendrick, Clarissa!" Frelia shouted over the melee. "How many of those astral hatchets can you make?"

"Erm," Clarissa called back from her spot on the floor, "how many do you need?"

"Two!"

In another moment, translucent magic began to coalesce in Frelia's hands. She gripped the burgeoning weapons tightly, not even waiting for the full spell before charging towards the wrestling garmr. She was vibrating with adrenaline and fury, could feel it rattling her bones, and the pain in her hip suddenly seemed an ocean away.

"Is she mad?" Markus' voice was high-pitched and terrified.

"Just angry," Vendrick told him.

Axe-fighting was a lot of circling, swinging, and waiting for an opportunity to strike. Frelia had never had the patience for it, but her older brother had been a natural. She hoped some of that talent had ended up in the blood archives, because Frelia was going to need it.

If the Grimsdalr Bloodrune activating was what it took to injure Geri, then Frelia would bet her last copper that Valerius would do it, too. And if she was betting on her bloodrune, then she'd simply slice into the garmr so many times she'd force the old magic to sing in her blood.

And she'd weather that storm as many times as it took to sever flesh from bone.

***

Vendrick knew, intellectually, what he was watching was a quite literal dogfight between two descendants of the Bloodrune Saints themselves and a divine beast of legend.

Emotionally, what he was watching was sheer fucking chaos.

Thera was the terrier to Geri's malamute, snapping at his flanks, his paws, his neck—anything she could reach. Frelia was even smaller still, her gait uneven as she rounded on the fighting darkbeasts with iridescent, arcane axes in hand.

Markus seemed to realize what was happening at the same moment Vendrick did—the instant Frelia raised both axes to strike.

"Oh, no she—*oof!*"

Whatever rune Markus had started to draw was cut off when Vendrick's Singularity pellet smashed straight through his left pauldron.

The worked metal cratered inwards, and gore splattered out the other side as the Singularity pellet worked itself free. Markus' scream was nearly as ungodly as the darkbeasts', and he scrabbled for his spellbook with his now-useless left arm.

"Enough, Markus." Vendrick tugged on his Singularity pellet, and the unholy knot of arcane energy came to rest in front of Markus' remaining unblemished eye. "What did you do to summon Lord Geri?"

He needed to compose himself, to bring his mind to heel and his full might to bear. Markus della Luciana did not deserve to get to him like this. But still, Vendrick's casting hand shook with unrestrained fury.

"Oh, fantastic," Markus muttered, beads of sweat visible at his brow. "I've always wondered how it felt to swallow a Singularity pellet."

To their right, the air burned with ozone a half second before Frelia's bloodrune activated.

She roared that battle cry that had once echoed across the battlements above, cleaving both axes into Geri's hind leg. She sheared its kneecap clean off, and the enormous darkbeast faltered, unbalanced. Thera let go of its foreleg with just enough time to drag Frelia sideways by the scruff of her armored coat.

Geri landed hard on its injured leg, still thrashing and snapping at where Thera had been.

"Put me down, dammit!" Frelia snapped.

Thera opened her jaws and Frelia tumbled free, pain pulling at her facial expression as she hefted both axes up to striking range.

"Again," she growled.

Frelia would clearly be fine while Vendrick sorted out this mess, and he trusted her to get it done.

"Merciful Saints," Markus spluttered, "you can't just let her ruin everything, Caecillion!"

Vendrick's eyebrow rose, but in all honesty, the outright entitlement gave him an idea.

"It's her people's legendary monster," Vendrick said with a shrug. "Let her and Grimsdalr tear it apart, if they wish."

Markus shot him a look like Vendrick could not possibly be so stupid, and blood dribbled from the corner of his mouth.

"She already took care of Huginn and Muninn," Vendrick said, lying a little. "I don't see what the fuss is now."

"You little...!" Revulsion and horror bloomed across Markus' sallow face. "What is wrong with you?"

Why did everyone ask that like they didn't already know?

"Shall we ask my mum?" Vendrick said. "I'm sure she'll have a litany for you."

That was about the time they both noticed Governor Deadcut was not standing near Clarissa at the far wall.

In fact, despite the lack of cane or physical assistance, Deadcut had somehow made her way around the edge of the cavern with a spare astral hatchet clutched in her undamaged hand.

They stared each other down for a moment, the black and grey mages of Octavia's Queenmakers, and the storied general of their parents' era.

"Oh, pish," Deadcut said, and threw.

The astral hatchet shimmered as it tumbled through the air. No sooner had it left Deadcut's hand than it embedded itself into Markus' shoulder, almost exactly where the Singularity pellet had exited.

Markus gasped, and somewhere across the room, Geri roared.

Deadcut continued limping towards them. "Prop him up, Vendrick, would you?"

Vendrick reached for the scruff of Markus' cloak just as the man began to topple over. He had to sheathe his spellbook to keep Markus upright in all his armor, and blood dribbled down his front and over Vendrick's forearms.

"Now, pay attention, Markus," Deadcut called. "You might learn something."

Deadcut gestured, somewhat unnecessarily, to the fight still going on across the grotto. Frelia and Thera were both sporting streaks of black darkbeast ichor now, and there was a chunk of reddish flesh missing from Thera's left hind leg. Frelia's hip was clearly paining her, and blood was flecking the swallow collar of her armored coat. But she was grinning like mad and Thera's growl was more of an incredulous laugh.

Because Geri was falling back.

Inch by inch, woman and monster pushed back the ink dark tide of legend. Geri's enormous paws left rents in the stone floor, as though he had dug in against gale force winds. His back paws were nearly in the water.

"Grand Duke Einar Winter's Heart Valerius was a master of siegecraft," Deadcut said, and Vendrick was stunned to hear the man's full name and title from anyone besides his daughter. "He made us pay for every inch we gained at Fort Anver with Volsinii blood."

The Winter War had, perhaps predictably, ended when the titular season had descended. The attacking Volsinii had been forced to fall back or be annihilated by the jaws of a Kaldiri winter they were neither prepared nor built for.

"What in Hypogia," Deadcut continued, "made you think his daughter would be any different?"

Frelia disappeared from view, her icy blue magic like an aura of frost in her wake. A moment later she snapped back into existence over Geri's enormous skull with the brilliant violence of a shooting star.

This time Geri's shriek rocked the grotto. Vendrick had to brace Markus against his hip to keep the man upright.

"Who's side are you on?" Markus hissed.

Deadcut's eyebrow quirked. "Whichever is opposite Vittoro."

She was in measure with them, now. The most dangerous place to be, with an axewoman.

"So listen here, you arrogant fop. I have had just about enough of you. You demand my time, impose upon my hospitality, threaten my children and my guests, and now you've attempted to kill me! I might have even forgiven all that, if you'd simply followed the cardinal rule."

Vendrick had to hold back a laugh.

His mother was the sort of person who would take the paved path the long way around, despite a perfectly good, more direct bootleg trail. She was the sort of woman who paid her taxes on time and donated to all the local charities. Who stood on ceremony for things like warrants and due process.

But there was another, almost more important, thing that Sulpicia "Deadcut" Verona was—absolutely rigid in her beliefs of right and wrong.

"But you have abused my faith in your family."

Deadcut's gnarled fist yanked the axe out of Markus' pectoral, and he slumped against Vendrick like a boneless sack.

"And that," Deadcut said, "simply will not stand."

Markus looked like he might be sick all over the esteemed governor of Northern Volsinii. "You're a right bastard, Deadcut."

She smiled, but it was thin. "Where do you think Vendrick and Clarissa got it?"

Vendrick couldn't help it. Despite everything, he actually did laugh. "Did you just make a joke?"

His mum sniffed. "It's been known to happen."

Anxious arcane energy skittered across Vendrick's knuckles as he shook his head, and Markus' grey eyes followed the motion warily. Vaguely, Vendrick wondered if Markus could still see out of the bloodruned one, if he knew what rune would be coming next.

But then the breaking waves stopped roaring.

Brow furrowed, Vendrick glanced, just for a moment, to the dogfight across the room. Frelia had stilled, atop Geri's back, and even the two darkbeasts had stopped thrashing.

Out across the water, in the last rays of a dying sun, an enormous, mottled grey shape had begun breaking the surface.

CHAPTER FIFTY-TWO

AT FIRST, IT WAS as though a craggy lump of hewn rock had gained the sentience to move around. And then a second lump joined the first, pulling a dark, mottled-grey shape out of the water and into the last few rays of sunlight.

And then the enormous creature opened its eyes—its burning, hollow green eyes—and Vendrick's stomach dropped.

"Are you serious?" he snapped at Markus.

Markus spluttered, somehow still finding the energy to sound affronted. "What makes you think I did this?"

Frelia's voice came from atop Geri's back—"*Did Markus summon the fucking kraken?*"—a half-second before the first of the creature's tentacles smacked wetly onto the shore.

Thera screeched a howl that echoed in the cavernous room, thundering towards the interloping tentacle. She smashed into it headlong, and at once, the tentacle slithered back into the sea.

Then a second one smacked onto the shore, and Geri seemed to realize what was going on. He screamed that same unnatural, subharmonic scream, and Frelia took her hands off the hatchet to cover her ears.

Time slowed to a crawl as Geri reared onto his hind legs, forepaws scraping at the air before him, and Frelia began to skid down its rancid spine. She twisted, reaching for fur her gloves would find no purchase in, and Vendrick desperately flipped through his mental spellbook for something—anything—that would help.

He had one thought, and it would have to do.

He dropped his hold on Markus even as his right hand snapped up to cast. He drew the first jagged lines easily, sketching the eye-like rune in the air before him, praying he was right because there was no time to consult his actual spellbook.

And then something jerked behind his navel, and Vendrick was no longer in the Waking World.

Through the crystalline tunnel, he could make out snatches of greenish light, rolling, azure hills, and—he could *swear*—Cillian Grimsdalr's raucous laughter. And then he was crashing into Frelia, sending the both of them toppling off Geri's back.

He hit the ground hard enough to spark stars, and Frelia hit *him* hard enough to drive the breath from his lungs. For a moment, they lay there in stunned silence, Vendrick frantically trying to catch his breath while Frelia scrambled off his ribs.

"You *dorchya*," she got out, and Vendrick had approximately a second to feel warm and fuzzy about it before Geri screamed again.

Vendrick scrambled to his feet like an ungainly spider, joints and limbs protesting as he hauled Frelia to her feet, too. She looked around for her hatchets, cursed when she saw they were still studded in Geri's back, and then drew the Sword of Hana.

But Geri was no longer looking at them.

He was rounding on the kraken, snarling and screaming like a wolf studded with arrows. Black ichor sloughed from his wounds and, at this angle, even Geri the Greedy was dwarfed by the sheer, gargantuan size of his seafaring cousin.

That hadn't stopped Thera, though. She was snarling around a mouthful of tentacle, the sound brutal and reverberating. She snapped her head backwards and ripped out a chunk of purplish squid-flesh, then spat it out somewhere towards the sea.

Froth churned around the kraken as it burbled in fury. A third tentacle came whipping out of the water and smashed into Thera's back. She sprawled on all fours, and Vendrick made an inadvertent noise of sympathy pain as Thera struggled against the tentacle's pressing weight.

And did not rise.

"Thera, no!" Frelia took two steps before her injured hip gave out, pitching her onto the stone. She tried to get up again, only to falter on her injured leg.

Vendrick hastened to help her back up just as a young voice cried out, "Kraken, stop!"

Force rippled through the kraken's mantle as though Faustine had smacked it with a war hammer. The creature tilted its mantle like an investigating bird, but kept its tentacles where they were. Even Geri cocked his head, confused and stumbling over his own paws in the shallows.

"Kraken," Faustine said again, this time not quite so loudly, "don't hurt her, please?"

Markus' disbelieving snort was disgusting. "Do you really think that simply by asking it you can—"

But the kraken had stopped moving. Its enormous, darkbeast-green eyes were roving, searching for something Vendrick would be prepared to bet was Faustine.

A growl sounded from somewhere to their collective left, and Vendrick glanced over just in time to see Thera's jaws snapping shut on the kraken's tentacle, even as she remained pinned beneath it.

Whatever cease-fire Faustine had brokered shattered; the kraken immediately resumed thrashing.

Thera whined again, still without letting go of her hold on its tentacle, and Geri shook himself, spraying the whole cavern with saltwater and thick, black ichor.

"Grimsdalr!" Vendrick shouted. "Let the girl work!"

Thera snarled again, her tail jerking from side to side.

"She'll never—" Frelia began, but the end of her sentence was swallowed by a snarled cry of surprise.

Two additional tentacles shot out of the water, surrounding Geri. Despite the enormous, wolf-like darkbeast's thrashing claws and snarling teeth, the kraken did not let go.

Inch by painstaking inch, just like Frelia and Thera had, the kraken pulled Geri into the water.

Squids, Vendrick knew, didn't have mouths as such. What they had were beaks, and he watched in horrified fascination as the kraken dug that chitinous protrusion into Geri's flank and heaved.

Geri screamed again as a long tear of rent flesh came free of its flank, only to slowly disappear beneath the water.

"Is it..." Vendrick stared at the two darkbeasts in shock. "...*eating* Lord Geri?"

The kraken bit down again, tearing into its cousin in a frenzy of fur and limbs.

"Why are you asking me?" Frelia's voice was as unsteady as her injured leg, and she leaned on him for support. "We don't have a legend for this."

And though Vendrick had seen and done several lifetimes' worth of awful things, none of it prepared him for this grotesque pantomime. He watched in morbid fascination as the kraken began, systemically and methodically, to tear Lord Geri apart.

It was more like watching a chef spatchcock a plucked chicken than a wild beast mantle a kill. The kraken had evidently done this before, and the water around it began to blacken with darkbeast ichor. Frelia leaned more heavily on Vendrick's side, staring in mute, horrified silence.

Whatever she was watching, it had a lot more context than Vendrick saw, but asking felt like a terrible idea when he wasn't even sure if combat was through.

Even Thera had stopped trying to tear the giant squid apart. She sat back on her haunches, panting heavily and whimpering softly whenever she shifted and jarred her injured hind leg.

"Markus...?" Faustine sounded on the verge of being ill.

It took him a moment, what with Deadcut holding him upright, but Markus eventually coughed out, "What are you looking at me for?"

"Oh, good," Frelia muttered. "He has no idea what's going on, either."

The kraken was down to Geri's ribs, now. It broke those apart like bundles of kindling, chomping on bone as surely as flesh. Bit by devoured bit, Geri ceased to move, except where the water rocked him softly against the kraken's mantle.

And that was about when Vendrick started to notice a chill in the air.

Not the usual sort of chill—it was, after all, winter—but the sort that was accompanied by the arcane and made the hair on the back of his neck stand on end.

"Do you feel that?" he murmured to Frelia beneath the cracking of bones in the kraken's beak.

"The rumbling?" she asked.

"The cold."

"It's *winter*, Vendrick!"

"I'm aware." He resisted the urge to huff. "I mean the... sort of... I don't know, arcane cold."

Frelia blanched. Vendrick hoped it wasn't from blood loss. "...No."

"Capital," Vendrick muttered.

The kraken suddenly let go of Geri's dwindled corpse. It pushed itself through the mess of darkbeast ichor it had made of the shallow water, sloshing waves in every direction, until it came to rest just in front of Thera.

It tilted its mantle again, one baleful, green eye fixed on the smaller wolf-like darkbeast.

"Thera..." Frelia called warningly.

Vendrick prepared to cast Dark Fire, but it turned out not to matter.

Quick as lightning, one of the kraken's tentacles broke the surface of the water and came to rest, gently, unthinkably, on Thera's great forehead.

And then the wolf-like darkbeast began to scream.

Not howl—*scream*. Sharply and abruptly, as though something had just bitten the woman Thera had once been.

The wind kicked up, and the unnatural chill practically forced Vendrick's eyes shut.

He squinted against the cold and the salt air, and found not an enormous, carriage-sized beast shaking in fury before the kraken, but a fierce-looking red-haired woman, naked as her name day. Her scars sucked in light as though the twilight had gone there to die, and her skin was the kind of pale that hadn't seen proper sunlight in years.

"What... the fuck?" Thera rasped.

Vendrick's jaw fell open. That had to be transmutation magic, did it not? He could smell it in the air—a sort of guttural ozone that the arcane always held—and at his side, Frelia had gone rigid in shock.

"Oh, Saints," Markus moaned, "Father's going to kill me."

It struck Vendrick as the most honest thing the man had quite possibly ever said.

Unsteady on her own feet, Thera took careful, mincing steps towards the water. She raised one arm like a supplicant, reaching for the heart of the monster and laying a very much human hand against the kraken's hide. The other pressed against her leg where an angry red welt had risen up around—

Vendrick blinked, as if to clear something out of his eyes. But, no, he'd seen clearly.

That welt had risen up around her bloodrune.

"Ow." Thera's rough voice echoed across the dark water. "I am... *here*... you... damn thing."

All was silent for a long, terrible moment.

"I see." Thera ran her hand along the kraken's slimy hide, exactly how they'd been taught to soothe wyverns, all those years ago at Silverwood. "You're in... terrible pain. And you were..."

Thera shut her eyes, then, and pressed her forehead against the kraken's slimy skin. For an awful, protracted moment, nothing moved but the wind across the mouth of the grotto and the waves beneath it. The kraken's innumerable tentacles slowed, and it fell motionless as its mantle pressed to Thera's forehead.

And then, inexplicably, Thera began to weep.

Vendrick and Frelia exchanged a wary, horrified look, but then Frelia jerked her head towards Thera.

"Come on," she said quietly.

There were few people Frelia trusted so much as a Grimsdalr, and few people she cared more to see whole.

With silent, assassin's feet, Vendrick crossed the empty grotto with her, past the point of no return and well into the kraken's grasping range. He undid the clasp holding his cloak together at the shoulder without looking at it.

"Grimsdalr," he murmured, holding the cloak out to her. "What's going on?"

"Look... at this," she rasped, and grabbed for Vendrick's hand to press into the kraken's side, too.

As soon as he touched it, his mind was flooded with the creature's alien consciousness and a garbled language he couldn't make any sense of. It took Vendrick a reeling moment to understand what he was even seeing.

There were snatches of other creatures like the kraken, other void-skinned, green-eyed monsters with spindly limbs and too many eyes. But they weren't darkbeasts—or at least, they weren't any darkbeasts like Vendrick had ever seen. There weren't almost-wolves and massive elk and whatever other forest creatures they mimicked. These darkbeasts were humanoid, even if they had too many arms and stood too tall and bent at impossible angles.

And then, one by one, the humanoid-darkbeast shapes fell away in the kraken's mind.

First went the one with a missing right eye and entirely too many arms, possessed of an internal light that seemed to shine through cracks in the ink of its skin. Then went the one with both eyes and straw-like hair, whose absence the kraken felt as keenly as if it had died. Then went the one with no left eye, with spines up its back and wicked-looking claws. Then went one with no eyes at all, a blind, formless darkness fading through a rune Vendrick couldn't quite recognize.

No right eye, both eyes, no left eye. Where had he heard that before?

"The Goddesses..." Grimsdalr rumbled. "I think they left it behind."

CHAPTER FIFTY-THREE

VENDRICK STOOD THERE IN the icy grotto like a dead thing, motionless and uncomprehending. The monstrous dark creatures in the kraken's memory were the *Goddesses?* How could that possibly be? Weren't they supposed to be the kindly (and in turns, cruel) women from legend?

That last image, though. It haunted him and had for years.

"Left it behind from what?" Vendrick managed.

"Helheim." Frelia stared at the Kraken in horror. "The Goddesses went to Helheim... but it didn't."

The kraken shuddered, kicking up froth in the freezing water.

"So it's an Old One," Vendrick murmured. "The step above Hypogean."

"That's not possible!" Markus scoffed.

"Shut up, you git," Faustine told him.

"What do you mean, not possible?" Frelia grit out. "Your own people told us that."

"The Sightless One has been sealed in Hypogia for a millennium! There's no way he could possibly—!"

Markus suddenly shut up, as if realizing what he'd just admitted.

"*I knew it.*" Deadcut's voice was the tolling of an iron bell.

There were too many revelations to keep track of; Vendrick was starting to lose his hold on all the threads.

"You knew what?" he asked anyway.

"I was, perhaps, not entirely truthful, earlier," Deadcut admitted, and Vendrick was not the only one stunned. "Not only had I heard of the Unseen, but I—"

"Have the fucking Maximus Bloodrune because of them?" Frelia growled.

Vendrick's gaze flicked between Frelia and Deadcut. The wounded Kaldiri warrior was hunched over her good knee, glaring daggers across the grotto. But the wounded Volsinii soldier held her ground, and met the challenge head-on.

"I should have known you would figure it out," Deadcut said, and she sounded almost amused. "I would expect nothing less of Grand Duke Einar's daughter."

Frelia's smile was all carnassials. "Don't try to slither out of this, Volsinii."

"Bloodrune?" Clarissa piped up. "What in Hypogia does she mean, *bloodrune?*"

Deadcut's hand moved to the collar of her delicate blouse and tugged her neckline to the side to reveal a scarred-over mark as red as blood. The twisting, star-like points stood out against her fair skin like an army at attention on a snow-covered hillside.

Markus stared at it with revulsion. "It can't be."

"Maximus," Frelia barked, "to keep humanity on the right path. I fucking knew it."

"Task of the... Undaunted," Thera added, sounding somewhere further away than merely the kraken's side. "'By your guiding hand... shall stability flourish.'"

Clarissa and Vendrick both snorted, and quickly went to put a hand to the offending noise.

"Okay, that is rather funny," Deadcut admitted.

"Mum, this makes no sense," Clarissa said. "We're runeless."

"You're runeless, dear," Deadcut said with delicate emphasis. "Your brother, as well."

Vendrick's eyes narrowed as he studied the twisting bloodrune on his mother's collarbone. The Verona family were famously runeless, and if any of those power-grubbing men and women had possessed a bloodrune, they absolutely would have ruthlessly pushed that advantage in the Senate.

Which meant...

"You got that later in life," Vendrick said, his voice very low. "Didn't you?"

Deadcut's smile was thin. "I've never told you about what I saw in the Winter War, have I?"

"No," Markus interrupted. "No, no, I refuse to believe this."

"Refuse all you like," Frelia told him. "Her thumb doesn't lie."

Deadcut stuck her hand in his face, mutilated thumb and all.

"I begged—*begged!*—for years," Markus snarled, "only to be denied. And you seriously mean to tell me Vittoro Caecillion lobbied to give his wretchedly nagging wife a bloodrune?"

Deadcut's laughter was chilling. "You're assuming I wanted it."

"So you what, stole it?" Markus snapped. "That doesn't change—"

"*You...* stole," Grimsdalr snapped.

It suddenly occurred to Markus just who was standing in the shallows beside a cannibal monster that had already heeded his little sister once. Vendrick could see the realization in Markus' unbloodied eye as all the color drained from his face.

"Me?" Grimsdalr added. "Or Cillian?"

Markus didn't say anything for so long a moment that Deadcut shook him by the shoulder. "Go on, then," the governor said. "Answer the woman."

When he said nothing, Deadcut thumped the axe back into the wound on his chest. As much to stop the bleeding as egg him on, Vendrick figured. He'd have done the same.

"It was a phylactery!" Markus burst out. "Saints, woman, I've no idea which of you the Unseen pulled blood from. They've had both of you imprisoned at one point or other!"

"I remember," Grimsdalr spat. "And it knows too."

She jerked a thumb towards the kraken and, as if on cue, the beast bellowed and the ichor-drenched sea erupted into froth. But it stayed where it was beside Grimsdalr, and no colossal tentacles came sniping out of the water.

"What's it still doing here?" Vendrick couldn't help but ask.

Grimsdalr's lips pulled to one side, and then she pointed over their heads. "It wants that thing out."

Vendrick craned his neck to squint up the kraken's enormous mantle. For a moment, all he saw was a wide expanse of mottled kraken hide.

"There's nothing there," Markus harrumphed.

"Yes, there is," Vendrick said quietly, having finally spotted it. "It's about this big."

He made a circle with his thumb and forefinger, roughly the size of a gold coin.

"Tell it to crouch down, or something, Grimsdalr," Vendrick said. "I can't get up there."

He wasn't keen on trying to draw the Grimsdalr Blink again only to punt himself into the cold, dark water.

"Who said you're going?" Clarissa said.

Vendrick glanced at his little sister, seated cross-legged on the floor near the far wall, her spellbook spread in front of her and a ghostly knight at her back. She would struggle to even reach the kraken, and so would Frelia. Deadcut was holding back Markus, who was under no circumstances getting anywhere near the beast, and Vendrick would be damned before he handed this off to a student.

"Well we're not sending Mum," he said instead of any of that.

Getting onto the kraken's mantle turned out to be the world's most bizarre rock-climbing excursion, Vendrick would later joke. He pulled himself up onto one of the tentacles after a few failed attempts that dropped him back into the shallows and onto the cave floor. The kraken eventually seemed to realize what he was doing, and slimy, octopodal muscle came down to assist. Vendrick was vaguely reminded of offering the Silverwood wyverns bacon strips in the palm of his hand as he stepped onto the tentacle, except he was the bacon.

Newly advantaged, he first tried to climb up the side of the beast. But his hands—with or without his gloves—couldn't find enough purchase on the kraken's smooth mantle. Markus was laughing hard enough that Faustine had gone over to yell at him, which was stressful to listen to, even if Vendrick appreciated the thought.

"You could try knives, like I do with garmur?" Frelia mimicked pulling herself up the creatures' backs with knife after knife dug into their spines. She was sitting on the cave floor now, her left leg outstretched at an awkward angle.

"I don't think I want to hurt it," Vendrick said.

"Don't!" Thera demanded from over by the kraken's enormous eye. She had mercifully put on Vendrick's cloak during his impromptu physical education class, so at least he could look at her again.

Beside him, the kraken shuddered. Vendrick nearly went tumbling back to the ground when the tentacle holding him up jostled.

"Then tell it to help me up!" Vendrick called.

An enormous, sucker-studded tentacle loomed towards him. Vendrick recoiled instinctively, but it merely tried to curl around his middle. Turned out, there was too much tentacle and not enough skinny grey mage.

"Hold," Vendrick said. "Just... hold on."

He reached up, bare-handed, and felt around one of the suction cups. They were strong and faintly squishy, but raised enough that Vendrick could curl his hands around them. The kraken held its tentacle steady as Vendrick tested it, and tugging on the suction cup didn't seem to bother it.

"Just..." Despite having fought Lords Muninn, Huginn, and also apparently Geri, Vendrick had no idea how in Hypogia one addressed a legendary monster directly. "...hold your arm steady by your head, would you, Lord Kraken?"

Below him, Frelia burst out laughing. "*Lord Kraken!*"

"I don't know what else to call it!"

"I dunno," Faustine called, "I think it likes it?"

Vendrick resisted the childish urge to stick his tongue out at Frelia, and began to climb.

It turned out to be more effort to unstick himself from the suckers than to grab them, Vendrick was annoyed to discover. The longer he hauled himself upwards, the deeper the bruises on his arms grew. He'd almost call it a hickey, if it weren't the size of a dinner plate.

He studied the kraken's mantle as he climbed, searching for the divot he'd seen earlier. Something was embedded in it its hide, glowing with a weak arcane aura, as though it were very old or not particularly powerful. Given the options, Vendrick would bet on the former.

Once he was finally level with it, Vendrick clambered off the tentacle and onto the kraken's mantle. The beast shuddered beneath him, and sent Vendrick tumbling back down its mantle.

Shit!

He scrabbled for something, *anything*, to hold onto, and managed to catch himself on its eye ridge before he went plunging back into the floor.

"Merciful Goddesses," Deadcut said.

"Easy, now," Vendrick said to the kraken, his heart beating wildly in his ears.

He found himself soothing the kraken in the same way Grimsdalr had been earlier, smoothing a hand over its hide as if to say hello. He felt a bit daft, but the enormous creature stilled.

"Good," Vendrick said. "I'm going to try climbing again, alright?"

He dragged himself towards the divot again, shoulders burning. He'd lost his knife somewhere in the struggle to climb up the first time, and his mind was a jumble of the kraken's ancient fear and modern isolation. He hoped his own strength would be enough.

It was all he had left.

Vendrick found the divot at last, where a small, coin-sized pebble lay pressed into the kraken's mantle like it had rolled over onto it. Vendrick's thin fingers wormed their way around the small protrusion, digging into slimy muscle.

The kraken roared, and there was pain in it.

"It's just a little thing." Vendrick pressed his thumb against the pebble with all the force he could muster. "Easy, now, Lord Kraken."

Funny, it didn't sound so silly now.

This time, Vendrick pushed against the pebble with both thumbs. He cursed his lack of nails, lack of knives, lack of *anything* useful. But if this thing wanted the ancient magic freed, Vendrick would just have to figure something—

He toppled forward with a yelp as the pebble finally slipped free.

Vendrick tumbled headfirst down the kraken's mantle, clutching the pebble tightly in his fist. He just barely caught his bearings with enough time to shut his eyes before he smashed into the shallows.

But instead of hard stone, he connected with a weird sort of ethereal space that made his hair stand on end. He opened his eyes and found himself staring up at one of Clarissa's ghostly knights.

"You're welcome!" Clarissa shouted.

She directed the ghost knight to set him down, and Vendrick's feet had just barely touched ground when a bright blast of rose-gold light burst to life to his right.

"Now, Vendrick," Markus began, his magic warping in front of him, "hand that over before you're tempted to do something stupid."

"Like this, you mean?" a feminine voice asked.

Vendrick was only halfway through his Singularity rune when Deadcut, with an exhausted eye roll, yanked the astral hatchet out of Markus' chest.

The Watcher staggered into his half-drawn rune, knocking himself onto the floor with the recoil blast. Deadcut's pink slipper-clad foot pressed lightly onto his throat, as if to ask if he'd had enough.

For a moment, no one moved.

Deadcut looked over to her children then—Vendrick, with his half-drawn rune, and Clarissa, cross-legged on the floor leaning over her spellbook—and said, "Restrain him, would one of you?"

This time when Vendrick drew the restriction rune, the astral energy coalesced around Markus' wrists and ankles without tripping a protection rune. He clutched the pebble tightly in his gloved hand, unwilling to take his eyes off Markus despite his unnatural stillness.

"Faustine," Deadcut said, and the girl snapped to attention. "Would you be a dear and run upstairs to inform my steward and Sir Mitri that we are in need of a contingent of guardsmen, as well as the castle physician? I think we shall need some help down here."

CHAPTER FIFTY-FOUR

FOR THE SECOND TIME in as many months, Frelia found herself showering clean of garmur ichor without even the time to enjoy it.

She dressed quickly, ignoring the day clothes Deadcut's staff had set out in favor of her own spare travelling clothes. Frelia did take an extra moment to scrub some of the grime and garmr ichor off her armored coat, though. She wasn't going anywhere without it and, well, there would be time to clean it and her sword with the wolfsbane solution later. She hoped.

It was around then that Vendrick reappeared, his hair still damp and curling against his collar. Frelia valiantly resisted the urge to curl her fingers through it and hang the stupid meeting they were supposed to be getting off to.

"Are you ready?" Vendrick asked, presenting an elbow as though this were a court.

She didn't know what to tell him. Part of her wanted to scream, to hit something, hurt something. Drag Deadcut out to the battlements by her frilly collar, make her stare out across Skjöldr's skyline and say *look what you've done to my city, my country, my* home, *you fucking zychnik.*

But it wasn't Deadcut who'd tried to summon Lord Geri and broken the cycle of the Sacred Tasks. It wasn't Deadcut who had stormed this castle half a lifetime ago and killed Hägen in his own throne room. And it wasn't Deadcut who had turned Einar Valerius into a monster and left his daughter to pick up those pieces.

Ironfang and his Unseen had done that. Ironfang was the one to blame.

"No," Frelia finally said, "but I don't think it matters."

Vendrick caught her easily, arms looping around the small of her back to steady them both. He made a surprised noise in his throat when she tugged him down into a kiss, but a moment later, Frelia felt his hand curl around her cheek in the way she was starting to learn he liked.

And then he pulled them apart, staring her down with concern etched into the furrows of his brow. "Of course it does," Vendrick said, softly. "Talk to me."

It was easier to stare at his waistcoat buttons than it was to meet his gaze. "Everything in this place is Volsinii fucking red, except for me."

It was starting to feel like when she'd first walked into Vendrick's office at Silverwood last year. That hopeless, ceaseless rage that bubbled deep inside her soul, and colored everything she did.

She felt her head tipped back, found herself staring into Vendrick's calculating gaze. "You and Thera," he murmured. "And, as cruel as it sounds, I do have an idea about how best to use that."

Frelia's eyebrow rose. "Eh?"

"I know you're not opposed to using your own trauma as a blunt force weapon—"

Frelia laughed, and it broke some of the ice that was creeping across her heart.

"—so let's find a way to be strategic about it, shall we?" Vendrick smiled, just a little, and Frelia's mind inched towards equilibrium.

"There are plenty of ways to make a government regret what it's done to its people without so much as a sword or a lie."

Frelia was torn between the urge to laugh in spluttering shock and ugly cry.

"Sometimes," she managed, "you Senators scare me."

Vendrick pressed a kiss to the top of her head—"I wasn't even a particularly good one."—and then let go.

"Are you alright?" Frelia asked.

"I'm fine," Vendrick said, too quick for it to be anything but automatic.

Frelia shot him a look.

"Alright," Vendrick admitted sheepishly, "I'm far too old to be falling off the kraken, but other than that..." He shrugged.

"You..." Frelia blinked at him a few times, trying to string together a sentence. "...your da attacked you in Helheim, Vendrick."

"So?" Vendrick raised an eyebrow. "He did that in the Waking World, too."

"*Ja*, so are you okay?"

Vendrick's facial expression softened. "You forget, love, I've killed him once before. I'll be fine."

Frelia didn't believe him, and made to argue about it.

"Besides," Vendrick hastened to add at the look on her face, "with what Cillian Grimsdalr told me?" He seemed to debate a few things internally before adding, "I've honestly never felt better about our odds."

Frelia sheathed the argument, for now—"*Ja*, he was good at that."—and they went next door together.

"Thera?" Frelia called, rapping on the door as gently as the motion allowed.

Silence.

Then, "Door's open."

Frelia had lived in the guest rooms of Castle Skjöldr approximately every other summer between the ages of four and twenty, knocking Thera and Cillian's doors to find something interesting to fill their time with. So when she pushed her way through the heavy wood and found Thera standing there barefoot and with her coppery hair flying every which way, it was like no time had passed at all.

Something wet tried to prick at the corners of her eyes, but Frelia blinked it away.

"How are you feeling?" Vendrick asked with polite, Volsinii interest.

Thera pulled a face that Frelia had been watching on her garmr for so long, it took a moment to recognize indecision on her very much human, very much like Cillian's face.

"Hungry," Thera settled on, and then she smiled. "I hope your mum has food at this ridiculous meeting, Vendrick."

Again, Frelia laughed and fought the urge to weep. Maybe moving forward didn't have to mean losing everything that had come before.

Together with her past and present, Frelia strode through the halls of Castle Skjöldr down to the governor's office.

Which, apparently, was the same as the king's. Frelia tried not to flinch as they approached the familiar mahogany door, and Thera actually growled. They looked at each other then, Valerius amber meeting Grimsdalr ochre for the first time since the Tyrant's War.

"Here goes nothing," Frelia said, and twisted the doorknob.

Clarissa and Mitri had already arrived, the former tucked up on a sofa and the latter bent over a side table laden with food. Deadcut was sitting at an enormous wooden desk piled high with paperwork, and Frelia suddenly saw exactly where Vendrick had gotten it from.

Vendrick raised an eyebrow at the side table. "Is this a party or a war meeting?"

Deadcut shrugged. "I don't see why it can't be both."

Thera snorted, and went to go help herself.

The side table was laden with a lot of Volsinii dishes Frelia didn't recognize and Vendrick had to translate, but the pile of crescent-shaped dumplings nestled in a warming dish near the end of the spread made Frelia's heart clench uncomfortably in her chest.

Never mind that she already didn't want Deadcut's charity, didn't need whatever passed for her kindness, and still didn't know why the woman was carrying a stolen bloodrune.

"Are you trying to bribe me with *varenyky*?" Frelia asked, glancing to the governor.

Deadcut smiled over the lip of a wineglass. "Is it working?"

Frelia held up a finger and, bare-handed, plucked a single *varenik* from the pile and bit into it.

For a moment, Frelia was assaulted by the warm, mealy potato-and-onion taste of childhood. It tasted of home, of moot summers and the weeks before the Battle for Skjöldr, of standing in the kitchen with her Aunt Brenn and trying to learn how much filling to plop into the doughy circle without the whole thing exploding.

Then she was pressing her hand to her mouth as silent tears finally broke free.

Frelia was distantly aware that Mitri was clucking at her about the serving spoon, and Faustine's voice inserting itself into the room, and Vendrick's warm hand squeezing her shoulder. But her mind was somewhere in the hollowed-out ruins of her hometown, dueling the draugr her father had become.

He'd loved *varenyky* almost as much as Frelia did.

"Professor?" Faustine said.

Frelia dragged the heel of her hand across her good eye. "Needs sour cream," she grunted, and reached for a plate.

To her left, Thera laughed, and you'd never know what it sounded like distorted through a garmr's rumbling throat.

They settled into what, for the Volsinii, passed for an informal meal.

"I'm sure you will all love to know that Markus della Luciana—or, for appearance's sake, the man calling himself such—"

Here, Deadcut had to pause while Vendrick and Clarissa cackled.

"—is safely behind bars in the dungeons while we send word to the Imperator."

Frelia refused to freeze mid bite. Not when it was *varenyky*. She finished chewing, swallowed, and then said, "Why in Helheim would you tell him?"

"Oh, I'm obligated to," Deadcut said, readily enough. "However there's little point in sending a letter all the way to Ascalon without evidence of who exactly is impersonating the Imperator's son. And I foresee that investigation taking a rather long time, particularly with the snows this time of year making letters so easily lost."

Frelia spluttered a begrudging laugh, and she wasn't the only one.

"I am a career bureaucrat, dears." Deadcut swirled the wine around her glass with a self-satisfied grin. "If I wish for an administrative nightmare to last forever, I will make it so."

Hard to argue with that, especially when Frelia had been subjected to Volsinii-style educational paperwork for a semester.

"So, Deadcut," Thera said, and Frelia was starting to remember how nice it was, not to have the be the only one dropping bad news in everyone's lap. "Why do you have the Maximus Bloodrune?"

Frelia would have expected harsh silence, but Deadcut only nodded, and set her fork down. "What do you know of the Battle for Ice Crown?" the old woman asked.

"Oh, um." Faustine piped up immediately, ever the eager student. "That's the one where ten centurions went into battle with their forces, and scarcely a hundred soldiers left, right?"

"Yes," said Vendrick. "Reina Einnaska also retreated unscathed, although she would eventually fall at the Battle of Prehl."

Deadcut nodded to the both of them. "It was to be our great triumph, yes." She sighed. "We would finally take down Countess Traust and Grand Duke Valerius, and the war would soon be over."

Frelia laughed, and the only sound more bitter had been the wind in the mouth of the grotto. "Then we sent Crown Princess Einnaska instead."

"I'd never seen anything like the Einnaska Bloodrune. Watching it in action is..." Deadcut shuddered, and it didn't suit her.

"*Ja,*" Frelia and Thera agreed, after a pause.

Mitri, already on his third plate of charcuterie, trembled.

"But again, Mum, we're runeless," Clarissa said. "Surely you could avoid orders given from it?"

"I could and did." Deadcut shut her eyes for a moment, took a deep breath, and then opened them sharply. "But by the time I had fully shaken the compulsion, I found myself deep in the forests of Traust Territory, alone."

Frelia could see, in her mind's eye, the deep, black forests of Geir and Gudrun's homeland. Hunting there wasn't like hunting in Valerius Territory; Frelia's family lands were harsh and wild, but they were fair. The Traust family lands didn't care who or what they ate.

"So that's why you 'abandoned' everyone." Vendrick put air quotes around the word.

"Quite." Deadcut stared hard at the wall, her half-finished meal, Faustine's shaking hands—anywhere but her children. "And in that forest, I saw a monster with horrible green eyes and spindly black limbs."

Clarissa froze with a fork midway to her mouth. "A darkbeast?"

"That's what I thought at first," said Deadcut, "then it spoke."

A chill to rival the Northern Wilds ran down Frelia's spine as she finally remembered, once upon a very long time ago, where she had heard a rumble like Garmr-Thera's.

"It had a woman's voice," Deadcut continued, "and asked me what I was doing out here, all alone in the cold. I told her I was terribly sorry, but I'd gotten lost somehow. Did she know the way back to Ice Crown?"

Vendrick snorted into his wineglass. "You apologized to a darkbeast?"

"Habit, you know?" Deadcut smiled thinly. "But she got down on what I can only assume were knees, and stared at me so long I thought I might pass out from sheer panic."

"That's what the one at Kjell did," Clarissa said, quietly. "Plucked Frelia from the air and just stared at her. Until she went to stab it, of course."

Frelia laughed, hoarsely. "That reminds me, I'm going to need to clean my sword and armor with a solution of wolfsbane, Deadcut. I can make it if you get me the materials."

"Of course; let me know what you'll need and I'll arrange for it." Deadcut moved to make a note of that in a motion Frelia would have called reflexive. "And anyway, I don't know what that creature was looking for, but then she bit into her own hand, and offered it out to me. 'Drink,' she said, 'and you'll find your way home.'"

Faustine's jaw dropped. "And you did it?"

Funny, Frelia was wondering the same thing.

Deadcut made a wishy-washy motion with her hand. "You don't really turn down that kind of thing from a monster that can snap you in half with its bloody fingers."

"Oh, Saints," Clarissa said, but it was muffled by the hand clapped over her face.

"I don't know why she did it," Deadcut added. "She could just as easily have eaten me."

"You keep saying 'she,'" Vendrick observed.

"I've always thought of it as such, given the voice." Deadcut shrugged.

"I do, too." Frelia could feel the eyes on her as she stared at her plate of half-eaten *varenyky*.

There were Volsinii families with bloodrunes, sure, but Deadcut had been an invader, a usurper in Traust Territory. There was no reason for its Guardian to help her—but then, maybe that was why she wasn't describing Lord Muninn.

Frelia hadn't seen the Watcher, either.

"Once," Frelia added, her voice soft as the wind, "when I was a girl, the twins and I got lost in the Northern Wilds."

Thera nodded, massaging her throat as though it hurt to speak.

"Couldn't have been more than a few hundred paces from Grimsdalr Lodge," Frelia added, "but I stumbled into a druid circle I've never seen again, and in it..."

Something in the atmosphere seemed to shift at her voice, listening.

"Well, in it, I remember flashes of gnarled, black fingers and gnashing teeth," Frelia said. "And a whispering voice telling me I do not belong. Then I was back on the Grimsdalrs' back porch."

She refused to shudder at the memory.

"And you're certain it wasn't just a darkbeast?" Vendrick asked.

"That's what I thought at first, but... your mum's right. Garmur can't talk—well except Thera and the Guardians..."

She looked to Vendrick then. His arms were folded across his narrow frame, and he stared down his mother with a calculating look Frelia knew very well.

"So what did it taste like?" Vendrick asked. "The blood, that is."

"Rust and grass," said Deadcut. "And she—the creature, that is—was right. I found my way out of the forest shortly after she told me to run along. Apparently, it had been days, and we'd been routed."

Frelia nodded solemnly. "Reina never left survivors."

Deadcut inclined her head in acknowledgment, and then continued. "After that, I tried to put the whole incident from my mind. I continued fighting, gaining ground for the Imperium, and then, one day, in the middle of a bloody battle, some lucky bastard chopped my hand clean off."

Everyone's eyes immediately dropped to Deadcut's hands. She held up the one with the severed finger, and sure enough, there was a pinkish, fleshy lump where there had previously been nothing, and before that, a thumb. The protrusion was starting to take on the color of Deadcut's actual skin.

"I managed to kill him, but I remember staring at the bleeding stump of my hand in disbelief." Deadcut stared down at her regenerating thumb, flexing the rest of her fingers and twisting them in the light. "You can imagine my surprise when the hand began to grow back."

Part of Frelia wanted to reach out and touch the regrowing nub. See if it were real or some illusion. But the other part of her resented the stares she got when the Valerius Bloodrune activated and, well, she wasn't going to do that to someone else.

"*Ja,*" said Frelia grimly. "That's Maximus. Their bearers will keep coming at you until you break enough of them to matter."

"And I presume the horrible, searing pain on my collarbone was normal, as well?" Deadcut asked, pointing to where the bloodrune lay beneath her shirt.

"*Ja,*" said Frelia. "Plus the three days of feverish nightmares afterwards that I assume you had?"

Deadcut made a face that, inexplicably, made Vendrick and Clarissa both laugh. "Is that normal?" the old woman asked.

"Tragically," said Frelia.

"So then what did you do, Mum?" Clarissa asked.

"Attempted to live my life ignoring it," Deadcut said primly.

Frelia and Thera snorted. But the second said, almost to herself, "Blood always outs."

"It does," Deadcut agreed. "Vendrick, Clarissa—do you both remember when I received the summons to Windmont Hold later that winter?"

"I remember thinking it was odd that you and father both left," Vendrick said. "That never happened."

Deadcut's smile was rueful. "I wasn't supposed to come back."

"Wait, wait, wait!" Faustine piped up. "Did they drag you into a blood circle with the late Count and some other folks?"

Deadcut nodded gravely, and Frelia felt her stomach drop through her boots.

"Vendrick," Frelia said, hoarse and hurried, "was your da Ascended?"

"Thankfully, no." Deadcut's smile was wicked. "They were so surprised when their magic went awry. They had their sacrifices, but the magic snapped in their hands. Nearly killed Vittoro."

"That would have been far too convenient," Clarissa muttered, and Vendrick visibly struggled not to laugh.

"Apparently I broke their circle." Deadcut was laughing herself, just a little. "It outright killed most of the mages casting it, and the handful who remained demanded to know why it hadn't worked. I stole an axe off one of their guards and told them all to rot in Hypogia."

Frelia's laugh echoed in the close room. "I bet they didn't like that."

"They liked discovering this thing..." Deadcut gestured to the bloodrune hidden at her collarbone. "...even less. My children's father attempted to sever my lower leg and was rather put out to find it growing right back."

Frelia's hand pressed, unbidden, to the lower edge of the scar across her chest. Where Ironfang had cracked her ribcage open at the Battle of Spirits' Fen. She would have bled out in the acrid muck, if not for Cillian dragging her to the medical tents.

What torture must that have been, to be so injured and not die?

"I figured he would just try it again without me," said Deadcut, "but he called it off. Got the sense they needed me for something else."

"You must have a bloodrune that's hard to find," Vendrick said. "My guess is that's why they haven't killed Frelia yet, either."

"And here," Frelia said mock-seriously, "I just thought I was hard to kill."

"Well, that too," said Vendrick, and Faustine laughed.

"So then... what happened?" Thera asked, her gaze intent on Deadcut.

"Their father tried to threaten me into silence," said Deadcut, hooking a thumb towards Vendrick and Clarissa. "But I forced him to make a deal."

A grin cracked across Vendrick's sharp face. "Now *that* sounds like my mother."

Deadcut smiled at him—really smiled—and just for a moment, she seemed, for lack of a better word, human. Frelia wasn't sure she liked it. "In exchange for my silence about this... mad cult of his, we would divorce."

Clarissa's jaw dropped. "Mum, that's brilliant!"

"Vendrick and Clarissa would go to Silverwood," Deadcut continued, as though Clarissa hadn't spoken, "so that he couldn't poison them with his 'Sightless One' nonsense while I wasn't around. I would keep my mouth shut about both this thing..." She gestured to her hidden, inexplicable bloodrune. "...and what happened at Windmont Hold, and we would claim the divorce sprung from my discovery of your father's affair."

"I always thought that sounded off," Vendrick said. "Father barely looked at anyone and was in his study all the time. When in hell would he have had the time or inclination for an affair?"

Faustine turned faintly pink at the decades' old gossip, and Frelia resisted the urge to ruffle her hair.

"You were always too clever by half, Vendrick." Deadcut suddenly sounded so, *so* sad.

"I thought it sounded wrong, too," Clarissa pouted.

Vendrick rolled his eyes. "Because I pointed it out to you."

Clarissa harrumphed. "Also Mum, if you can regenerate, is your cane fake, then?"

"No, that's real," said Deadcut, patting the head of the cane in question. "For some reason, the leg never healed. And, well, I suppose I could test it by cutting off the injured one and seeing if it grows back without the limp, but frankly, I never felt the need."

Clarissa grimaced, alongside Faustine, but Vendrick, ever practical, pressed forward. "Why are you telling us all of this now?"

That was a damned good question that Frelia also wanted to know.

"All those years," Vendrick continued, softly building the lance of his argument, "of tense family dinners and split holidays and 'your father' this and 'your mother' that, and never once did you think to tell us this?"

Even Frelia knew, General Deadcut was cautious, sure, and politically inclined to a fault. But stupid? No, Deadcut Verona was not stupid. She had a reason for staying quiet beyond cruelty or fear of Vittoro Caecillion's retaliation.

"I am first and foremost, a general," Deadcut said, her eye resting first on Frelia's eyepatch and then Thera's entire being. "And therefore, I am aware of a losing battle when one strikes me across the face."

Frelia laughed so hard, her hip twinged, and she cut herself off with a groan of pain. Deadcut's castle physician had seen to them all before the showers, but Frelia hadn't been the most injured by a mile.

"And it occurred to me," Deadcut continued, "while Markus della Luciana was so desperately trying to avoid giving up the party game, that if Ironfang has implanted a bloodrune in his own son, then he must have what he wants—or close enough. Elias wouldn't allow for such an obvious move without the endgame in sight."

Faustine fidgeted with the hem of her borrowed skirt, clearly uncomfortable. Frelia wished she had anything remotely helpful to tell the girl.

"So here, I never thought I'd consider treason the reasonable option," Deadcut added dryly, "but I'm afraid the Imperator has left me no choice."

"Treason?" Faustine's head jerked up. "Where'd you get that from?"

"This is a rebellion," Deadcut said, a touch of horror and pride both, in her voice. "We are actively going against the orders of the Imperator Volsinii and the Senate, and we've sided with the Kaldiri to do it."

Deadcut gestured to Frelia, now chewing on a *varenik*, and Thera, hunched over her second plate of food like an anxious dog.

"So the question, my dear son..." Deadcut glanced back to Vendrick. "...is what's our next move? If you don't have one, I have an idea."

"Our?" Clarissa sounded like she didn't dare hope.

Deadcut let the question hang, and Vendrick carefully set aside the remains of his dinner to lean forward on the sofa, his elbows on his knees. "I could have used this attitude a decade ago, Mum."

"And for that, I am sorry." The statement rang with honest regret. "But if I'm to all-out assault something, all other options must be exhausted."

Frelia couldn't say she respected that, exactly, but she understood it. Considering conflict the last-ditch option was a luxury afforded to those who hadn't grown up with eight months of winter.

So while her stomach churned with dread, and resentment—and *varenyky*—at the thought of working alongside the Butcher of Traust Territory, there was relief, too. Frelia was no longer the first line of defense, no longer a loose sled dog wandering the world alone.

"Well, first thing." Vendrick reached into his inside coat pocket and retrieved a wadded-up handkerchief. "Anyone have any thoughts on this?"

He un-wadded the cloth to expose the small, pebble-like thing that he'd pulled from the kraken. Ip close, there was no mistaking the aura it emanated.

"Bloodstone." Frelia grimaced at its proximity. "I don't see a bloodrune, though. They're normally see-through, not a rock."

Staring with trepidation, Thera set her plate aside and padded nearer to the grey-gold rock in Vendrick's hand. "That... looks like... an eye," she said, unevenly.

"I was thinking the same." Vendrick's hands were steady, his tone wary. "So what was an extra eye doing in the kraken's mantle?"

All eyes went to Frelia, and she tried not to feel annoyed about it.

"What, do you want me to sing the *Ballad of Hana?*" she snapped. "Trust me, if we had a story about this—or about the kraken eating a Saints-damned garmr—I'd have told you all by now."

Vendrick leaned forward to lay the bloodstone—still nestled in the handkerchief—on the coffee table.

"I want to take a look at that, while we're just hanging around here," Mitri piped up. "The vials we recovered, too."

"What will you require?" Deadcut asked.

"A laboratory, preferably with staff Vendrick has vetted and a place for Lady Clarissa to sit. I'll need her expertise on the bloodstones."

"Oh, and I'll need somewhere to work on Frelia's shield," Clarissa added, "as well as my own prosthetics."

"There is an alchemy laboratory in the lower floor of the castle," Deadcut said. "I'm sure you'll find it suitable."

"Capital," said Vendrick. "Now, second order of business—Grimsdalr, any ideas on what happened to you?"

Thera shrugged, even as she folded herself into a pretzel to poke at the bloodstone on the coffee table. "I felt... strange, when my bloodrune went off. Like it was trying to reach me through layers of stone, or sleep.

And when the kraken touched me, I felt... I don't know, something... *in* me react?"

"Do you recall what the Unseen did to you?" Clarissa asked, more kindly than anyone except maybe Faustine could have. "Perhaps there's a clue there."

"Not really. I can only think, whatever's in here that makes me a garmr ..." Thera thumped her fist to her heart. "...was reacting to Lord Geri. Like knights to their generals, or pups to their dam."

Silence came then, broken only by the quiet clatter of silverware.

So not only did Frelia have no idea what had happened, it sounded like Thera didn't, either. For some reason, that was more terrifying than if the woman had come right out and said the Unseen had stuck some kind of arcane abomination in her guts that allowed her to change forms.

"That's horrifying, Thera," Frelia managed to say. "What the fuck?"

The other Kaldiri woman shrugged. "You said it, not me."

"Alright, we'll table that for now," Vendrick said, and he sounded so normal Frelia fought the urge to laugh. "Third order of business—we'll need to determine a half-decent cover story for why we're all here, given that we're in no state to leave."

"And have nowhere to go," Clarissa pointed out.

"Oh that's an easy one," Deadcut said, and Vendrick's head snapped around to look at her. "Dovetails rather nicely into my idea, in fact."

Frelia had no idea how she was supposed to interpret that and, apparently, neither did Vendrick.

"You," he said, a note of guesswork in his tone, "who hates all things remotely dishonest, have a dishonest idea?"

"Oh, Saints no." Deadcut waved the idea aside. "You've been waging war in the shadows too long, Vendrick. I propose an ambush."

Frelia made a face. "And how the fuck are we supposed to do that? Ironfang's as paranoid about the Unseen as Vendrick is."

"Simple." Deadcut's face lit up, and Frelia didn't trust it one bit. "We throw a party."

She looked, very pointedly, at Vendrick.

"For what?" Mitri asked. "Yule's already passed and the next holiday won't be until nearly summer."

The color began to drain from Vendrick's face. "No, Mum, you can't—"

"Oh Vendrick, there are very few reasons why you, let alone you *and* your sister, would be visiting your dear old mum," Deadcut pointed out, with no small amount of sarcasm. "Particularly since your father is already dead. Why else would you both, Valerius, Grimsdalr, and Mitri be here?"

"No," Vendrick said firmly, "no, absolutely not. You had best not be about to suggest what I think you are."

Frelia was too tired for this shit. "What are you both on about?"

"She's talking about an engagement party," Vendrick said, stiff as an alley cat.

Frelia blinked. "Who could possibly be getting married?"

"Why, Valerius dear—" Deadcut turned her most grandmotherly smile on the warrior. "—you."

Also by Evelyn Hyde

Want more of the Wolf and the Viper?

Prequel: A Dark and Ancient Evil
Available for free when you sign up for the newsletter!

Book 1: Some Kind of Hell
Available from Amazon

Book 2: Bring Down the Sky
You are here!

Book 3: Hour of the Wolf
Coming Soon

Book 4: Last Queen of Kaldr
Coming Soon

ABOUT THE AUTHOR

Evelyn Hyde is an indie author, editor, and the founder of Tag Your S#@!. She is a Midwestern native with the tragically Ohio penchant for leaving the surface of the Earth by any means necessary, but no head for NASA. When not at work, Evelyn can be found in her kitchen experimenting, digging into a new story in whatever form it takes, or annoying her loving husband. She is also an excellent Game Master.

You can find her at https://evelynhydewriter.com/

If you want to hear about all her latest novels, new works, and nonsense (and psst get a free copy of *A Dark and Ancient Evil,* the prequel novella to The Wolf and the Viper Saga), you can sign up for her newsletter on her website.

AUTHOR'S NOTE

ONCE, WHEN I WAS in high school, I was perusing the used bookstore like usual when I came across a guy with a whole-ass Samoyed in the video game section. This was in the era before ESAs were really a thing, so I was surprised to find a dog in there that wasn't a service animal.

Like any self-respecting animal person, I wanted to pet the dog. But I was also a high schooler, so I was afraid of asking the guy if I was allowed to. I don't remember why, exactly, anymore, but probably just because he was an adult.

Then a little kid ran up to him and asked, breathlessly, "Can I pet your dog?"

And the man beamed and said, "That's what he's for!"

So as the kid excitedly scratched the dog behind the ears, I awkwardly shuffled over like, "Um, can I pet your dog, too?"

And sure enough, the guy said, "That's what he's for!"

That story has lived in my friend group lexicon for *years* now. (I won't tell you how long ago high school was, but I will say there have been a few reunions since then.) Partly because it's just hilarious—Samoyeds are surprisingly BIG dogs—but partly also because "That's what he/she/I'm for" has become our shorthand for "Genuinely, you're welcome."

"Can you take out the trash, please?"/ "That's what I'm for!"

"Thank you for sending good vibes this week, I needed them." / "That's what I'm for."

"I can't believe you went out of your way to make a ravioli casserole for me because I had knee surgery." / "That's what I'm for."

The implication is not only that you don't mind whatever it is you've been asked to do, but that you're glad to help. It's your purpose.

So when people ask me why I became a writer, the answer is, simply, "That's what I'm for."

Truly, I am a Samoyed in a bookstore that way.

And I would like to take a moment to thank the otherSamoyeds who helped get this book out there.

My favorite bookstore Samoyeds are my husband, Jack,and our dog, Roy (who is not a Samoyed but kind of looks like one, if Samoyeds came in Chow Chow cinnamon). Thank you both for all your love and support.<3

There's also the incomparable Writer Coven. Jill,Becca, and Phoebe. I'm grateful to you all from the bottom of my heart. This series would not exist without your thoughtful critique, cheerleading, and general badassery.

I also want to thank my fantastic beta team. Heidi and Anna (the outstanding Gaydies), Deb, Alex, Becky, and Mike—thank you for being bookstore Samoyeds while I struggled to get this book out!

My editor, Heather Rubert, was also a huge help in getting this book off my computer and into your hands. Their suggestions,critique, and comments are what really brought this book to life. Thank you,again, for your support!

I also want to thank the artists who brought Frelia to life—Maria Spada for her awesome covers, Shivnath Productions for the beautiful map, and Alex Spreier for his lovely and expressive bloodrune art.

Lastly, I thank *you,* dear readers, for your enthusiasm and curiosity. A writer without readers is as purpose-less as a loose sled dog.

If you're curious about what I'm up to, there are links to my newsletter, website, and social media on my bio page. I'd love to hear from you there, or via reviews on Amazon, Goodreads, Storygraph, and the rest.Reviews are like magic to a writer—*the fuck you mean someone read my book and liked it enough to tell other people?*—and I'm grateful for every single one. Yes, even the ones that say the book is "just okay," because, hey, I don't just read the five star reviews on Amazon, either.

Go forth, ye Samoyeds, and do what you're for!

-Hyde

P.S. – For anyone wondering, Roy is a Husky/Chow Chow mix whose husky shenanigans frequently feature in my newsletter. He's named after Roy from *Fire Emblem: The Binding Blade.*

www.ingramcontent.com/pod-product-compliance
Lightning Source LLC
Chambersburg PA
CBHW022233020726
47496CB00004B/886